NOTHING ELSE IS LOVE

Gina Linko

Relax. Read. Repeat.

NOTHING ELSE IS LOVE
By Gina Linko
Published by TouchPoint Press
Brookland, AR 72417
www.touchpointpress.com

ISBN-13: 978-1-952816-74-1

Editor: Jenn Haskin
Cover Design: ColbieMyles.com
Cover Images: Alexey Erofalov

Connect with the author online GinaLinko.com

First Edition

Printed in the United States of America.

In loving memory of
Astrid and John

Part I
Alice

Chapter 1

Chicago, 1978

THE LITTLE GIRL WITH STRAWBERRY-BLONDE curls sits on the black office chair, her legs dangling. She is small and cherubic. She holds a stuffed giraffe in her hands, alternately hugging it and picking at its fabric eyes. She looks into the camera lens with a serious stare, and she answers the man's question.

"*Je parle le francais.*" Her accent sounds perfect. Her eyes are a sandy brown color, framed with the lightest of lashes.

"How did you learn French? Were you taught by your mother?" The man's voice is off-camera, but the girl's eyes follow him.

She shakes her head. "Mama can't speak French. But I know it from *l'avant.*"

"*L'avant?*" he asks. "What does that mean?"

"The before. I know French from the before."

"What is 'the before' exactly? Can you explain it to me?"

"It's when I was a different me. I lived in the place with the lavender and the *parfumerie.*"

Off camera, there is a low hum of voices, the sound of paper shuffling.

"How did you first tell your mother about the before, Alice?"

"I don't know. Mama?" Her brow furrows a little, and Alice looks past the camera, searching. "Mama?" The girl presses her fingers against the inside of her opposite palm, a nervous gesture, the giraffe forgotten, tumbling onto the floor.

"I'm right here, Alice," the mother's voice answers. "You're doing great, honey. Do you remember the picture you drew? Can you tell Dr. Lewellyn?"

Alice's eyes light up, but she quickly draws her brow again. "It was a scary picture. Lots of blood on the grass. I drawed a picture, and Mama worried about it."

Dr. Lewellyn asks, "Do you have a copy of this drawing?"

"Of course, at home," the mother answers. Alice listens, biting on her bottom lip.

"Alice, can you tell me what other things you know from your time in the before?"

"Um, lots of things. They weared hats all the time." The little girl jumps down from the chair to retrieve her giraffe. She hugs it tightly and maneuvers back into her seat. "I umm . . . I want to go home." Alice looks past the camera again. "Mama?"

"Just a few more questions, honey, I promise."

"I can play *le piano*!"

"The piano?" Dr. Lewellyn asks.

A woman with bright red hair enters the camera frame, and she kneels in front of Alice. She has the same upturn at the end of her nose as the girl. She holds Alice's hands and whispers to her.

"We have the keyboard from the other studio," Dr. Lewellyn offers, now also in the camera frame.

"She's never had a lesson, but a few months ago, at a friend's house, she just started playing," the mother says. "It's probably not that compelling to you, but I never . . . I . . . can't explain it."

A blonde woman moves into the frame carrying a large, freestanding keyboard. She sets it up in front of the girl, working to lower it to a child-friendly height. But Alice doesn't wait. She jumps from her chair and begins to pluck out a melody using two fingers. After the first three or four notes, it is clear that she is playing "*Frere Jacques*."

She finishes the song, while the adults clap for her. Alice joins in applauding herself, smiling.

"Ms. Grier, this is interesting." Dr. Lewellyn says. "Skeptics, of course, will conclude she could have picked up such a simple tune, but she–"

"It scares me," the mother says quietly. "I don't want–"

She is silenced as Alice begins to play another song, her hands set in perfect middle-C position, her fingering skills a wonder as she hits full chords and shows the advanced skills of a serious pianist. The mother's hand goes to her mouth in surprise.

The room is silent for a few more bars of complicated music, until Alice hits a wrong note. This trips her up. She pauses. "Oh, the cow!"

"I think you mean, holy cow, Alice," the mother whispers, clearly shaken by the piano playing. She turns to Dr. Lewellyn. "She always gets that saying wrong."

"No, no," a woman's voice adds from off-camera. "It's French. *Ah, la vaca*. A colloquialism. Literally, it means Oh, the cow. But it doesn't really translate. It means something akin to, Oh my gosh!"

"*Oui. Ah, la vaca*," Alice whispers, once again hugging the giraffe.

The mother shakes her head. "We need a break. Turn it off. Please," she says, and then, the camera goes black.

Chapter 2

St. Paul, Minnesota
1998

I SPREAD MY MAP ON THE LITTLE OUTDOOR bistro table at which Serena and I sat. We were new to St. Paul, transplanted for the summer from University of Chicago, each here for our own separate graduate research projects. I'd photocopied this map earlier at the St. Paul Historical Society, and now I tapped a finger on the handwritten cursive label of an immigrant neighborhood near the Phalen River. The neighborhood didn't exist anymore, but back when it did, it was known as Swede Hollow or *Svenska Dalen.*

In real life, sometimes there were no signs. When I was younger, I was constantly looking for signs, making them up. *If it's a good song on the radio, then Mom won't drink too much after her day at the storm-door factory. If the light stays green, then I'll dare to ask* Mom *for the field trip money.*

Sometimes there are signs though. A sense of *deja-vu*, the feeling of awareness that tickles the tiny hairs on the nape of your neck. Or is it that extra *da-dum* beat of your heart when you first see his face? Or even the feeling, that pull, that magnetic *zing*, that lures you somewhere different . . . but not exactly new?

The devil's advocate in me questioned—when you're so aware, seeking out signs, do you create them, bring them to fruition with the sheer power of your will?

I was guilty. Either way. Both ways.

My mother, Isabel Grier, had confessed, right away, once I was old enough to comprehend. Isabel told me that it was all a clever ruse, this previous-life nonsense, another of her money-grubbing schemes. And it had worked too well. "You had that birthmark," Isabel told me, gesturing to the strawberry mark covering half my hand and fingers that crept up my forearm. "And I thought to myself, I could run with this. I could make some serious dough. I taught you a few French phrases. You were a natural on camera. It was too easy." Mom had given me her signature wink then. She'd sucked in a drag of her cigarette, her red lipstick already staining the filter, and I believed her. Of course I believed her. She was beautiful, like the newscaster on the local Chicago station, with red hair that never frizzled. I idolized my mother. Loved every quirk of her eyebrow, every word from her mouth.

Like every kid loves her mother. I did. I hated her a little too, of course. But I mostly loved her. And believed her.

I still did, some days, even now as a twenty-five-year-old grad student, with my mother only two months in the ground.

"I'm just saying I wouldn't mind a lumberjack," my friend Serena said, sipping her coffee.

"We're in Minnesota, not the Pacific Northwest, you know. There are no lumberjacks." We sat on the main drag of downtown St. Paul, in the neighborhood of Summit Hill. We'd somehow finagled our projects to be in the same city, hers an internship in psychology, mine a research project in local history. It was convenient, and it anchored me. Serena did that for me, had been doing that for a few years. She knew Isabel well.

But she didn't know my secret. No one did.

She continued, "Christ, Alice, let me have my fantasy. And admit it, it feels very lumberjacky here."

"It's all the flannel." I dug in my backpack for my current map of St. Paul and placed it on top of the old one. I'd annotated this one with the areas I needed to focus on: the many Hamm's brewery buildings, the Victorian homes on Planck street, the speakeasies, the most famous of which was housed in the Wabasha Caverns.

Serena scratched her nose. "I'm probably going to get hives being so far from the El. From the lake. The bustle. It's so quiet here."

"It isn't exactly the middle of nowhere, Serena. We'll deal."

"I haven't been a lot of places, Alice. This whole nice Midwestern, suburban thing is throwing me for a loop. I mean, who takes on boarders in their own, actual home for God's sake. It's like a set-up in a small-town horror flick."

I laughed and gave Serena a look, shaking my head. We were both staying at a quirky Victorian boarding house up the road that sat atop the sandstone bluffs above a picturesque green-space community park.

I compared my current map of St. Paul with the photocopy of the older turn-of-the-century map. *Swede Hollow.* I had learned about it in my earlier research, even before I came here, and I could've seen it as a sign. Sure.

The whole Swede thing.

It could've factored into my decision to come here to do my research, to write my thesis, rather than to go somewhere else—anywhere else, really.

He was a Swede.

I remembered the stiff click of his consonants, the reluctance to form the English "j" sound. I remembered everything about him.

Whether it was real or not.

There were many Swedish immigrants in this area, families dating back to the 1920s, but there were also many other pockets in the Midwest thick with Scandinavian heritage.

It might mean nothing.

But rebirth was happening in Swede Hollow, in St. Paul, a trendy metamorphosis of reuse, with brewery buildings being turned into hophouse restaurants, Prohibition caverns turned into mushroom farms, speakeasies into swank banquet halls. This was a 1990s thing, a new idea, the rehabilitating of the old, rather than the standard "new-is-better" raze and redo.

And this gentrification, this retelling of the history, remodeling into something new while keeping the tradition of the old, was the focus of my thesis and research: history retold and rewritten through architecture, through urban settings in their transformations and rebirth.

I'd chosen St. Paul because it was rich with these ideas.

And . . . this city had tunnels running under it, caverns and pathways winding deep and down and up and around. Beneath the city's heartbeat was another life, another storyline, equally as interesting as the conspicuous one featured aboveground—if not more so.

The tunnels intrigued me. From an academic point of view. Of course. Their use in a historical sense.

But also . . ..

I was looking for a tunnel. I was. Of course I was.

From my "memories." Where I'd last seen *him*.

I told myself in my sanest moments that I chose St. Paul because it was close to my home in Chicago, and because Serena would be here. Because it made sense.

The tunnels had nothing to do with it.

But when it was the middle of the night, and I was alone in the dark, and I was missing my god-awful just-deceased mother, who loved me the very best she could've, at least in some moments, well, then, I knew. I didn't lie to myself then. I knew I was looking for an answer.

I had to know. One way or another.

What had happened to *him*?

To me.

And Jesus Christ, was it real? Or was my mother just better at thorough and lifelong deceit than I gave her credit for?

"Red rum, red rum," Serena croaked. And I snapped back to the here and now.

I sighed. "Really, Serena, Mrs. Signy seems very nice and not at all horror-movie-ish. There are no identical twins about to walk down our hallway and spout Stephen King horror lines."

"Why would you even say that out loud? You're tempting fate. Plus, have you seen that house? The stairs creak more than my granny's arthritis. Seriously, there's probably like a secret bookshelf trapdoor. Who knows?" Serena faux-pounded her fist on the little bistro table.

A group of patrons dressed in suits and office-wear walked past us toward the coffeehouse, and Serena eyed them lazily. She lowered her eyelids and sipped her coffee. "I mean, he doesn't have to be a lumberjack, but a goatee would be nice. Muscles. Must look good in a suit. Must be available for summer fling."

Another man caught up to the group of businesspeople, his long strides grazing right past our little table. Serena eyed this one up and down with vigor. I fiddled with my hair. It was so much shorter, as I'd just lopped it off to my chin after my mother's death. I'd felt the need to mark the occasion. I felt different, so I should look different too.

I noticed the businessman who'd caught Serena's attention carried an umbrella, tapping its end on the cobblestoned sidewalk like a cane. My eyes shot to the clear blue Minnesota sky. It didn't look like rain—but then I forgot about the weather. In that moment, I had a memory, a flash:

Our old apartment, the first I could remember when I was super young, before Isabel's doublewide trailer. The counter-top was a mottled orange and brown. On it sat Isabel's fringed leather purse. Next to it, a stack of large child-like flashcards. The card on top was a cartoon drawing of an umbrella, purple with blue dots. Parapluie.

"Earth to Alice," Serena said, snapping her fingers in front of my face. "He's handsome in that nerdy, I-read-poetry-and-pretend-to-like-it kind of way."

I laughed and tore my eyes from the man's umbrella, tore my mind from the memory of the French flashcards.

I tried to recover quickly. I didn't want to have to explain myself. "You have to stay open to a little nerdiness," I joked to Serena. "That's your problem, Serena, going for looks only."

Had my mother really been teaching me French with flashcards? Could I trust this *memory*?

"Oh right, I'm the one with the problem," Serena said.

"What's that supposed to mean? I don't need a lumberjack," I told Serena. "I just want to get my project research off on a good foot. Get some good data, photos, etc. I need to do well and get—"

"You always do well."

"You don't have to interrupt me," I said, but my mind was still back with the umbrella. Why else would my mother have French flashcards? I tried to go back in my cache of memories and uncover more, but I couldn't get anything much. My mind, my memories, all of it was always imperfect, confusing, filled with nonsensical juxtapositions.

"Alice, you could let your guard down a bit. I'm going to need a wingman here in this god-forsaken suburb-looking city, or I'm never going to get any the entire summer," Serena eyed me, tearing a piece of her blueberry muffin, and eating it. "When's the last time you got laid?"

I tried to force the *parapluie* from my mind, and I weighed telling Serena the truth. I sighed. "1996."

"That's two years ago!"

"Dry spell."

"Woman, this is an emergency."

"Less entanglement, less problems."

That goddamn *parapluie*.

And you know what? I'd already been in love. In France, a century ago, and I couldn't go out with one more goateed moron wearing a Nirvana t-shirt. I just couldn't. I couldn't pretend or even sort-of-pretend that I didn't know what it was like to feel something destined, otherworldly, fated.

It was that serious.

At least in my faux-memory.

"Right, you don't do relationships," Serena went on. "You've got the Isabel Complex. I forgot."

"Those who don't learn from history are doomed to repeat it."

"There's a whole lot of space between your mother and you, Alice. You know that. Why you so hard on yourself?"

"Adam Griffin."

"Oh please."

"He was my advisor. And married."

"Separated."

"Slippery slope and all that."

"I know, I know. One more man like that and next thing you know you'll be working the front desk at a storm-door factory, slapping your daughter in the face if she takes too long running up to the Shell station for your cigarettes. I get it." Serena held up her hand to stop me from listing the many reasons I didn't want a relationship, didn't want to become Isabel.

It's not just Isabel, I wanted to add. *I secretly dream about a man who may or may not have been real, a man who smelled like almonds and coffee, wrote me poetry, carved wood as a hobby, and basically adored me. Surely, he was a figment of an imagination, started in Isabel's, then passed to me. Surely, I had embellished him to the point of perfection.*

"A summer fling would not an Isabel make," Serena explained.

"I know."

"And listen, I loved Isabel too, but she never ironed her jeans. Or her underwear. You're eons away from becoming her."

"Ironing makes me feel in control," I said, scowling at Serena for always making fun of this fact about me. That and how I liked to wear my Doc Martens with everything, including dresses.

And, yes, I was aware that my ironing habit gave much away to my psychoanalyzing friend Serena, but rather than retort, she clucked her tongue. Surely, she had many theories about me, and my complicated relationship with my mother. Thankfully, she kept most of them to herself.

"You *are* in control," Serena said finally, and her voice had changed now. Gone was the teasing, but here was the Tender Serena, the caring one. And I almost couldn't take it.

I shook my head and studied my map, feeling tears burn my eyes, embarrassed.

I loved and adored my mother, thought she was the greatest, most vibrant thing in the world, except, of course, when she wasn't. She wore dresses everywhere, cinched at the waist, full skirted dresses that made her look like a 1950s film star. Her lips were always perfectly stained red, and her cigarettes were in a silver monogrammed case. The initials on it weren't hers, of course, as she found it at a yard sale, but the cultivated look, the façade, it was all Isabel. She never had enough money for eggs, for milk, for school field trips. But her shoes were always expensive designer heels.

I smiled at Serena, pushing away the vulnerable feeling inside me, the voice that told me to tell her everything. Tell her about *him*. About the *parapluie*.

Serena was breaking me down, and I wanted to tell her things I really shouldn't.

I had never, ever, not once in my entire life spoken to anyone besides Isabel about my previous life, *l'avant*, the tunnels, about any of it.

See, Mom had me selling make-up door-to-door as a nine-year-old, doing third-rate commercials for a local auto business when I was even younger, and collecting quarters from the neighbors every payday for some kind of lottery scheme at age eight. So the idea that Isabel had taught me French, spun a yarn about a harvester accident, invented a whole story, a whole life, I could believe it. Everything was a-okay if it meant coin in Isabel's pocket.

But then I got older, and the memories came at me fast and hard, so many of them, I couldn't explain them away. I mean, I could speak flawless French. I inexplicably knew how to knit—one handed, no less. I knew exactly how many milliliters of *rose absolue* it took to hit the just-right note in an elegant *eau de parfum*. And these were things I just . . . *knew*. Like instinct.

I mean, Isabel Grier was good. But was she that good?

Of course, I'd asked Mom about it all when I'd gotten older, when memories had started to surface like mad, around the onset of puberty.

Isabel referenced the whole thing, as that "load of shit." She had laughed her most obnoxious laugh, the one that I'd come to hate. The one that had made my cheeks burn hot and felt a lot like scorn.

That's all she'd said.

I'd kept promising myself I would ask her again, when I was in college, or now that I was an adult. I'd reminded myself that her laugh couldn't do anything to me anymore. But before long, she got sick. And she stayed sick. And then . . . before I even understood that the end was really coming, she was gone.

And for one last kicker, one last fit of shits and giggles, Isabel left me the damn puzzle box. From *l'avant*.

How?

When it was all supposed to be a ruse?

It was a sign I could no longer ignore. I had to weigh it, against so many other things. But now, especially, against the memory of the French flashcards.

Parapluie.

I had some serious investigating to do.

I still hadn't been able to open the puzzle box. I'd brought it to St. Paul with me. I'd gotten to the third move. I could remember that much. But, of course, I couldn't remember all the moves to get the mechanism to release. I'd contemplated forcing it open—hitting it with a hammer or prying it with a crowbar—just to see what was inside. However, really, it was too precious to me.

But what could be inside? One last letter from my dead mother? A lone Winston Light? Jesus, I could see that from Isabel. She did have a wicked sense of humor. Or would there be some kind of cosmic explanation, an answer?

"You ready to go?" Serena asked, leaving a tip on the table. "I have to get to the hospital by 2:00 PM, a patient with schizophrenia, then at 3:00 regression-therapy hypnosis." She waggled her eyebrows. She was excited about her internship placement. "Meet you back at the boarding house for dinner?"

I nodded. "Yeah, definitely. I have a lot to do as well." But my thoughts were, of course, still caught in the past. And not in terms of my research project. Maybe I would go back to my room and see if I could get further on the puzzle box.

Really, how could I even doubt *the before* anymore?

When I had first seen that Isabel had left me the puzzle box. I couldn't believe it. It was one of those moments in life, one that stops you dead in your tracks and you have to blink a few times, anchor yourself in the moment, and test out whether you're really sleeping or not, prove to your mind it isn't a dream.

It wasn't. It was real.

I took one look at that puzzle box, dragged my fingertips over the smoothly sanded and oiled wood. And I don't know if I was overjoyed or terrified, because it felt very much like both.

But my only thought was, *It's all real. Every last thing.*

Chapter 3

France, 1921

I WANTED TO PLAY ESCARGOT, BUT MARTINE-MARIE was a year older and she said we were too big for that hopscotch game now, that we should play petanque instead. I didn't feel too big. I felt seven, and that seemed pretty perfect for escargot.

I didn't know what to do with those stupid petanque balls, so I just rolled them around the patchy lawn near the distillery, liking the way the wooden balls sounded when they clanked against one another. Martine-Marie tried to explain the petanque rules to me, but I stuck out my tongue and continued to do it my own way.

"You'll start school this year, after the harvest, Lolotte," Martine-Marie said, her dark eyes serious, as she gave up on petanque and stretched out on her stomach on the weedy grass. She took a blade of it and put it in her mouth, between her teeth.

I gave up on the balls and did the same; mimicked her posture and chewed on the bitter grass. "We'll walk together." And it was high time, in my opinion. I'd been kept from school because of my staring spells, the times I went quiet. Martine-Marie was a year older than me and forever getting to do things without me. Her mama and papa let her walk down to Lac Pommier on her own and fish. She went to l'acadamie. She had her own jobs in the main building of the parfumerie, sweeping up and running errands.

"No," Martine-Marie said, flipping onto her back, stretching her arms behind her head. "You won't go to l'academie. You will have private tutors here on the grounds." She didn't seem too put out by this bit of information, but I was not happy. I sat up and thought on this.

"But I want to go with you." I didn't like being little, in size or in age.

"Lolotte, you have to quit pretending we're the same."

"What do you mean?"

"Look at your house."

I did as she said. I looked up to the main house, past the fields and distilleries, past the enfleurage and the lab. It was just my house, but then I saw it anew somehow. How big it was, with its balconies and white-pillared porch, sprawling against the lavender plateaus behind it. And there was Anneke in her white-aproned uniform tending to the rose garden out front. I thought of Martine-Marie's house then, down the road toward town, red-brick and without pillars, and with only one servant inside.

"Shut up, Martine-Marie," I said, and I pulled out two fistfuls of grass and threw them at her, because I didn't want to be different.

Why hadn't I noticed all this before?

Probably I was too busy climbing trees and caring about actual important things. Like playing pranks on Adelaide, my baby nurse, who spent a lot of her time looking the other way, reading novels, and smoking cigarettes.

"I will so go to your school," I told Martine-Marie, and she answered with a shrug.

I didn't know what I was angrier about, the school, or the fact that Martine-Marie was trying so hard to act like she didn't care. I stood up and scuffed my patent-leathers in the dirt, kicking up a cloud of dust. Martine-Marie coughed and fanned the dust from her face.

"Don't act like such a baby," she said.

I stuck my tongue out at her.

"It's not my fault, Lolotte."

"It's not mine either."

"Why are you being so mean to me?"

She looked all hurt then, wobbly-chinned, and unsure of herself. I couldn't take it. I balled my fist and, quick as a pheasant, I punched her in the arm. I ran off into the citrus orchard, where I climbed a bitter orange tree and cried, chewing on the peel of one of the fruits, staring up at the main house where my fancy mama and my busy, tie-wearing papa were deciding things that were not any of their business, hurting me right in the pit of my stomach.

Chapter 4

ISABEL'S DEATH HAD COME OUT OF NOWHERE. She and I had talked about it and prepared for it, of course, but those were just words. She'd been sick for so long that I'd internalized it as our new way of life. She'd slowed down of course, but I hadn't understood. Hadn't wanted to.

It was finals week of the spring semester, and I worked as a teaching assistant for three classes, plus my graduate work. I'd just had a hospital bed delivered to my studio apartment in Hyde Park. This round of chemo was a particularly tough one, and the hospital bed seemed like a temporary move—or at least I convinced myself it was. I'd moved Isabel into my place only weeks ago, as driving out to Evergreen Park every day had become too much of a hassle, and I was still trying to keep from registering for a leave of absence. The semester would end soon and Isabel would be on an upswing again, I told myself, her red lipstick back in place, her health and vigor only partially blanched by this cancer we'd been forced to accommodate into our lives. It all seemed par for the course; we'd been through these ups and down over the last four years again and again.

I'd just come out of a meeting with my advisor, where we'd gone over some revisions to my research proposal for the summer, and Serena was waiting for me outside the building. "Alice," she said in greeting.

"I have to go deposit my mother's check at the bank. Want to walk with me?" I asked.

Serena nodded. "We can hit up that bakery."

"Yum, cannoli. It might take me a few minutes at the bank. Isabel wants me to check if I'm actually on the account too. So I have to go inside and see an actual person."

Serena stopped short. "Whoa. She wants you on her bank account?"

"Yeah." I kept walking and Serena eventually caught back up to me, but the scrunched look of worry on her face stood fast.

Serena grabbed my elbow. "Isabel's circling the wagons."

"What do you mean?" My heartbeat sped up.

"What I mean is that Isabel knows that it's coming, Alice."

"No," I said, giving Serena an incredulous look. "That's not true."

"Her numbers were really low last week. The nurse told you that. I was there."

"They've been low before."

Serena started to say something, but then she stopped herself.

"What? Just say it." I was irritated. We moved to the side of the sidewalk to let a group of students past us, and Serena took the opportunity to grab my hand and give it a squeeze.

"Alice, when I visited last weekend, when you went to bathroom, Isabel made me promise I'd . . . take care of you." Serena's voice had turned into a whisper at the end of that sentence.

I took a deep breath. "She's Isabel. She's being dramatic." I started walking again, pulling Serena with me.

Serena hooked her elbow through mine, and she slowed our pace. I let her, as we were almost at the bank. She spoke low, hesitantly. "I watched my mother go through this same kind of illness with my aunt, and I know what things mean. I don't want you to–"

"You're wrong." I jerked my arm from hers.

She gave me a look, not angry, no, more like sympathy. And I hated it.

I stalked away, but Serena followed. "You might want to postpone your summer quarter, Alice. You'll never get this time back, and I don't want you to have regrets."

"Stop, Serena, okay? I know you mean well but—"

"You think I don't know how much you love her? You think just because she was a shitty mom growing up that I can't see that you're in denial?"

We were right by the university library then. Only a block or so from the bank. I stopped, moved over to the side so other people could pass us, and I let Serena's words hit me, really hit me.

Was this it?

Was I not seeing Mom's reality for what it was?

Would Mom not rally this time? We'd been in battle mode for so long, it was natural to assume she would come back.

"I like denial." I collapsed onto a bus bench then.

Mom's concern with the bank account was a sign, of course it was. Maybe I was too good at keeping secrets from myself, especially when they hurt too much.

Serena flopped down next to me. "I know."

I touched Serena lightly on the hand. "I'm sorry."

"I'm here for you."

After a few moments, I stood back up, and we walked in silence. When we got to the corner, I nodded. "You get the cannoli. Double the order, okay?" I turned toward the bank to make sure that my mom's measly $236.13 checking account would be willed to me after her death.

• • •

SERENA WAS INDEED RIGHT. Mom went downhill fast.

Serena called or visited me daily. She remembered to do the dishes, take out the garbage. She bought me groceries and tampons. She even filled in as TA for a few of my classes, helped me grade the final essays.

She kept me from falling apart.

Then, on the Thursday after finals, I sneaked out to my thesis seminar, as Mom had had a good day. But when I came home, there was a different look on the hospice nurse's face, some kind of forced optimism. I wanted to label it as hopeful, but it wasn't. It was afraid.

"It won't be long now," she said, her voice a warble.

I was seized with the urge to slap this nice woman across the face. I clenched my fists instead, drew in an uneven breath. "How long?" I asked.

"Hours. Maybe not even."

"No. You can't be right. She just fed herself yesterday. She laughed when the Jell-O fell off the spoon." A far-off part of me, the sane part, could hear the unhinged note in my voice.

The nurse gave me a tender look, full of pity. She stood slowly, and she placed a hand on my shoulder. It terrified me. I jerked her hand away, took a step back.

Suddenly there was so much I hadn't done, hadn't discussed. "But . . ." I said, and panic shot down my spine in a course of adrenaline. *We didn't settle on the shoes. Which ones, Mom? And what is the flower you loved from Kelly's wedding, that orchid with the pink insides? How can I order it for the funeral if I can't remember the name?* And of course, the biggest question: *How am I supposed to go on without you?*

"Alice," the nurse said, "it's always a surprise. *Always*. We're never ready."

I shook my head.

She lay asleep in the hospital bed. The purple-bronze moonlight hit her profile in exactly the right way, her features soft and peaceful.

I collapsed into the chair next to her. I took Mom's thin hand in mine, and it was cold. She squeezed my fingers so lightly. "Alice," she whispered, her eyelids working to open.

"Mom," I said, and I moved to the edge of her bed, leaned in.

I couldn't stop the tears now. Big sloppy tears hitting the eyelet bedspread. "Mom, I can't . . . I don't know what to—"

"You do. And when you're ready, look in my old sewing box . . ." Mom fought against something then. "It's from . . . from *him*." Mom coughed a terrible, rattling cough. It shook her entire body. It scared me like nothing had ever scared me before. Suddenly, I gave in.

In a very real way, that moment was when I first accepted that my mother was truly going to die.

I had fooled myself, somehow, some way, even in the face of all the facts, even when the past four years had slowly morphed into nothing but the sour smell of hospital-disinfectant waiting rooms, with our strained last-ditch hopes hammered thin as we waited for test results that never truly surprised us. My mother bore the evidence every day; it was carved into her sunken eyes. But I found a way to ignore it, clutching only to the doctor's newest, next Hail-Mary treatment, even as Mom so slowly—and then too quickly—disappeared in front of our eyes, pound by pound, day by day.

Mom gasped hard, her breath catching in her chest. "Alice," she whispered, closing her eyes. Then something swept over her features: an odd peacefulness. In that moment, I saw the child she had been, the innocence there, the hopes and dreams she had borne. And then, the moments, both tiny and grand, that had made up her life, flashed across her face—the pain and joys, struggles and triumphs. All of it played over her face in a tender second, a blink, and she looked both grateful and relieved.

Here it was. The end of my beautiful, redheaded, hot-tempered, flighty, harebrained mother. My throat pinched; my vision tunneled. "Mom," I said, useless.

"I can see it," she whispered, her eyes suddenly focusing over my head, past me, beyond me.

I leaned closer, fighting my own rising hysteria. "What, Mom? What can you see?"

"What's after. I see what's after." She laughed this high twitter of a laugh, and her eyes refocused on me. "It's beautiful." She squeezed my hand again. "You see before, Alice, and now I've seen the after."

"Mom."

"Al," she whispered. Her throat worked.

"No, you can't go. No, Mom. I'm serious. This isn't okay." I knew it was childish. I didn't care.

Her breath hitched. Her eyes closed.

"Please don't go."

"Alice." She crinkled her nose at me, a gesture that meant many things between us, a conversation, a secret code.

I crinkled mine back, and I laughed a terrible, rib-aching sob.

I draped myself on top of her then, burying my face in the space where neck met shoulder, breathing her in, pleading for her to stay with me, begging her.

Her skin was paper-thin, dry, and so very cold. I cried.

I sat up. Mom breathed in a long pull of air, slow and deliberate. I found a scrap of courage. "I love you, Mom."

The slightest of nods. Her eyes took on that other-worldly quality again, unfocused and . . . a little scared. "I smell . . ." she whispered, "roses."

And then she exhaled, longer and slower than a usual breath, a full emptying of the lungs, and then it was finished.

I waited, my own breath held tight in my chest, listening, watching, certain she would inhale.

The old-fashioned windup clock on her nightstand ticked loudly. It read 1:24 AM. I placed my hand on Mom's chest. Surely it would rise.

It didn't.

I watched the second hand make its route around the face of the clock. Once. Twice.

How quickly my mother's face went slack, her body inanimate, so . . . uninhabited.

Where was her soul now?

I stood, my knees knocking, my limbs vibrating with a specific, useless rage.

I turned toward my bookshelf. I lifted an antique carnival-glass swan from the top shelf. I weighed the amber-colored object in my hand. I pulled my arm back, and I threw it hard, so very hard, across the room, straight into the mirror on the wall.

The hospice nurse gasped.

The swan hit the mirror with a hard thunk, then landed on the ratty carpet, rolling around for a second before stilling on its side. Amazingly, neither the mirror nor the swan chipped or cracked. I had wanted them both to shatter loudly, exploding into a million little shards. A great, loud, violent mess.

But, no, it didn't happen.

I took one last look at my mother, her shell. Then, I glanced at the hospice nurse who had the sense to be quietly crying into her handkerchief. I turned and left her bedside. I stood in the kitchenette for a long moment, motionless, and then headed out to my little apartment balcony.

There was one last thing she had asked me to do. So I would do it.

The base of Isabel's perfume had to be vanilla essence, I just knew it, so I took out a clean dropper and I added fifteen drops of vanilla to the little beaker, my favorite glass beaker with the funny little filigree on it. My hand shook while I counted out the drops, and I had to swallow against a sob, but I refused to fall apart until I had done this. For Mom.

I mixed the vanilla with a smidge of cinnamon, which gave it a little more depth.

The head scent was easy. I used two-parts lavender and one-part bitter orange. This was a favorite blend of mine, and it always reminded me of Mom. Sophisticated, contradictory, with a bright splash.

Now, the head scent is the one you usually smell first, that first whiff of a perfume. It hits you right away. It doesn't usually linger around forever, but it's often the one people judge first. Some noses—or perfume makers—think that the head scent is the most important.

Not me.

For me, it's always the heart scent, what's in the middle, holding it all together that is the most important. For Mom, it took me a while to get the right heart. I had to really think about the substance of the chord, the heart choices. Because wasn't that always the way? Wasn't the heart of something—of someone—the most difficult, most enigmatic part to know and to truly understand?

I mean, how well do we even know the true terrain, the ins and outs, the deepest corners, of anyone's heart?

Even the people closest to us? *Especially them.*

Of course, I had to use roses, since they were waiting for Mom in the *after*. Whatever she might mean, although I admit I wanted to picture pearly gates and long-lost relatives greeting her. But roses were almost too recognizable and pretty. And Mom was that: pretty, charming, but also over the top. Contrary. She was complicated and layered, difficult at times, easygoing when it suited her—prickly and proud, a force. I wanted her fragrance, her last fragrance, to show that. It had to be nuanced.

She was so many things—smart and silly, ruthless and goddamn selfish, and a very, very good liar.

So I searched and tried different combinations. I spent a long while out there, on our little balcony.

I quelled that nervous flicker of panic, blocked it all out, by focusing on the perfume. On some level, I knew I was teetering on the edge, about to lose my shit, just really fall apart, but for some reason, the perfume . . . the *doing* kept me somehow bolted down. Steady. I had played with these scents, listened to the clink-clank of the tiny glass bottles of essential oils so many nights with Mom, it was like I could almost pretend . . ..

I sat out at the little bistro table, playing with my droppers and beakers, trying desperately to get it right, because I couldn't do anything for Mom anymore, not personally, not directly, except for this. And it sort of mattered.

Then I got it. Two parts tuberose, one-part clary sage, and just a dash of geranium. It shouldn't have worked as well as it did. The amber coolness in the clary sage seemed to magnify the singular top note of the geranium, and the scents married, creating something different, unexpected. Then, when that was added to the base and the head blends, it . . . worked. A scent that was inviting, open, lush, but with a cool hint to it, a note of mystery, a tease that there was more under the surface.

It was a scent worthy of Mom.

I would put it on her wrists and behind her ears at the funeral parlor, and I would know that I got this scent finished. I would keep this small amber bottle, labeled Isabel #1, and I would know that I finished what she had asked me to start those precious months ago, and this was a tiny, good thing inside a very, very bad time.

As I made my final batch, the one I'd actually bottle and use, I chose the expensive perfumer's alcohol and not the vodka I usually used. Even though my experience with my at-home perfuming seemed to show me that it didn't really matter. I couldn't tell the difference. Using vodka as an alcohol substitute worked very well. It had virtually no smell, so it didn't mar the scents that you were marrying.

I hadn't found the vodka-substitution trick on the web or in any of my home-perfumery library books. It was something I just knew. From before. My *grand-pere* told me about it one day when I was playing in his study. I remembered the ivy-printed wallpaper on the walls. The smell of the wood burning in the fireplace. But that was so long ago, probably close to a hundred years. From *l'avant*.

Chapter 5

France, 1922

GRAND-PÈRE TAUGHT ME THE TRICK TO *training my nose. "It is a Guillet family tradition," he'd told me many times. I'd done it so often, spent so many hours blindfolded that now I was passing on the trick to my closest friend.*

"Here, Martine-Marie," I said. "Tie this around your eyes. No cheating."

We sat at the outdoor table near the enfleurage. I had taken my time in setting up this experiment, sure that Martine-Marie would never be as good at it as me.

Martine-Marie grumbled and complained, but she folded the linen strip over once, twice, three times until it was thick enough and would block out her sight. I helped her knot it behind her head.

Then, I lifted the first item from beneath the picnic cloth on the table. "No touching," I said, and I lifted the object beneath her nose. Martine-Marie instantly sniffed and a smile broke over her face.

"That is a lemon."

I started easy, because I didn't want to hurt her feelings too badly. "Oui!" I praised her. "Now the next one."

"Hmm," she said "That is sharp. Vinegar?"

"Oui!"

Grand-père would often praise me and my scenting talents in front of Maman and Father, at the dinner table, or while we rode in the carriage to church. It never failed to anger Maman. "Must we call her Le Nez? We already nickname her as Lolotte, as she is tiny, now this?"

She didn't like my working as "the nose." She had other plans for me: learning needlework, and worse, lessons on the behemoth of an instrument, the harp! To Maman, I was a debutante in need of shaping, for Father and for Grand-père, I could be more.

Father let me tag behind him some days. He asked one of his employees to fashion a chemist's leather apron small enough for my frame, just for these times when I would shadow him in the lab. He explained the many details of parfum to me. And I listened.

"Olfactory memory is the strongest type of memory. One sniff of something, and you can be right back somewhere, lost in a long-ago moment. Experiencing your first moment of the sea, dipping your toe in the surf. Or bringing your scythe down smoothly, easily through the tall stalks of the tuberose plant in the early moments of dawn. Cleaning the creek mud from an expensive leather shoe because your daughter didn't listen to her maman *once again."*

He'd winked at me with this last one.

I knew what Father meant. Some scents mean something to you and others just sort of . . . don't.

First, you have to learn the families. There are your orientals: musks and spicy scents. Your florals: roses, jasmine, magnolia. Your chypre: oakmoss, citrus. But there's something more important than the families. It's how those scent families are going to mix together. Because a typical perfume has a lot of notes in it, from nine to ninety-seven. Perfumes are like chords on that blasted harp—different notes put together to make a beautiful sound. And there are always three parts of this chord: the base, the heart, and the head.

I presented Martine-Marie with another object beneath her nose, smiling to myself, as I knew she would never, ever get this one, although I had on my very first try.

“Leather?” she asked.

“No.”

“Um.”

“It’s pencil shavings.”

“Oh, oui. *Can I take this off now?”*

“No, I have a mixture now. So two things. Please guess.”

I moved the bowl near her. “Lavender, of course,” but then she screwed up her nose. “Mint?”

“Very good, Martine-Marie.”

“The next one has . . .” but then I felt it coming on as it often did. I had no control over the staring spells. No more than a moment or two of warning. I knew enough to sit down. I felt a strange calmness, a closing down of my senses. And then, it was like I was there, with Martine-Marie *and not.*

I heard her voice, tinny and far-away.

But I heard her, nonetheless. “Again? I will get your maman.”

I could not move my body, couldn’t as much as blink, but I didn’t panic, as I knew it would only last a moment or two . . . maybe a few more.

It was nothing but an interruption, one that would leave me worn, a bit cross, but that wasn’t the worst part. No, Maman *would begin her worrying anew.*

If only I could stop Martine-Marie *from alerting her. Ah, how I liked to keep these episodes a secret.* Maman *liked to use them as ammunition, as evidence to win her arguments, that I was to live a quieter life, one that required many more petticoats and hours of drudgery inside the fancy parlor.*

One that required much of the essence of Lolotte Guillet *to suffocate.*

Chapter 6

OF COURSE, ISABEL'S FUNERAL WAS OVER-the-top—and shabby—but planned for and even paid for ahead of time from her hospital bed, which surprised me. A magician performed graveside, releasing two surly-looking doves. Isabel's friend Arnie played the accordion. And friends brought balloons to release into the sky.

I hated and loved it. Serena held my hand the whole way through.

Mom's funeral: eccentric and barely respectable—like the rest of our patched-together lives.

When all the hoopla was done, I stood at Mom's graveside, her casket now lowered into the muddy earth. I knew Serena was saying the goodbyes, the thank-yous that I should be doling out, but I couldn't leave her yet.

Mom.

I scrunched my nose in just the right way—*I love you; I need you, please see me still, and are you onto another life already?*

My one final goodbye.

A blackbird landed on the bough of the pine tree above Mom's grave—that open, gaping mouth of a grave, ready to swallow Mom, to swallow me too, our entire ramshackle lives. The dirt was black and wet with rainwater from the night before, barely drier than mud. The bird cawed, looking down with its indifferent, beady eyes.

I felt a rising sort of panic.

Mom would be cold, Mom would be trapped, Mom wouldn't be able to breathe. Then I shut myself off, like a switch. *I'm not here. I'm not here. I'm not me. This isn't real.*

I live in France with a mother I don't like much at all and a parfumerie *I love. I'm another person, a better one. And was it real, Mom? Was it even real?*

I will never know now.

Something tugged at the edges of my consciousness then. Had Mom referenced *l'avant* in those last moments we'd had? She'd talked about seeing the after . . . and me seeing the before.

Had that been some kind of admission?

My reasoning couldn't spin the wheels right now. My head was muddled and exhausted, hazy with grief.

I could only watch that blackbird, its glossy black wings. I watched as if outside of myself, as if I could be that bird, that blackbird on the bough, just passing by, an onlooker, nothing more.

Suddenly, I was crying and I was kneeling next to the grave, in the wet earth, imagining Mom in that casket, in her purple dress with her peaceful expression, and the beautiful and horrible scent of Isabel #1 mingling with the singular fragrance of death.

I picked up a large clump of the black dirt, and I held it in my hand, crumbled it in my palm. I wanted to become that dirt, fall asleep underneath it, swallow it, breathe it, and die in it, right here, right along with Mom.

The blackbird above me cawed in agreement.

I looked up at the sound of its voice, and there were two blackbirds now, sitting on the bough above the grave, side-by-side. They seemed to be watching us, and I didn't like it. Their beady, black-oil eyes.

Birds were always associated with death for me, for some reason. They seemed too fragile for this world, their tiny frames, and feather-light skeletons.

Or maybe it was the other thing. Maybe they were too powerful, with their ability to fly over our little earthly lives, to hover above, to see it all as it really was. And what did we look like from that vantage point? From above?

The blackbirds took flight, in one smooth motion, together, in perfect tandem.

And there it was.

A memory, from *l'avant*.

As I sat there, quelling my shuddering sobs, I welcomed the memory in all its too-shiny and bright falseness, wishing there was a way to escape into it, forever.

Chapter 7

France, 1923

THE BIRDS FLEW UP IN ONE SYNCHRONIZED motion from the lavender fields, hundreds of them, dotting the sky in crow-black patterns.

I swallowed the last of my blueberry patisserie, and I watched them disappear beyond the orchard.

"They call a group of crows a murder. At least in English they do," Martine-Marie said.

"I know," I said, although I didn't. "A murder of crows." I figured she knew this from Gillian, her American cousin, whose father was some kind of rags-to-riches story, a pauper-turned-businessman. Gillian and her family were spending the summer with us. Mostly Gillian was bragging about all her worldly travels, keeping Martine-Marie from me, and generally getting in my way.

"We need to get back to work," Martine-Marie said, putting away the last of her egg sandwich, crumbling up the brown paper and string that she had wrapped it in.

I stood up and straightened my dungarees, a hard-fought win over my mother's insistence on skirts and dresses, even now with the world bending, turning itself inside out with modern changes, with women like Coco Chanel and Josephine Baker in

Paris reinventing what it meant to be a woman, and even country women like Mrs. Parcell and Martine-Marie's mother discussing women getting the vote. Seemed like the whole world was getting smarter, just not my mother.

I was eleven now, more cunning and diplomatic in my dealings with my parents. I had agreed to the tutors, of course, seeing as I was pounding my head against a brick wall, but it meant I got to work here, in the parfumerie lab, always. Each afternoon and all summer. No exceptions. That had been my bargain; I would quit fighting them about l'acadamie and about the occasional doctor, and they had to quit fighting me about the parfumerie.

I took one last swig from my canteen. "I want to show you something," I said, getting up and grabbing Martine-Marie's hand.

"But it's time," she said, gesturing toward the other workers, their backs bent over the lavender, pulling weeds, their heads covered in straw sunhats not unlike our own.

"Come on," I said, and we took off hand-in-hand for the enfleurage building. We ran past the sign by the door that read, "Interdit." We knew it was forbidden, but there had to be some perks to being the boss's daughter.

We walked in, and it was a rush of scents, jasmine and tuberose, lavender and orange blossom. Inside this small ramshackle barn building, the oldest on the grounds, dating back a century, there were stacks of wooden frames, hundreds of them, which held the linen screens. These were the enfleurage screens. Workers had spread animal fat on the linen, and then covered it with scads of flower petals. This was an old-fashioned way to draw out the essence of a flower. It was clearly the right way, if you listened to Giles Abraham, Martine-Marie's father, which I did.

We weren't supposed to be in here. You didn't disturb the flowers when they were giving over the scent. It was common knowledge. It was common law.

Martine-Marie and I moved slowly, reverently, between the aisles of stacked frames. This aisle held stack after stack, frame after frame of purple petals. Lavender and its cool, calm scent.

"Isn't it something?" I said.

Martine-Marie nodded in silence. Her parents were Father's assistants, his trusted leaders. And Martine-Marie and I were the same in how we felt about this place and what was made here, how such beauty could be grown from our dirt. She loved it too.

"My papa says we may go to America."

"No," I answered. Martine-Marie on another adventure without me.

"Well, you as well, Lolotte. The whole parfumerie to move, to expand?"

I didn't know how to feel about this. America meant progress. Could I like this idea? I didn't like that Martine-Marie knew about it before me. That was for sure.

We turned down another row, this time the large white petals of jasmin were stacked on either side. Their exotic scent filled our heads. I pictured my grand-pere as a younger man, even then his red kerchief always at his throat, standing proudly on his first plot of land, up on the western plateau. My father told this story often, how he started with two acres and fifty enfleurage frames. How he fled the big city and his job as a butcher for a new life, to work the land.

The sliding wooden door near the rear of the building made a creaking noise, and Martine-Marie and I froze. "Ow," someone said, and I figured they had gotten scraped by the jagged metal of the half-broken handle on that sliding door. I had ruined many an apron on that thing.

We heard footsteps. Martine-Marie squeezed my hand. But no one appeared. We looked at each other. I raised my eyebrows.

"Hou!"

She jumped out from behind a row of frames, all gangly legs and ears and teeth, startling us both. But her white-blond hair gave her away.

"Boo yourself," I said, punching her on the shoulder. " You're not supposed to be in here, Gillian."

"Neither are you two," she said, smiling.

"Maman is going to give me a hiding," Martine-Marie said.

Wagon wheels crunched on the dirt outside, and Gillian grabbed our hands, yanking us toward the rear door. "Come on!"

She pulled us out toward the large barn that housed the distillery machinery, and when we crouched behind it, I saw something small moving at our feet. "Oh *no," I said, and I bent down. "It's a swallow," I said. It was pink and leathery, no feathers yet. "Its mother must be around here somewhere."*

"Your scent will ruin him," Martine-Marie said. "Don't touch it."

"Let's find its mother," I said, climbing up the nearby apple tree, trying to find the nest.

"It's not going to make it," Gillian said. "I think I will step on it to end its pain."

"No!" Martine-Marie said. "Leave the bird alone, Gillian. And Lolotte, we need to get back to work! Maman will knock me senseless if she catches me back here."

"Oh hush," I told her, hopping down from the tree.

"You said it's a sparrow?" Gillian asked, now crouched down next to it.

"No, a swallow," I said, spying the bird more closely now.

It was indeed hurt, with half of its body nearly flattened into the cobblestone walkway. Its one wing sat there, immovable, lame. It was a terrible sight, its beak opening, closing, looking for something, someone.

"Somebody needs to hold it, comfort it," Martine-Marie said.

"What?" Gillian said. "It's just a stupid bird."

"It's not stupid," I said, feeling tender in my heart, wondering why I cared so much for this creature.

"He can't be so alone at the end, can he?" Martine-Marie asked, and Gillian laughed.

"I'm going back to the field to get you in trouble," Gillian said, taking off toward the lavender. We let her go.

"Do you think the bird is scared?" I asked.

"I'm sure. Wouldn't you be?"

Martine-Marie picked it up in her hand, gently, cupping it against her chest. "I'm here," she told it, and I watched Martine-Marie as she furrowed her brow, trying to think of something to say to the bird. Martine-Marie settled on humming a tune instead, and, after a moment, I realized I knew the song, from church, some old organ piece. I hummed along.

"You know what they call a group of swallows in English?" Martine-Marie asked me.

"No. Probably something crazy."

"A flight of swallows."

"Huh," I said, and I peeked into her hands. The bird had given up the fight. It lay there, lifeless. We both stared at it for a second. I sighed. "I'll get a shovel." And when I ran away toward the shed, I heard Martine-Marie whisper something to the bird. I couldn't make out the words, but it made me feel better for the bird anyway.

Chapter 8

MY THIRD FULL DAY IN ST. PAUL, I SPENT it touring and photographing the grounds of the old Hamm's Brewery. One outbuilding was a gorgeous octagonal horse barn, with rustic quarry stone walls and a barnboard roof that sloped drastically to the east. The tour guide spoke of the brewery tunnels in which dairy farmers now aged bleu cheese and a famous local gorgonzola, and the deeper caverns where other farmers grew rare species of puffball, stinkhorn, and morel mushrooms, the humidity and temperature fitting for these ventures. The tunnels, according to urban myth, were dug because of Prohibition and its need for transporting illegal liquor, but that, of course, was not true, as the labyrinthine maze of tunnels was first part of a design of silica mines, used for making glass.

I ate all this information up, took copious notes, photographs, but I was crestfallen to find out that there was no longer any tunnel access offered with tours to the public. It was a triumphant day for my research, however, even if I couldn't poke around in the tunnels, to see if these were indeed the same tunnels.

From the before.

Him.

I came back to the boardinghouse that evening, a bit weary, and I found

Serena and Mrs. Signy sitting in the parlor, surrounded by doilies and antique furniture, their heads bent over what looked like a photo album, a glass of wine in each their hands.

I paused in the doorway of Mrs. Signy's foyer, studying the parquet pattern of the original wide-plank pine flooring, trying to think of how I could excuse myself and go up the stairs to my room without being rude.

But I quickly understood this wasn't going to happen. Serena spotted me, "Toots, get in here!"

Toots?

How long exactly had they been drinking?

It was then I noticed the two opened bottles of wine on the coffee table in front of them, along with an array of homemade pastries. And also several other leather-bound albums, large and crackled with age.

"Miss Alice, please come join our party. What did you learn today?" Mrs. Signy asked. She was elderly and barrel-shaped, with the most jovial of faces. A pink-cheeked Mrs. Claus, with a teased white beehive, she spoke with a true Minnesota accent.

She leaned over toward Serena and said something I couldn't make out. Serena laughed her loud guffaw-of-a-laugh and swatted Miss Signy on the shoulder. The whole scene was so far from Serena's earlier take of this place being a horror movie set, I found myself smiling, drawn into their scene. I took a seat in the matching black-and-white toile armchair across from the sofa.

Mrs. Signy moved to pour me a glass of wine, and the plastic cover on the sofa cushion gave a little squeak. "You like red?" she asked.

"Red is fine. Thank you," I said, accepting the glass. "How long have you two been at this?" I gestured with my wineglass to Serena, who smiled with glassy eyes.

"Long enough for me to know I love Molly, here—love in, like, a deep, deep way. She came from Ireland in the forties, first to New York of course, where she worked as a cigarette girl on Broadway! She's lived a *life*, Alice."

Molly?

Serena was indeed drunk. But God, she was great. So friendly, so open.

"I'm so very sorry to hear about the recent death of your mother," Mrs. Signy said, pursing her lips into a concerned look for me, just as a tiny, high-pitched burp escaped.

This took Serena into a fit of giggles.

"Thank you." I sipped the wine.

"That's right," Mrs. Signy said. "Drink . . . and quickly. You have to catch up." Her vowels came from far back in her throat, hovering somewhere geographically between Chicago and Canada.

"Her husband passed away," Serena said, refilling her own glass.

"Oren." Mrs. Signy nodded. "He wrote erotica. Some very popular titles, no doubt you've read him."

I nearly spit the wine from my mouth but recovered just barely with only a cough. Serena watched me with wide eyes, like, *Can you believe this?*

Mrs. Signy continued, gesturing toward a bookshelf on the far parlor wall. "He was very good, actually. Male/female. Male/male. He had a way about him, you know? Like some people do. A romantic at heart. He actually won quite a few awards." She flipped a page in the album on her lap and moved to show me. "This is Oren here." She pointed to a robust man with a ruddy complexion and a shiny bald head.

"I'm so sorry," I offered. "Very handsome."

"No," Mrs. Signy said, but she brought her hand to her mouth in a gesture of affection, pressing her knuckles to her lips. "But he was a thorough and creative lover."

It was Serena's turn then to choke on her wine.

"And Lordy could he bake. Try this," Mrs. Signy said, pushing a plate toward me with a flaky pastry. "It's Oren's recipe. I'm not quite able to get it perfect, but it passes, eh?"

I bit into it, nodding, assuming I would have to be polite. But, oh, it had the texture of a croissant, and it was . . . fresh, flaky heaven, carrying a hint of saffron. "This is wonderful." I took a second bite.

"My husband made it every Tuesday, only because he knew I loved it. *Vetebrod.* Swedish flatbread. Oren came over as a child in the thirties, and I, of course, am Irish through and through. Born here though. You can imagine the problems that caused so long ago, but you are from a different age and you young people don't understand the pressures of heritage. Swedish, Irish, not always peas and carrots."

"How long has he . . ." My voice trailed off.

"Lost him before last Christmas holiday," she said. "We bought this place and made some changes so many years ago, modified it for business. We didn't have children, and we needed a project, so . . . It was his dream. He was full of ideas; you would've liked him." She gestured to me. "You're the one writing about the rehabbing of the old spots around town, right?"

"Yes ma'am."

"This house was his baby for a while." Mrs. Signy got a wistful look in her eye. "I'm mostly used to the loneliness now, but I still find I make the *vetebrod* every Tuesday, just like he always used to. It keeps me busy, doesn't it?"

I nodded, bringing my wine to my lips.

Mrs. Signy sipped her wine. "Your friend here has been telling me about her research at the hospital, so I suppose that you should tell me about the brewery."

I nodded and summed up my day for Mrs. Signy. "I'm going to visit the Wabasha Caverns tomorrow," I offered. I took another sip of wine and I welcomed that warm fuzzy feeling from the alcohol. It was what I needed on this night, so that I could find some sleep rather than lie awake and think about a purple-and-blue *parapluie* and the puzzle box. And *him*.

"Make sure you go for the actual tour, not just a visit. Quite an interesting place, Wabasha. You know Dillinger hid out there in the 20s, Capone frequented the dances, all that gangster mumbo jumbo."

I nodded. "The tour starts at 9:00 AM."

"It's a Wednesday tomorrow? Oh, you're in luck. Eli Braithwaite will be there—he'll be the tour guide at the caverns. He'll take you underground.

He's a professor at St. Catherine's, grandson of a friend of mine, went to school with Hillary Jones whose mother owns the Laundromat, does tarot cards too, but that's hooey. He was engaged to the girl, I believe, but that went south somehow. But Father God and Sonny Jesus, he's a looker. I've had him for tea a time or two, helped me when I was renovating the downstairs bath. He's good with his hands. Might be tough to keep your skirts on, Miss Alice."

Serena dissolved into a fit of laugher, while I just gaped.

Mrs. Signy didn't notice. "Eli doesn't believe in the ghosts or the other legends though."

"There's a ghost?" Serena asked, refilling her wine glass, and of course, spilling onto the coffee table. I watched as one of the delicate doilies absorbed the reddish-purple wine. Serena wiped it up with the hem of her shirt.

Mrs. Signy didn't seem to notice. "Oren heard the ghost."

"There's supposedly a ghost at the Wailing Arch which is in the tunnels," I explained to Serena. I read a lot about the area.

"Oren heard it on several occasions, if you believe him." She turned to me specifically and said, "He did have a writer's imagination, you know, God bless him. But he loved the tunnels. Was even toying with writing a romance based on the Lovers' Legend, you know, after he found his first paper scrap of poetry."

"What poetry?" I asked, trying not to sound too interested, but my heart thumped against my rib cage, the wine suddenly making me feel flushed, a sheen of sweat on my upper lip.

Poetry?

Tunnels?

Swedish immigrants?

Mrs. Signy heaved herself from the floral-upholstered couch, and she held up a finger in a just-wait gesture. I watched as she walked her side-to-side waddle into the kitchen.

I looked at Serena who shrugged, but I could feel Serena's eyes on me. She could sense I was interested in this story. Did I seem *too* interested?

After a few moments, Mrs. Signy came back with a shoebox. She set it on the coffee table as she settled back on the sofa. She rifled through the box, which held papers, index cards, and several cassette tapes, as far as I could see. She lifted one tape. "This one here has the Wailing Ghost on it. Oren taped it back in the 80s, I think. Poor quality, but there nonetheless." She set it on the table, then shuffled through the box again. "This was his favorite. I think he was the second person, no, . . . wait, maybe the third to find a poem." She handed me a small plastic bag. I took it from her and saw it had a small rough-edged piece of paper encased inside it, flattened and yellowed, the typed printed on it faded with age.

"Other people have found poems?" I asked.

"Oh yes, they're hidden in the tunnels. Very romantic-like. Love poems. Some people say that it was a way that two star-crossed lovers communicating, *a la* Romeo-and-Juliet. There's even a letter. Mary Nearhouse has the original. It was quite the topic years back."

I stood up to get a better look at the baggie's contents in the light of the parlor lamp. My hand shook a bit. Serena stood and was now looking over my shoulder. The poetry was typed.

Just one line.

A beautiful one.

I recognized the verse.

Not from *the before* though. Or was it?

So many of my memories from the before were fleeting, circling only the edges of my consciousness for moments at a time, only landing for a blip, like a hummingbird in motion.

But my love of poetry had spilled over to this life, so I knew a classic when I saw it.

For this is love and nothing else is love.

It was Robert Frost.

I wasn't sure but I thought it was from "A Prayer in Spring." And my breath caught. I had always had a special place in my heart for Frost, his lyrical, Modernist beauty.

I had the overwhelming, childish urge to cry.

Because it reminded me of *him?*

Or was it simply the words affecting me . . . how Frost could dig deep inside you and get at something so delicate, so guarded, so protected?

I took a deep breath, and I let Serena take the tiny scrap of paper in a decades-old sandwich baggie from my hands, but when she did, the light from Mrs. Signy's parlor lamp caught the edge of the paper. And that sparked something in my memory.

Something happened then. My heart seemed to both stop and speed up at the same time. The hairs on the back of my neck bristled.

Serena's voice, Mrs. Signy's as well, they faded to the background.

And I was there, in the boardinghouse parlor, but I was somewhere else as well – *l'avant?*—and I saw that same thick, ecru writing paper from the baggie, rolled tightly into the carriage of an antique typewriter.

And I saw another line from the poem as it was being typed out, each key forcing the type hammer to hit the paper, leaving a freshly inked letter, then a word, then the whole line:

Like nothing else by day, like ghosts by night;

The typewriter had a "g" that hung too low on the line. I saw it, clear as day. I knew it.

That was it.

I couldn't see any more, couldn't replay it in my mind to refocus my gaze on the fingers pressing the keys, or to turn and face the typist.

No, but it was . . . something.

Did I know this poem from the before after all? Or was this something else?

Could *he* have written this? Typed this? Left it in the tunnels for . . . who? Me?

For this is love and nothing else is love.

My knees buckled and I flopped onto the armchair, Serena giggling behind me, now at my shoulder. "Too much wine already? You lightweight."

I started to say something, but then I didn't. Mrs. Signy kept talking though. "You might want to look through this old collection, Alice. Oren loved those tunnels. Was down there half the night sometimes. He'd wake me once in a while with a few loud knocks, because that darn blue door would stick—weather, eh? Well, surely, there's room in your research paper for old sentimental notions about history and—"

"Wait, what do you mean he would wake you? The blue door?"

"Oh, there's a door that leads into the tunnels from my coal cellar."

"There is?" Serena asked, sitting on the arm of my chair. She elbowed me. "Like a trapdoor? A secret bookshelf that swings out?"

Mrs. Signy laughed. "No, but it is hidden by a curtain. It's from back in the days of Prohibition. There are tunnels like that all over the city. Not just under the big speakeasies. I mean, someone had to be making the hooch in their bathtubs, eh?"

Serena laughed. "Cheers to that." She clinked her glass with Mrs. Signy. But then I could feel Serena's eyes on me. She knew me better than she let on sometimes.

And I couldn't stop staring at that poem, so much so that Serena gave it back to me.

For this is love and nothing else is love

I steadied myself and stood. I added the poem back to Oren's box. "I think I'm going to turn in for the night," I said. "You sure you don't mind if I look through this?"

"Oren would've loved for someone to be interested."

Chapter 9

France, 1930

THE LAB SAT SEPARATE FROM THE OTHER BUILDINGS. It was made from stone and had been an old farmhouse, with additions here and there, held together with spit and dirt and crumbling stone. Inside, it was like a maze with many small rooms and ante rooms, cubbies, and offices the size of closets, all littered with racks of test tubes and glass beakers, pipettes and mixing rods, hot plates and Bunsen burners. And in the closet, as it was known, the large rack up against the northern wall, sat dozens of amber perfume bottles, all labeled in Mrs. Abraham's hand. These were our absolutes. Our starting points, the essences. We had our own lavender and tuberose, jasmine and orange blossom, sandalwood and more. But we also had imported ambergris, which came from whales and anchored a scent, gave it a good base. We had a kilo of iris absolute that cost a rumored fortune. We had African civet, a true rarity, and many other essential oils, ready to become more than a scent . . . a parfum.

We also had a small section of synthetics too. It was all very controversial, and another thing that my parents and I fought over constantly, but Mr. Abraham agreed with me. Mr. Abraham was a good businessman, and he understood the need for progress, so once he knew that all the big perfume houses were doing it, we did it too.

We had a team of chemists come in to teach our noses how to mix aldehydes, and how to incorporate them into our mostly natural accords.

It did seem wrong to make perfumes from chemicals at first, but once the chemist showed Mr. Abraham and me how to mix the exact scent of a lily, we were floored. Lilies were selfish, beautiful flowers, keeping their scent for their own. They didn't give up their fragrance. Not through distillation or enfleurage *or anything.*

"Oh mon dieu!" *Mr. Abraham had cried. "Henriette, come quick!" And Mrs. Abraham could barely believe it either.*

A synthetic lily fragrance. Truly, progress had come to Grasse.

I loved it. All of it. The new and old. The old farm house. The synthetics. The enfleurage. *Mr. Abraham and his northern accent, rolling his r's so hard. Everything. But most of all I loved that I got to be part of it. For a long time, the fields drew me, and I worked there, sweating in the sun, long, hard hours, feeling at one with the land and the soil, the germinating seeds and the magical scents hidden within. But soon, the next step of the process called to me too. I started spending my free time in the labs, helping anyway I could, washing glassware for the chemists, measuring, jotting notes in a little leather notebook that my father gave me. Mr. Abraham liked how interested I was, and I think he noticed how I turned down countless invitations from Martine-Marie and our friends to go out and be young and frivolous, so he finally took me seriously. He let me take up an unused corner on the second floor of the lab.*

I had a desk and a stool, some hand-me-down equipment, and a ceiling only five feet high, because the thatched roof was in dire need of repair at this end. The other chemists teased me, about how I fit here so perfectly because I was so petite, but I didn't mind. I was here, in the lab, and I often spent entire afternoons and evenings lost in mixing scents, in trying to copy scents from memory. This was my new love, second only to the fields and the plants they produced.

Mr. Abraham was amazed at how closely I could copy a fragrance, down to nearly the exact drop-to-drop ratio, from only ever having smelled it. I could break it down into its essential components, usually with just a few tries.

Coco Chanel, the feminist icon and absolute hero of mine, had invented the glorified Chanel Number 5. I'd smelled it once, on a day trip to Paris with Martine-Marie and my mother, all gussied up in our Sunday finest. I remembered two things about that day, the horrible way my feet pinched into my shoes, and the gorgeous, ethereal smell of that parfum. *It took me close to a week, but I got it. The trick no one knew was the addition of a synthetic aldehyde. It added a little sparkle, rounded out the floral scent, bit back the cloying nature of the tuberose.*

I told Mr. Abraham that I hadn't written it down, the exact measurements, when I finally got it right, because I didn't want Guillet Parfum in the business of copying. But of course, I had written it down.

But what good was perfuming if you were only going to copy? To invent, to create, that was something else entirely. So here I was, with my shoulders bent over my workspace, the low ceiling pressing down so hard I could smell the moldy hay of the roof.

I began with a cocoa and cognac base, something so masculine you'd never hear of perfumers using it for women, but I was going to. There were no rules anymore, were there? Hadn't the 20s taught us that? Hadn't Coco Chanel and the American flappers gotten rid of rules?

I added the peppery scent of coriander and a light citrus lime, and I knew that I was on to something. Sometimes, it was what shouldn't work, that absolutely did.

That, right there, was the difference between reading about something and doing something. You just never knew. I sat on this for a long while, putting a test paper in the blend over and over, getting a fresh sniff of the scent, trying to determine what it was that I needed to add next. I had the base, and the head, now I needed the heart.

*I was gone, lost in thought, when I heard a throat clear behind me. I stood up, startled, hitting my head hard on the low ceiling. "*Ah, la vaca!*" I cried out.*

Martine-Marie laughed then.

"How long have you been there?"

*"Long enough to hear you swearing under your breath," she said with a smile. "*Merde, merde, merde,*" Martine-Marie teased. "Can you hurry up? Or we'll never get to the cinema in time." She checked her watch. "I want to ride in Jean-Luc's motorcar, don't you?"*

But I was already showing her my mixture. "Look," I said. "Smell this. It is coriander and lime. The base will be cocoa and cognac. But what it really makes me think of is coffee spoons." I sat down at my desk and I wrote that on a piece of paper.

"I don't smell coffee," she said, taking the paper from me and sniffing it, perching herself on the edge of my desk.

"No," I said, "not coffee per se, but it reminds me of the poem by T.S. Eliot. Surely l'academie *has taught you something. Even my conservative tutors teach me these radical poets."*

"I do know Mr. *Eliot, yes. Oh, the lovesong one,* oui*?" Martine-Marie asked.*

"Yes," I said. "That is the poem. It is about life passing you by, and how we get caught up in other people's conventions and expectations, and we forget that we are to live. You know?" I stood, and I walked over to the lone window at the other end of the little second floor, and looked out at the lavender fields, stoop-shouldered and feeling something stir within me.

"J. Alfred Prufrock," She said. "Right? That's in the title?"

"Yes, that's the one."

"Measuring his life out in coffee spoons."

I looked up toward the main house, its pillars and manicured gardens, the terrace where my mother took her tea every afternoon. "My mother would prefer that I measure out my life in coffee spoons. Preferably wearing a skirt below the knee, silk stockings and a corset, and a fashionable new hat, yet not anything even remotely flapper." I laughed, but it sounded bitter. It was on the tip of my tongue to tell Martine about the big row with my mother this morning, how I was supposed to be at the house right now, getting ready for some dinner with a very eligible bachelor in attendance. How we had raised our voices so loudly to each other that Father had come in and shushed us, intervening on my behalf. Something Father rarely did.

Martine-Marie asked then, "If you don't want coffee spoons, what is it that you want, Lolotte?"

"Well, to grow my own scents and make perfume, of course."

"I think you already are doing that."

"That's it!" I said, and I ran down the stairs, in a hurry, nearly falling over, and

I stood in front of the closet, searching. "It's supposed to be in alphabetical order. People don't put things . . . Ah ha!" I turned and ran back upstairs, with Martine-Marie at my heel.

"I've got it," I said. "That note, right there in the base. The one that's already there, leading your nose, the one you're already smelling, that's the one this needs. Just stronger. And what brings out cognac? Spearmint."

I decided on a ratio, did the math on some scratch paper, and I added the seventeen drops. I stirred it. Put in a testing strip and then I brought it to my nose.

"Dear God," I said. Martine-Marie took the paper from me, without hesitation bringing it right to her nose.

"It's . . ." she said.

"It's god-awful. It's blasphemy." And I laughed, big guffaws of laughter making me double over.

She joined in too. "It's terrible," she said as she caught her breath. "How? Why?"

"I guess," I said, sitting back on my stool, finally getting ahold of myself, "that's what makes it interesting. You just never know until you try."

"Exactement!" *Martine-Marie exclaimed. "Let's go ride in Jean-Luc's motor car!"*

Chapter 10

I SHUT THE BEDROOM DOOR BEHIND ME. I sat down on the bed and looked through the shoebox. The cassette tapes were each labeled with the words *Wailing Arch*, along with dates that stretched from 1979 to 1996. Three folded newspaper clippings about the St. Paul neighborhood sat in the box as well. A handful of index cards with verses of poetry written on them, in the same hand that had labeled the cassette tapes, I assumed Oren's. Had he copied these poems from the original found in the tunnels by other people? I didn't know, but I recognized Langston Hughes:

Hold fast to dreams
For if dreams die
Life is a broken-winged bird
That cannot fly.

And then Walt Whitman:
Sullen and suffering hours
(I am ashamed–but it is useless–I am what I am)

And, of course, Emily Dickinson:

I felt it

shelter

to speak to you

I could only think of *him* . . . of all I had in *l'avant* . . . of all that burned brightly in my heart, from memories incomplete.

I slid down to the floor, and I grabbed my backpack from near the door. I pulled the puzzle box from my backpack, and sat with my back against the mattress. I ran my fingertips over the smoothed and curved pieces that made the elongated rectangle, the many different shades of wood. I brought it to my nose and sniffed.

He always smelled of almonds, of coffee, of the outdoors.

I got to Move 7 on the puzzle box last night. The hexagonal piece of light birch wood near the right-hand corner popped out when you applied pressure to its center, but only if you knew to do the same to its twin on the underside.

I still didn't know how I had this puzzle box, this relic from my other life. I told myself it might not even be something real, just a prop in Mom's elaborate, sociopathic lie.

But it had to be real, didn't it?

On her deathbed, Mom told me to look into her sewing box, but I hadn't thought of it, hadn't remembered anything about it right after her death. Those days were fogged with grief. But when I was packing up Mom's trailer, deciding what to save in the storage unit and what to toss, I saw the sewing box.

Of course, then I remembered.

She told me there was something *from him* in there.

In that moment, while Mom was passing away from me, I thought she was talking about my father for some reason, even though I hadn't thought about or really wondered about who my father was in many years. But, of course, during my adolescence I had been obsessed, trying to figure out who he was, hounding my mother.

So when Mom said *from him*, my mind went to that. My father.

Mom only ever answered my questions about him by saying that he was useless and not to bother about him. I tried on my own, of course, on the sly, to find out about him as I got older, and I never got very far. My birth certificate didn't list his name.

The last time I had asked Mom about my father, she'd gotten real quiet, in a moment of complete seriousness—rare for Isabel—and she'd answered, "He's not worth your time, Alice. He never was."

Anyway, the sewing box sat on her closet shelf, as it had when I was kid, then filled with needles, thread, fabric scraps and rolls of felt. It was large, its sides wicker with a yellow gingham top. When I hefted it from its perch, I realized it was heavy, heavier than usual.

There was something substantial in it now.

I lifted the lid, and inside the sewing stuff had been taken out, and there was nothing inside but another box.

A beautiful, multi-toned, hand-decorated puzzle box. It was about six inches long and four inches wide. It had the most gorgeous mother-of-pearl inlay on the lid in a stylized floral pattern, and the box itself was made up of at least six different shades of wood, with a parquet pattern, moving from dark mahogany to the lightest, almost white, of birch. It was extraordinary, a real testament to craftsmanship.

I held it in my hands, and turned it around and around, and I could barely breathe at the sight of it, because this was not just a pretty gift. And this had nothing to do with my father.

The "he" that mother had referenced that night of her death, it was not my dad. And I wasn't even disappointed.

Because I knew this puzzle box. I had held it before, when it was new.

I lifted it to my nose and sniffed, and I could smell the deep cedar, the sharp cherry wood, the sting of the varnish, and I could smell *him*.

He had made this box. All those years ago. In the before.

But how in the world had my mother gotten ahold of this box?

I held it in my hands, brought it to my heart. The box. Right here, in my hands. It was like my old life, my before, had superimposed itself onto this life. This sort of crossing over, it was . . . insane. Absolutely crazy and impossible.

This box, it shouldn't exist at all, because my previous life—it was all a ruse. Supposed to have been, anyway. A joke. A scheme.

She fed it to me as toddler. She gave me the framework, the suggestions of a life, and I ran with it, filled in the blanks. I was a creative child, she told me, with an imagination that could run wild. A cute little girl, believable and charming.

She could sell it for a buck.

Or so I'd been told.

But this box was real. Here, in my hands, the wood smooth, the edges discolored and worn. It was tangible. Three-dimensional.

Had Mom . . . always had it? Or had she found it at some flea market, used it as inspiration for her lies?

How could she make it all seem so real though? Or did I just fill all that in, with the wanting, with the worshipping of anything that might take me out of the sometimes-nightmare I lived with Isabel Grier, her revolving door of suitors and wild dreams.

This puzzle box, it made no sense. Defied everything I held as true. Or did it?

I still could hardly believe it, as I held it in my hands here in St. Paul. It proved my mother was a liar.

Didn't it?

But why would she lie and say she made up *the before*?

I unlocked the seven moves I could remember.

Then, suddenly, I understood I was all in. The moment in Mrs. Signy's parlor with the poem. That flash of the typewriter working, pounding out another line of Frost.

Holding this box in my hands.

This was real. I was tired of vacillating. Tired of doubting.

I heaved a heavy accepting sigh, and I set the puzzle box on the bed, next to Oren's shoebox. The puzzle box had wooden pieces sticking out of it now, slats moved this way and that, looking half-deconstructed. I wondered how long I would be able to hold out before I took a screwdriver to the thing.

I changed into my pajamas and then I thumbed more carefully through Oren's Lovers' Legend collection. I read one newspaper article, and learned there were thirteen poem scraps found, some handwritten, some typed. One love-letter was quoted in the article, but not in its entirety. Miss Mary Nearhouse held the original and hadn't agreed to the printing of the whole thing.

I made a decision then. I put on my terry-cloth robe, covered with whimsical clouds and cupids, a gift from Serena, and I found the skeleton key that fit my bedroom's lock. I shoved it in my bathrobe pocket. I pushed my feet into my gym shoes, and I crept out into the boardinghouse hallway, hoping that the wine and late hour might keep Mrs. Signy and Serena from horning in and asking me too many questions.

I just wanted to look.

I wanted to stand in those tunnels, smell the air, feel the atmosphere on my skin.

Was it here in these tunnels that I knew *him*? After we moved to America from France?

Could it possibly be true?

Out of all the cities in this great country, was this really where it had happened?

And how had we ended?

And why? My chronology with him was heartbreaking, I knew that. But I had so many gaps and questions and even some competing information, and I wanted to know the specifics. Was it too much to ask?

To know how it all played out?

To know what happened . . . to him. To me.

I wanted to be in the places that Lolotte had been. I wanted to bathe in more signs that this was all real life, like the *parapluie* told me, like this puzzle box.

I wanted to confirm it all.

Or not.

Sometimes not at all.

I wanted it to be true so badly, but also not true. Not true at all.

Right now it was both, so very true in my heart and so very preposterous that I didn't have to do anything about it, didn't need to change anything about myself, or live with any serious, confirmed knowledge. It didn't have to mar any of the good moments with Isabel.

I straddled the line of *maybe.*

Isabel Grier could stay the harebrained mother who fessed up and came clean to her daughter before things got out of hand. She didn't have to turn into a lifelong liar in my mind.

True. Not true.

Straddling the line, even now, with the actual puzzle box lying on my bed.

I'd liked living in this in-between for so many years, but suddenly . . . now, in the dark of night, standing right above the possible tunnels, I knew I needed more.

I grabbed my flashlight from my backpack.

Chapter 11

France, 1931

I FILLED MY BASKET QUICKLY, SCUFFLING ALONG the dry dirt between the rows of famed French lavender in the Grasse hills of the Guillet parfumerie, *knowing this lavender would make the best and most expensive perfumes of Paris, along with a few of our very own brands. The buds would be dried and the scent steam-distilled, right here, only yards away, and I wondered at this. How lucky I was to be here, now. How lucky I was to be my father's daughter, my mother's child, to have claim to this beautiful land. It was a blessing and it was a curse, to want so badly to work the land, to press the scent from the rind, to work in the labs, to do the work of the laborer or a chemist, when all you were expected to do, all you were any good for, was wearing the perfume at useless, constant tea dates, with constantly useless women and girls. Society. A fancy word for a bunch of boring women. And this in 1931, when the world was changing. Why, Martine-Marie spoke of seeing women wearing pants in Paris, on the street, in cafes!*

I thought of Maman's pinched face as we argued over my summer, for the twentieth time. About my social calendar, about my duties as an heiress, to attend events, to represent the family. I could tell Father was bending. Abraham had showed him my last perfume. Father was going to do it. He was going to stand up to Mother and let me work here, really work here, in a position of power, run the place even someday, not just marry someone who might want to do it for me.

Because I might only have been sixteen, but I knew what I wanted: To pluck the jasmine from the stem. To feel the weight of the sickle in my hand and sheave the lavender from its base. To invent the new accords. A tiny cog in the machine of such olfactory beauty.

I leaned my face close to the lavender and I breathed in slowly, letting the calming scent fill my nose, my head, my thoughts.

The lightning flashed through the sky, and thunder exploded around us. Before I knew it, I was on my feet. Father found me running back into the enfleurage, *seeking shelter.*

"Lolotte!" he called, and I stood under the overhang of the building, dripping rainwater on the steps, knowing better than to enter the enfleurage *itself. It would not do to damage the level of humidity inside, to intervene in the sacred process of scent removal that occurred within that room.*

"Yes, Father?"

He sheltered with me beneath the overhang. Lightning flashed again, and I waited for the rumble of thunder to follow.

"Your mother has agreed. With Grand-père *gone now, the time is right to travel to America to expand, to work in synthetics."*

My heart lurched with excitement at the idea of America, but also with loss over my grandfather's recent death. Plus, how could I leave Grasse? "This year?"

"Next." Father watched my face. "We have many plans to make."

"Where exactly?"

"We will finalize the location soon. Will this trip make you happy, mon fille?*"*

"It is not forever?"

"No. It is an adventure."

"Will Maman agree to let me work as a true employee, a chemist?"

"Will you agree to see the doctor she has written?"

"Oui." I was good at bargaining. "No ballrooms though," I told him, with a smile.

He gave me a look.

"Only a few ballrooms," I amended.

"Anything you wish. It means a great deal to me to have your support in this." He kissed my cheek then.

"It is no longer Guillet Parfumerie, but Guillet Worldwide Empire?" I gave him a cheeky smile.

"Ha!" He laughed. "Abraham has agreed, so of course, Martine-Marie and her family will travel with us."

"Merci, Father."

"I cannot start anew without Abraham, as you know, he is important. But I'm glad to make you happy, Lolotte. Anything for you." He took off toward the main house, holding a newspaper above his head to catch the rain.

"Can I have a pony in America then?" I called, only half-joking.

• • •

"SHE'S SICK? MARTINE-MARIE is never sick. What is this madness?" I said, pushing past Celeste, Martine-Marie's sister, throwing open the door to the Abraham house, still dripping from the rainstorm, but needing to tell Martine-Marie the news about the move. We had speculated for months now. Surely, she was also excited for our new lives to start in America.

"Martine!" I yelped, walking through the kitchen, then the hallway. I stopped, knocking on her bedroom door. "You will not believe it, Martine-Marie. I have confirmation, from Father! Have you heard?"

She did not answer, so I opened the door of her bedroom. I figured I would have to nurse her from another late night–too much champagne, too much dancing with Jean-Luc and his rich friends at the coast. Hadn't she and the Parcell girls, with their cousin Pierre, been on his boat this past weekend?

But she was not in her room. The sheets on her bed were mussed, but then I heard the retching from the bathroom. It was a horrible noise, and when I looked up, I saw Celeste's knowing eyes looking at me from the hallway.

My heart thudded into my throat. No.

Martine-Marie was not sick.

"No," I said. "It can't be."

Celeste only nodded.

"Do your parents know?" I asked.

"Oui," Celeste said. "It has all been arranged. She will marry him on the third Sunday of March."

"Jean-Luc?"

Celeste shook her head. "No, it is Pierre. The Parcell cousin." My spirits fell. Martine-Marie would not get out of Grasse, as she wished. She would not come to America with me. She would not travel; she would not see stamps on her suitcase. She would become a baker's wife.

I felt my childhood slipping away then, as I took the few steps into the hallway, opening the door to the bathroom. I knelt down on the bathroom floor, putting my arms around Martine-Marie's shoulders.

She did not look up at me. I didn't say anything. I just held her as she finished vomiting. Then she collapsed into me, heaving a sigh that could only come from someone carrying a burden too great for words.

Chapter 12

I FOUND MRS. SIGNY'S BASEMENT OFF THE KITCHEN easily, because she'd gestured toward the breezeway explaining she had an unfinished basement, when she had given us an initial tour. We hadn't gone down there. I hadn't thought anything of it then.

Tonight, I did. Quietly, I moved toward the breezeway, feeling all kinds of criminal for not asking permission first. But sometimes you had to take advantage of your nerve when you had it. In the morning light, I would be too chicken again. I knew that about myself.

The stairs were steep, covered with the same curling linoleum as the breezeway. The basement itself had a low-slung ceiling, the floor simply tamped-down dirt. The whole of it was packed with boxes here, the occasional piece of old furniture there, and it smelled like earth and mold. Off to the left, there was a cistern that caught rainwater, to the right a small room that could be a coal cellar. I tried the door. It wasn't even locked.

Inside, the coal cellar was mostly empty, a small square of a room, filled with dust and two empty wooden crates. A long, narrow rectangular window sat in the upper corner of the room that must've faced the back yard, through which the coal had likely been delivered back in the day. A small wingback chair with mouse-eaten upholstery sat on its side at the far end of the room, a broken leg sticking out like a wounded animal, its end splintered and sharp. Behind the chair, there hung a plaid bedsheet like a curtain, covering most of the far cinder-block wall. I moved around the upended chair and lifted the curtain to the side, holding my breath. Sure enough, behind that curtain, there was the door.

I stepped forward. It was a strange door, only about three-quarters as high as a normal door. It was painted a royal blue color, with an ornate geometric applique near the top. Much of the paint was peeling away to reveal a different blue color beneath, indigo, nearly purple. The hinges and knob were made of a tarnished metal, with a floral engraving surrounding the keyhole. The overall impression was that this door was old. Very old.

I touched the door with the tips of my fingers. It was cold. I grabbed the old metal knob and gave it a turn.

Nothing.

I slipped the skeleton key from my pocket. "It can't be this easy," I whispered to myself. But it was. It fit into the lock and the knob turned reluctantly at first, the door sticking in its warped, aged doorframe, but giving in with only a slight nudge from my shoulder.

I was not prepared for the whoosh of cold air when I opened the door. I gasped, surprised. The flashlight shook a bit in my hand.

Rough-hewn stone steps led the way down. I ducked through the door and took the first step. I left the door open behind me, hoping for at least a little light from the coal-cellar window.

The stairway ended after eleven steps, and it opened into a space, a tunnel, I suppose. But it was small, not what I had imagined. To go any further, I would need to move onto my knees.

But I was in this now. I wasn't going back.

I checked out the tunnel with my flashlight, and from what I could see the walls were darker, more dirt and clay, less sandstone, but as I crawled further into the tunnel itself, this wasn't true anymore. Quickly, I could tell I was surrounded by stone. It was cold on my knees and hands, harder, sharper, with little jagged outgrowths digging into my knees through my flannel pajamas.

I held the flashlight in one hand and scuffled along, switching hands every few yards. After what seemed like a really long time, I heard something skitter on the gravel ahead of me, and my heart thudded into my throat.

I talked myself down. Worst-case scenario, it was a rat, but the tunnels seemed strangely clean. Not too many bugs or detritus.

I pressed onward.

Soon, the tunnel opened up into a large cave, larger than I'd imagined could be down here. I took my time surveying the place. I wished I had a better flashlight.

There was evidence here of present-day shenanigans. A stubbed out joint, beer cans, some kind of graffiti-drawn devil figure in red spray paint on one wall, with two horns and a forked tongue. This cave had two offshoots of tunnels leading away from it. One tunnel held a slant of light at the other end, beckoning, ever so slightly. The other looked dark and curved sharply to the right, promising nothing, hiding its destination.

I followed the one with the light. After what seemed like no time at all, the tunnel widened, and I stood in a tall opening, one that opened up into a sandstone bluff, obviously the bluff on which Mrs. Signy's Victorian stood up on Planck Avenue. I moved carefully to the ledge, and I used my flashlight to sweep left and right. I was about twenty feet above the ground, standing inside a sandstone cliff, with the waning light of the upper-bluff streetlights lighting the green-area of the park below, which held a cobblestoned path, a water fountain, and a futuristic–looking jungle gym in the shape of a rocket ship. I tried to get my bearings, and I thought I was probably due south of Mrs. Signy's.

I shined my flashlight around some more, and there, in the middle of the park, sat a circle of large rocks, with a narrow pillar of sorts in the middle. It looked like some kind of purposeful collection of rocks. Man-made. It reminded me of tiny-scaled Stonehenge in a crude way.

I made a mental note to check it out in the daylight. For now, I was heading back for the other tunnel. I needed to know where that led.

I stopped myself for a moment and made myself register how much *deja-vu* I was having. Did I think these were *his* tunnels?

Was this where it happened? Our last moment together? Where I'd smelled gunpowder? Where I'd seen the blood on his dungarees?

I was in that no-man's land again. I couldn't tell.

For all I knew about Lolotte, for all I thought I had put together, I had ten times the questions.

I didn't know if these were *his* tunnels. I sighed. I probably never would.

I backtracked into the cave then. I entered the opposite tunnel, the dark one, and I could tell right away this tunnel was different. Darker, for one thing, as it led away and farther into the bluff, and it seemed . . . dangerous too.

I couldn't explain it, but all of a sudden my ears didn't pop exactly, but the pressure increased. Was it because I was getting lower? Deeper? Or was this my sign? My skin seemed to stretch tighter on my body, adjusting to some kind of weird change in the atmosphere.

Soon, there was a small cavern off to the left, then another adjacent one on the right. There were old boards stored in ramshackle piles here and there, more rubble in the next few offshoots of caves. Nothing but junk. PVC piping. Chicken wire.

Stacks of old newspapers molding from the eighties. Cardboard boxes decomposing into dirt.

Surely, anything good had been foraged and salvaged long ago.

I didn't really believe that though, or why would I be down here? So I looked through the junk, kicking things around with my feet, wishing I'd brought a pair of gloves. I found nothing, aside from a zillion centipedes, some kind of small brass pipe fitting, and a piece of iron equipment that looked like an old-fashioned apple-corer.

I followed the tunnel farther in, pushing away any worries about getting lost, and I noticed that the tunnel started to descend quickly, a steep decline, and it felt wetter. Beneath my feet, it got slippery, with thin, little stalactites dotting the ceiling of the tunnel, in groups of three of four, here and there.

It was definitely moving downhill fast. I came to a T-intersection, and I chose the one furthest to the right, hoping to go even further in. If there was anything good—scraps of poetry? more love letters?—surely it had to be this way, in the direction furthest from the surface, right?

I trudged along for a very long time, until I realized that my breath seemed shallow. Did that happen when you got deeper under the ground? Was the air thinning?

Then, there, on the right was a small inlet, and on the ground was an old slot machine. Rusty, old, but intact, its surface was heavily gilded in tarnished silver. I knelt down next to it. I pulled the lever, but nothing moved.

The three windows across the front of the metal machine were covered with so much dust I couldn't see what had shown up on its last turn. I was wiping the dust from the windows with my sleeve when I heard it. There was no other way to describe it, other than wailing.

It was too long and drawn out for a sob. The noise was high-pitched, a woman, surely.

I jerked backward from the sound, scaring myself in the process, tripping over the slot machine, landing next to it, hands first. The sound stopped for a moment, its echo fresh in my ears, along with the rapid pounding of my pulse.

The voice had startled me, and, not just that, it *scared* me too, because I couldn't tell where it was coming from. Had I somehow circled near the Wabasha Caverns and Wailing Arch?

It began anew then, loud and fever-pitched, worse than before.

I searched for the source of it, the direction, turning my head. But the acoustics were unsettling; it wasn't coming from anywhere in particular. Rather, it was around me, moving through me. I could feel the vibrations.

That voice. It held so much pain.

Suddenly, I had to get out of there, that little alcove, and the tunnels altogether. I clutched at my throat; the air was too thin.

I couldn't breathe.

My mind knew I was illogical, but my heart pounded, unsure.

I panicked, hyperventilating, scraping my hands on detritus on the ground next to the slot machine, the wailing voice still thick into its frenzy around me.

I turned, tripped again, and fell to my knees, dropping my flashlight. It rolled away from me, creating disorienting shadows on the wall. My palms landed squarely on a small rectangular object, along with the detached lever from the slot machine, which I must've knocked off when I tripped over it. The wailing abruptly stopped, and I held my breath, waiting for it to start again. I was shaking, a mess.

After a few moments, it didn't start up again, and I began to relax bit by bit. I pulled a stuttering breath into my lungs.

I sat back on my heels, and I picked up my flashlight, wiping off the cave's wetness on my shirt. I shined the flashlight on the rectangular object still caught in my fist.

But when I looked back on this moment, as I would, over and over, I knew from the first feel of it in my fist, when I had rubbed my thumb over its shape, its design.

I knew before the beam of my flashlight revealed it.

It was a pocketknife, the handle a carved bit of ivory, with floral filigree. I flicked it open with the jerk of my wrist, like I'd done it before a dozen times, more.

Because I had. In another time. In another life.

Chapter 13

America, 1932

THE WOOD SHAVINGS CURLED AND FELL TO THE DIRT porch of the tin shack, joining the others in a fragrant pile underneath his three-footed stool. We sat, him carving and me in the rocking chair, as we looked out onto the lane, workers arriving home from their day shifts at the railyard, lunch pails in hands, children greeting fathers with outstretched arms, dinner bells ringing, dogs barking.

He worked his knife, in his calm and patient fashion. I marveled at the trust his hands had in one another, the way one hand pulled the sharp knife so quickly and forcefully toward the other hand, never even nicking it, just peeling away a smooth, curlicued piece of wood. He had always been good with wood, he told me, carving little birds from wood scraps when he was younger, but this was something altogether different.

He was so large and long-limbed, dwarfing all of the men from back home surely, and most others here in America. There was something so interesting in watching his big frame tucked on to that small stool, his broad shoulders hunched over the delicate work of his hands.

As he worked, he spoke little, but I could get him to talk, if I wanted to. It didn't take much. I only asked him of poetry.

Today, I read him Whitman as he worked:

"I hear America singing, the varied carols I hear,

Those of mechanics, each one singing his as it should be blithe and strong,

The carpenter singing his as he measures his plank or beam—"

He interrupted me, "Your pronunciation sounds very good; your accent nothing but a tiny bit of music in the background. It doesn't distract, only adds."

He was sixteen and I eighteen. He had been here in America for so much longer than I had. His grasp of the English language, its intricacies, was much better than mine.

I smiled at him. He spoke with the best of accents; it was Swedish like so many of the others here, of course, but different too, an accent all his own, something I couldn't exactly place, but I could pick his voice from a hundred, a thousand, its rich quality always reminding me of coffee, the best of coffee, a sharp and rich blend, its aroma unmarred by cream or sugar. But deep and dark the way it should be.

"When you left home to come here, did you think of it as an adventure?" he asked me. He lowered his eyes then, as he said the rest, for he was shy. "Like a new start? A rebirth of sorts? I thought so when I first came to America."

"I am a progressive girl. I liked the idea of progressiveness in America. Oui.*"*

"Oui,*" he agreed with a chuckle.*

"You know this about me so surely, yes?"

"From the moment I first met you. It is written in the jaunty step of your walk."

"Is it?"

"Oui. Bien sur."

His French was adorable.

There was nothing more precious to me than when he let his guard down a bit, when he joked with me, let me in.

I wanted to kiss the scar on his eyelid. Just press my lips to it once. Watch the blush reach even the tips of his ears, watch the knowledge seep in that I liked both of his eyes, the one damaged, the one not.

I didn't kiss him, for I didn't want to scandalize him. But I did scoot my rocker closer. "What do you smell like?" I asked. I leaned toward his shoulder, and I breathed in deeply: wood shavings, sweat and skin—a nutty flavor. The length of his neck was only inches from me, the sharp jut of his Adam's apple. I watched him swallow, the muscles of his throat working. And I talked myself out of laying my head on his shoulder and closing my eyes, breathing him in.

Two pink spots appeared on his cheeks, and I tried not to giggle at the ease with which I could rile him.

"Nothing bad," I told him. "Of wood and almonds. Coffee too. That is your scent. I shall make you a cologne."

He seemed not to know what to say.

So I spoke, "When will you visit my parfumerie *with me?"*

He shook his head. He didn't like this topic. We had been friends for months. Many months. I still didn't know all of his secrets yet. I did know his mother died a few years ago, her name was Birgit, and his face changed into something so serene and dreamlike whenever he mentioned her name. But I didn't know about his father, or why his every muscle tightened whenever he came up.

But my love for the parfumerie *was a secret he knew about me. I missed Grasse, the grand state of our century-old operation there, the fields that rolled for an eternity above me, below me, and how the lavender grew in tight rows, curving in a horseshoe pattern upward, giving the hills a uniformed, curlicued look. The billowy plants, green and greyish, slightly purple at the edges, fuzzy.*

It was too early to know if our small fledgling crops and parfumerie *would succeed here in America, but I was proud of it, invested in it, nonetheless. I wanted him to see it.*

But he answered my question as he always did. "Your parents will not . . . appreciate me."

"I don't think that's true."

"What are you two sots up to?" Inger, his neighbor—and his brother Gunnar's paramour—asked as she joined us on the porch. She tossed me a piece of her mother's toffee, and she sat down on the steps. "What're you making?"

"He's carving," I answered for him. "He learned to make different kinds of puzzle boxes, whatever in the world those might be, from the blind man at the railroad crossing."

"No, you make me sound like a master," he said. "I hope it will finish into a puzzle box. It is difficult, a very detailed process, and I'm only a novice, but if I'm a success, when I'm done, you can hide something in there, something secret or close to your heart, and it will be nearly impossible to get open. The trick isn't in the carving so much as the mechanism. The puzzle."

"I don't believe it," I said. "Anyone will be able to open it."

Inger scoffed, "Put that thing under a wagon wheel, I'll crack it open, lickety-split."

"Ha!" I laughed.

"No, no," he explained. "To open it, you'll have to slide pieces around, up, down. Move a whole side one way or another or find some hidden trigger to loosen a piece in order to move it. It is very complicated. Some boxes can take thirty moves or more even."

"Really? Thirty moves?" I asked. "And there's no key?"

"No key. It's very intricate," he said. "Like the game up at the pharmacy, where you have to move the pieces around in the frame, to make the picture."

"Oh," said Inger, "I get it. Like that, but it's an actual box. Like a rectangle or a cube."

"Three-dimensional. Yes. But it's made with lots of little pieces, like this one I'm making will have twelve moves and–"

"Who is it for?" Inger asked, raising her eyebrows in a suggestive way.

He didn't answer, but I watched how he worked his jaw. Was the box for me? Did Inger know this and she was teasing?

He ignored Inger. "Anyway, this one will have small pieces of wood, all different kinds, different geometric shapes, and I will meld them together in a pattern, to form a three-dimensional box."

"It's almost like a quilt pattern," I said, helping to change the subject, looking at the half dozen or so pieces of wood he'd carved into smooth pieces lying there on

the porch. It made me think of the fancy quilts my mother ordered from catalogs, and their ridiculously involved patterns. I mean, who had the patience?

"I think that's a good way to think of it," he said.

"But what's the point?" Inger said.

"Ah, la vaca!" he said in a mocking tone. "What's the point of any art?"

"That's a good question," Inger said, egging him on. "If you can't trade it for meat and eggs, I don't know. If you can't age it into hooch, or plant it in the ground, bah!"

"There is beauty in creation, not just in usefulness," I said, watching him as he pulled his knife down a particularly long, slender piece of wood. "The natural world and our interaction with it, our glorification of it," I said, thinking of the necessity of my hours in the parfumerie lab, coaxing mathematical mixtures of scents to sing, "they're not at odds at all, rather the opposite."

And I liked how I'd put words to this. He brought this out of me, the best of what was inside.

It was something dear to my heart, this feeling, after working with the flowers, their petals, their essences, for so long, and now I had just voiced it. Brought it into fruition. The idea that there was more to the land—this life—than existence, moving forward, sustenance, it echoed the arguments that I had with Father all the time.

We didn't just plant and harvest so that we could sell the flowers or the essences and feed ourselves for another winter? Did we? It was more than that. It was about the beauty found in just the right mixture of scents, the perfect balance of notes, in creating that special parfum.

The art of it.

It was what I loved to do, and my mother wanted to forbid it. She wanted me to attend to debutante balls and enroll in finishing school, for endless afternoons filled with teas and the pianoforte. And worse, she wanted Father to bar me from the lab.

"You know," I said softly to him, as Inger wandered inside the house, yelling for Gunnar. "This puzzle box is . . ." And it was like the slippery thought already had jumbled up in my mind, fallen away, just out of reach, fleeting, like a dream upon waking.

"You'll run that box over with a wagon wheel and you won't need twelve moves to open it?" he joked.

But I didn't laugh. "Never," I said, and I looked him in his eyes. "I would never."

His face fell then, went serious. Did he know what I was saying?

Did he know what he meant to me?

Inger reappeared on the porch. "You want some more toffee?" Inger asked, offering some to us both. "Later you two want to go to the bonfire down at St. Peter's?"

"Oui," *He and I said at the same time.*

We shared a look.

Inger bounded down the lane, whistling to herself, and just then, he swore in Swedish.

"Skit," *he said, and I saw that he had blood coming from his hand. A lot of blood. I got up quickly and I pulled a handkerchief from my pocket, and I knelt in front of him.*

"Which finger?" I said. "Let me see."

"It's my thumb," he said, and I pressed the cloth to his hand, held his thumb between my two hands. His flesh and blood were warm.

We stayed there, just like that, for a long moment. Me kneeling in front of him. Him sitting on his stool. Me holding his thumb in between my palms. He looked even more handsome up close, older, the beauty of his face so stark, the lines carved so cleanly. My favorite curve of his face was in the slope below his cheekbone, how it hollowed out a bit before the hard line of his jaw. The grace of that line, it made my ribs ache from the inside out. His beauty, it jabbed at me, hurt me somehow right beneath my breastbone.

Didn't he know what I felt for him?

Of course not.

He didn't know his worth. He only knew his imperfect eye, its droopiness, the stares from other people.

I wanted to shake him, tell him, make him believe me.

How his eye, that scar, meant nothing in the full sum of what he was. The way his eyes watched me, the way his mind worked through the classics, both literary and poetical, and rolled their meanings and questions into conversations about ideas that at once seemed much too big for me, and yet, the only things worth contemplating.

And his face.

He led with those blue eyes of his, all inquisitive intelligence, hidden away behind his uncertain silences.

I suspected the marred eye, of course, as the root of so much of his . . . hiding. But I knew there was more to it. His parents, perhaps.

Even his scar was beautiful because it was his.

That twisted white line of skin. It didn't do anything but call out for my lips to kiss it. It cut a jagged path down, vertically, over the tender skin of his left eyelid, starting in the eyebrow and finishing on his cheekbone.

And really, he had such a good face, with large open features, a strong nose, a manly square jaw like an American film star, complete with a slight shadow of a dark beard on his chin at this hour in the evening. It was a face that showed every emotion, so often missed though, because he didn't call attention to himself. He was quiet, so quiet, until it was just him and me.

As I held his wounded thumb between my hands, I thought, There will never be a face I love more.

This thought. It jarred me.

It did something to me, both scared and excited me, in the pit of my stomach, not unlike the talk of beauty and art a few moments earlier. I moved closer to him; I bent my head toward him.

"Thank you," he said. "I'm fine though, I'm sure."

"Merci," *I said, not knowing exactly what I meant. I checked his wound.* "Merde." *The bleeding had slowed, but not stopped. He would be fine, but I didn't want to give up my hold on him. I pressed the cloth, his hand, between mine again.*

"When will you visit the parfumerie *with me? Meet my parents?" I asked again.*

I saw then that it was fear that crossed his features. Or was it . . . shame?

Whatever it was, I hated it. So I did what I'd been wanting to do. I rose up on my knees and I leaned in, closing the inches between us. I heard the sharp intake of his breath.

I watched his eyelids flutter closed, and I kissed the scar on his eyelid. The lightest touch, brushing so softly.

I whispered his name like a secret, my lips still against his skin, trying hard to pronounce the second syllable as he taught me, somewhere between an "ah" and "eh."

My breath fanned his face, and he shivered against me. He exhaled, his shoulders relaxing. I pressed my forehead to his. Our eyes locked.

"Say it again," he said.

I smiled. I whispered his name again, this time even more quietly. "Rune."

Two syllables of want.

I heard something clatter to the ground then, and when I pulled back, I saw that it was his pocketknife. It sported a lattice edge, with roses carved into its ivory handle, a delicate carving.

I reached down and picked it up. It was still warm from his hand.

He spoke again, his voice serious. "I'll do anything for you, Catarin."

Chapter 14

THE WABASHA STREET CAVES WERE KIND of famous, an old hotel-gone-speakeasy that was built into the side of the St. Paul bluffs, looking architecturally Tudor from the outside, with the inside being the natural interior of the sandstone caves.

The tour guide was indeed handsome, as Mrs. Signy had warned. It was his eyes. They were striking, large and dark, and rimmed with thick lashes, giving his face a puppy-dog kind of look. Or they would've, if the rest of his face wasn't so severe, all hard lines and angles, a stern jaw. And he moved with a certain coolness, a reserve about him. Or maybe that's just how I interpreted him because he didn't smile. He didn't look unpleasant exactly, but he didn't smile.

He was an excellent guide, however, with details upon details about the caverns, about St. Paul in general. I realized listening to him that I hadn't asked Mrs. Signy what kind of professor he was. Surely it was within the history department. He seemed enthralled with the living, breathing history of this place: from its initial construction to the supposed famed criminal meetups that occurred below stairs.

He listened closely to all the questions asked from our motley assortment of tourists on this Wednesday morning. He gave thorough answers. He offered his elbow to the one elderly lady who was part of our tour, when she had trouble climbing the three marble steps into the famed ballroom. So the guide was okay, even though I had a hard time imagining him sitting in Mrs. Signy's parlor, drinking tea, and discussing Oren Signy's erotica.

I followed along on the tour cataloging away all the information I could glean from other people's questions, but I was really hoping he'd give me a few minutes afterward. I wanted to pick his brain, and I tried to tell myself it was for my research project, for my thesis, but after last night, now that I had what I thought was *his* pocketknife in my backpack right now, well, really, it was hard to kid myself anymore about what was more important.

I had more pressing questions than which gangsters had set foot in the Fireside Room or how many tons of dynamite it took to open up the cavern for its ornate entrance.

Had our tour guide heard of the Lovers' Legend? Had he personally found any poems? Could he take us into the actual tunnels? Right now, this very instant? Were all the tunnels connected? Could I get here, beneath the Wabasha if I started at Mrs. Signy's or were there separate routes?

I swallowed back my eagerness though. I had to bide my time.

Our tour guide led our small group into a long, narrow ballroom, with gorgeous antique crystal chandeliers, and dining tables set in porcelain and silver. It was easy to imagine the flappers and the gangsters, the music and the booze flowing. I snapped photo after photo. I knelt onto the ballroom floor, below one of the large chandeliers, taking a shot straight up from below, listening to the tour guide speak.

"What is strange and wonderful about the place is, and I'm sure you noticed on your way in, that the exterior is all brick and Tudor-work. Inside, you're inside the natural cavern." I looked up from my camera to check, but the tour guide still hadn't smiled, although I could hear the affection in his voice for this gorgeous room, this hallowed architectural triumph.

And it was beautiful, the juxtaposition of the place; the walls and ceiling rough-hewn sandstone and limestone, dotted with support arches, composed of fancy brickwork designs. It was beautiful, the contrast between the natural and the manmade.

I zoomed in on the intricate brass-work on the chandelier, with the stalactites hanging off the ceiling in the background. It was a great shot, both jarring and pleasing.

Next, the guide walked us through the parquet hallways, with rows of black-and-white framed photos of gangsters who had visited the Wabasha during the Prohibition years. These photos were nailed into the sandstone walls of the hallway that connected the great dining room to the sitting room with the enormous limestone fireplace. The other people voiced lots of questions about the gangsters: *Did Dillinger really hide out here? Were there really murders that took place in this Fireside Room? Is this picture really signed by Al Capone?*

I took more pictures. My favorite was of a group small cone-shaped stalactites, reddish brown in color, hanging from the ceiling in front of a gold gilded mirror.

I mentally forced myself to hone my thesis: the life and death and life again of architecture and the history it preserves. I knew I needed a portfolio of photos. As many as possible.

A teenage boy asked, "How do we get to the actual tunnels?"

The guide brought a hand to the back of his neck. "Ah, of course."

"Are there any tunnels?" another woman asked. "Like secret sorts of tunnels that lead different places?"

Our guide made a noise like, "Hmm," and nodded. "Of course." He maneuvered us into the corridor/cave that led into the well-stocked gift shop. "The tunnels are not part of the tour anymore though," he answered.

"Aw," the teenager complained.

"Can you show us photos?" I asked, my shoulders slumping with this information. I thought for sure I was going to get into the tunnels this morning.

"There is an actual booklet with all the appropriate photos. Free to all tour-takers, and truly, I used to love taking people down there, but there was an incident last year. And well, insurance, liability."

"An incident?" the elderly lady asked.

"Kids using the caves for parties," the teenager offered. "They were stupid and started a fire for God's sake."

The guide nodded. "They weren't the smartest."

"We really don't get to see them?" I asked, feeling a terrible stab of panic in my gut. I couldn't quite explain it, but ever since last night, it was like I just had to . . . search.

Nothing else mattered.

Nothing at all.

"My apologies," the guide said. "But the kids, you know, one of them was in the hospital for several days, and, well . . . It was serious. They lit a campfire in a cave, or a small off-shoot of a cave, and it wasn't properly ventilated. I have strict orders. Below-ground is off limits to the public." To his credit, the guide did seem unhappy about this.

He took off toward a glass-cased counter, returning to the elderly lady with a leather-bound book, pointing out something on the cover.

I walked around the gift shop hesitantly. I looked at this and that, fingered a keychain in the shape of the state of Minnesota, flipped through a book about the Valentine's Day Massacre.

I would just go through Mrs. Signy's coal cellar each night, every night, if I had to. I would search those tunnels within an inch of my life. I would get . . ..

What was it that I needed?

Didn't I have enough evidence?

Wasn't it all real? Hadn't I proved it to myself?

So now . . . what?

I couldn't quite explain it to myself, how necessary it was to me to explore those tunnels, to find the spot, to touch my hand to the wall, have my feet stand where they had once, so long ago, where it all ended.

Where my heart broke.

So, I decided I was going to wait out this tour guide. Sure, he was a little imposing, but I was determined. The guide talked to us about a few more topics, local lore that surrounded the caves—the ghosts that liked to frequent the men's room, wearing fedoras and three piece suits, the legend that a local crime boss hid his treasure somewhere below the city, that kind of thing. He rolled his eyes when someone asked about the Wailing Ghost. Same reaction when someone else asked if it was true a gangster named Lassiter bricked another guy into a tunnel, alive, as punishment for ratting on a fellow mobster.

He handed them another pamphlet from behind the desk. "That's one of the myths about who's doing the wailing down there," he offered.

As the rest of our group milled around in the giftshop, buying up Dillinger postcards, taking photos in front of the black-and-white gangster photographs, I tapped the guide on the elbow.

"Hi, I'm Alice Grier, and I'm a grad student from Chicago—" I stuck out my hand, and he took it, shook it nice and firmly. He looked me steady in the eye. He didn't say anything, so I continued, "I really, really need to get into the tunnels. Could I somehow hire you to take me? Off the books? I mean, you're a professor, right? History?" I waited for some kind of answer, and he did, after a second, give me a nod. "You know how important things can be for research . . ." He still didn't say anything else. Just looked at me with those eyes, this entertained expression on his face, coming as close to smiling as I'd seen yet, his mouth quirking up a fraction at one corner. "Or is there someone else I could ask?" I ventured. "Someone else who I could hire?"

Or I'll just go myself tonight through the coal cellar.

Finally, he let out a half-laugh, half-chuckle. "Relax. Mrs. Signy already called me this morning."

"She did?"

"She did."

"Huh," I smiled thinking of Mrs. Signy calling this man on my behalf. "Does that mean you'll take me into the tunnels?"

He tipped his head in a noncommittal answer. "I suppose, even though I could get in big trouble for it. Truthfully, though—and don't tell anyone—I think I'm more scared of Molly Signy being unhappy with me."

This bit of humor surprised me, and I let out a laugh, loud and bark-like. He smiled then too, for the first time. Not really a smile, but a grin, a pleased expression.

Maybe he wasn't as grumpy as I'd first assessed, but then I realized he knew who I was from the get-go.

"So, you, um . . . couldn't have told me that you knew Mrs. Signy right away? You had to let me go through my whole spiel and beg?"

"Would you have begged? Is going below that important to you?"

If he only knew. "I think I already was begging."

"Nah, you just implored." His mouth wasn't smiling anymore, but his eyes sure were. "So you really want to see the tunnels?"

I nodded. "Absolutely. Yes please."

"I'm Eli, by the way," he said, giving me a nod.

"I'm so grateful," I said. "And I'm Alice, although you probably know my life story from Mrs. Signy."

"More or less." He shot me a look then. "But I hear it's your friend, the other boarder, who we all have to watch out for."

"That much is true," I agreed. "And Mrs. Signy herself."

"You have no idea."

"So, um, not to be pushy, but when can we go?"

"Right away."

"Really?" He moved toward the back of the giftshop and I followed. "I feel a little guilty because those other people wanted to go too. How come I get special treatment?"

"People come here for the gangster and the ghosts. A story to tell at a cocktail party," he said, shrugging his shoulders. "You . . . well . . ." He stopped speaking then, squinted his eyes at me like he wasn't sure he should go on.

"I . . . what?"

"Well, Molly said you really cared about the real history of the city, not just the fantastic stuff." He brought a hand to the back of his neck then, in a gesture of thinking. "I guess I'm tired of the people who only want to say they heard the Wailing Arch, but don't give a shit about the souls who lived here in Swede Hollow, who toiled, who tried, you know, believed in the American Dream, sweated and worked toward it, gave it their level best, and then . . . I don't know. The silent ones, the ones who don't get to haunt us with their wailing, I don't know. They lived too. They endured their own stories and heartaches and . . . lives lived."

I licked my lips to answer, to say something, but I came up short. Something pinched beneath my ribs. I felt out of breath. This, this right here. He'd put words to why I loved history, about why I chose to study it in the first place.

The common tragedies, the everyday triumphs.

This guy got it.

I was dumbfounded really, and I watched something flicker over Eli's face when I didn't respond. Was it embarrassment? No, maybe regret that he'd wasted his words on me.

Eli motioned for me to follow him into a small room beyond the giftshop, and I did, shrugging off the awkwardness of my speechless moment. Eli led us into his makeshift office, with a desk and piles and piles of paper, a Greenpeace poster, stacks of vinyl LPs, and a humongous plastic jar of red licorice.

He grabbed a threadbare blue backpack from the floor and kicked around a few piles of books before he bent and picked up a camping lantern. He didn't say anything, and I didn't either. I followed him to the back of the Wabasha dining room, and we entered what was a state-of-the-art restaurant kitchen, with stainless steel surfaces and a six-burner stove. "It's still rented out as a banquet hall. It's a busy place," Eli offered. He took us to the back of the kitchen.

"This used to be a big walk-in pantry," he explained, and he opened a heavy metal door. Back in the corner, beyond the pantry shelves, there was another door, wooden, unsuspecting. But I knew.

That thrill of excitement shot up my spine. I was going to get to see the actual tunnels again.

And maybe I'd find the spot.

The location of . . . the last of us.

"This takes you below?" I asked, as he opened the wooden door.

He nodded and led the way. "Here," he said, handing me a flashlight from his backpack. The stairs were stone this time, uneven and difficult to descend, half-natural, half-manmade.

I grabbed Eli's shoulder in front of me. "Do you mind?"

"Not at all." I knotted some of his t-shirt into my fist. It made me feel safer.

When I did though, some of a tattoo showed on his arm. I aimed my flashlight at it. A torch, with orange flames, a name in elegant script: *Persi*.

"Who's Persi?" I asked, as he led us forward.

"My daughter," he answered.

I wanted to ask more. I didn't.

I waited for him to volunteer more information. He didn't.

It seemed that we descended for a very long time. The smell went from sandy and dry, to musty and wet, the air from cool to cold. My ears registered the pressure of our decent, and when we got to the bottom of the stairs, they popped, as if I'd been on an airplane.

Lit only by Eli's lantern and my small but powerful flashlight, we stood in a small cave, much more primitive than the ones upstairs. It was rough and dirty, with walls that billowed out in a ruffled pattern of stone, natural and gorgeous in their striated colors. Either these were way better flashlights, or I had my wits about me more, now that I wasn't alone and scared, buried beneath the earth's surface. Because today I could take in the details.

The sandstone went from burnt sienna near the ground to white and bright yellow marbled together on the ceiling. I stood close to the edges, studying the formations. I didn't know much about geology, but this was Mother Nature at her best.

"This is below the Wabasha, and the offshoots lead toward the brewery, mostly." Eli used his lantern to gesture toward the three openings that led away from the cave. "One goes off toward Pig's Eye Lake." The shadows were inky in the tunnels themselves, and Eli's voice rang out against the small cave, creating an echo, contorting it. The overall effect was spooky, and I liked it.

"Do these connect to the ones underneath Mrs. Signy's?"

"They all connect. I could draw you a map."

"I'd like that." I took a few steps around the cave itself. An old file cabinet stood in the far alcove. I pulled open a drawer and it creaked loudly. I fingered through the files, mostly decades-old invoices for plumbing equipment. A tipped-over stack of wooden chairs sat next to the file cabinet.

"Could I take some photos?"

"They probably won't turn out so well. You need more lighting."

"They're just preliminary." I bent down low and aimed my camera to get a shot of the tunnel-like hallways reaching out from the main cave. "Can we follow one of the offshoot tunnels?" I asked. I knew I was pressing my luck.

"You really want to?" Eli gave me a skeptical look.

"Yes. I would love to. I need to."

"It gets pretty tight in places."

I shrugged. "I'm game. It doesn't scare me." It did scare me. It really scared me, but not because of claustrophobia. But just because I might find myself at the exact spot where my life – my previous life – fell apart.

Those last moments.

I clenched and unclenched my birth-marked fist, not even knowing I was doing it, pressing my thumb into my closed fist, a habit leftover from another time.

"You're not injured? That doesn't hurt or . . ." Eli was looking at my strawberry mark.

"Oh? No, it's nothing. I was born with it."

He nodded then. "Well, let's do this then," he said, giving me a look. "I love hiking below here."

"Why do you love it?" I noticed my voice had taken on a whispery quality, in deference to the beauty of this place, I supposed. Or maybe because I felt something coming.

I did.

"Being down here, I feel like I'm being let in on somebody's secrets, all the big moments that probably went down in these tunnels—don't you think? Can't you just imagine?"

Eli moved toward the tunnel on the far left. I followed.

I could imagine.

The ceiling became lower, so I bent over slightly to fit, but Eli had to practically crouch.

I ducked my head very low for several yards, and my lungs pressed inward when we got further into the tunnel. I tried to focus on the sound my boots made, the crunching of the sandstone gravel, and on my breathing. Not on panicking.

"The heyday for this area was of course the twenties and thirties, before World War II," Eli said, shooting me a glance over his shoulder. I was happy he was going all history professor on me.

"Go on," I said.

"You should talk to some of the old folks in town. They'll have stories for you, I'm sure."

I'd already asked Mrs. Signy to track down Mary Nearhouse with the love letter. I wanted a look at that like nobody's business.

"I'd love personal stories that link to the tunnels themselves to add into my research project."

I followed Eli silently into a larger opening, not quite as large as the cave we'd been in before, maybe half the size, but the ceiling was tall, uneven, with several recesses that went higher than the arch of my flashlight. In the middle of the ceiling was an extremely tall arch. "It was built by the brewery," Eli explained. "A little further north and you'll be in the main caves that held the kegs, refrigerated them, so to speak. It's a cool forty-seven degrees down here, give or take, and that's a perfect temperature for the beer."

"This is gorgeous." The bricks of the arch held a rich patina, reds and oranges. And the brickwork was in a strange parquet pattern. I would remember this if I'd seen it before. I hadn't. In the before or last night.

"Architects don't agree, but people swear this one arch is what keeps most of these caves from collapsing in on themselves."

"So it's an important structure?"

Eli nodded. "Yeah, but it's known for another reason. The best ghost stories come from here. This is the Wailing Arch."

"Yeah?" I asked, snapping picture after picture.

"It's more sound than visual, as no doubt you've heard people say. People report someone crying, a woman. That happens often, a lot when there's a full moon. I know it sounds crazy, but it's what people say."

I stopped, stood still with my camera. "I heard it last night," I admitted. "When I was down here."

Eli's brow shot up. "You did?"

I nodded.

"You were down here? When? Who was with you?"

I averted my eyes and didn't answer, walked the perimeter of the space instead. After a few seconds, I decided on honesty. "I was by myself."

He let out a slow breath. "Alice."

I could hear the censure in his voice. So I changed the subject. "You don't believe in the ghost though, huh?"

"No, ma'am."

"So what makes the noise then?"

"Water coursing through the layers of sandstone and limestone, with acoustics in just the right structural form to magnify it, stretch it out. Maybe couple that with strong winds. I don't know exactly, but I'm working with a team from St. Catherine's—a geologist and acoustics expert to actually figure it out. We're in the grant-application stage right now."

"Really?" I was impressed. He nodded, crossed his arms over his chest and watched me. His research, his inquiry, with a cross-departmental approach, was the kind of university study that I dreamed about. It seemed . . . progressive.

"I kind of like the idea of the Wailing Ghost," I said, dragging my hands over the striated edges of the cave, enjoying the texture beneath my fingers. "Something so awful you have to stick around and complain about it even after death. Kinda badass, you know? But I like the idea of explaining it scientifically even more."

He was too quiet.

I swung my flashlight around to look at Eli's face.

"Which entrance did you use to get down here last night?"

So he was still on that.

I sighed. "I know. It was stupid. It's dangerous to be here by myself, and I know that now. I won't—" I stopped myself from making that promise, because I knew I would be back down here alone, again. Probably tonight.

Eli took a step closer to me, his arms still folded across his chest, emphasizing his size. He squinted his eyes at me. "A decade ago, a college kid died down here from asphyxiation, smoke inhalation. They think he got turned around and couldn't find his way out. So, a worse turnout than even that group of kids a few months ago. People forget . . . until the next casualty." Eli gave a me a look then. "Let me come with you next time."

"We're here now," I said.

"But you'll be back. I can tell. I can see that this place has gotten under your skin." He shrugged, like he understood. "It happens."

"Yeah."

He nodded. "What's your thesis about anyway?"

I explained, as he leaned onto the cavern wall and listened intently, his brow pinching, as he really paid attention to my ideas. I liked the way he gave me all of his attention, like what I had to say was really important. It was a singular thing, to have all of this serious scholar's attention, that intelligent gaze.

I finished explaining which buildings I was focusing on, what their repurposing histories were like, and then I added, "But I also think it would make my whole project more interesting if I could intertwine the history of these structures with actual human tales of love and loss, growth and death, the buildings and structures mirroring the circle of life. That kind of thing."

He nodded like he was thinking this over. "I think I could let one of my students work on that." I was half-annoyed and half-pleased that he was giving my project his blessing.

"What's your specialty? What did you study?"

"Hellenic Greek history. With a minor in mythology."

"Really? And you want to come across like you're not a romantic?"

His mouth quirked up again. It was funny how much I appreciated that he liked my jokes. "You know," he said, "the wailing . . ." he stopped like maybe he shouldn't go on. Then he took a step closer to me, and leaned in, like he was going to tell me a secret. "One time, when I was down here, I heard it. And then, I swear to you, a voice asked for a drink. Just like that, 'A drink?' And then, out of nowhere, I could hear piano. Not a tune, just three or four keys, being tapped randomly."

"Piano?" A shiver crept up my spine. Was it my imagination or did this cave just get colder? Was it possible for a breeze to flit over the back of your neck when you were *under the ground?*

"People say it's the daughter of one of the high-society money-men. She had some sort of condition, was locked away in her later years. I don't know exactly. Maybe a mental illness. The records are spotty."

"You don't believe it?"

"I don't."

I studied Eli for a moment. "What was this cave used for?" I asked, moving toward the other side of the arch for more photos, trying to ignore the unsettling feeling I had, the way my skin seemed to stretch tighter on my skin, more aware of . . . my surroundings and its hidden history. Was this my subconscious telling me something?

"A lot of people say this room is where some of the bigger deals went down."

"So during Prohibition?" I tried not to blind Eli with my flashlight as we spoke, but it was difficult, as the darkness was so thorough, so thick. I settled for focusing my flashlight up at the ceiling, on the arch.

"Yeah, this place is deep below the surface, hard to get to."

"So, like, Ma Barker or Dillinger or—"

"More like the locals. They really ran the bootlegging. The big names just passed through here."

"Did the Hamm's Brewery continue making beer and hide it somehow or . . . ?"

"No. They kept themselves in business by making different soda pops and things, but the bootlegging, it was all small time. Smuggling and home-brewing. Moonshine. One family in particular, a wealthy one, kept St. Paul wet during those years."

"Which family?" Would I recognize names?

"The Thranes. They were old money, were invested in lots of things in St. Paul at the time. Owned a chain of hardware stores. Brought the first automobiles to the area, that kind of thing. Had ties to banking. Just bigwigs in general."

"Thrane," I tried it out on my tongue, in my memory. "Are there any relatives still alive?" Thrane, Thrane, something prickled at me, a memory, a name? A face with a chapped upper lip. Was this anything?

Eli answered, "I'm sure there are relatives. It wouldn't be too hard to find out."

"Huh."

Just as I was about to follow up with some more questions, many more questions, something chittered, a strange insect-like sound.

"What was that?" I froze.

"A bat." His voice was nonchalant.

I moved my flashlight up and around the arch, toward the higher inlets of the ceiling. I saw motion inside several of the larger crevices, black leathery motion. Bat wings folding in and around small furry bodies.

More of them began to chitter. It was a terrible sound, nails on a chalkboard.

"Holy shit," I said.

"What happened to all that bluster from earlier?" He eyed me, one side of his mouth turning up into a teasing smile.

"I believe all that bluster is having an existential crisis."

Eli laughed then. It was such a good sound, a rumble from his chest, and his eyes crinkled up at the corners when he laughed. "You ready to go?"

I shook, keeping my eyes on the horrible mass of bats, backing away. "No way. You must have me mistaken for some kind of chicken."

"Oh really? And what if I tossed a pebble up there and one of those bats came swooping down here just to say hello?" Eli reached down to grab a stone, and I yelped.

"No, please!"

"They're just tiny little winged mice."

"That want to nest in my hair."

"Come on," he said, grabbing my hand, and he led us into a deeper tunnel. Suddenly, he went down on his knees, and I realized if we were going to move forward, that was the only way. I crouched low, then we were crawling for at least twenty yards.

"Good thing you're not claustrophobic."

"Good thing," he said, "and you should know, I actually am. But only on airplanes. I'm terrified of the things. I avoid them at all costs."

I smiled. I kind of like knowing that this burly guy had a fear. "Really? Airplanes?" I teased.

His shoulders shivered. "Yes. Airplanes."

I smiled, and when he stopped in front of me, abruptly, I bumped into him. He turned around.

"We have to kind of shimmy down, a short jump."

I tried to mask my fear, just nodded.

Eli maneuvered himself so that his legs were out in front of him. "It's not too far down." And then he pushed off, disappearing into the dark below.

I swallowed hard, listening for the thump of his boots onto the ground, which happened quickly.

"Now, this is the goods," Eli said, dusting off his jeans, pointing his lantern toward me. "See, no tourist wants to crawl through that muck. This is for serious historians only. You earned some real field points. You didn't complain once."

I moved to a sitting position, and I hesitated before pushing off.

"Let me help."

I shook my head. "No, just let me land on my own." He gave me a quick nod.

It was only ten or twelve feet. I landed squarely, bending my knees to absorb the shock.

"Good," Eli said.

I swung my flashlight around. The cavern was filled with a mass of junk: wooden barrels, a stack of horseshoes, several piles of bricks. I scuffled around the detritus, slowly taking in the thick blankets of sandstone dust, lifting this and that, trying to imagine how or why these things had made their way here. And all the while, I understood that I was . . . close to something.

I felt it, in the way that a current ran just beneath my skin, an awareness.

Eli wasn't looking around, I realized. No, he held his flashlight on me, watching my reactions.

I ran my hand over a dozen or so rolls of paper leaning against the farthest edge of the cavern. "What are these?" When I touched them, I realized they weren't paper at all, but cloth.

"Old Hamm's Brewery advertising," Eli explained. I unrolled one of them, and it began to fall apart even as I did, just at the edges. It was canvas, heavy and crumbling, curling up and brittle from many seasons of moisture and temperature change. Eli moved toward me, and he held one edge while I unrolled the whole thing. Eli flashed his lantern over the length of it, probably twelve feet of it. There sat the simple, smiling cartoon bear that Hamm's had made famous and used in advertising for years.

"I'm surprised no one has looted this place."

Eli shrugged. "There are still some gems left here and there." I let go of my end, and Eli started to roll it up carefully.

Gems.

As if that was a cue, I began to unroll the next canvas, and there, fluttering to the ground like a tiny forgotten butterfly, was a folded square of paper.

"What's that?" Eli asked.

My throat went dry, and I couldn't find any words.

No.

It couldn't be.

Before I knew it, I was on my knees, picking it up with shaking fingers.

I unfolded it, stuck the flashlight in my mouth so I could use both hands. The pencil was faded, nearly gone. But it lived. Still.

This time, it was Dickinson.

Hope is the thing with feathers -
That perches in the soul -
And sings the tune without the words –
And never stops – at all

I sat back on my heels in that cave and shined my flashlight on that barely-there yellowed paper, watching even as its edges crumbled between my fingers, and I read those words again, and my world spun.

I felt my lives slip and steady, flail and recover. The before and the now, she and I, her and me.

Both of us the same.

Any lingering doubts, any half-cocked theories about mass produced ivory pocketknives, about mothers with hidden money-grubbing agendas, they all slipped away, gone into the cold air of the St. Paul tunnels that night, disintegrating into dust, much like the Hamm's canvas advertising.

I held this piece of paper in my hand.

So delicate, so ready to become nothing but a memory itself.

But here it was. It existed.

It lay in my palm.

The handwriting, it wasn't cursive, no, it was printing. But the printing of a person who was always in a hurry, some letters connected simply because the writer couldn't be bothered to lift the pencil from the page. It was the handwriting of a person whose mind worked so much faster than his hands.

It was *his* handwriting.

Of course it was.

Here I was, Alice Grier, in 1998, below the bluffs of St. Paul, Minnesota. And I was holding Rune's paper in my hand.

Part II
Rune

Chapter 15

Goteborg
1921

GROWN UPS' WORDS WERE TRICKY, FICKLE. When Farmor said that Papa was a proud man, a good man, for going ahead of his wife to America, and that, of course, they shouldn't pry as to why he hadn't sent for them yet, Mama agreed wholeheartedly. She nodded her head, and she spoke reassuring words to Farmor, but she was lying.

Rune knew it.

At five-years old, he wondered *how* he knew.

Rune always thought about these things, almost as if he was outside himself, looking in, watching his extended family, his close neighbors, and family friends interact, searching their motives and their humanity underneath all that was varnished on top: manners, chivalry, etiquette.

Even from a young age, he could see that there was always more going on in a person, in a situation, in a moment, than what was said. Words were liars.

Faces too, but not as blatant. It was harder to lie with your face. Impossible to lie with your whole body. So Rune got busy watching, and watching closely, and he learned quickly what was true, what was only partially true, and what was absolutely false.

Because he was a mostly silent child, because he was different, fading into the background was easy. People forgot he was there, or they dismissed him. "It's just Rune. Who's he going to tell?" they probably told themselves with a chuckle.

So he was often privy to conversations and interactions that the other children, his brothers especially, would never get to hear.

The two grown-ups stood in the kitchen, over the tub of heated water, Uncle Isak helping Mama with the dishes. It was a Sunday, like any other Sunday.

Except.

"Has he written?" Uncle Isak asked.

Mama shook her head once. "Not since last you asked."

Rune sat underneath the wooden table, playing with his tin soldier and petting Sötnos, his scrawny wet-nosed mutt of a dog. Rune kept his eyes on his uncle. Isak stood very still, watching Mama. He reached out to Mama, touched her forearm, only barely, just for a moment. Mama leaned into it, sighed a heavy breath. Isak's voice sounded jagged, pained. "I can't help being glad he hasn't sent for you."

Rune listened, and he catalogued this away.

His brothers waited on bated breath for their father's call for them all to join him in America. Even without word for months and months, it was an active longing that his brothers had for Papa. One that Rune's brothers prepared for daily.

If they found a good stick, they put it aside, maybe to bring to America.

If they had extra hardtack, they saved that for their trip.

Farmor spoke of America too. Of her son, of their eventual trip over the ocean to join him.

For Gunnar and Anders, the recurring discussion of Papa was like a church hymn, the same phrases repeated over and over, worshipping Papa like a hero, his years in America only serving to widen his grasp, strengthen his shoulders, turn him into some kind of mythical, almost Biblical, creature. Gunnar even liked to tell a certain story about Papa fishing and grabbing a great silver trout, the size of a small child, straight from the river with his bare hands.

Gunnar liked to tell stories, and Rune liked to listen, especially because Gunnar was actually old enough to really remember Papa, unlike Rune and Anders.

Rune had never met him. Rune never told stories about him, of course, or longed for him, really, because Rune heard the other stories about Papa, the ones that weren't said aloud. These were told in Mama's silences, in her still, quiet, watchful eyes.

Yet, his brothers took no note of this. Did they not see it? Or did they ignore it?

Rune noticed. He saw the hollow look in his mother's face when Papa was discussed. Her eyes went flat, her posture stiffened. Rune also noticed the way that Isak and Mama rarely, if ever, touched. Always staying at opposite ends of the room. Never looking at each other easily. This was noticeable, different from the way that the rest of his family interacted with each other: the easy slaps on the back, the booming laughs and the arms rested on shoulders. The tender taps on the hand while cooking with each other—uncles, friends, and in-laws alike.

Rune watched how his uncles and the other field hands propped each other up on the long walk back from the fields, the way men always offered their hand to a lady as she got out of the horse carriage, whether that lady was your wife, sister, or a stranger.

But never Isak and Mama.

That's why the day over the dish tub was branded into Rune's memory.

Rune noticed many things. And he knew this made him different, but he didn't think it was because he was a particularly skillful observer or because he was of above average or even average in intelligence. It was simply because he had less to do.

Less to talk about, since he rarely spoke.

Less responsibility since he was the youngest of his brothers.

Less depended upon because he was . . . well, imperfect.

He had heard the story of his birth so many times from his brothers, especially Gunnar, that it seemed to him that he had been there, observing that too, like any other day in the kitchen, sitting under the table with Sötnos, watching members of his family come and go, to and fro.

• • •

HIS MOTHER, BIRGIT, LABORED HARD with him, deep into the night. The sun still shone, low in the Goteborg sky, as it was summer, the time when the daylight refused to give up its grasp on the day. The sun and its hold continued to stretch long past the dinner hour, giving the farmers and field hands more hours of work, and casting a rust-orange glow on the barley in the field.

The Kasparsson main house stood upon the hill, large and regal in stature, if not a bit worn around the edges. But Birgit Kasparsson and her boys lived in the modest clapboard house, hidden behind a copse of threadbare Norwegian pines. The silver-haired midwife stood on the ramshackle porch, deciding. She produced a small tin flask from her apron.

Her rough hands shook as she brought the homemade barley liquor to her lips. "*Skit*," she swore under her breath, taking a large gulp, registering the presence of one of the small tow-headed boys at her skirts.

"Your grandmother is not at home?" The midwife gestured up toward the main house. The boy shook his head. "Any of the other women?"

Anders shook his head again. "They are in town. Mama told them to go."

The rhythmic sounds of Birgit and her labor carried on inside the house, the heavy, desperate breaths, one, two, three, four, and then a deep, howling grunt, bearing out through the pain, lasting and lasting, finally trailing off into teeth-gritted silence.

The midwife sighed deeply, as if she were accepting something difficult. "Did your father leave any tools? Or did he take them with him?"

"There are tools in the shed."

"I need something flat, long, and any good knives." She turned to the older boy, Gunnar, standing in the open doorway. Just then the mother shrieked, high and piercing, jarring the nerves of even the steely-eyed midwife.

"Fetch the boiling water from the stove. Bring it to the bedroom," the midwife ordered. The boy stood there frozen, eyes wide. "Now, *kille*, hurry!"

The midwife turned back toward the door and walked inside. The back bedroom smelled of blood and iron, of sweat and urine. Birgit's eyes were glazed, her fists clenched around the quilts beneath her. She took the third, then fourth large gulp of breath, and then she opened her eyes. A scream, more animal than human, emitted from her lips, as her slight body bowed hard off the bed. The sheet slipped from the top of her and the midwife saw the hard, contracted shape of the woman's middle. She heard a terrible sound then, a crunch, a snapping of what could only be bone. The sound was something the midwife had heard before, and it was singular, organic, and it shot the midwife into action. The time for deciding was done.

The midwife took her tools from her pack and placed them on the bed. She grabbed Birgit's wrist and checked her pulse. It thudded hard, erratic against the leathered flesh of the midwife's thumb. The older boy entered the room and settled the pot of boiled water at the foot of the bed with a clank. The younger boy followed, handing the midwife an ax, a large wooden spoon, and something that looked like a railroad spike.

The midwife cursed under her breath but quickly scrubbed each article in the boiling hot water. You never knew what might come in handy.

The midwife spread the woman's legs, ordering the boys from the room, and she checked the woman's progress as Birgit breathed her grunting breaths. One. Two.

Birgit's eyes flashed open, the whites turned a deep red from broken blood vessels, her pupils wild and unseeing. "Do something!" she gasped, gulping in breath. "Save him!" she whispered, as the scream crept back into her voice, taking over the end of her words. Her voice rose and cracked into a hoarse shriek. Then, at the peak of it, she passed out. Her limbs fell and sagged, her stomach, tight, rippling with the new contractions.

The midwife grabbed Birgit's wrist again, found her pulse, weak but present.

She moved to the large, tightly contracted abdomen, swathing it with iodine. She had only performed a few caesareans. The risk of infection afterward was great.

Birgit's stomach went lax for a moment, only a split-second, then contracted violently beneath the midwife's hands, and it was then that the midwife saw something that stopped her in her tracks.

The baby's large purple-red hand was now birthing from the woman's canal. It moved, opening, closing, part of the bloody mess that was between the woman's legs. "*Skit*," the midwife breathed. She pressed the tip of her knife to the woman's belly, then stopped.

She had assumed the baby was breech. This was not the case. The baby was head down if the arm was already coming down the canal. The baby was possibly transverse, or his shoulders were just too large to pass. Whatever the case, the baby was enormous, judging from the size of the hand.

In the few seconds that she paused, the midwife saw that Birgit's color was gone, her face ghost-white, her breathing nearly nonexistent. The midwife changed her mind.

She nodded her head once to herself, and she grabbed her large forceps. She maneuvered them inside Birgit's canal. She grabbed the shoulder of the baby, and she yanked.

The midwife knew what death during childbirth looked like. She knew the color of it, the sound, the silence of it, and she knew the smell.

All of it filled Birgit Kasparsson's bedroom now.

The midwife tried again, angling the forceps differently. With the upper side of the tool, the midwife quickly found the baby's other shoulder wedged against its mother's pelvis, and she pulled to no avail. She grabbed the large wooden spoon, swearing under her breath, and she used it as leverage. With this, along with the forceps, she brought the baby's body farther down the birthing canal. She pulled and maneuvered, her hands slick with blood and life, but she could not get the baby to budge any more.

She felt Birgit's pulse and it was weak, so weak. It was now or never. With a small prayer, Greta Holmquist, the midwife of Goteborg's rural outskirts, birther of hundreds of babies, mother of eleven herself, she prayed. For the first time in a very long time, she prayed to God. And she forced the forceps up into the woman and she grabbed hold of the baby, in the direction of the wedged shoulder and she yanked. On the first pull, she got nowhere, but on the second, she felt some give.

"Boys!" she yelled, and they appeared instantly in the doorway, the older one's face a study of concentration, the younger one in tears. "Both of you take one of your mother's legs." The midwife pushed each of the mother's legs up, bent at the knee, and she waited for the boys to hold them. "Hold her there," she barked.

"There's no time for crying!" she spat, as the younger one eyed the bloody mess that was between his mother's legs.

The boys held on and the midwife pulled, and God Bless, the baby came barreling out, sending Greta to the floor, baby in her arms, forceps tumbling, then falling with a decisive clank, onto the wooden floor. The curling, blue-white rope of an umbilical cord pulled at the mother's body, taut and unforgiving, as the midwife struggle to stand up, eyeing the wriggling, wet mass in her arms. He was fine, pink in color, with a round belly, four limbs, tiny scrotum. But, Lord, he was large.

The midwife ran a thumb inside his mouth, cleaning it, and she made sure he took several breaths. He didn't cry. But he was breathing easily.

The older boys watched, horrified, each still holding a leg, as the writhing, bloody mass of their brother lay in the crook of the midwife's left arm as she got up from the floor. With her right hand, the midwife found her knife, cutting the umbilical cord close to the baby's body, cleaning it deftly with a rag dipped in the boiled water. The midwife used another rag to clean his face, his nostrils.

"Take your brother," she said, handing the baby to the eldest boy. "He's breathing. He's fine. Clean him up. Wrap him, place him in the basket."

The midwife knew she didn't have time to waste.

She turned back to the mother, but the smaller boy was in her way. There he was, tear-stained and shaking. He held up the sterilized railroad spike as a weapon. It was nearly as big as he was. The midwife stifled a laugh, even in that desperate moment, for this little boy and the spike . . . it was ludicrous.

"Save my mother! Now!" he yelped. "Right now!" The fear came off of him in waves. It nearly broke the midwife's heart.

"You don't have to threaten me, boy," the midwife said, pushing the railroad spike away. "Let me do my work. You should leave the room, Son."

If she hadn't been in the throes of the moment, the midwife may have remarked on the little boy's gall, at his loyalty. But there was no time. She moved to the mother, checking her breathing, her heartbeat. Next she palpitated her belly, waiting for the afterbirth, which slithered out of her easily, as if mocking the difficulty that the baby had with this same path.

The midwife cleaned Birgit methodically, stitching her carefully, thankful for the midnight sun of the summer months.

Stitches in the dark, by the light of a lantern, were difficult now that the midwife was in her seventies. Her hands ached in the wet weather, and her knees hurt by the sound of the dinner bell every day, but she knew what would finish her, in the end, what would make her hand her midwifery bag off to a new, younger woman. It would be her eyes.

But today, she didn't need to worry about that. She made her clean, little stitches, as perfect as any needlepointing, cross-stitching champion, and she washed the flesh tears vigorously with her grain alcohol. Next, she applied clean rags to the areas, covered in the cooling salve of witch hazel.

Birgit would have a time of it. The bleeding stopped quickly, easily, and the midwife was glad of that. She did worry because of the size of the child. She had seen large babies unknowingly maul their mothers from the inside, irreparably.

With the mother cleaned and stitched, the midwife gave her attention to the older boy who was still cleaning the baby. "It won't stop bleeding," he said, grabbing another rag.

The midwife moved toward the baby, and before she saw what it was that the older boy was speaking of, she marveled at the size of the child in the basket. He dwarfed the bassinet itself. She had been working with mothers for close to forty years, and she had never witnessed a larger baby. He must've been close to fourteen pounds. This baby's fists were small potatoes, his head as large as a head of cabbage.

The older boy brought the rag to the baby's face, and the midwife took it from his hands. The baby had some kind of injury to his face. The fluids of birth masked his injuries, but now the midwife could see blood on his temple, maybe a cut on his forehead. She cleaned the blood away and saw that it was actually the baby's eye that was hurt.

It was difficult to see exactly what was wrong, as the blood kept swelling in the way, but once she truly got it cleaned off, it was obvious what had happened. The midwife had inadvertently torn the delicate skin of the child's left eyelid during the extraction. "*Skit*," she said, hoping the eye itself was unblemished.

The mother made some quiet grunting noises behind her, and the midwife turned back to her. "Hold the rag to the baby's eye," the midwife told the brother.

The color crept back into Birgit's cheeks. The midwife gave her some smelling salts and tipped a bit of whiskey down her throat.

She came to with a scream, hoarse and breathy. "Is he?" she said, her eyes blood-filled but focused.

"He's fine. You are fine," the midwife answered, with a small smile.

She picked up the baby and placed him in his exhausted mother's arms.

Birgit took a long look at her third son, and a soft, exhausted smile spread over her face. "God bless you," Birgit whispered, tears flowing down her cheeks. She kissed his head, laughing, smiling at the large baby in her arms.

"He is a giant, surely," the midwife offered.

"He's half as big as Anders," Birgit said, smiling at her middle son, who had come back in the room, this time without the railroad spike.

Both boys watched their mother protectively, giving her small smiles, the air of disaster lifting slowly from the room.

"I have injured his eye," the midwife said. "It was an accident as—"

"I will have no apologies, Greta," Birgit said, her voice small and tired. "You surely saved us both. I will never be able to repay you for that."

"I think I will have to give it a stitch or two."

"Let him nurse, then I will give him to you." Birgit took the rag from the midwife, cleaning away the blood from the newborn's eye. Birgit unbuttoned her nightdress.

"Run into town," the midwife told the boys. "It is late, but with the sun up, Dr. Nillson will still be able to attend. He can assist me with the stitching, and he can make certain his eye is unharmed."

Birgit grabbed the hand of the other woman. She closed her eyes as her newborn son latched onto her breast and suckled greedily, making small grunt-like noises, the first noises of his life. A wave of relief washed over Birgit's petite features. "I thought . . . You know, earlier I saw . . ."

"It was not his time, Birgit. It doesn't matter what you saw. He is with us."

"I didn't hear him cry."

"He hasn't cried." The midwife held the mother's gaze then for a moment. "Let it not worry you. I worried that he wasn't breathing, as that is usually the case if the child doesn't cry at birth, but he was breathing, pink in color."

Birgit nodded, and she cleaned the blood away from his eye again. "You know what they say of a baby who does not cry—"

"No, do not say it." The midwife ran her knuckles gently down the cheek of the newborn. "From the day we are born, some of us are better at bearing life's hardships. That is all."

Birgit pressed her lips together. "Yes," she answered. "Yes, this is true."

"Dark hair," the midwife murmured, running her hand over the child's large, melon-sized head. "What a surprise."

Birgit did not meet the midwife's eyes. "His grandfather was dark haired." Her voice was tight, defensive, but the midwife did not notice.

"You rest," she told her. "I worry you may have a fracture in your pelvis or some such. You need nothing but rest now."

"I am fine." Birgit said, but she let her head loll back against the headboard.

"Dr. Nillson will also have something for the pain. I'm afraid that you may have quite the recovery ahead of you."

The midwife went about the business of cleaning up the room, piling dirty rags into a laundry pile, wiping down the mother's legs, covering her with a fresh sheet. The quiet snores of Birgit broke the silence in the room, as did the greedy noises of the newborn, his appetite surely larger than most if judging by his size.

The midwife cleaned her tools, slowly, methodically, with iodine and boiled water, a ritual she had done dozens upon dozens of times, bringing a certain calm to the old woman in its familiarity.

The sun finally began to give up its throne in the sky, the room darkening slowly, filling with the strange, purple-tinted light of twilight.

Birgit spoke quietly, her eyes still closed, jarring the midwife as she placed her best knife in her ancient leather pack.

"Surely you know I do readings for people."

"Yes, Birgit, I know."

"You don't believe then?"

"It's not that I don't. It's . . . maybe this time you were wrong."

"I'm never wrong. I don't make mistakes with these things."

The midwife considered. "If you can forgive my mistake," she gestured to the baby's eye. "Then, surely you can forgive yourself. None of us can be correct or perfect all of the time."

Birgit opened her eyes, and she looked hard at the midwife.

"Are you not glad he is okay? Alive and well?" the midwife asked.

"Of course I am," she said, bending to add a kiss to the baby's temple. She picked up the rag to clean the blood from his eye, which was slowing but not completely stopped.

"What was it that had you so convinced that he was going to die?" the midwife whispered, because she suddenly felt like she shouldn't jinx it. It was stupid to think it, but a little shiver slipped over her body. She looked toward the open front door, the darkening sky. A cooling wind slipped into the room, rushing over the midwife's skin.

"I saw him. He was my son, running, running through a tunnel, dark and wet, forbidding. He struggled to get through it, and eventually he was too large, so he had to crawl on his belly, and . . ." her eyes looked up from the baby then.

"And what?"

"I don't know exactly. Something was after him. Someone? Death was after him, I think."

The midwife considered this. "Isn't death after us all, Birgit?"

The wind blew harder then, a sudden gust, and the bedroom door shut closed with a loud bang. The midwife jumped and then quickly admonished herself with a shake of her head. "My dear, this seems vague and shouldn't trouble you. Now or ever. It was nothing."

"You know me, Greta? Did I not warn your youngest daughter of her husband's death at sea? When she questioned me—did I not see it?"

It was the midwife's turn to keep her eyes down. "Yes, but . . ."

"I thought I knew what the tunnel meant. It seems so . . . obvious, but I must've been wrong. It foretells . . . something. In time, it will be revealed."

"In time," the midwife agreed, drying the last her tools and placing them back in their leather case, feeling the skin at the back of her neck tingle and tighten. She wanted to change the subject. "Shall I have Mr. Algott's daughter send word of the baby to America, to your husband? Do you have an address?"

The boys came through the front door then in a loud tumble, along with Dr. Nillson, and the eldest one opened the bedroom door tentatively with a shy knock.

Birgit greeted them with a tired smile, beckoning them inside. The shoulders of both tow-headed boys relaxed the moment they saw her looking better, farther away from death. They ran to their mother. "Meet your brother, officially, boys. His name is Rune."

Chapter 16

THE FIRST YEARS OF RUNE FOLKESON'S LIFE WERE spent outside Goteborg, in the same clapboard house he was born in. He lived with his brothers and his mother, raising chickens and tending to their barley fields, playing with the multitude of farm children nearby. These were happy days for Rune.

He would remember them as happy, as his true home, even if he were soon on his way to America. He would hold snatches of memory, moments of Sweden in his heart forever.

The golden sun reflecting on the pond's surface near the stand of birches in the west field.

The feel of the soft tuft of mottled fur on the neck of their mutt, Sötnos.

Anders' cold feet snuggling against him when they slept as a family in front of the fire, those worst cold nights of winter.

He wouldn't remember everything of his homeland, the sights and sounds slipping away from him as the years spread out like the ocean between his new life and old. But when he grew older and his brothers or his mother would mention those first few years in Sweden, it always filled Rune with a certain feeling. A calm warmth, a security that all was good and all was golden.

Because although he didn't form the words to say it, or even have the thought consciously, he felt this truth in his heart: His father—in all the important ways—was and always would be Uncle Isak, with his gentle way, his quiet, low rumble of a voice.

So beyond his conscious mind, beyond his six-year-old wants and needs, there always circled a question that he almost asked. Why would we ever want to leave here?

But he never voiced it, as he knew that it lay in the way of a dangerous space, an unspoken problem, a litany of what-ifs that his mother, his uncle, and probably even his brothers couldn't meet head on.

For they were always on the verge of going to America, when Rune was a child, to join Papa. When he was two years old, although he didn't quite remember it, he'd heard the stories. They had all been planning the voyage when Anders came down with a severe case of the mumps and that had put an end to their travel plans.

During Rune's third spring, there was talk of taking the steamer again, but Farmor was in poor health, and they were unsure she would last much longer. Rune had heard Uncle Isak and his cousin Lars discussing this one day in the barn when Rune had been playing in the hayloft.

The trip loomed large in all the family's lives, but for Rune, it was something he could ignore. He could wait to meet his father.

He was a dark-haired and quiet child, with a slight scar on his left eyelid, drawn vertically down the middle, giving his eye a perpetually droopy, sleepy look. In his first few years of life, Rune grew so large so quickly, that his brothers and mother were astounded. He ate more food than either of his brothers, and he grew steadily, the size of his hands and feet rivaling that of his petite mother's by age three.

By then, he was spending time away from his mother with his two brothers, like an older child would. Whether it was that Birgit was too busy because her husband was in America, or if it was that she assumed he could handle himself because of his size, it didn't matter, Rune was his brothers' child during the day, and his mother's baby at night, when he slept curled into her side in her bed each night.

His brothers took him into their fold easily, like brothers do, as their mascot, their project, and they taught him the finer points of living in Goteborg River area. Before he was three years old, Rune could trap a fish, scuttle under the rocks and catch crickets, kick a ball with amazing accuracy, and hit a glass bottle from the fence with a slingshot, and of course, curse.

Gunnar would goad him on, a sour-candy for a treat. "Say it, Rune."

Anders would elbow Gunnar. "Mama is going to beat you."

Gunnar would shrug. "Come on Rune."

Rune didn't say much, but he wanted to please his brother, and on that day, and a few others, he would work hard to form the word that Gunnar had taught him. Rune watched his brother's mouth and he tried hard to get the sounds just right. "*Skit*," he said, a whisper. And his voice sounded far away and hollow to himself, almost like it was all in his head.

But his brothers had heard him. Gunnar and Anders laughed so hard that first time Rune said it, that they fell into the dirt, with Gunnar holding his side while he cackled. That was how Rune's first word ended up being *shit*.

Although speaking was hard for Rune, thinking was not, and he knew that he would not say this word in front of his mother. When they returned for dinner, after hearing Mama's call for them when she blew the old oxen horn from the back porch, they washed the morning's dirt and grime from their hands at the pump near the chickenyard. Gunnar poked Rune in the chest and told him, "Don't say that in front of Mama." Rune gave him a look, a scowl. What did his brother think? That he was soft in the head?

Anders pulled Rune close, put his arm around the boy's shoulders, although he was nearly as tall as his five-year-old brother at not-quite-three-years-old. Rune bit the candy from Gunnar in half and handed the other half to Anders who took it with a smile. "*Tack*." Thank you.

• • •

ON ONE EARLY SPRING MORNING, just after his third birthday, Rune woke howling, holding the side of his head.

Because Rune rarely said a word, never cried, never complained, Birgit woke with a start, and the boys rushed into the room to see if Rune was okay.

Rune held his right ear, cupping it with both hands. The pressure in his head was enormous, and the pain in his ear was sharp, thudding with each pound of his pulse. It scared Rune, and he watched as his mother spoke to him, placing her hand on his cheek. Gunnar asked him a question.

Rune could see their lips moving, but he could not make out the words. Gone were the sounds.

The buzzing, shuffling background noises of the house, the distracting whoosh of the wind. Where had it all gone? The hard-to-hear voices, the incessant bark of Sötnos tied to the tree in the morning, all of it. Gone.

He looked to his family, feeling scared, suffocating. It was as if his mother and his brothers moved their mouths to trick him, keeping any sound from being made. He could hear nothing but the sound of his own pulse, the intrepid boom, thud, of his pulse in his ear, as it pounded against his skull, each beat of it a fresh bloom of pain in his right ear.

See, he knew that his left ear was his silent ear, but he heard things in his right ear. Didn't everyone just have one ear that worked?

But now he had neither. It scared him. Plus, it hurt. God, it hurt.

He blinked his eyes.

"Mama?" he said, and his voice was alien sounding, not just because he rarely spoke anything, but because he could barely hear himself. It was a strange sound, hollow and breathy.

"Ear," he said, and he pointed.

Birgit said something and she turned her head. Rune reached out then and grabbed her face turned it toward him. He gave her a hard look, and Birgit seemed to understand then. The color drained from her face and she spoke slowly, exaggerating the movements of her lips.

"I'll send Gunnar for the doctor. You'll be fine." Birgit went about checking Rune's right ear, finding infection there, and she cleaned it as well as she could with witch hazel, as they waited for the doctor.

Dr. Nillson arrived to see Rune holding a warm rag to his right ear. They all greeted each other. For Rune, it was all in a painful, silent haze. He wanted to close his eyes against the drumming pain in his ear, but he couldn't. He needed to watch their faces, their mouths.

"You boys shouldn't swim in that pond, before it warms up," Dr. Nillson admonished. Rune could read his lips, although it was difficult below the doctor's gray mustache. It was true. Rune and his brothers swam in their pond near the stand of birches even when it was cold and gray and the sun refused to show itself.

The doctor took a look at Rune's infected ear and motioned for him to lie on the bed. He dropped something into the fiery ear that felt cold and oily. Rune stared at the doctor's mouth. "It's surely an infection from the swimming hole. I see it a lot. He'll be fine."

Rune's mother nodded, and Rune watched as his brothers yanked on their own ears nervously.

The liquid in his ear cooled and fizzed, and Rune registered a pop, and then he could finally hear again. He stuck his finger in his ear and moved it around a little bit, the bubbles of the liquid itching him. It was slick and wet. It hurt, it hurt a lot, but at least he could hear some.

"Turn over," Dr. Nillson told him. "Let it drain." Rune did as he was told and then it was like the world went silent again. This was his quiet ear; Rune already knew that. It was easier to fall asleep this way at night. If he had his quiet ear, his left ear, off the pillow, then the world fell away easier and he would fall asleep easily. If he laid the other way, with his quiet ear lying in the pillow, he could still hear the world through his other ear, his right ear. It kept him up.

Dr. Nillson stuck his little tool in Rune's quiet ear. He rummaged around in there for what seemed like a long time. The doctor finally stopped. Then, he said something to Mama, but Rune couldn't see his face. He felt the rumble of the doctor's voice, knew that he'd said something, but couldn't understand it.

But Rune saw Mama's face when it stilled. Her mouth turned down.

She came to look into the quiet ear. After a few moments, Rune turned toward them, so he could see, moving his head so he could hear.

"It's scar tissue. It probably started at birth," the doctor said. "Things like this sometimes go undetected, just building on themselves, until . . . He's likely got some hearing damage."

Birgit said, "The way he tilts his head sometimes, that sweet little tilt. I always thought he was just listening, like a cute habit. But he's been angling his right ear to hear."

"I see," the doctor said.

"Is there anything to be done?"

"I'm afraid not," the doctor explained. "It may stem from his injury at birth." The doctor motioned to his eye, Rune's scar and droopy eyelid. He cleared his throat, hesitated. "Does his speech sound . . . irregular?"

Birgit shook her head. "He's only three. He speaks . . . rarely."

"He may be delayed because of the hearing problem. He may have difficulty intellectually as well. I think you will need to prepare yourself for this eventuality." Rune did not like the look that Dr. Nillson gave his mother. "He has no lasting problems with his vision? Just the scar and the dilation of that pupil?"

"I believe his vision is fine." Mama stared hard at Rune.

The doctor seemed pleased with this news, as he packed up his bag, writing out directions for the small amber bottle of liquid that he handed to Mama. "He'll need this twice a day in the infected ear."

Mama nodded and thanked the doctor, paying him in eggs and rhubarb pie, since the doctor had recently lost his wife, and consequently twenty or so pounds. He thanked Birgit and apologized for not catching the situation with his ear earlier. "I think we were just so concerned with his eye. Plus, sometimes these things don't show up until later. The scar tissue must've started over his eardrum long ago and built on itself. These things, they have a way of hiding themselves until . . . until they are ready to be known to the world."

Birgit nodded, and she and Rune's brothers saw the doctor to the door. She waved as he pulled away in his small carriage, the horse's hooves playing a *clip-clop* rhythm that Rune could hear, now that his ear was beginning to already feel much better. Rune sat up in the bed.

And in that moment, Birgit shooshed her older children out into the yard, and she came to the bed, pulled little Rune to her arms, and held him close to her. He snuggled into her lap and looked up to his Mama's face.

She rubbed her nose against his. "My little Rune."

She looked out the small bedroom window, watched the backyard as Gunnar and Anders wrestled in the weeds, and she pulled Rune closer to her, his dark curls tickling her neck. She kissed the little shell of his scarred ear. She kissed his droopy eyelid, and for some reason, though she hadn't thought of it in many long months, she remembered the tunnel.

She saw Rune's clear blue eyes, the fringe of his lashes, against a grown-up version of his face, and he was running, the bulk of him making advancement difficult in the tight tunnel.

"These things," Dr. Nillson's voice echoed in her mind, "they have a way of staying hidden, until, well, until they are ready to be known in the world."

Mama ran her hands through Rune's hair, resting her hand on his cheek. "Does your ear feel any better?" she asked, looking him right in the eyes.

Rune nodded then. And, almost as if to show the doctor up, to prove him wrong, Rune spoke then, a little whisper of two words. "*Tack, Mama,*" he said, and it was a salve to her mind, to Birgit's soul. *Thank you, Mama.*

• • •

RUNE'S INFECTED EAR RECOVERED VERY quickly, but according to his mama, it healed slowly. She checked it faithfully every morning and night, and she continued the drops and clucked her tongue for several weeks after the incident.

His ear became the newest problem to keep Birgit and her boys from planning their voyage to meet Papa that spring of 1921. Rune couldn't be sure, for he was only a small boy, but it seemed to him that his mother seemed happy about this delay.

The following spring, they had their tickets purchased, and Mama had actually begun to stockpile things in her cedar chest. Her family bible, her newly finished quilt, canned lutefisk, tins of crackers, a small glass jar of a peppermint concoction—a homemade cure for seasickness.

The family, all of them, felt the reality of the trip upon them, and for the first time, Rune's brothers fell silent about their voyage.

But then a storm, an ice storm, the likes of which hadn't been seen in Scandinavia for decades, damaged the hull of the ship, the great *Stockholm*, which the Folkeson family had booked passage aboard. It would be in port for months in order to be properly repaired.

They would receive credit toward new tickets. The steamer company wanted Mama to purchase for the fall, or to travel in the summer, just aboard a different ship. But she would have none of it. She cited superstition, wanting to sail on the *Stockholm* as Folke, her husband, had years before. Plus, she wanted to only travel in the spring. "It is the safest season; it's always been our plan."

So the trip was put off for yet another year. It seemed like the whole extended family, the neighbors, everyone seemed happy about this. Mama whistled quietly to herself as she emptied her trunk, displaying her new quilt at the foot of her bed again. She wrote to Papa with a somber look on her face, but she hugged Aunt Malin tightly, so tightly, after the news first got to them of the *Stockholm*.

Rune's brothers seemed happy as well, the far-off idea of travel much more enthralling than its realities.

Only Farmor found their postponement unsatisfactory. She peered down her nose at Mama, and she told her that people were "going to talk." This phrase was lost on Rune because he, for one, was not going to talk. And what did she mean anyway? People always *talked.*

Rune was happy they were staying. He was relieved.

For many reasons.

He hadn't known how he'd ever say goodbye to Uncle Isak for one, or how it was that he'd be able to smuggle Sötnos on the ship. Because, surely, his mother would look the other way when he did. Surely, they didn't expect him to leave his dog.

Also, the lambs were coming soon, and Uncle Isak had promised Rune and his brothers that they could help with the lambing, that they could oversee the process.

It was dark in the night when Gunnar shook Rune awake, with Anders mumbling beside him. "Get up! It's time."

It took little Rune a few moments to remember what reason they might have for waking in the night. But it came to him quickly. He and his brothers dressed quickly, making their way out to the smaller of the two red barns. Uncle Isak was already there, waiting for them.

"The mother knows how to do most of the work," Isak explained. The mother, for this, the first baby of the season, was Hettie Lamb. She lay in a fresh bed of hay, her swollen middle looking larger even than yesterday. She mewled some quiet, complaining sounds, and Isak just nodded along with her, and spoke soft, encouraging words.

"If there is a problem, we intervene. Much like when you were born little Rune."

Isak ruffled Rune's hair then, and Rune leaned into the rough, callused hands of his uncle. "But mostly, the mothers know what to do. Just like with us humans, if you have a problem, the mother is the best resource. Don't you forget it. You've got yourself an extra good one, an especially good mother. They know all kind of things about tricks and solutions, how to sew things up tight and strong, how to soothe your nightmares, how to bake an apple crisp just right."

"They also know how to gut fish," Anders offered.

"And win at whist. Always." Gunnar frowned at this.

"How do they know? How do they know everything?" Anders asked, looking worried, biting on the pad of his thumb.

Isak thought on this, rubbed the lucky coin he wore around his neck. "I don't know exactly. See I'm not a mother, I don't have the same special magic." He looked away then, toward the mother sheep. "Look boys, it's happening."

And sure enough, there on a pile of hay on the Kasparsson family barn floor, Hettie Lamb gave birth to one small black lamb, its wool wet and curly as it came from its mother. One minute it was not in the world, and in the next, there was a low braying sound from Hettie, and here it was, lying on its side in the hay, a tangle of limbs, and wool, and fluid.

Isak moved in to help clean the little lamb, and before Rune knew it, the lamb was up on shaky, wobbly legs, only for a second, and then it was down, splayed onto the ground, nose in the hay. Rune moved to help it, but Isak held Rune back with a tender hand. "Let it try," he said. "That is what you must do. Let the lamb try." And sure enough, the lamb slipped around for a few more times, but then it was up and it was moving awkwardly, gingerly on its newfound legs.

Hettie moved to the new baby and began to clean her up, with soft curls of her black tongue.

"You should name her, boys."

"Does it begin with an L?" Gunnar asked.

"Yes, this generation will have L names," Isak explained, as last year's lambs all had names that began with K. It was easier this way, one of the rules Isak instilled to keep order in the vast workings of the Kasparsson farm.

"Lilja," Rune offered. He always loved when Mama sang him the lullaby with all the different flower names. *Lilja*. Lily. He wanted to picture lambs on a hillside, eating all type of flowers, just a full blanket of blossoms, laid out like a buffet.

Gunnar and Anders' eyes brightened at the suggestion. "Lilja!" they both agreed.

Isak was busy cleaning up in the stall, and he ordered the boys to put out fresh water and hay for the lamb and its hardworking mother. But when the boys finished all their helpful chores, they sat close to the lamb, touching its silken wool, and playing with the new creature. Lilja seemed particularly taken with Rune who sat cross-legged in front of her. Lilja approached Rune slowly, baaing a small hello, and she pressed her face to Rune's, nearly nose to nose. The brothers laughed when Rune stayed very still and said, matter-of-factly, to the lamb, "*Valkommen.*"

Soon, the boys tired, and they lay on their own pile of hay, sprawled out and yawning. They leaned back, getting comfortable, silently agreeing the walk back to the house was much too long, especially because they would be up to milk the cows in a matter of hours. In moments, Anders snored his little, soft whistle of a snore. And Lilja nursed at her mother's teat.

And Gunnar flopped from his side to his back and back again, finding his most comfortable position.

Rune watched Isak, as he finished his chores. And when he finally finished, he put out the lantern, and he came and joined the boys on the hay, his burly body stretching out behind all three of them.

"Can you come with us?" Rune asked. "To America?" This was a question that had been bothering Rune, tugging at his insides, for a long time, and he needed to know the answer. He thought he did know the answer, but he wanted a different one. So he figured he would ask. This was the most elaborate string of words Little Rune had ever put together, and in the dark of the barn, this was the first sentence spoken in his young life. And Rune felt Isak stiffen and sit up behind him.

"Rune," he said, and he pulled the boy into a rough embrace. "You know I can't. I wish I could but I can't. I'm sorry, Son, but I'm not . . . your father."

Rune breathed in Isak's scent then, hay and hard work and the outdoors. He rested his head against Isak's chest, and he sighed. He knew this was true. He knew his father was someone else, this man's brother, off in America, working on the railroad, saving up for their arrival.

He knew this all to be true.

But it didn't feel true in Rune's not-quite six-year-old heart.

• • •

THE STEAMER CABIN SMELLED LIKE SALT-water and Anders' vomit. Rune's family, Birgit and his brothers only, boarded the great *Stockholm*. Farmor's health still wasn't at its best. She declined the trip to America but made certain that Mama wouldn't join her in staying. "There are to be no more excuses," she had said to Mama, her eyes shooting over to Isak, across the dining table.

Farmor had even purchased Mama and the boys a first-class room. They did not travel as peasants, sleeping below-deck in bunks with many other immigrant families, but rather in their own state-room, one that held two sets of bunks, its very own wash basin, and fresh linens, towels, and paper-wrapped cakes of soap in a tiny closet behind the door.

The boat was luxurious, decorated in thick, velvety fabrics, and the food decadent. Gunnar, at their first buffet luncheon, counted six different types of potatoes. But the trip was hard, the waves rough and jarring. The reality of steamer travel proved to be grueling at times.

Rune watched in the damp, gas-lit darkness as his family fell asleep those first nights on the ship, watching all the objects—his brothers included—as they listed left then right, then left, then right again. The give and take of the sea, the sway of the waves, it was a music that Rune could understand, a music that calmed him, soothed him.

But he watched Anders as he retched yet again into the pot on the side of his bunk, and Gunnar swore again under his breath when the smell wafted up to him. Rune wished he could comfort Anders somehow.

He hopped down from the bunk above his mother, who was blessedly asleep, for she also suffered from seasickness those first few days, and Rune snuggled up next to Anders. Rune at five, though two years younger, was nearly larger than his brother now, and he wrapped his arms around him. Rune breathed in deeply, pressing on his brother's chest with his palm, urging Anders to find the rhythm with him, something Mama would do when Rune had bad dreams about the bear.

Anders sniffled and sobbed, but he took a deep breath and matched his breathing to Rune's.

It didn't help.

After several minutes of hoping, Anders propped his head over the side of the bed and heaved the last few remnants of the fresh bread and veal soup from dinner. But then Anders curled his head into Rune's shoulder and fell asleep, too exhausted to be sick anymore. With everyone else finally asleep, Rune let the sway of the boat overtake him, that soothing push and pull, and he let himself wonder again about his father.

He thought of the one photograph that Mama had of Papa, their wedding photo. He was tall and broad-shouldered with the square jaw of Gunnar and the thick blond strap of hair of both of his brothers.

Gunnar told the same handful of stories about Papa over and over, about fishing, about shooting. Anders told them too. How Papa let Gunnar shoot his shotgun one glorious morning when he was five, the spring before he left, in the clearing near the river.

How Papa chewed tobacco, rather than used snuff, which was nearly blasphemous in their native parts of Sweden.

How Papa cracked Gunnar with his belt for eating butter out of the larder without permission.

Was he truly going to get to meet his father? Folke Kasparsson?

Rune was nearing six years old that spring on the steam ship, and he had lived most of his young life knowing that this trip hung out in the future, something that was surely to be done, to be accomplished, but never truly occurring.

In a very real way, until recently, Rune hadn't ever truly believed they would leave Goteborg.

What worried him most, aside from leaving Uncle Isak, was the expression that Mama wore when she spoke about the trip to America those few months before they really, truly left, because this time they were really going. Farmor had made certain. The shadows played over Mama's face when their friends and acquaintances would question about Papa. Mama lost weight. Rune noticed a few strands of grey in her golden hair as well.

These pieces of evidence worried Rune. They were much more real than the stories his brothers told of his father.

Rune liked to think that he was an expert when it came to people's stories, their true stories, not just the ones that passed over their lips and formed into words.

Words could be the enemy sometimes. He knew this in more ways than one.

Rune was quiet and his speech was plagued by the rounded-out consonants of those with hearing deficiency, the just left-of-center pronunciation of his vowels. He could easily be understood, but also the listener understood something that wasn't said—Rune was imperfect. He behaved oddly, tilting his head to hear, staying silent when he could. He looked poor, with his scar on his eye.

These things were all checks on a list of evidence to so many people, children and grown-ups combined, and when the evidence was added up, summarily, the same conclusion was reached: He was dumb.

And that word felt bad in Rune's mouth, on his tongue. It felt untrue, a lie. Was it?

Rune accepted that this was his "story." It was his fact, true or not, in the eyes of others. Just like how people thought of Gunnar as brave and strong, and people liked to tell Gunnar he was like Papa. Also, people called Anders handsome. He made girls and grown women twitter and giggle.

Rune would often fade into the background, playing near the woodstove or under the table in the kitchen with his marbles or Sötnos. Mama was a tough one, she never let much pass by her lips, but Rune knew her. He could watch her face, the way her shoulders tensed, the way she hissed air through her teeth when she was trying to keep her temper.

She did that the day Aunt Malin came to visit, just before they left for America. "I will not hear any of that," she told her.

"If you just refuse, write to him, tell him it is not so bad here. It isn't, is it?"

"It is starting to look bad. A few seasons is one thing."

"It started to look bad long before now, Birgit." Malin gave her sister a serious look.

"I cannot stay. Folke's family cannot keep supporting us."

"They do no such thing. You do plenty with the chickens and—"

"Selling eggs is not enough to keep my boys in clothes and food. They have been more than gracious. Especially Isak."

Mama's eyes did not look up from her teacup, and Auntie Malin cleared her throat, her eyes shooting toward Rune at the woodstove. "Birgit," Malin said finally.

"We must go and there will be no more discussion about it."

"What about the drink? If Folke still—"

"It is outlawed in America, you know this."

"So it is decided." Malin sighed deeply. "We shall look upon it as a great adventure. I will send you with—"

"You will not reconsider and come with us, Sister?"

"The farther I am from Folke Kasparsson the better." Malin leveled Mama with a stare, and Rune wondered then again at Folke.

What could make his mother shrink so? And how could his brothers not see it, feel it, in every step closer to that steamship across the ocean?

Rune's stomach twisted and dropped as he tried to match his breathing to his sleeping brother's in the cabin of this great steam ship barreling across the Atlantic Ocean, toward America, toward their new life, toward their father. Rune was conflicted; excited to finally meet his father, to greet this new land and all its promises, yet stretched out, hammered thin, a tenuous string of himself still grasping tight to Goteborg.

America. The kids back in the old neighborhood were in awe, jealous of their trip.

It was a glorious adventure, but he couldn't fully enjoy his sense of excitement, because even in her sleep, his mother wore a furrowed brow, a pursed mouth, an expression of worry. There was no doubt about it.

She was scared.

She turned over in her sleep on her bunk, making a small sound. Her fist unfurled and she dropped something onto the floor of the ship, and it landed with a *clink*.

Rune got up from his bunk to retrieve whatever it was, and he swayed left with the boat, then right. He got on his hands and knees to find the object. He could hear it rolling, along with the heft of the ship. His hand found the object, warm and metallic. He picked it up, squinted in the darkness at the small round disc in his palm.

It was attached to a thin leather cord; it was a small bronze coin, old and tarnished. It was a lucky coin, one that Rune himself had rubbed many times before he shot a big marble or rolled a big number in jacks. But, of course, only with his Uncle Isak, because it was Isak's lucky coin. He wore it always around his neck.

It made Rune feel somewhat homesick in his belly holding that coin. He thought of his uncle's easy smile, with his big front teeth, the way they overlapped a little bit. The way he always smelled like hay. It had been hard to say goodbye to him, most of all. Him and the dog.

Uncle Isak was the one who had taught Rune how to thread a fishing line, how to whistle with his fingers in his mouth to call the dog, how to braid the reeds in the river nice and tight into a basket for all the fish he caught. Isak was big, tall like him, and he had a deep booming laugh, one that vibrated through Rune himself when he sat on his lap.

Isak had promised and promised that he would come visit them, but now, in this dark room on this vast ship, something like a visit from his family in Sweden seemed so impossible. Rune and his family were starting over.

He understood that now. More than he had understood when they'd said their goodbyes to everyone. His mother had cried, hard, salty tears, her shoulders shaking. Malin and Farmor had cried too, but now, in that moment, he understood why.

They would never see them again.

Not Isak, not Malin. Not any of the neighbor kids.

But looking at his poor mother asleep on that small bunk, with its lavish bedding and feather-filled pillow, Rune knew he needed to put this coin back in her bed, for her to find in the morning. There was something important about it, desperate even. Mama could not know that Rune had seen it. Rune was sure of this, even if he wasn't exactly sure *why*.

So he placed the coin on the cord gently next to her head, on the cot, and he climbed back into his bunk with Anders. "You okay, brother?" It was Gunnar's voice in the darkness.

"Yes," Rune answered.

"It's going to be okay, Rune. Don't be scared."

Rune didn't answer.

"I will protect you," Gunnar said.

Rune placed his arm over Anders' shoulders and he answered, "Okay." But what exactly was it that Gunnar was going to protect him from?

Chapter 17

AMERICA DIDN'T LOOK TOO DIFFERENT FROM Sweden to Rune's eyes, just flatter. But *jösses*, it felt different: hungrier, more tired, and a little bit sad. Gunnar tried to explain that it was just homesickness, when Anders had started crying that first night in New York at the hotel, after all the filling out of paperwork and waiting in line after line after line, standing next to so many passengers who'd just deboarded their ships, their clothes wrinkled, their breath sour, their spirits bouncing between bedraggled and exuberant.

To Rune, homesick seemed like a thin idea or a flat word, and the pang in his gut was much more real, more tangible. He wanted more food: potato sausage and rye crisps. He wanted a comfy place to curl up next to Mother. He wanted a warm fire, and he wanted *not* to feel this strange clench of what-is-coming-next in his stomach.

Rune liked his routines at home. He liked to wake up with Sötnos in his bed, he liked to smell that warm spot on her neck, he liked to read until the rest of the house awakened, and he liked his breakfast with warm milk, a special indulgence that Mama afforded him and only him.

But it had been two weeks since he'd had any routine, any comfort, and in many ways it was like forever. Anders felt it too, he knew. Rune could tell by the way Anders was moved to tears over stupid things on their train trip from New York: Gunnar's teasing, spilling his afternoon tea on the train, losing his third button on his vest.

Rune didn't like how *he* felt loose and unraveled like the threads to Anders' button. And he didn't like how America looked out the train window. It was like God had taken America and flattened it out with a rolling pin, like Mama used when she was baking her *pepparkaka*.

There was just so much of it: America. It went on for days, flat and stretched out, green from one end to the other, with nothing interesting in between. A few small mountains at the beginning of the trip, but then nothing. For many, many hours. Just wheat fields, the sun, and the horizon, with nothing breaking it up. Did people who lived here even know the sea? This seemed nearly criminal to Rune.

And their language, it sported different vowels sounds, a strange staccato rhythm. And how did they say the letter *j*? It was completely different than the Swedish *j*, much more aggressive . . . vicious even. Rune knew he was going to have to learn a new language when he came here, but no one had told him about the completely different *j* sound. Rune felt swindled.

Rune studied the mouths of the passengers on the train, trying to figure out how they made the odd sounds of English, what it was that they were doing with their mouth and tongue to get those sounds out of their head. It was an assault on his ears. Whereas Swedish sounded so musical to Rune, the English around him was like a steady beat of torture.

With his diminished hearing, Rune convinced himself at first that he was just not hearing it correctly. But no, the more he studied the English, the more he learned it was as odd in sound and cadence as it seemed.

Aunt Malin had told Rune and his brothers that they would pick up the language easily, much more easily than older people, as children held an advantage. Children absorbed it. But Rune wasn't so sure. He didn't want anything about this new language *absorbed*.

They rode for a full day and a night on a train from New York to get to Swede Hollow, a place that held so much in those two words. For years, the Folkeson boys had talked about Swede Hollow and dreamed about Swede Hollow. Rune thought it strange that this new place in this vast country of America would be named a bit after his home country. He both liked it and he didn't. Like it was somehow cheating. But it was where their father lived. It was the place of everything to come—where they would be reunited as a family, where they'd grow into men, where they would blossom.

When bad things, small things, happened in Goteborg, Rune would often remind himself of his brothers' oft repeated phrase. *I bet it'll be better in Swede Hollow.* If they were too poor for more paper and pencils for Rune's drawings, Gunnar would tell him, *I bet in Swede Hollow, we'll have them.* Or if they curled around each other, too cold, in their bed at night, Gunnar would pipe up, *I bet it's warmer in Swede Hollow.*

Gunnar was always looking ahead. So when they got off the train in St. Paul, Minnesota, bedraggled and exhausted, Gunnar was the first one to spot him.

"I think it's him, Mama. Is it him?" Gunnar pointed across the station's landing to large man, broad-shouldered and thick, with the same strap of wheat-yellow hair that Rune saw in his brothers every day. He had the generous mouth of Uncle Isak, the same thick brow.

"It is," Rune's mother said, breathless, her cheeks pink and her smile working at the corners of her mouth. Rune took this as a good sign.

They moved together across the station, and before he knew it, his father swept his mother up in his large arms, pulling her right off her feet, spinning her around. Their lips met in a kiss, and Gunnar chuckled, but Rune had to look away. There was something he didn't like in this display. He didn't appreciate how this stranger of a father acted toward *his* very own mother. Rune knew this was babyish of him, nonsensical, but he couldn't help how he felt.

After what seemed like too long, his father put his mother down, and he took Gunnar by the shoulders. "Look at you, *kille*! So grown!" He pulled him into a rough embrace, and Gunnar's cheeks pinked like Mom's.

Next, it was Anders' turn. He looked up at his father eagerly, hoping for the same sun to shine on him, and he wasn't disappointed. Papa switched to Swedish then, "Even more handsome than your mother writes, Anders!" Papa got down on one knee and ruffled Anders' hair. He pulled him into his embrace, grabbing Gunnar again as well. Papa spent a long moment smelling Rune's brothers' hair, just inhaling their scent, with his eyes closed, and Rune began to feel self-conscious, both wanting this man's attention and dreading it. Rune scooted closer to his mother, half-hiding behind her skirts.

"Let me have a look at you," Papa exclaimed, standing and walking over toward Mama and Rune. But suddenly it was more than Rune could take. He hid completely behind his mother.

"He is quiet, Folke," Mama said. "You are new to him."

Papa stepped around Mama anyway, and Rune was glad he did. The man beamed, the sun catching off the blue of his eyes, and he gave Rune the warmest smile. Rune smiled back, just a little, tentative.

"You don't have to embrace me yet, Son," he said, quietly, his voice tender. "I've waited many a long year to meet you, my dear boy. I can wait until you're ready. I know it must be strange." And he stuck out his hand. Rune considered it then, and he shook hands with his father.

Rune didn't know why, but his eyes filled with tears, and he quickly grabbed his hand away from his father and dried his eyes on his mother's skirts.

"Such dark hair," Papa said to Mama, placing his arm around her shoulders and grabbing her suitcases, nodding to Gunnar to get the trunk.

"His hair is like your father," Mama answered.

"Like Isak too," Papa said. And there was silence between them for a few steps, and Rune followed, listening, wondering at this large man.

"He is a very big boy, Birgit. You are right about that. He's nearly Anders' size."

"My heart is so glad to see you again, Folke, to finally be together as a family."

Anders took hold of Rune's hand then, gave him a smile.

"Papa," Rune whispered, trying out the word.

Anders squeezed Rune's hand and nodded. "We're finally here, Rune. This is home."

It seemed both strange and familiar at once, as if he'd found himself inside a dream he didn't know he'd had. Rune was home. In America. With his father.

• • •

SWEDE HOLLOW, OR *SVENSKA DALEN*, sat in a ravine below a famous brewery, with a couple dozen ramshackle, claptrap houses stretched out, sitting right up next to Phalen Creek, their outhouses on shaky stilts, sitting out over the water. Rune thought about how back in Sweden, they didn't have to shit in a river. They did it more civilized, in a true outhouse, with a hole in the ground.

Mostly Swedes lived in the Hollow, hence the name, but there were some other foreigners as well: German, Polish. But the Irish lived down river, in Connemara Patch, just beyond the Seventh Street Bridge, and it was quickly learned that the Irish were looked down on, that they lived "downstream" of the Hollow, of the stilted outhouses, and that was enough said about that.

The Hollow was home to immigrants who were making their way in the new world, working at the brewery, which of course, being 1923 was struggling, only making near-beer and soda pop, or they worked at the nearby railroad, which is what Folke Kasparsson had been doing for six years.

He had managed to put together one of the nicest homes in Swede Hollow, from cast-off scrap lumber, tin sheeting, and months of hard work.

There were two bedrooms in the back, and a large living area in the front. No one in the Hollow had running water or electricity, but this was nothing new to Rune and his family. They had never known such luxuries.

The first night in the Hollow, it stormed, and Rune startled, sitting up in the bed he shared with Anders, as the raindrops hit the tin roof with sharp, echoing sounds.

"It's nothing," Gunnar said in his sleep-muffled voice.

But Anders looked at Rune wide-eyed, and scooted closer, and Rune scooted closer to him.

For Rune, and often Anders too, things took some getting used to. The rhythm and tone of English. The sounds of the roof. The low timbre of their father's voice in the other room as they drifted off to sleep. All the sounds of this new home, they were . . . strange.

If Birgit was disappointed by the state of their home in Swede Hollow, she never let Rune or his brothers know this. From that very first day, she set about rattling around the kitchen, cleaning things up, beating rugs on the front porch, airing out sheets, making the rounds to meet the other womenfolk in the Hollow, learning when the vegetable wagon came through, and the general day-to-day ins and outs of the place.

Rune was careful to watch Birgit, and he found nearly none of the visible signs of worry that he had cataloged those weeks and months before they left, aside from how she would jump when the heavy wooden front door would slam shut in the wind.

Mostly, his mother seemed happy, humming beneath her breath, going about her work, with high pink color in her cheeks, and this was enough to calm Rune, to soothe him, in those first strange days in America.

Mama began right away resetting the routine for the boys, and no one appreciated that more than Rune. By the second morning, she already made toast and warm milk for Rune, his jelly laid out like he always had, and it was like something in Rune relaxed a little bit.

It was that day, that second full day in the Hollow, that Papa returned from the railroad on his lunch hour, and he brought home a kitten. Just a little orange ball of fluff, with a small bite out of his left ear, but Papa presented her to Rune.

"For you, Son," he said, and he handed the kitten to Rune.

"*Tack* . . . Papa," Rune added the last word, cautiously.

"He speaks!" Papa said, with his smile that looked so much like Uncle Isak's, minus the overlapped teeth. Papa took his place at the lunch table.

"What will you name her?" Gunnar asked, petting the kitten's ears.

"Aprikos," Anders offered.

"What about Killer?" Gunnar said.

"No, you should name her something in English, Son," his father pressed. "In English, Aprikos would be Apricot. That is good, eh?"

Papa reached out and ruffled Rune's hair, just as he had done Anders' the other day. Rune liked it and he didn't. Uncle Isak used to do that.

Rune kept his eyes on the kitten's fur. He stuck his nose in her neck and smelled, but it smelled nothing like Sötnos's thick collar of cozy fur. It smelled like dirty socks and rotten beets.

"She needs a bath," Rune said, wrinkling his nose, and for some reason, the whole table erupted in laughter then, and Rune smiled along. He watched as Mama laughed, her eyes crinkling at the corners, and she watched Papa. Papa, he didn't watch anyone. He just finished laughing and dug into his boiled fish and potatoes.

• • •

THE BOYS WENT OUT INTO THE Hollow that morning, and they walked around the place, digging near the creek, climbing the steep ladder-stairs that took you up to Planck Avenue, and they snuck around the nearest outbuildings of the brewery. They were boys, exploring their territory, and of course, Rune had Apricot with him, and she searched around, sticking her nose in all kinds of shrubbery and mud puddles, proving her courage right along with Rune.

And Rune, for the first time since coming here, started to feel wholly good about this place. Outside with his brothers, he could sense the adventure this new world had to offer, the freedom. He knew that there were things to be done here, and that they, as brothers, would do them together.

They saw a pair kids, fishing near the *bluffs* (as Papa called them), and the girl called out to them in Swedish. Rune picked up Apricot and stuck her under his arm.

"I got just the thing," Gunnar told his brothers as they made their way up the rough incline to where the kids were casting their lines. "Uncle Isak gave me something before we left."

"Want some chewing gum?" Gunnar asked the girl and boy, speaking in Swedish, of course, but for the first time ever, feeling strange about it.

"*Självklart*," the girl said.

And that was how the Folkesons made their first friends in Swede Hollow.

The girl had long, stringy hair, the color of burnt toast, but she spoke Swedish and she smiled at the brothers, showing off a wide gap between her front teeth. "This here is Johann, my brother. And I'm Inger."

Gunnar stuck out his hand and they shook, in an oddly formal exchange. Gunnar gave the kids his name and his brothers'. "We just got here."

"We know," Johann said. "Everybody knows everybody's business in the Hollow."

"I've only heard about this," Inger said, about the gum, as she took a stick from Gunnar. "You just chew it?"

"Yeah. Until the taste goes bad."

"Then what?"

"Stick it to a tree," Anders offered. "That's what we do at home."

"Were you near Goteborg?" Johann asked, taking a stick of gum and giving it a once-over before he put it in his mouth.

Anders nodded. "You guys too?"

"South of there, closer to Malmo."

"We were north of the coast," Gunnar said. "How long since you came over?"

"Near a year," Inger said. "You guys going to school in the fall?"

"Mama says we have to," Anders said.

"Him too?" Inger asked, pointing to Rune.

"Yeah," Gunnar said.

"He's . . . okay?"

Rune's cheeks turned to fire, but he put the cat down, and busied himself with petting his head.

In Sweden, everyone knew everything about Rune. There were no questions. His bedraggled eye, his silence, they were nothing special.

In America, on the boat, the train, he registered the stares, heard the quips. They'd questioned Mama about him mercilessly in one line at the immigration office.

But somehow when they got to Swede Hollow, Rune had so much to take in, he had forgotten about his appearance again. He had simply forgotten to be self-conscious.

"He's fine," Gunnar said, a slight challenge in his voice. "He's just quiet, and his eye has a scar, that's all."

"I didn't mean . . . Sorry," Inger fumbled. "I like your cat. What's his name?"

"Her," Gunnar said.

"Aprikos," Rune answered, in his usual whisper, and he answered in Swedish. Not English as his Papa had told him to, and he saw Gunnar and Anders' exchange a look. Rune let the kitten go then, so she could do some exploring.

"You got any poles?" Johann asked. "You want to fish?"

"We didn't bring any. We'll have to make some," Gunnar said.

"Why don't we get looking for some good sticks," Inger said, propping her pole against a stone and hooking her arm through Rune's. "I got a scar too," she offered to Rune, pulling up the sleeve of her blouse. "That's from a dog. Bit nearly through my arm when I was six."

Rune nodded at her, unsure of the proper response.

"Are there really caves around here?" Gunnar asked, picking up a stick and breaking it over his knee.

"Yeah," Johann answered. "All over in the bluffs. Brewers use them for . . ."

"For keeping beer?" Anders asked. "Isn't that illegal here?"

Inger and Johann exchanged a look. "Yeah," Inger said.

"Of course," Johann mirrored.

"So that brewery up there is still making beer?"

"Not the big brewery, no," Inger answered. "Doesn't mean somebody else isn't still making it."

Rune stopped and picked up a large, straight stick. He began picking off the bark. He could imagine this as a fishing pole. He could shape it a little with Gunnar's pocketknife, grab some twine from the spool on the porch. His father had to have hooks, didn't he?

"Catch up, Rune!" Anders yelled. But of course, Rune needed to find Aprikos, and carry her with him. She had her nose in a hollow stump, but Rune picked her up. He shoved the kitten in the front of his overalls. She seemed to curl up there, to nestle into him. He charged forward.

Anders had picked up a stick too, but when Rune caught up to the group, there was a lot of talk of the caves, and Rune gathered that fishing poles had been forgotten for now.

They had to climb up, onto a thistle-covered, thick, weed-filled area, and Rune started to feel that slick curl of fear in his belly, but he stuck close to his brothers. They would know how to get back. The incline was steep and filled with brush and thorny plants, but Rune followed his brothers' footsteps, forgetting his birch pole, and he focused on keeping up, on not getting left behind.

By the time they got to the cave, Inger was red-faced and smiling. "Here it is!" she announced, as if she were responsible for the place.

They stood up at the top of the hill now, and another hill, no, not a hill. It was something else, something new to Rune. Flatter and made of stone, it jutted up toward the sky. Right in front of them though, there was a hole—a cave—an opening into this strange structure.

Sweden didn't have this landscape.

The mouth of a large cave looked dark and menacing. It gave Rune the creeps, like it was a gaping mouth letting out a wail. Just as the boys were about to follow Inger inside, a pair of boys appeared out of the darkness, startling everyone in Rune's group.

"Hey ya," one of them said, in a sneer of a voice.

Rune took a few steps back, clutched at Aprikos in his pocket.

The pair of boys wore porkpie hats low, and they squinted at Rune and his brothers through their cigarette smoke. Rune instantly put them at older than Gunnar but he wasn't certain.

"Get out of here, *Stinger,*" one of the boys chided to Inger, in brittle Swedish. He was the bigger one, taller, with mean little slits of eyes. "This place ain't for babies."

The other boy, the one with the red hat, took his cigarette out of his mouth with two fingers, and he spit on the ground, dangerously close to Inger's feet. Rune immediately shot his eyes over to Gunnar. This was not the kind of thing that Gunnar could let go.

Sure enough, Gunnar's fists formed at his sides, and he stepped forward, moving in front of Inger, practically into the boy's face. "That isn't right. You apologize to Inger right now."

"It was an accident. I didn't mean to get it on her shoes."

"So apologize."

The tall boy stepped in then, saying something sharp and short to his friend in English. Then he pushed Gunnar once, just two hands on his shoulders, a light push, a warning.

"Gunnar!" Anders warned, his voice cracking over the word. Anders was going to cry, and Rune, even at his young age, knew that this was a terrible situation for their first morning on their own around the Hollow. Because the universal language of bullies had been spoken in Sweden too, and Rune knew that this test, right here, it would set the tone for how they were treated here in the Hollow.

"I'm giving you one more chance to apologize," Gunnar said, and his eyes were dark, blazing. Rune knew there was no messing around with Gunnar, and at only eleven years old, Gunnar was nearly as broad as the tall boy, though a few inches shorter.

Red-Hat narrowed his eyes—he was the spitter—and he looked Inger up and down. She watched, her arms crossed in indignance. He took his red hat off his head, and then he took one step closer to Inger. He looked like he was about to say something, but then he changed his mind, and he stepped right up to Anders, bent down into his face. "Wah, wah, little baby, you gonna cry?" And he spit on Anders's shoes, just like that, like it was nothing.

Gunnar wheeled on Red-Hat, but before he laid a hand on him, Rune came out of nowhere and he clocked the kid right across the jaw.

Just one fist, without really planning it or thinking it through, Rune brought his fist up and into Red-Hat's jaw, naturally knowing how to put all of his weight behind him.

It was a thing of savage beauty. Rune threw his first punch like he'd been made to do it. Like he was Gunnar, or his father, and it leveled the spitter. Just laid him out inside the gravelly cave.

For a moment, everything and everyone held still in the mouth of that cave. Something momentous had just happened. Gunnar stood, his fist cocked, his mouth hanging open. Johann hid behind Anders, and Inger held her hand over her mouth in disbelief.

The tall one broke the silence with a sharp shove into Gunnar's back, and then it was like everyone came back to life, the black-and-white photograph went color.

Gunnar got the tall kid in the ribs with an uppercut. Red-Hat scuttled backward in the gravel away from Rune, shielding his face, and Rune, without realizing it, had taken a few steps forward, and charged toward Red-Hat, yelling profanity and challenging him to get up.

From far away, almost as if he were underwater, Rune could hear Red-Hat apologizing, over and over. "Inger, I'm sorry. Really. I won't . . . ever again."

But then Anders' was pulling at Rune's arm. "Let's go," he said.

Gunnar had the tall kid by the collar and he shoved him down into the dirt with his buddy.

"Ha! You like that?!" Inger was yelping. "You better leave us alone now, Ian, you bum. We had enough of you all!"

Gunnar grabbed an ebullient Inger by the elbow, and they all scurried away from the cave, taking much less care to scour the incline on the way down, falling on their knees, rolling through the brush, but no one seemed to mind too much.

"Jesus, Rune," Inger said, when they finally made it back to the Hollow. "You got yourself quite a right hook."

"*Helig skit*," Johann kept repeating.

Rune smiled at Inger. And he felt both his brothers' eyes on him.

For the rest of the day, they made makeshift poles and fished in the creek, getting four big walleye that Mama would love for dinner, and one, of course, for a very excited Aprikos.

Of course, Johann, Inger, and Gunnar spent the whole afternoon going over the events of the cave, detailing the look in the kid's eyes when Rune clocked him, the sound of the tall kid's breath as it came out in one big huff when Gunnar got him in the ribs.

Rune couldn't help but smile along with them, and he liked the attention, although he couldn't really explain where his nerve had come from . . . or his anger.

"Hey, you okay?" Anders' asked him later in the day as they walked back to their house.

Rune nodded carefully. But something was bothering Rune a little bit, although he wouldn't put his finger on it until much later.

It was only their second full day in Swede Hollow, and the Folkeson boys had already made a name for themselves. Especially Rune.

That afternoon was the stuff of legend, and Rune would hear kids at school, kids in the Hollow talk about it for years to come. They would always say the same thing from that day on. "That Rune kid, you don't wanna mess with him. He's tough."

And Rune knew that it was true. It wasn't necessarily a lie or even a half-lie. He *was* tough.

It was just that he wished he didn't have to be.

Chapter 18

GETTING USED TO AMERICA WAS HARDER IN SOME ways than Rune had expected. In other ways, it was easier.

The air was different. The scent of the ocean, its salt and life, was robust in Rune's memory when compared to the flat, dusty air of America. Even outside, Rune thought that if he took a deep breath, he could smell cobwebs.

Here in Swede Hollow, Mama still cooked the same kind of food, her salted meats and potato cakes, the boiled fish and rice, the sweet, gooey *kanebullar*.

Food seemed like home right away—maybe a river trout substituted for salmon in a pinch, but mostly food was a comfort. But the water they drank tasted different. More earthy. Rune could imagine Uncle Isak blaming it on more iron in the soil or some such. All Rune knew was that water here tasted slightly of earthworms.

The boys had to fetch their drinking water from the natural spring a good walk northwards up Phalen Creek. It was a twice-daily chore, and it was hard work, compared to the convenient well back at Kasparsson Farm.

They had no farm animals here either, and that meant a lot less work, but *jösses*, Rune missed the whey butter Mama used to make. He'd even dreamt about it a few times.

But mostly he dreamt about the bear.

These same nightmares had followed him from Sweden. Rune didn't know exactly why, but sometimes, the bear would speak to him in his nightmares, which was new. And it spoke in English, saying things like, "Come here, little Rune." Its voice was low and scratchy, often a vibration to be felt rather than heard, and it sounded a lot like his Papa.

Gunnar followed Papa around like his shadow from the moment that they arrived in Swede Hollow, chopping wood for the stove with him in the mornings, waiting at the railyard to walk him home for lunch each noontime. Something about it bothered Rune, but like always, Rune said nothing.

The people of the Hollow were friendly and mostly Swedish, bringing casseroles and cakes, meatballs and coffee, and this funny jiggly dessert they called gelatin. And more coffee. Everywhere was coffee. Every neighbor came to say hello and wanted to sit down and have a *fika*. This word, Rune learned quickly enough, didn't have an English equivalent. Sure, the drink itself had an English word—coffee. But the Swedish act of *fika*, that ever-so-important act of taking a break in your day to talk, to just *be*, with a cup of *kaffe,* that ritual didn't have an English word. So the Swedes here kept the word *fika* in with their new English vocabulary. Swedes needed this word. It was necessary every afternoon, as well as some evenings, of course, to sit and have coffee and cake.

Rune could walk down the Hollow lane and smell *kaffe* wafting out of the kitchen of nearly every house at all times of the day. He joked to Anders that this place should be called Kaffe Hollow.

That first year, Mama seemed content, and that went a long way in making Rune feel comfortable. In Sweden, they hadn't attended church very often, but here, in the Hollow, it became a Sunday ritual. And Mama made all the boys dress nicely in starched, collared shirts and attend services with her, services that always seemed to run on forever and ever, with always one more verse of "Lift High the Cross" or an after-service meeting for the congregation or the eternal potluck dinner.

Rune didn't say a word about it though. He didn't complain like his brothers did or fidget in the pew, because he saw that Mama liked church, the social part of it, and he figured that she needed it. If she was missing Auntie Malin even half as much as he was missing Uncle Isak, well, then he could sit still for a spell and try not to itch at his collar once a week.

By the time school began in the fall, Rune and his brothers had fallen into a good summer routine, playing out at the creek with Inger and Johann each morning, and hitching rides on the slow-moving train cars up on the shunting plateaus, jumping from one car to another, in the afternoon. Sometimes, they would swim in Lake Phalen. Or they would hike out to Pig's Eye and fish for catfish, spending hot, hazy afternoons underneath a funny American tree called a weeping willow, whose leaves looked like long, narrow feathers drooping to the ground.

It was here, under the willow leaves that Rune would read his one letter from Uncle Isak. *Dear Rune,* it said. For Uncle Isak had written another letter to his family, for everyone, but this one was just for him.

It told of the farm, the animals, little Lilja Lamb. And it felt solid and good in Rune's chest to hear these things about his homeland; the news was a comfort. He missed the farm, yes, but it felt far away. His brothers, the tin shack, they were here, immediate. The last few lines of the letter troubled Rune though. He wasn't quite sure why, but they made him want to cry.

Be good to your mother. Please take care of her, Son.

Rune kept this letter under his pillow, reading it only in the privacy of the willow tree, showing it only to little Aprikos. He would run his thumb across Isak's signature, the choppy curves of his handwriting, thinking of Uncle Isak's humming when he would milk the cows alongside the boys, the way his soft eyes were buried deep in the hard angles of his face, of the way Isak would cluck his tongue when Rune threaded his fishing pole incorrectly. Isak would pull the line out, thread it again, showing Rune his mistake, tying the knots slowly, patiently.

Rune missed Uncle Isak so much, the heft of him, his bulk, the way Rune could lean into him and feel . . . safe.

It was a surprise to Rune, to come to Swede Hollow and *like* this place, to feel at home in the strangeness of all of it. For Rune had easily traded the backdrop of the farm for this strange *Svenska Dalen*. That had been easy. He didn't miss the farm too much.

But he missed his uncle. Desperately.

Isak wasn't so easily replaced.

• • •

SCHOOL CAME UPON THEM QUICKLY, interrupting the brothers' summer routine.

At first, school was especially a problem for Rune. It wasn't that he couldn't keep up, although that was what his teacher thought. That was what the other kids thought, surely, maybe even Gunnar.

Anders knew though. Anders always knew everything about Rune.

Their school sat squarely atop the bluff, situated on Greenbrier Avenue. The boys climbed the makeshift staircase from the Hollow up to St. Paul proper each morning, walking past the garbage and debris that the Plank Avenue dwellers discarded down into the Hollow, reminding Rune and his brothers that they were not to think too highly of themselves.

Word spread quickly at school about the Folkeson boys, and they were spared the usual hazing of new students because of Rune's show of gusto in the cavern that first of days. They were all three brothers in a class together at first, a class designated for immigrant students still learning English.

They had an energetic teacher, and she worked to integrate them in the language, so that they could move into the appropriate grade for their age, in a classroom that would speak solely English. Luckily for the boys, Inger and Johann had yet to make the leap up, so they were in class with them as well.

Over that first summer, Rune surprised himself by picking up the strange, new-sounding language of English much more quickly than his brothers. The assault that the new sounds, especially vowels, made on his ears never softened completely, but he did get used to the rhythm and cadence of the language. And it was easily sorted out for him, while he played a mental game of translation each time he heard people speak, whether it was in English or Swedish. He was constantly challenging himself to flip the spoken sentence to the other language, and in that game, he found success. Always listening, always mentally translating.

He had quite an advantage because he was rarely expected to respond, to participate in conversations. He was, after all, Silent Rune.

Also, Rune deciphered the structure easily—the noun came first, the verb next. It was much like Swedish in its building blocks, and once Rune figured this out, he was nearly there, because he was, and always had been, a keen observer.

Sitting in class with Ms. Michaelson, he understood everything. He was often bored, to tell the truth, but he never responded. He never spoke. For although he had parsed his way through the first steps of *understanding* English, speaking it was a different task entirely, especially for Rune and his bad ear.

He feared the way his voice would sound to the other children. He knew his vowels were not correct. He saw the looks, the narrowing of the eyes, from the other kids in the Hollow on the few occasions in which he spoke.

He didn't want to have to get in any more fights. He hated the way he felt after he had punched the Red-Hat kid. He hated the way his stomach rolled when he would hear one of the other kids talking about it, bragging about Rune and his right hook.

So for Rune, he found that silence was his best choice.

Ms. Michaelson had her hands full with a class of over twenty immigrant children, all at different levels, ranging in age from five to fifteen. She wasn't unkind, but she was overworked, and like so many others who met Rune those first years in the Hollow, she chalked his silence up to him being a "big, dumb Swede."

Until Inger's mother stepped in.

Inger's mother, Miss Vendela as everyone in the Hollow called her, helped the situation. She was a large woman, with a big bosom, and a bigger laugh. She had two thick, gray braids wound up around her ears, permanently rosy cheeks, and no husband. She ran the Hollow's only speakeasy right out of her front room.

This, of course, was something the brothers learned by hanging around with Inger and Johann, for they were happy enough to boast about their mother's status in the Hollow.

One day, as the boys sat in Miss Vendela's front room, eating potato cakes and drinking milk after school with Inger and Johann, which had become their custom, Miss Vendela asked Rune to come back into the kitchen. Rune looked to Gunnar nervously, but he only nodded. When Anders offered to come with him, Miss Vendela shooed Anders away. "Only Rune," she said. This made young Rune feel nervous, unsure of himself.

He got up from the table and followed Miss Vendela into her kitchen, which was clean and smelled of vinegar and onions. Miss Vendela had recently received the very first running water in the Hollow, which was, of course, due to her status with many of the city officials and law enforcement workers who looked the other way when it came to her front room bar. They even visited it sometimes, and Miss Vendela was a shrewd businesswoman. She knew whose palms to grease.

Rune sat silently on the wooden kitchen chair opposite Miss Vendela and eyed the strange contraption on her table.

"Rune," Miss Vendela said, her accent thick, and her snuff box at hand. "I want to help you with your speech. I spoke to your mother about this, and she has given me her blessing. I had a little brother, not unlike you, growing up." Miss Vendela eyed Rune for some sort of reaction.

Rune swallowed around a thick lump in his throat. He had hoped his speech wasn't so terrible. But this acknowledgment, it hurt him, his pride, and his eyes filled with tears.

"You speak pretty well, Rune. And I have heard your English. It's much better than most Hollow residents. You are a smart boy, but I know you feel insecure with the way you sound." Miss Vendela clucked her tongue and passed Rune a rag to wipe his tears. "Buck up, Son. Anyway, you know the *aaah* sound instead of *ayyh*, the *uuuh* instead of *oooh*. These slight differences were hard for my little brother because he couldn't hear too well; the tiny differentiations were lost on him."

Rune blew his nose, hating how affected he was by Miss Vendela's intrusion into his worst, most central worry in his heart. Miss Vendela stopped, reached her hand across the table to grab Rune's. "Son, I know it is hard to talk about. But hear me out, I only think it will help. I don't mean to embarrass you."

Rune looked up now, cheeks heated red. He had thought he was getting by, not truly outing himself as an idiot. He had thought he was passable.

Did he though?

He rarely spoke.

And he knew, deep down, that his silence was not taken as intelligence. His silence didn't keep people from thinking something was wrong.

In fact, it was the opposite. Instead of hearing a slight speech problem, they thought worse of him.

It was easier that way. He found people gave him a sort of pass then. They assumed his scar, his eye, his silence, equaled an impaired mental state.

Mother often would tell him, "Don't hide behind it." And it wasn't until this moment that he understood. He had been hiding. Sometimes, even milking his status as a big galoot.

This was a revelation to little Rune. And not a welcome one.

"Do you read lips?" Miss Vendela asked.

Rune nodded. "I tilt my head too. My right ear is good."

"That's what your mother said. I have this for you to try." Miss Vendela held up the strange object on the table. It was metal, shaped almost like a cone, or a cornucopia. "It's an ear trumpet. It was my brother's."

She showed him how to adjust the small end all the way into his bad ear, fitting it into his ear canal itself. Then she spoke. "What does it sound like?"

Rune jerked, pulling the trumpet from his ear. "It's so loud."

Rune couldn't believe how clearly he could hear out of the thing. It was jarring, so clear. He took the metal cone and looked more closely at it.

"The shape helps trap the sound, deliver right into your ear," Miss Vendela explained. "My brother had a much easier time learning language when he used this. When you have two ears to hear, even if one ear only hears some, it works much better. You can drown out the background noise easier, and I'm told this helps magnify if there is any hearing going on in your bad ear."

"Thank you," Rune said, his eyes wide with amazement, blinking hard at how much fuller the sounds were, how different, when he could get at least some of it through his silent ear.

"Would you like to borrow the horn? Use it?"

Rune nodded. "Could you read something to me?" He couldn't believe how clear it was. And he wanted to hear more, to study the clearer sounds of someone's speech. He wanted to listen to the vowels as Miss Vendela shaped them. He wanted to practice her pronunciation, right there, right then, with the sounds so clearly delivered into his ear. He needed to watch her mouth and listen to the sounds, then mimic them.

He was certain, in that moment, that he could clear up the problems in his speech, round out his vowels, if he only had some quiet time with this cone to study the speech of others.

He thought for the first time . . . if he tried, if he studied, if he really gave his all to this . . ..

He could read aloud at school.

"Please, Miss Vendela, could I practice a while?" Rune worked hard on the vowel sound in "while," and the "*a*" sound in "practice," trying to match the softer sound of these vowels to how Miss Vendela sounded.

He was amazed at how closely the vowels were formed near the front of his mouth. This was his most obvious mistake, now that he listened in the cone.

He usually made his vowels much farther back in his mouth, using his throat even.

He stared at the cone, but then he realized Miss Vendela was reading, a passage from an old Swedish cookbook. Just a list of ingredients.

Rune held onto the vowel sounds. The hope he found in them. The soft *u* sound of cup. *One and one-half cup of sugar.*

He practiced, "Cup."

"Almost," Miss Vendela answered. "More air with the *u*. Cup." Rune repeated it. It felt different that way, the shape of the air in his mouth, against the roof of his mouth.

"Half," she said.

"Half," he repeated.

"Less in your throat. Hear me. Half."

He listened through the ear trumpet, and he repeated. And he watched the little dimple at the corner of Miss Vendela's smile deepen.

And he realized he was smiling too. "Miss Vendela, *tack.*"

Then she answered Rune in Swedish, with a funny little saying they used back home: *Ingen fara pa tacket*. It meant: *No harm done.*

It made Rune chuckle. Such a funny saying. There was no English translation for that.

"Thank you, Miss Vendela."

"It's nothing, Little Rune. We here in the Hollow stick together."

• • •

ANDERS WOULD COME TO RUNE FOR help with his English homework. They would sit by the stove in their front room and they would work in their schoolbooks together. Even Mama probably thought that Anders was helping Rune. It was an easy assumption to make.

One day, not long after the ear trumpet revelation, Ms. Michaelson asked Anders and Rune to stay after class, and she spoke directly to Anders, as if Rune would not even be capable of conversation.

"You should not be helping him," Mrs. Michaelson said. She spoke completely in English, not translating into Swedish afterward.

Anders nodded.

But he had a twist to his mouth that Rune recognized.

He wasn't completely understanding the teacher. They had only been in America for a handful of months, and Anders was still struggling. Each of the boys was capable, many strides ahead of their mother, but Anders still needed things repeated sometimes.

He shot his eyes to Rune, and Rune cleared his throat. Rune had been practicing hard with his ear trumpet, both with Miss Vendela and his mother. He thought that his voice was making great strides. He had written to Uncle Isak about it, enthusiastically, but he hadn't yet tested it out in public.

"Answer me when I am talking to you," Mrs. Michaelson said to Anders.

Anders looked nervous now, and he fumbled around for an answer. "Um . . . apologies," he answered in Swedish. *Ursäkter.*

"He speaks for me so I don't have to," Rune said, in precise English, his voice ringing out clearly and loudly in the schoolroom. His vowels were crisp, nearly perfect, aside from the *"a"* in *have*. That one still gave Rune trouble.

Mrs. Michaelson actually took a step back, her eyes going wide.

Rune continued, "I don't like to talk too much. My eye. My ear." He pointed to each of them. "My voice. Kids make fun of me. You know, big dumb Swede and all that."

Mrs. Michaelson gaped at Rune. She didn't say a thing, so Rune turned to Anders and translated the conversation into Swedish so he could keep up.

"So, you are capable."

"Yes, Ma'am," Rune answered.

Her face changed then; apology, empathy, so much, washed over it. "But you can't let the other kids . . . You shouldn't . . ."

Anders had regained himself. "He does speak when he wants to. He has hearing loss, Ma'am. But he knows English better than all of us. He can read quicker than me. Better than Gunnar. He's just . . . shy." *Blyg.* The word for shy in Swedish made Rune cringe.

Was he *blyg*?

He was. It seemed like such a sin.

Papa would not like it.

"Okay," Mrs. Michaelson said. Her lips pressed together, her eyes a penitent look in them. "I'm sorry, Rune, for not understanding the situation."

"I've been looking at your stove," Rune said, changing the subject, both for Ms. Michaelson and to take the pressure off of himself. He pointed to the pot belly stove in the corner. "The grate needs to be cleaned and it will warm this place much better. Can we help you?"

Mrs. Michaelson, still shocked, nodded.

Rune and Anders took to work, cleaning out the pot belly stove, and Anders kept eyeing Rune, giving him this knowing smile.

That next school day, there on Rune's desk sat a dog-eared copy of *Treasure Island* by Robert Louis Stevenson, and when Rune looked up at Ms. Michaelson, she gave him the slightest of nods.

And to Rune's utter surprise, Ms. Michaelson didn't call him out, didn't force him to answer out loud, as he had been so sure she would. She didn't send him to the all-English classes without his brothers either. She let Rune go about his days as he had done before, save for one change: Ms. Michaelson would ask Rune to come to her desk once in a while, pair him off with a student, and Rune would quietly help them, with their reading, with their writing, mostly with their English skills.

Between the tutoring and the books that found their way on to his desk, Rune wasn't bored at school anymore.

• • •

OTHER THINGS WERE LESS EASILY conquered that first fall in America. They'd been here in the Hollow for several months, and the shiny veneer was chipping away from Papa, revealing a sliver of something frightening beneath. Gritted teeth, flashes of fiery anger in his eyes. Papa would catch himself, sometimes, his face smoothing over into the normal Papa-mask, nearly indistinguishable from before, and Rune could once again see the resemblance to Uncle Isak—Papa's angular jaw, the wide smile. But other times, Papa would not catch himself. The mask would slip away, and he would turn into something altogether different, far, far from Uncle Isak. He would stand and yell, spittle flying from his mouth, pounding his fists on the table, his size overtaking the small house.

Rune would wince and watch him, frozen in fear, certain Papa was a giant, growing in his red-eyed anger, right there in front of his eyes.

Usually, this was all over something small, minute even, like Gunnar forgetting to fill the water jug before dinner.

Often, Mama would give the boys a look to shoo, when Papa's mood would turn black, and the boys would grab what they could from their plates, pocketing biscuits and ham, shaking, frightened, and they would make themselves scarce, leaving the small house for their *other* home—the Hollow itself, the creek, the caves.

Rune worried about his mother taking the brunt of that anger. He would sometimes linger at the table, watching his father yell and carry on, turning shades of red and purple. Rune thought of Uncle Isak's letter, of protecting Mama. But Mama would shoo Rune out the door, with a hushed, insistent tone, placating him. "I'll be fine, Rune. Just go."

Rune was always worried now, in all moments, waiting for . . . well, he didn't know, but he knew it was coming. Papa had turned. This was for certain, and the knowing that something was coming, the feel of it in the air always in their tin shack, it was a yoke around Rune's neck, heavy on his shoulders. What could he do?

How could he protect his mama?

His Papa scared him.

He tried to remember the Papa that first met them there at the train station, those few months ago, of the gentleness there, the sunlight hitting the golden tones of his hair, the way he breathed in his sons' scents like he had waited an eternity for just that.

But Rune didn't know where that man had gone, and it scared Rune to think that this was not the end of Papa's changing. Rune could sense that Papa was holding back, that he was only going to get much, much worse. Rune knew this, deep inside himself, like a terrible sin he didn't want to admit. It soured his stomach, made him feel guilty somehow.

At night, Mama and Papa talked, when the boys were already shut in their room. Their voices began civilly, sometimes staying that way. But once in a while, Papa's would become increasingly irritated, and the thin walls of leftover scrap lumber were no protection.

Eventually, Papa's words came out in a horrible sound, a growling snarl, like the devil himself trying to keep his voice down. It made their tin roof rattle and shake, as if Papa's huffing and puffing could make the whole place fall like a house of cards.

Anders cuddled up next to Rune and Aprikos in their bed, and Gunnar whispered over to them from his bed, in the dark, to make some excuse for Papa. "He's just had too much to drink," he'd say. "He'll sleep soon."

All the while, Rune couldn't help but think, *Uncle Isak never scared us like that. He never scared us. He never scared Mama.*

• • •

"I'M NOT SURE I WANT TO live like a pioneer, away from cities, " Mama answered over the dinner table. Her tone was light, but Rune could see the old shadow in her eyes. Papa was getting to her as well.

"I've been saving a lot of money, Birgit, to get us out of the Hollow."

"Well, we could just get a nicer house up on Plank Avenue, one with a true toilet, or heated water! What will they think of next?"

"We will have all this and more. In the west," Papa said, his eyes darkening, his voice lowering.

"Or we could save that money for university, Folke. Our boys have become quite the readers. They could attend right here at St. Mary's, maybe become doctors or a–"

"So working on the railway like their father isn't good enough?" Papa's voice was dangerously low, menacing. This is how it was with Papa now. He always seemed to be looking for a fight.

During his first years in America, Papa worked as a brakeman for the railroad, which he often told Rune and his brothers about. It was the most dangerous job in the whole railroad. He had to ride on top of the cars, and when it was time to brake, he would have to turn a big iron wheel, several times clockwise, in order to manually brake the car. Then he would have to hustle and jump to the next car, continuing the process. This was repeated dozens of times in a row, in a monumental hurry, and it was treacherous work, with many brakemen dying from the conditions of the job. The railcars were often icy and slick, and many brakemen fell to their death.

Not Papa. He worked this job for years, before he was promoted to his job as switchman, which was what he did now. As a braker, he traveled to many different Midwestern cities, and even out to several states in the west. Papa told stories of wild horses, of a funny thorned plant called a cactus, and he talked of land. So much land out west, ready to be claimed, ripe for the buying.

"We could farm, like in Goteborg. Maybe cattle, dairy. It will be our choice," he told Mama.

With the mention of farming, Rune thought of the thick, homemade butter he loved back in Sweden, his mother's little tin butter churn. The tiny mechanical noises it would make.

"It feels like we just got here, though, Folke. Must we move on already?" Mama asked. Mama's mouth set into a hard line.

Rune pushed away his memories of Sweden, of the little things he missed: butter, his uncle, Sötnos. In moments like this, he became aware, tensed, each muscle contracting, ready to defend her if her had to.

Rune and his brothers stared silently at their parents.

"We will move from the Hollow when and where I decide," Papa said, and his jaw set in a tight line. He continued with a strained growl, "My boys will learn to live off the land. They will not waste my fortune on dreams that cannot truly be realized by immigrants or half-wits." He stared hard at Rune when he said this. "University! Birgit, you need to get your head out of the clouds."

Rune stared hard back at his Papa, not giving him the satisfaction of seeing him flinch. He was still only a child, but he was getting braver by the day, and he just stared at his Papa, his jaw set hard, the sound of his father's insult—*half-wit*—echoing off the walls of their home.

"Your brother has written. He will be visiting this summer," Mama said, her eyes meeting no one's.

Rune saw something then in the tilt of her chin, and Rune wasn't sure, being such a young boy, but he thought he recognized it as courage.

Rune looked toward his brothers at the table, their uncertain smiles. It was hard to believe that Isak could set foot in this house, on this soil. It was in moments like this, with Papa grumbling and groaning, looking for a fight, about to explode, that Isak and their homeland seemed so far away to Rune and his brothers, like golden memories too happy to be real.

"Isak," Papa growled to himself, but then there was a hint of a smile at the corner of his lips.

This was what it was like now. Papa, teetering between anger and pleasant indifference. The boys and their world always coiled, ready. For what?

Rune was unsure.

"Will he stay with us?" Gunnar asked. "Here in our house?"

Little Aprikos chose that moment to appear in the kitchen, her fur thick with burrs from her outdoor adventures, and she pressed her forehead against Rune's legs, meowing for a lick of butter from the tip of his thumb, as had become their custom at the dinner table.

But when Rune bent to give the cat her treat, Papa's boot came out of nowhere and kicked the poor animal. Hard. The sound of his boot meeting her tiny ribcage was thick, blunt. She mewled a sound of surprise, as she skittered over the floor, away from Papa, and then she ran and hid in the boys' room, the brothers all staring, open-mouthed, at their father. "I do not labor in the railyards so an animal can eat my wages," he hissed.

Mama swallowed visibly and looked as though she were attempting to bite back her tears. No one said a word.

It was right then, at that moment, that Rune understood that those first few months in America, they had been like a dream—like his time playing pirates underneath the canopy of the weeping willow out at the lake. But now, the veil was lifting. This was life. This was his America. This was what he was up against, and it was only going to get worse.

Right now, things were not as bad as they could be.

Rune thought of the see-saw up at the park near the church, the old, worn wood. The up and down of things.

This was Papa, his moods. Things were not terrible, no. Not yet. Because sometimes, Papa diffused. Somehow. A comment from Mama, another swig from the bottle. Something, somehow, would tilt things back toward Papa's mask of indifference.

Like tonight.

He was already calmed, his attention on his plate, nothing more.

In a little while, dinner would finish, Papa would begin his drinking. And Rune would find little Aprikos, and he would comfort her. She would be fine.

Things are not terrible, Rune told himself again. They were bearable. Especially with the thought of Isak and his laugh, his smile, his large, square face filling up the emptiness of this house.

But Rune knew that someday, probably someday soon, things might tip further into the dark, black place of Papa's anger, irretrievably into that space, and then this time of not knowing, this in-between phase, it would be over.

And Rune would miss it. Because there, in the true blaring light of Papa's rage, Rune knew that things would not be fine, and he would think of this day, this evening, of the kick Papa gave Aprikos as nothing. Compared to what could be.

The things that were coming.

Rune woke often in the night, from the rumble of a far-off train. He would listen to it—its whistle, the rhythmic click-clack of the wheels on the track. When he first got here, he would try to figure out how far away the train was. He got pretty good at it after a while. He could tell which trains were up on the northern plateau, which ones were off farther to the east by Pig's Eye, or the trains on the tracks right down by Connemara Patch. He could tell which trains were passenger cars, or which engines were pulling heavier loads, like coal and lumber. They each sounded different.

He could tell which trains were coming from where.

But this thing that was coming from Papa, his anger, his breaking, whatever you wanted to call it, it was not like the trains.

Rune didn't know exactly how far away it was. Or exactly *what* it was. Rune just knew it was coming. And that when it got here, things would not be bearable anymore.

Whatever it was, it would be bad.

Chapter 19

SEASONS BLURRED FROM ONE INTO ANOTHER, the boisterous green of spring and summer, along with the cacophony of cicadas and crickets turned into the autumn crunch of purple and gold leaves underfoot. Then finally came the hushed insulated silence of their first frozen-white Minnesota winter. This season seemed Swedish to Rune; it felt familiar. The boys were happily surprised, however, to find that they had to adjust to the measured sunrises and sunsets of all seasons here, as opposed to the grueling dark that grew slowly, intrepidly into a stretch of nearly sixteen-hour nights of darkness in Swedish winters.

Their first Christmas in America came and went, which they spent with Miss Vendela, Inger and Johann. Mama even sewed a Lucia, queen of light, gown for Inger, this heavy white velvet, with a blue and yellow embroidered hem. Miss Vendela could barely hold back tears when she saw her daughter in it, and then she could barely hold back her laughter when Inger's traditional crown of candles almost lit the curtains on fire. Papa, in a rare easy mood, used a dishrag to tamp out the sparks on Miss Vendela's curtains.

They sang Christmas songs together, and they ate many Swedish delicacies for a true Swedish Christmas. It was a success on all accounts, and

Rune thought that their first holiday here somehow cemented their family as Americans.

Soon after the holiday, Isak wrote of Farmor's death. Papa said they could not afford to return to Sweden for the funeral. Mama arranged a quiet service for the family, here at their Lutheran church, where they honored Farmor's memory.

Mama cried for many nights after the news of Farmor's death, but Rune suspected it had more to do with how this delayed Isak's trip to visit than it did her grief over his grandmother. If she felt at all like Rune did, she had been holding that visit from Isak out ahead of her, as a beacon, as a prize. Something to work toward.

Without it, Rune felt an emptiness, almost like a homesickness, but worse.

It was around that time that Rune woke to strange noises in the earliest of morning light. He listened, cocking his good ear toward the front room, trying to decide if he should get up and inspect what was going on or if he should wake Anders next to him.

Then he thought he heard a voice. A swear word. Mama's voice.

He got up, his feet cold against the boards of the floor, even through his heaviest woolen socks. Anders snored lightly in the bed. Gunnar stirred, turning over in his bed. Rune crept into the front room. He could see Mama's shadowed form through the front room window, as she made her way toward the outhouse.

It was then he saw the blood on the floor. Two thick droplets, more black than red. He bent, studying them, feeling his body quiver with anger, his fists curling in on themselves.

Papa's voice was in the doorway, thick with sleep. "She's lost the child."

Rune looked up at his Papa then, his mind trying to understand exactly what his father was saying to him. Gunnar appeared in the doorway of their bedroom. He took one look at Rune, his fists, and he looked at his father. Hard. "What happened?"

"Your mother was with child. Early on, but it's lost now. "Papa gestured to the blood on the floor. "Nothing worse than a nosebleed." He went back into his room.

Mama returned from the outhouse, in a rush of cold wind, looking pale and red-eyed. She spied the boys, the drops of blood on the floor. She grabbed a rag from her pocket, bent to clean up the spilt blood. "It's nothing, boys," she said, but her voice was off-kilter, tight. "Get yourselves to bed. Go on now."

Rune climbed back into bed with a snoring Anders, nearly lying on top of a purring Aprikos, and Gunnar whispered. "She is fine now."

Rune closed his eyes and he wondered if that was true. He wondered at the little child that had been inside his mother. Had it reconsidered? Gone back to wherever babies came from? God? Heaven? To another family? Had it heard Papa's voice rise too many times, from inside its insulated womb, felt the shaking of the walls and decided, *Well, no thank you.*

Once a baby got inside, how exactly did it become *lost* anyway? Why was there blood?

These were terrible questions that Rune circled around in his mind.

Rune didn't like the way that Papa said Mama *lost* the baby. Lost seemed like a terrible thing for a tiny, too-early child, and it seemed like it put the blame on Mama, as if she was supposed to be looking after the child and hadn't. Rune knew that couldn't be true.

All Rune knew was that it made him sad for Mama. That along with the loss of Isak's visit. Rune was worried.

Nothing worse than a nosebleed, Papa had said. And for some reason, even though Rune was still only a small boy and he didn't quite understand what had happened, he hated his father for saying that. Surely it was much worse than a nosebleed.

Rune had many nosebleeds. They were nothing. A nuisance. A bother that made him have to stop playing for a bit, pinching his nose and sitting still for ten minutes, with his head tipped backward.

Surely, this was a child, and to Mama, this was much, much worse.

Before Rune fell asleep he had a terrible thought. One he tried to push away to no avail. It was this: he realized that when Papa had explained the blood, Rune was disappointed. Something in Rune wanted it to have been Papa's fault, blood at his hand. Then Rune could have done something about it. Reacted. Defended.

It shocked Rune how ready he was, how willing.

Chapter 20

TIME PASSED IN THE HOLLOW. The boys grew taller. They grew together. They grew up, into young men. Mostly they didn't notice any of this because they were too busy watching Papa reveal himself one slitted eye, one bared tooth, one growl at a time.

Always, they kept one eye on him, one ear pricked to hear his voice.

Papa drank more and more, either at Miss Vendela's or right in their very own front room. He drank homebrews from bootleggers in the Hollow. He drank moonshine that he bought from an Italian on the railroad. All of it smelled like ammonia and piss to Rune.

The brothers lived their lives in this in-between, heightened purgatory, waiting, just waiting, for Papa to crack. Mama jumped at the smallest sounds as she worked in the kitchen. She stopped inviting her friends from church home for coffee, as she just never knew when Papa would come home from the railway, already half-pissed.

After the lost baby, Mama shrank in on herself, seeming to get smaller. Her hair lost its golden sheen, her eyes their sparkle. She became a ghost of the woman that Rune could remember laughing, pink-cheeked in the fields of Goteborg. She lost weight consistently, even as the boys grew taller than her.

Anders was now tall and lean, his cheeks hollowing out, only lending his features an even more handsome angle. Girls began to notice him, and Anders played at this, walking girls home, carrying books for them. Anders never did another lick of homework for the rest of the year. He was never short of licorice ropes and other treats that the girls would bring him either. He began to wear a jaunty pancake hat and a confident smile and gone was the teary brother of Rune's recent memory.

Gunnar, on the other hand, only had eyes for one girl. Inger, of course. When he wasn't home, he was with her. He was sixteen years old and nearly as tall as their father, and he worked weekend shifts at the railway. He'd save his money to take Inger to the cinema, to the dances at the downtown VFW. No longer did Gunnar follow Papa around like a lost puppy dog. Gunnar was busy, barely at home, always on the go.

But Rune didn't think it was all because of his newfound interest in the opposite sex. Gunnar held himself in a strange, defensive posture around the house. Gunnar's eyes only met Papa's when they had to. Something had changed in his oldest brother, and Rune wondered if it had been something distinct, an event or conflict he'd missed somehow, or if Papa's insidious anger and drunkenness had just worn him down. Either way, Papa wasn't the hero he had been to Gunnar.

Before Gunnar was going out for the night, he would pull both of his brothers to the side, and he would make sure that at least one of them would be home with Mama the whole night. But it was an agreement that Rune and his brothers really didn't even have to talk about; one of them would always stay at home in the evenings. They shared watch.

Even at just ten years old, Rune knew he could fight Papa off if he had to, especially a drunk Papa. Rune was tall now, broad, still legendary in the Hollow for his right hook. But for Rune, none of that mattered. His growing up had to do with the expanding of his mind. After *Treasure Island*, Rune kept going. *Swiss Family Robinson*. Then Dickens. A biography on Charles Lindbergh. Sherlock Holmes mysteries. And the list kept growing. He read every book in the school library and was thrilled when he and his brothers were moved into the school proper. Finally. He threw himself into his new subjects, like algebra and world history, and he discovered the downtown library.

For Rune, the easiest way to handle the state of his home was to live somewhere else completely: in his mind. He had adventures. He traveled to far-off places. He grew in experience. His viewpoint became widened, his mind a constantly-expanding machine. All from the pages of books.

Each of the boys was growing up in their own way, all the while they weren't even noticing. Not much anyway. They were too busy watching Papa, waiting. And there were moments, times, when Papa was that same man that had met them at the train station—charming and pleasant. He'd laugh with the boys or pull Mama in his lap and they'd share a look that made Rune avert his eyes to give them privacy.

There were these flashes of the old Papa, mostly when he wasn't drinking. But these moments, they were rare. And the thing was, *they* were the surprises. Not the other way around. The grumbling, the violent temper—these were the norm.

That apprehension inside Rune, the wariness, it grew as the months passed by. It turned into something worse, something that put a sour taste in Rune's mouth. It was . . . fear.

Rune had a feeling, a premonition almost—the next time, the blood on the floor would not be accidental.

• • •

PAPA TRULY BROKE DURING THE WEEK BEFORE their fourth Christmas in America. He came home from a long day working in the rail yard, and Mama had ham, pig's feet, and au-gratin potatoes on the table, a bread pudding for dessert. She hummed a nervous little tune, and Rune watched her carefully.

Mama knew too. The way you knew when your shoelace was going to break soon. It had been pulled tight, taut, too many times. Given all it could give.

The pressure in the little tin shack had become palpable. With heavy snows making Papa's railroad work more difficult, with freezing temperatures keeping them all inside, together, huddled in front of the stove, there was too much tension.

In the summer, at least, the boys could get away from it all. Skinny dip in Pig's Eye Lake. Hike up in the bluffs, hide in the cool tunnels carved out in the sandstone. But in the winter, there was nothing but time at home. And the incessant creak of his rocking chair next to the stove. The *clink-clank* of his empty liquor bottles, and the grumbling rattle of his voice as he shouted for Mama to get him another.

It wore their nerves thin, each one of them.

It even wore on Aprikos. She had been gone now for close to a week, and Rune had begun to wonder if she'd ever appear again, or if maybe she found the cold and snow more bearable than Papa's boot.

Tonight, they sat at the table and ate quietly. Gunnar was not there yet. He was late coming in, from school, from Inger's—somewhere. This happened more and more lately.

Anders sat nervously playing with his napkin, and Rune knew why he was nervous. He had seen Anders and Johann steal cigarettes at Lottie's store just the other afternoon, and Rune didn't like it. He had wanted to tell Anders he knew, but something had kept him quiet about it.

Tonight, Papa looked agitated, his heavy brow furrowed, the twin gray rings under his eyes a darker shade, and his mouth was set in a firm grim line. Rune knew that Anders was worried that Papa knew about his recent escapades. Papa had a way of knowing everything.

Rune worried as he cut up his potatoes, reaching for the butter. Is that what this trembling silence from Papa was about?

Or was it because Gunnar was late, yet again?

Laughing came from outside on the stoop, and Rune knew immediately it was Inger's. Anders shot Rune a glance. Gunnar called goodbye to Inger, and he barreled in the front door. "I'm late. I'm sorry, Mama." He said it in Swedish. He bent and gave her a kiss on the cheek.

He took his hat off his head, and he went to take his place at the table, but in a moment, Papa was out of his chair and he held Gunnar by the collar. He pulled him up out of his seat and he pushed him up against the wall, his tomato-red face inches from Gunnar's.

"You're late?" Papa growled. "Don't you have any respect, boy, for your mother, for the meal she prepared?"

Mama was next to Papa now, pleading, pulling on his shirtsleeve. "Folke, please, do not hurt the boy. It's nothing."

"No, it is something," he spat in English, his bulging eyes staring at Gunnar. "I will beat the piss out of you, Son. Don't you forget it." Papa made a fist and he bashed the wall, right next to Gunnar's head.

"I'm sorry, Papa," Gunnar said, tears streaming, his voice choked and his face purple from being choked by his collar.

In one powerful and scary motion, Papa took Gunnar by the shoulders and shoved him hard into the floor, Gunnar landing on his face and shoulder with a scraping thud. Anders and Mama moved toward him.

Rune stayed stock-still. He hadn't even known that he'd stood up, but he had, and he was in a ready stance, a coiled spring.

Papa grabbed Mama sharply by her elbow. "And we speak the language of *this country* here, Birgit. Not Swedish anymore. Enough of the ignorant immigrants in this house. We speak English." For a moment, Rune thought his father was going to strike his mother. He could see his Father's cocked fist, and Rune braced himself to intervene.

Rune saw then the look on his mother's face. He saw more than that; he saw years of this, back in Sweden. He saw the roots of all those flat looks on his mother's face, all her wasted hope and beauty.

As if it was in slow-motion, Papa cocked that fist, and Rune moved quickly knocking his chair out behind him. In the same moment, Papa thought better of it. He just pushed Mama back into her seat roughly. She sat, eyes wide, breathing heavily, gripping the edge of the table with white knuckles.

Rune stared down his father. Papa pretended not to notice. He sat in his chair. Rune watched him cut up his pork and feed it into his mouth. He watched him shovel the potatoes in, watched him wash it all down with a glass of milk and then of course his ever-loving liquor. Rune watched as his mother's shaking hands buttered her potatoes.

Rune's eyes followed Anders' gaze to Gunnar's. Both of his brothers kept their heads down, and their mouths quiet, but they too stood. A silent protest.

"Sit," Papa growled. They stood.

"Please sit," Mama asked in a whisper. His brothers did as she said. They ate their dinner, trying to disguise their shaking hands, their sniveling noises.

Rune did not sit. He stood, chest heaving.

Rune watched his father, eyes squinted. And when finally Papa looked up at Rune, he placed his fork onto his plate. "What? You half-wit?" he said to Rune, a wicked grin flashing across his face. "You need to be taught a lesson too?"

But Rune didn't flinch. Instead, he lowered his voice to a whisper, "If you ever lay a hand on Mama, I will kill you."

Everyone at the table stilled, and Rune watched his father swallow hard, the whites of his eyes yellowed with drink. Rune saw the moment, that beat, in which his father considered if he was telling the truth, and his thoughts flashed over his grizzled face, a true moment of fear.

"Are you threatening me?" Papa said, but his bluster was gone. He squinted his eyes at Rune. But Rune's gaze didn't budge.

"Yes."

The others at the table watched as Papa considered this. He let out a sigh and he continued eating his dinner. And the moment passed.

Rune sat back down, and he ignored his food. Rune continued to watch his father, he watched every last bite, the pork juices dribbling down his chin and hitting the front of his shirt. Every last swallow, Rune's eyes never left his father. He had suspected that this was the true center of this man that he was supposed to know as *father*. Rune had suspected it long before he had even met him.

Rune actually felt something akin to relief as he watched his father there at the table, the truth now out in the open. Confirmed.

Rune meant what he said. It was not an empty threat. And Rune would never stop watching.

That night, Rune wrote a letter to his Uncle. Up until this point, he never let himself write about the bad stuff. He didn't want his uncle to worry, to be burdened with their trials. But this time, he had to get it out of his heart, out of his mind, and the only way he could think to do it as to write it all down.

Tell it all to Uncle Isak.

When he was finished telling of the night's events, Rune added one more line.

It is with a heavy heart that I ask myself each morning when I wake and find I am not back at the Kasparsson farm as I had dreamed, "Why? Why did we ever journey to America when our home is most certainly wherever you are, Uncle?"

Rune tore the letter up on his way to the post office in the morning. He knew that his problem was not his Uncle's to bear. It was Rune's. It was Gunnar's. It was Anders'.

It was their yoke, and their charge to protect their Mama. And they would somehow do this, and persevere, as men did. As Swedes did. This much he had learned from his Uncle, the man his heart still called Father.

Chapter 21

AS RUNE GOT OLDER, HE READ MORE AND MORE. He challenged himself with hard texts, the classics: Homer, Shakespeare. The natural outgrowth of his quiet nature, coupled with his keen observational skills, was a mind that was active, with theories and questions, lots of them large in scope. He began to read the great philosophers. He swayed toward Existentialism. He loved Thoreau, Emerson.

He moved onto more scientific writing. Darwin. Linnaeus. He read everything he could get his hands on—scientific journals, mathematical proofs, world history.

He found he couldn't get enough information. He read, and read, and read. And if he found something too difficult, he would set it aside, always returning to it after further study, until he could make sense of it. He was a thorough scholar, a dedicated one, trying to apply himself to life's larger questions: What is man? What is happiness?

Rune, now fourteen, was deep in his academic pursuits, but it confounded him how much space his brain had parceled out for thinking about one certain thing, one specific topic that didn't have any academic value: girls. The way they smelled, fresh and clean, their hair always full of some mesmerizing perfume. Their long, willowy limbs, and the graceful way they moved. The timbre of their twittery laughs. Girls at school. Girls at the soda fountain. Inger's friends.

All of them. How they overtook his mind.

The idea of girls. The notion of sex. His desire. They were always thrumming in the background of his brain. He understood now, firsthand, that these were driving forces, not just for him, but in the world around him.

It was there in the way his classmates teased each other, in the way the railway men whistled at the girls in the commissary. The way Papa tried sometimes to curb his nature for Mama, his voice gentle and soft while speaking to her.

It was there in the way that Gunnar looked at Inger now, the way she batted her eyelashes.

It was also there in the way Rune cocked his head when speaking to someone, especially a girl. Yes, it was the same old tilting of his head so that he could hear with his good ear, but it was more than that. He was embarrassed of his eye. Even if it was unconscious, he was tilting his head away from the girl's eyes. His imperfections always on such blatant display for the world.

Anders and Rune talked about girls, late at night, in the dark, when they couldn't see each other's faces, when it seemed safest, with Gunnar out secretly meeting Inger, as he often did in the middle of the night. This way he couldn't tease them for their questions.

"Do you think about *it* all the time?" Anders asked. He laid in the bunk above Rune now, one that Papa had built them last winter.

"I do," Rune said. "I think it is natural." Rune's face heated red and he was thankful for the darkness.

"Aren't we supposed to feel bad about it? About how much we want it?"

"Yes."

"At church they talked about keeping your hands off yourself," Anders said. "Sometimes I can't," he confessed.

This was a surprise to Rune. He had just started to wake up from sweat-tangled dreams, his heart pounding, his chest heaving, his shorts wet. *You mean, you could do this to yourself even if it wasn't part of a dream?*

"I think that's natural too." Rune agreed with Anders, to make him feel better about it, but really Rune had no idea.

The world of sex and all that it encompassed was perplexing to Rune, his knowledge incomplete. But he was glad for this newfound window into the world, the real grownup world, for now he saw it everywhere, how it motivated so much in the books he read, in the lives around him.

He had so many questions, with really no one to ask. But it seemed for so many things, sex was the answer, the motivator, the reason, the why.

Rune tucked this away in the back of his brain along with so many other interesting facts and figures.

Rune thought of the Greeks he'd been reading. He was trying to put their theories into some kind of structure that would make sense in a modern, American setting. And Rune kept coming back to one idea: that man needs a driving purpose in his life. For many in history, it was about dominion, glory, or piety, fulfilling God's purpose. He was thinking about these things in terms of what the great leaders of the world had been motivated by. He found he couldn't quit considering sex as a purpose, as a motivator, a great one. Now, here in the present, or even back a thousand years.

One that lead to a higher, more noble purpose of raising a family? Was this the selfless angle?

To what end was sex such a powerful means?

He was thinking about these things in the abstract of course. But he was also thinking about it, concretely, specifically, because he started to wonder about his own purpose.

It seemed about time. He was changing into a man. Best to start planning on what kind of man he might want to be, although he was pretty certain he knew the kind of man he *didn't* want to be, and that was a start.

• • •

ON A WINDY, COLD MORNING IN JANUARY, Rune and his brothers had to make their own breakfast. Mama was with child again, and she had begun the pregnancy with terrible morning sickness. Her trips to the outhouse to vomit interrupted the English lessons Rune still gave her every morning. This had gone on for weeks back in the summer.

But that had been months ago. She had gotten over that part of the pregnancy, hadn't she?

"She's not feeling well." That was all Papa would say this morning.

No one had lit the morning fire.

The house was cold and there was frost on the inside of the washbin. The boys set to doing their own and their mother's chores, and Papa sat at the table, his beard unshaven, his hair unkempt, and he stared into his empty coffee cup.

Rune noticed as Papa put his hand around the cup that Papa's knuckles were injured, with rust-colored blood stains and shredded skin.

At first, Rune's mind went to the railroad, and all the things that could go wrong there, the injuries, the commonplace deaths.

But then Rune froze in the kitchen, dropped the firewood he'd been carrying from the porch. He went directly into his parents' bedroom without knocking.

She lay there, asleep, her face angelic, the cold winter sun hitting her golden hair, now with its one grey stripe. She was small, so small, underneath the quilt, the one she had sewn with Farmor all those years ago.

Papa followed Rune into the doorway, and when he leaned onto the doorframe, it creaked. Mama turned her head in her sleep, revealing her left cheek, with a large swollen lip, a black and yellow bruise on her jaw, and dried blood caked on her neck.

How? When they were right in the next room, all night? How?

Rune didn't think any more. He simply reacted. In a flash, he was on his father, tackling him to the floor, using every bit of strength he held in his broad and towering frame. But Papa was sober by now, and he got one good punch on Rune's jaw, then a strong fist to his collarbone. Rune pulled back, unaware of his injuries, and he pummeled his father's face, his body. Rune saw nothing—just rage, blind, blind rage.

He worked his fists, tasting iron and hate.

He heard yelling, he heard profanity, he had no idea it was actually him. Rune continued to land punches in his father's ribs, on his jaw, in his kidneys, his eye. He knew he was being beaten as well, but it was as if Rune had no more feeling in his body, no more sensation.

Only hot, molten anger that had simmered inside him, barely contained, for years.

This went on for a long time, and just when somewhere far-off in the back of his mind, his non-animal self began to notice that Papa was now barely fighting back, Gunnar and Anders worked together to eventually get Rune off Papa. As they did, Papa rallied and brought a thick hook right up into Rune's ribs, a cracking noise echoing in the small house. Now, Mama was awake. She stood in her nightshift, holding her arms around her swollen belly, screaming for them to stop.

Gunnar, now nearly equal in size to Papa, shoved Papa up against the wall, his forearm at his throat. "Don't you—" Gunnar growled, but then something flashed over Gunnar's face, like he realized the time for words was done, and he brought a knee up into Papa's groin.

Papa went down hard, and Gunnar gave him another hard kick in the abdomen. Papa crumpled. Then from behind, a crash of water, a puddle, and Mama buckled over.

"It's the baby," Anders said, letting go now of Rune, who had finally calmed some. "She's having the baby."

Rune stood frozen. *The baby? It wasn't time yet.*

"Go," Gunnar yelled. "Get Miss Vendela."

Rune broke from his trance, moving then.

Gunnar got the extra quilts, Anders put on a pot to boil. "Get some more water. At the spring," he yelled to Rune. "Hurry." Inger's mother was, of course, the Hollow's midwife.

Rune left and ran. He got to Inger and Johann's house somehow, and when Inger saw his face, she blanched. "The baby . . . now," Rune said, breathless. Rune stopped then at the spring, filling up the tin water bucket.

When he got back to the house Miss Vendela was there. Papa sat against the wall where Rune had left him, with a dazed look on his bloodied face. Gunnar and Anders stood in the doorway. "Rune!" Mama called between her heavy breaths, her prolonged grunts.

He went to her at once. She pulled him close. "Rune," she said, pulling his face close to hers. "Thank you. Rune, you are my little secret. Do you know that?" She spoke in stilted Swedish, between the teeth-grinding pain.

Rune didn't know what she meant, why he was crying, but he nodded. "Yes. Mama," he whispered, feeling five years old and a hundred years old, ancient, and all the years in between.

"I love you, Rune."

"Mama, don't."

"Take care of your brothers. Gunnar will be fine. But Anders, he is. . . He needs you. He is special in that way."

"Mama, why . . . why are you saying this?"

Mama struggled through a contraction, her hands gripping into Rune's forearm, her jaw locked as she keened, a low terrible noise. When it finally let up, she gasped. "Rune, the tunnel. You . . . remember."

"Mama, it is nothing. I am fine."

"Dreamt it again. Last night." The pain over was climbing again, her teeth grinding. "This time, it was me."

"No." Rune watched as she struggled against the contraction. He shook his head. "No, it means nothing. Mama?"

"Boys?" she whispered, as the contraction receded. She looked frantic, hurried, her eyes darting around the room for Gunnar and Anders. The brothers crowded around their mother then, and she said her breathless goodbyes to Rune's brothers, quickly, as if she knew there was no time.

Gunnar and Anders, too, seemed to be in denial, wide-eyed, shaking their heads.

"You are talking senseless, Mama. You will be fine," Anders told her, brushing her forehead with a cold rag.

And with that, the contraction built again, and she screamed, a scream so terrible, so primal, that Rune registered a terrible shiver down his spine. His mother's body bucked off the bed, once twice, then she looked at him and her eyes rolled back in her head, the whites of her eyes shone, and she passed out.

He watched as her skin turned dusky, then blue, then so, so pale, all the while Miss Vendela was swearing, moving, pressing gently on Mama's abdomen. Rune stood, helpless, and Miss Vendela shooed the boys away so she could attend to Mama. Rune stayed where he was.

Miss Vendela checked Mama's pulse then. She gave her smelling salts. She slapped her twice on each side of her face. Mama did not wake.

Miss Vendela moved between Birgit's legs then. She pulled Mama's skirts high above her waist to get at the baby, and when she did so, Rune saw the bruises, horrible, mottled bruises—yellow-green, blue-black—along her swollen abdomen.

Rune swore under his breath, turning toward where his Papa had taken a beating only moments ago. Rune would finish him, by God. He would. He would put his hands around his father's neck, and he would press.

And he would press harder still, against his father's windpipe, and he would watch his father's eyes as they registered exactly what was happening to him.

But Papa was no longer there. He was nowhere.

Rune looked quickly in the front room, out toward the outhouse. He was nowhere.

Rune went back to his mother. Her hand was cold. So cold. Rune's own hand shook with rage, with horror, with fear.

Miss Vendela began pulling, trying to free the baby, just as the midwife had done so many years ago, freeing Rune from his mother's body.

Then something stilled Miss Vendela. She brought her bloodied hands to press on her own chest, in a terrible gesture of shock. She let out a long, slow breath. She called to Gunnar to get the doctor. Anders backed away then, crying.

"Hurry, Gunnar! *Skynda*!"

Rune followed down his mother's body, from her ashen white face, to what was between her legs, and he saw there the purple snake of umbilical cord. The blood, so much blood, and he saw the baby, with the cord wrapped in knots around its neck, and it too was white and purple.

It was not breathing. It was a girl, with hair golden as the Swedish sun. It was a terrible, terrible sight.

Miss Vendela spoke to herself then, in muttered Swedish, every shade of profanity that existed. She cut the umbilical cord and gently wrapped the baby in a cloth and laid her on the bed, tucked close to her mother. She checked Mama's breathing then, placed her hand on her wrist for a pulse.

She swore again, and she began to compress Mama's chest.

The doctor entered moments later, ordered them all out, and Anders' sobs racked his body, and they frayed what was left of Rune's nerves.

Rune ran so far from that house and the Hollow.

He ran and ran. He wore no coat. He felt no cold.

The snow and ice crunched beneath his feet. The brambles and thistles caught on his pants, on the bare skin of his arms, his cheeks.

He felt nothing.

He climbed the bluffs, and he repeated the word, "No."

"No, no, no." His voice was angry, so angry.

It wasn't until he was inside that cave, the cave from their first day here in the Hollow, that he truly let himself understand.

He sat, pulling his legs up to his chest, resting his head on his knees, and he cried. He repeated the word again, "No, no, no." But it was only sad now, only knowing—no longer angry.

He knew. The baby was gone.

Mama was gone.

Forever.

Papa, however, was not.

Chapter 22

THE VISITATION, THE FUNERAL, ALL OF IT WAS A BLUR. A long string of faces, both familiar and not, thrust into Rune's own, offering condolences, along with many tepid handshakes, and so many tears. Of course, Anders cried, always Anders, and Rune himself. Sometimes even Gunnar.

Papa didn't cry. He didn't cry when he came back that terrible night, drunk and smelling of moonshine and sweat and piss. He didn't cry when he found his three boys numb and hollow-eyed on the porch, with their dead mother and dead sister inside the house, being cleaned and wrapped by the doctor, ready to be taken to the church.

He didn't cry when they lowered her plain wooden casket into the ground. Or when they followed it with a tiny one for his stillborn daughter. When the church bells tolled in the background. He didn't cry when Rune fell onto his knees there at the cemetery, begging his brothers, in tear-strangled Swedish, for just one more look at Mama. One more moment.

"No, Rune," they told him, joining him on his knees, joining their tears into his.

Mama. Her shoulders bent over the table as she prepared a meal. Her hand absentmindedly petting Aprikos as she drank her coffee. Her head tipped back in laughter, her hand at her throat.

Rune missed his mother.

With a terrible, heated agony under his ribs. Every breath hurt.

Folke Kasparsson didn't cry while he was packing his things in the house in the Hollow that very night, taking the last of the canned goods, taking his shotgun, taking their best quilt made by Mama's hand. He packed it all up, and he gave the boys a hard look.

Rune knew his father was leaving them. The other boys knew it too, he figured. He knew that, like him, his brothers didn't give one single shit.

Papa attempted to shake hands with Gunnar, some misguided last attempt at good will. Gunnar only shook his head once, looking at him hard. Papa lowered his eyes and said, "I'll send for you kids when I get up to Canada. There's money to be made logging. Once I get us all set up, I'll send word."

"Don't insult us," Gunnar seethed. "You've killed our mother and sister. Now leave before we do the same to you."

Part of Rune wanted to pummel his father, to beat him within an inch of his life, to make good on his promise to kill him if he touched his mother. But now, that promise seemed pointless. Rune himself felt pointless. Life was pointless. All of it. Everything . . . pointless.

Truly, Rune almost felt a pang of pointless pity for his Papa when Gunnar said his parting words. There was something that flashed across Papa's face, a moment of humanity, that made him look so much look Uncle Isak. But then Papa sneered, and he spit on Gunnar's shoes. "You ungrateful sons of bitches." Gunnar stepped close to Papa, eye to eye with him, a challenge.

"Please," Anders pleaded. No one wanted any more blood spilt.

Papa backed away, picking up his pack. Rune stood there with Anders, shaking so hard his teeth chattered, and watched his father leave. Anders' hand dug into Rune's elbow, and when the door closed behind the father, the boys let out their collective breath. They looked to one another, looking in each other's eyes, maybe for the first time in a long time, holding each other's stares. They were here. Alone, but together. Their faces said many things to each other.

I'm so sorry.

I am here.

I am always here.

The three brothers looked at each other with hollow, wounded eyes.

"What will we do?" Anders asked. "We're orphans."

"I want to go back home," Rune answered.

"To Sweden?" Gunnar asked, shocked. "No, you don't know what you're talking about, Rune. We are here, in America, this is home now. I am going to start working full-time at the railroad. I am nearly nineteen now. We will have plenty. There is nothing to worry about."

Anders asked, "You are staying?"

"Of course," Gunnar answered. "Of course I am. Don't act so surprised. You're my brothers." Gunnar's voice changed then, became a little shaky. "And I may look like him, but I'm not Papa. I'll never be Papa. I will stay here for you." Gunnar gave Anders a hard look.

Anders continued, "But you've been gone so much lately, never home, and you just—"

"It was best for me to be out of here, so I wouldn't kill the bastard," Gunnar spat. But then he thought better of it. "Maybe, maybe I should've. Mama would still be here then, and—"

"Don't say these things," Rune interrupted. But Rune felt it too, that wish inside him that he'd protected his mother, killed his father, done something, anything differently. But he told his oldest brother, "None of this was your fault."

"Or yours," Gunnar said, eyeing both Rune and Anders.

"I miss her," Anders said.

"We will always miss her," Gunnar said softly.

Rune sighed and added, "I keep thinking I hear her, at the sink or on the back porch, humming under her breath."

"It is going to be hard," Gunnar said. "But we stick together, and I mean to marry Inger eventually. You know this, don't you?"

Anders and Rune exchanged a look. "We didn't know that," Anders said. "But I guess we did somehow."

"I will marry Inger, and we will all be a family, proper and happy, until you make your own way in the world. This is a good place, brothers. Swede Hollow. And it can be a happy place. I have found happiness here, and you will too, out from under that monster. Surely, it will take us some time. We will miss Mama. All of us." He looked especially at Rune. "But we are family. Papa was not family. We grew up with family in Goteborg, and we know how to be family together, to love each other, and we will do that now. We are so sorry to have lost Mama." Gunnar choked up then, and Rune's eyes pinched closed against more tears. "But we are not sorry to have lost Papa. We will flourish now; do you hear me?"

Gunnar pulled his brothers roughly to him, and Anders and Rune cried against their big brothers' shoulders, and he soothed them. Rune had never been more thankful for Gunnar before. He realized that he had overlooked how important Gunnar was to them, how strong, how giving, how much he obviously had learned from Uncle Isak—never Papa—about how to be a man.

Rune would learn from Gunnar too.

"I should've intervened sooner," Gunnar said. "I should've gotten Mama away from him." Gunnar brought his hands to his face. "I just thought I'd have a chance to defend her or I figured—"

"We all did," Rune told him, putting a hand on his shoulder. "We all thought we'd be able to step in, to stop it. It's no one's fault."

"Except Papa's," Anders said, and he pulled his brothers close again, for one more hug.

Gunnar gave each boy a squeeze and a kiss on top of his head. "Let's clean this place up, get some firewood and water."

Rune held onto him, for one more moment. "Mama would be proud," Rune told him. And he meant it, so very deeply.

• • •

IT WAS ONLY A MATTER OF DAYS AFTER the funeral when Rune and his brothers received the telegram from their Uncle Isak. He had sailed from Sweden, unbeknownst to the boys, and he had written when he first ported in New York. "Surprise!" the first line of the telegram read.

The boys looked at each other with solemn faces. Isak was on a train, currently on his way to Swede Hollow, and he would be here tomorrow. He would not have heard word of Mama's death, of father's leaving, because he had been traveling.

Rune's stomach roiled when he thought of Uncle Isak, of his excitement to see the family, of the planning and preparation it must've taken to travel in secret, in order to surprise his brother and his family.

Jösses. Rune felt a terrible, sick anger at Isak, for being too late, for living right now in ignorance, and for the suffocating guilt because Isak had been the one who'd told him to watch out for his mother, to protect her. Rune had failed her, had failed Isak. This he knew.

Rune thought of this as he waited, hat in hand on the St. Paul train station platform, surrounded by others, the expectation in their faces recognizable. But for the three brothers, it was a terrible mixed blessing.

As the boys watched the passengers leave the train, Rune found his warring emotions nearly unbearable. He desperately wanted to see Isak, but the shame he carried, the sadness he knew he had to impart was awful.

But then appearing through a tangle of passengers, he was there, in front of them. Large and imposing. Isak Kasparsson. In America, in their Swede Hollow. In the flesh, looking just as himself, save for more silver threaded through his dark hair. He hugged them each, there on the train station platform, marveling at their size.

Rune's memory played tricks on him, superimposing the scene of him and his brothers years ago, meeting their father here at this same station. His mother had been so young, so vibrant.

Rune tried to be strong. But when Isak held him to him, calling him "*Min pojke*," Rune shook in his arms, desperately trying to stifle a sob. The familiar firewood and hay smell of his uncle took him back to Goteborg, took him back to his family, to his mother. It unraveled him.

Rune pulled back from Isak's hug, feeling embarrassed, feeling young, weak.

"Tell me," Isak said. "Your faces are grave, my boys. Where is your father? Your mother?"

No one could meet Uncle Isak's eyes. Gunnar cleared his throat once, twice. "Can we go to the café? We should sit down."

Anders and Rune busied themselves with the task of carrying Isak's trunk, and they walked in silence to the corner, went into the corner diner. The cheery *clink-clank* of the dishes, the background chit-chat, all of it was out of place. There was nothing to soften this blow to their beloved uncle, who had traveled weeks over the ocean to be here now.

The timing was unbearable, as was the loss.

"Uncle, we are so glad to see you . . ." Gunnar began, as soon as they were seated in a red-vinyl booth. "But we have to share the worst news."

Isak seemed to steel himself. He gave one curt nod.

"Mama has died," Rune said, spitting it out quickly, feeling he owed that to his brothers, to take the brunt of it. "At the hand of father. The baby as well. It happened nine days ago."

Isak let out a breath as if he'd been punched in the chest. "No."

Rune found that he couldn't meet Isak's eyes now. That he couldn't bear the accusation that he'd feel in them. "I'm sorry," he said. "I'm so sorry, Uncle."

"*Min Gud*."

"We are all so sorry," Gunnar added. "He was a monster, waiting for an opening. We didn't realize . . ."

"Mama must've hid it from us. How awful he really was," Anders said. "We're so sorry."

"What are you sorry for?" Isak said, his voice gruff, choked with tears.

"We should've protected her," Gunnar said. "We tried. You have to believe us–"

Isak's fist came down on the table, not hard but hard enough to jangle the silverware. "Look at me," he hissed. Rune and his brothers brought their eyes up to his, finally. "I never want to hear you blame yourselves again. You loved your mother. You tried." Isak brought his shaking hands to his face then, dragged then down his face. "Have you had the funeral?"

"Yes."

"*Min Gud*," Isak repeated.

Now Rune noticed that upon closer inspection, Isak looked more ragged, older. The skin around his eyes had aged. It hung lax, in folds.

He reached his hand across the table and grabbed Rune's. Isak looked at him hard, a terrible wince of pain crossing his features. He dropped his eyes. "I loved her too."

Rune saw this as a confession. He looked to his brothers, but they too had cast-down eyes. Did they know? Rune squeezed Isak's hand. "She loved you too." He thought of the coin then. He had found it, after much searching through the tin shack. He had found it in a silk drawstring bag, along with her thimble, in her sewing kit. Rune had made sure to slip it into her casket. She would've wanted it.

"And where is my brother?"

"Left. Said he was going north. Canada."

"*Bra riddance*."

They sat in silence as the heavy realization settled onto Isak's shoulders. "You are such good boys," he said. "I should've come earlier. The farm kept me–"

Rune interrupted. "Uncle." Rune gave him a look, shaking his head.

Isak seemed to understand him then. He nodded. "Boys, can you show me where she is buried?"

Chapter 23

ISAK STAYED ON WITH THE BROTHERS. They would rise in the morning, Gunnar for work and Anders and Rune for school, and Isak would already have been up for hours, with sausages made on the stove, a patch newly affixed to the tin roof, and the floor swept clean.

The boys began the tumultuous journey back into real life, now without their mother or their father.

They rose to the challenge, like true Folkesons. True Swedes. And it was easier to do with their uncle there to oversee them. For Rune, especially, it anchored him to the tin shack.

To the world in general. When everything inside him seemed to be awash in chaos.

The hole left by their Mama's absence was hard to ignore, impossible to fill, but they waded through it, as it was the only true answer. At times, they found it best to ignore the grief, to tuck it away and get busy with something else, chopping firewood with Uncle Isak, learning how to make beef stock from bones. Isak had a whole list of things they needed to learn before he left.

"Times are turning, getting tougher here." Isak wanted them to be prepared for life when it got harder.

The brothers didn't think things could get harder. Losing Mama was the worst possible case. But their little family worked together, helping each other through the worst of things. With company. With distraction. Their little four-person family, plus the often-included Inger, was a tight entity, a force to be reckoned with.

And nobody cherished it more than Rune, as he pushed through the fog of grief. He would often find that he was daydreaming, staring off into space, sometimes for moments, sometimes for much longer. At school, he was inattentive. He lost track of time. He couldn't concentrate on his readings, on his studies. He was a mess.

He was clumsy. He dropped things constantly. He tripped up the steps and cut his eyebrow on the porch. He dropped firewood on his toe. Isak chalked it up to Rune not sleeping well. But Rune knew. Even his limbs were heavy with grief.

• • •

"I DON'T THINK YOU WILL NEED stitches or anything," Anders said, washing the wound with some of Gunnar's moonshine.

They'd spent the morning fishing at Pig's Eye, and Rune had gotten the idea to try and spearfish some of the giant silver trout near the eastern end. It had gone well, with a birch pole sharpened to a deadly point with a pocketknife. They caught more trout than they could eat in three days, and that was saying something with all three of the boys' appetites, but what they hadn't counted on was Rune, in his exuberance, spearing his own foot nearly clean through.

"Thanks," Rune told him, eyeing the wound and the bandage, pulling his sock over it. "I'm just a big dumb Swede." Rune was beside himself for doing something so stupid.

Anders got up and rinsed the rag in the clean water and came back to the table. He looked at Rune. "You know? You need to quit saying that about yourself, Rune."

"It's true, isn't it? Who else spears their own foot?"

Anders laughed. "It was a mistake. Lots of people make mistakes." Then Anders folded his arms in front of himself. "Rune, look at me."

Rune did so. "Last week you used the word *horticulture*. I didn't even know what it meant. I had to ask Maeve later on. I felt too stupid to even ask you about it."

"So? It's one word."

"Listen." Anders waved it away. "What I'm saying is that growing up, I'm sure you heard that a lot: dummy, galoot, all that *hästskit* like that."

Rune nodded. Anders continued, in a serious tone. "Well, listen. You are big. You are a Swede. And you have a scar and some hearing damage. Understood. But Rune, you are not *dumb*. You are far from dumb. Haven't you proven that to yourself yet? With all your tutoring and reading and . . . your insatiable curiosity? You're quiet, yes. Dumb, no. Do you understand me?"

He knew Anders was right. Rune knew he had an active mind. But he wasn't blind to what others saw in him. Or didn't see.

Rune opened his mouth to say something just like that, to explain it all to Anders, but Anders wasn't done yet. Rune liked this new, confident Anders. He wanted to thank Gunnar, over and over, for the new beginning he had afforded them, for the way he pulled them all up by their bootstraps.

Anders was up from the table now, pacing. He had lit a cigarette, and he ran his hands through his golden hair. "I mean, brother, people think that they know you, that there is a certain idea of you, and that's what you are." Anders stopped pacing, and he looked at Rune, cigarette hanging from his mouth. "I say no. We have a lot in our hearts, all of us, Rune. We have a secret place inside us, wherein lies the real person. The essence of us." Anders pounded on his chest to make the point. "Nobody knows us. Nobody can limit us." Anders squinted his eyes. "Do you know what I'm saying?"

Rune almost did. He knew what it meant in terms of his own self. But what was Anders saying about himself, exactly?

Rune nodded because he wanted Anders to keep going. He wanted to know what was in Anders' secret heart. He almost asked, but then Anders seemed to come back to earth, to return to the little tin shack. "I think your foot will be fine," he said. "I'm meeting Maeve tonight. We're going up to Abbottville."

Anders spent a lot of time with Maeve these days. He and Johann had sort of drifted apart, and in his place was this buxom, red-lipped flapper. She was foul-mouthed like a sailor, and she was a lot of fun.

Anders and Maeve got along well. But there was something odd in the way that Anders and Maeve looked at each other, like they were in on a secret.

Rune had a hard time putting together what their relationship was. He'd seen Anders kiss her square on the mouth in greeting many times, but there was something so completely unromantic about it.

He'd seen looks pass between Inger and Gunnar, a blink or a glance that held more in them than entire embraces or kisses between Maeve and Anders.

Rune chalked it up to one more thing he would have to figure out. Some kind of intricacy that evaded him.

"Okay," Rune said. "It's a long walk to Abbottville. Be safe." He watched his brother put on his jacket and hat.

"You want to come with us? Dance with some girls?" Anders waggled his eyebrows at Rune.

"Not tonight, brother. I put a spear through my foot. I will stay and play cards with Uncle."

That night, as they played gin rummy, Isak held up something in the light of the lantern, between his two fingers. "I found it in the bureau. He must've left it for you kids." It was Papa's wedding ring.

Rune felt a sudden pang of guilt in his belly. "I took Mama's off. I kept it. I didn't think she'd want to be buried in it." Rune dropped his eyes. "I buried her with your coin instead."

Isak sighed, and he rubbed at his beard that he'd grown since he'd shown up here weeks ago. He looked at Rune and he squinted his eyes. He opened his mouth as if he wanted to say something, but then he stopped himself. He played a pair of jacks.

"I know that you're my father. My real father," Rune said. He hadn't planned on saying it, but now that he had, relief washed over him.

Isak met Rune's eyes, and there was something there that Rune couldn't quite place. Something besides sorrow? Was it shame?

"If I had to do things over again . . ." Isak stared past Rune now, through him. Rune swallowed hard. He couldn't bear it if Isak finished that sentence.

"Don't say it." He didn't want Isak to say that he was sorry for loving Mama, for anything like that. He couldn't bear the weight of that, for his own heart, or for Mama's.

"I would do things differently, Rune. I would keep your mother from coming here. I should've kept you boys, all of you, with me. That is my failing, the weight I have to live with now. That I did nothing."

His eyes. It was *regret*.

"For a few years in Goteborg, I had you boys as my own, and I should've . . ."

Rune tried to hide his surprise. He knew that such things, a divorce, a remarry, these things happened, but not in respectable families. He almost couldn't believe what Isak was saying. Because Rune never had questioned Isak, or he had tried not to. Some things you couldn't fix. Some things you couldn't take back.

But Rune studied the jut of Isak's chin, the way that he squared his shoulders against something while they sat there, thinking, wondering, if . . . Rune understood then Isak *should've*. Isak, if he could, would do it again differently.

"Learn from me," Isak said. "There are no rules. Look at me, Rune. This is important. You find love like that. You seize it. Protect it. There are no rules." Isak shook his head. "Maybe you are too young for me to plague you with this talk."

"I am not. I'm fifteen, Uncle."

"You will sell your parents' wedding rings. Don't tell your brothers. They are loose with money." He shook his head and waved away Rune's disagreement. "Anders will buy cigarettes and piss it away at the bars. Anders is running with a troublesome crowd. Gunnar is better, but you . . . *you* are my son." Isak looked at him hard, and Rune wondered if Isak could see how those words warmed him, from the inside out. "I love you, Rune. You will keep this money, and you will keep it safe. No banks. Keep it hidden. Save for harder times. Live close to the bone. You and your brothers will be prepared for the worst then."

A realization hit Rune then. His stomach folded in on itself. "Where are you going?"

"I'm going to find Folke."

"Uncle, that isn't wise. You'll—"

He held up his hand. "I will hear none of this. I will stay on, until you are ready to be alone. But I have to find him. I have to look my brother in the eye."

"And that is all?"

Isak didn't answer Rune then. Instead, he discarded, slapping his card on the pile. "Your turn, *min pjoke*."

• • •

AT FIRST, THE NEWS OF THE STOCK market crash seemed to exist for people with money in banks, for people who lived up above on Plank Avenue. It seemed unimportant to the likes of the Folkeson boys and those living in Swede Hollow, but soon, it was apparent that hard times were coming to everyone.

At the railway, Gunnar's wages were cut, but his hours lengthened.

Prices of their food staples began to rise, and the boys found themselves with bellies that were never quite full. They began to survive off of sardines and beans, with real meat only a treat for special occasions. Isak showed the boys how to cut corners, how to make a broth and thicken it with flour to keep their bellies from rumbling too much. Isak showed them how to mend their own clothes, how to bake peasant bread.

Isak taught Anders how to roll his own cigarettes, to save him money, and Gunnar began to take on odd jobs, chopping neighbors' wood, mending brewery fences, just in case. They were preparing. For Isak leaving, for financial mayhem. For adult life.

Anders suggested to Rune that they both leave school and take railroad jobs. Isak huffed and puffed about it, but, in the end, he too agreed. "Best to jump on that idea before others do it and there are no more jobs."

And although Rune was surprised, hadn't ever thought of himself as a railer, he agreed. He would do anything if his brothers thought it was a good idea. Plus, school had started to take its toll on him. He was learning nothing new there, and he found that his time in school, his inevitable list of pupils to tutor, all it really did was interfere in his own rigorous schedule of studies at the library.

It was time for Rune to start pulling his weight, and things had been so peaceful with the three boys alone and together, Rune would do anything to preserve it.

They both found a job at the railroad. Rune and Anders were together on a section gang, along with two other men. They had their own handcart and were responsible for keeping a thirty-mile section of track in good working order. They replaced rotted lumber, did replacement iron work. It was hard work, work that required strength and stamina. But it bolstered their bodies and put more food on their table.

Together, the brothers would be fine.

It wasn't an easy day's work, by any means, for any of them. Money was scarce, their tin house always cold. And their appetites were bigger than their budgets, but as winter melted into spring that year, the boys found an easy rhythm to their lives. A hardworking, busy, sometimes exhausted rhythm.

It was during this time, when Rune had been at the railway for less than a month, that Miss Michaelson tracked him down, waiting on the stoop of the old tin shack, when he and his brothers walked back for their evening meal.

"Excuse me, Rune? May I have a word?" she asked. And she looked up at Rune with what looked like almost surprise. She hadn't been his teacher for a few years, and now, at sixteen, Rune had gone from a large boy to an even larger and more imposing man.

"Yes, Miss Michaelson?" Rune asked. "Would you like to come in? Have some *kaffe*?"

"No, thanks, Rune," she said, seeming to relax, now that she heard Rune's voice, she seemed to recognize something about him.

"We need a tutor for the young people's English program. We do extra sessions now, in the evenings. Sometimes on Saturday mornings. I was wondering if it might be something you'd like to do."

Rune thought about this. "I did a lot of tutoring, at school. For Mrs. Woolman."

Ms. Michaelson looked hard at Rune. "You would be paid for this, Rune. Maybe not much, but this wouldn't be like before. You would be the actual teacher."

Paid? The thought had never crossed Rune's mind. This changed things for Rune. He could see himself preparing lessons by the fire at night. He had worked enough at the railway to understand that this was not a thinking man's job, and it would do Rune good to have something to keep his mind occupied. Rune agreed immediately.

His brothers, having heard the conversation from the porch, clapped him on the back.

"Mama would be proud," Anders said in Rune's ear.

They moved inside, and Rune was excited to tell Isak. But when they entered the front room, they saw it was empty.

There, on the table, was a note from Uncle Isak. "*Ingen fara pa tacket*. I love you, boys." He was gone, as he told them he would be.

But still, the emptiness, the shock of it, hit Rune hard in between his ribs.

The boys were now alone.

"I hope he doesn't find Papa," Anders said.

"I hope he does," Gunnar said, his voice hard. "I hope he kills the son of a bitch."

• • •

THE DEPRESSION WORSENED; everyone got poorer.

This put off Gunnar's marriage plans. He said it was for Inger, so she could have more time to plan. But Rune knew it was so that he could stay with Anders and Rune longer. Gunnar took responsibility of his brothers, and he wasn't going to leave and start a life with Inger until he knew his brothers would be fine on their own.

Rent in the Hollow began to increase, and the county declared they were putting public sewers and running water into their homes. This baffled the residents, as they didn't know how they would ever be able to pay for it. But the Folkeson boys worried little and focused on working instead.

Rune relished the physical work at the railroad. The heavy lifting, the driving of the iron spikes into the ground. He was good at it, and mighty tired at the end of the day, when he came back into the Hollow aboard the work train.

Each of the boys thanked God for Miss Vendela. She would often send Inger over with pork chops, with chuck roast, a stew. Something. Although the Hollow was hit and hit hard by the Depression, her business was not suffering. People still had money for their drink.

And Rune found that Isak was right. Gunnar and Anders still found money for their entertainment. A few coins for a night out here, a few more for a moving picture there. But Rune did not begrudge his brothers this. A sliver of distraction was necessary. He knew this.

The evening hours were lonely for Rune. They left Rune plenty of time to prepare for his tutoring or, his one luxury, to read.

The library became Rune's evening routine. It was during this time of Rune's life that he, more and more, left the heavy texts of Thomas Aquinas and John Locke, and he turned to poetry of all things.

He found comfort in the verses, the way they could capture a fleeting emotion, how they could forever hold a moment's feeling in only a few syllables.

Dickinson, Whitman, Eliot, and of course, Robert Frost. It was like these poets stripped things down to their barest essentials and whispered their truths right into Rune's ear.

Even as his body was growing hard and lean with heavy work in the railyards, his mind was growing, through poetry, turning more elastic, able to understand so much about the world around him. Here in Swede Hollow and beyond. Life. Love. Morality. Purpose.

The serious texts of his earlier years had given him a basis for original thought now, and he found he thought best in verse.

He became a student of humanity, of what it is that makes us alive. He found that he had question upon question, and as he read, some were answered, even as some were discarded for better questions.

What is man?

What is life?

What is good and evil?

How did we get here?

These questions seemed appropriate, given the state of confusion and depression that his mother's death had left him with.

He approached those questions the only way he could see fit, by not answering them head on. Rather, he came at the questions around the corner, with poems, with feelings conjured in words.

He read, and he wrote and wrote.

Mrs. Krall, the Irishwoman at the reference desk, began to set things aside for Rune: novels, but mostly poetry volumes, and he became a fixture at the library.

Rune began to have the itch to talk about the ideas he was reading, and once, while he and his section gang were having lunch in the bright heat of the May sun, he brought up the idea of a book club to the men on his work detail. He had wanted to hand out a copy of his favorite poem by Robert Frost, but he had decided to stick with something more mainstream.

"Have any of you ever read *Gatsby*?"

"He was born right here in St. Paul, yeah?" Louis asked.

"No one wants to read books with you," Anders laughed, elbowing Rune in the ribs.

The other fellows joined in, laughing right along with Anders. And Rune didn't take it too personally.

They weren't going to keep themselves up at night, deliberating over Darwin's theory of specificity, or Whitman's barbaric yawp. This surprised Rune, and it didn't.

Anders had been a reader, had read every book that Rune recommended to him, for years. But things had changed. Anders spent his nights out with Maeve and their whole group of friends. He came home late, smelling like booze and cigarettes, and Rune understood this.

Anders had discovered a different hobby than Rune. He'd given up books, for now, in favor of dancing at the clubs with lipsticked girls who bobbed their hair and talked about Josephine Baker and did flappers dances. Rune got it. Everyone was on fire with something, with change and progress! And Rune understood. They all needed something. A distraction from their manual labors. From the loss of their mother.

They were growing up, filling up their lives with the distractions of men.

Rune understood.

Chapter 24

AS THE GRAY SLUSH OF LATE WINTER MELTED into the green St. Paul spring, there were more things to do, more events, more reasons to be outside, away from the house. Gunnar went off dancing with Inger and to the moving picture shows. Anders and Maeve went dancing, drinking—out.

His brothers were always pomading their hair, ironing their collars. Even when they were home, they talked of where they would next be going. Rune realized that what it came down to was this:

Girls.

Rune missed his brothers. Their company. He felt alone, more alone now than ever. His mother was gone. He missed his uncle with a sharp worry. Where was he? Would he . . . ? No. He wouldn't.

The tin shack all of a sudden became too small, too haunted.

Suddenly, his books, his studies, they weren't enough. Rune needed out. He needed something else.

So he began to throw himself into tutoring. Rune needed it.

Rune was a natural at it, and Ms. Michaelson soon hired him for a Thursday evening class as well. It was a difficult job. Because so many of the kids, Swedish or not, thought about things differently, processed language in different ways. If they saw words in their mind while they were speaking, if that was the process of brain to mouth that Rune was dealing with, then he knew to approach the learning of English in what he coined the slip-and-change routine. These students needed vocabulary building. They needed flashcards and a large well of words to choose from, because they needed to see them in their minds.

Other students needed to understand the workings of the verbs first, the conjugations, and then they could go from there, once they had these underpinnings. And others still needed to hear it spoken, and they absorbed it somehow. The rhythm of things. These were most difficult for Rune to understand, yet the easiest to teach.

Before long, Rune had full classes, with some of the students bringing their poor immigrant parents along, because Mr. Rune—word was getting around—could teach English to a rock.

Mrs. Michaelson was bursting with pride about it. She spoke with the headmaster of the school about expanding their English program, and before he knew it, Rune was assigned a small section of actual adults: problematic immigrant adults who couldn't seem to grasp the language.

Mrs. Michaelson was over the moon. Rune was terrified. He was only sixteen years old, and he was going to stand in front of a classroom of adults.

He spent long hours in the night and on the weekends, going through books given to him by Mrs. Michaelson, weighing different teaching strategies. And Anders began to call him "Scholar" as a nickname.

Rune didn't like the tension and the nervousness that this new job was giving him, but he did like the money. Gunnar liked the money too, but even more than that, Rune was so happy for the timing of it.

He needed this monumental distraction.

Because with the other boys out of the house so much, finding new outlets for having fun, socializing, and just plain gone, Rune was lonely.

He'd begun to squirrel away a little of his money each week, in an old lutefisk can beneath his bed, along with the money from pawning the wedding rings. Rune hoped he and his brothers wouldn't need it. And maybe, maybe when Isak showed up again, they could both go back to Sweden.

The idea of Sweden soothed Rune. To see the farm, run his fingers over the edges of the rough-hewn fence. To see Sötnos, who upon the last letter for Aunt Malin, was gray in the muzzle, but still getting along. And of course, Uncle Isak. If he could only see him, hear him call him Son again. He'd not heard from Isak. Rune hoped both that Isak had not found Papa, but also had.

That first night of the new tutoring session, Rune nearly chickened out. "I can't do it."

"Yes, you can, brother," Anders told him. "You've been doing it for months."

"Those were little children."

"These are bigger version of those same people. They will love you."

"Kids ask about my eye."

"Yeah? Is that hard for you? Are you scared—"

"No, I like that they ask," Rune explained. "They ask and get it out of the way. Then we move on from it. Older people, kids, adults, they just stare, then look away all embarrassed."

Anders looked at Rune carefully then. "You want me to come? I'll come. That's what brothers do."

Ah, the soothing effect of those words was something Rune couldn't quite explain. Anders had always been his biggest source of comfort, because in many ways, Anders seemed like Rune's mirror image, his other half, his better one. Where Rune was shy, Anders was smooth. Where Rune was book smart, Anders would struggle. Rune was ugly, Anders unbearably handsome. And because they lived in this world of opposites, of making up for the other's shortcomings, they understood each other and their places in the world.

Gunnar, yes, he was always on Rune's side, always there for him as well, but he would never volunteer to come to the library with Rune, to sit in his first class. That was Anders, giving the one thing Rune needed, offering it before Rune even realized it was exactly what would help.

• • •

THE ROOM IN THE BASEMENT of the library was long and narrow, with a dozen wooden chairs, barely any of them matching. There was a small stack of slates, a box of half-used chalk, and Rune.

He cleared his throat several times, as he waited for his students to enter. Anders busied himself rearranging the chairs from their tidy rows into a semi-circle. "Maybe make it more like a conversation? At least for the first night?" he asked.

Rune thought about it. "Okay," he answered. This was a good idea, with the coffee-and-cake exercise especially.

And he let Anders continue his work. The people trickled in. They greeted Rune shyly, with nods of their head, or a strained hello.

Rune reminded himself that these were people who were having trouble with the new tongue. They needed his help; they were eager and coming here of their own accord. Mama would want him to help them; they were her, in many ways.

Just as he was about to introduce himself, a blonde girl, who looked to be a little older than Rune, walked into the room. "Sorry!" she said in English, with an accent Rune couldn't immediately place. She took a seat at the right-hand side of the semicircle. She wore her hair in one long braid down her back, and her cheeks flushed red as Rune continued to stare. She was small, built like a tiny fairy from a folktale, with round cheeks and deep dimples.

Anders elbowed him in the ribs. Hard.

Rune tore his eyes from the girl.

"Hello, I am Rune Folkeson, your tutor," he said, trying to make himself meet the eyes of the students, trying not to imagine their thoughts, their worries, their questions as to whether they could possibly learn anything from this big dumb Swede with the strange, scarred eye, the too-loud voice, the odd manner.

"You're so young!" an older woman said in perfect Swedish.

Anders broke in in Swedish, "Yes, he is my brother. He is young, but he has quite a knack for this thing. He has instructed many students. Mrs. Michaelson at the school sings his praises. You will be quick learners here. You are in the best hands. And please," Anders said this in his way that he had, as if he was already close friends with them all. "Please forgive the eye. It was an accident during childbirth. It is of no concern. Rune is the best of us." Anders gave the crowd his trademark charming smile, and Rune didn't know whether to be proud, glad, or angry at his brother.

And when had Anders turned into such a slick, polished version of himself?

But the class seemed to settle in then, to believe in every word that Anders said. So, Rune gave Anders a quick nod of his head in thanks, and he began by serving coffee and cookies, as Mrs. Michaelson had suggested. As the students helped themselves, Rune wrote the appropriate vocabulary words on the board.

kaffe—coffee

tarta—cake

socker—sugar

mjolk—milk

Mitt namn ar—My name is

"Take a moment and discuss your treat with someone," Rune told them. "Meet your neighbor." Rune worried about the girl with the strange accent. She wasn't Swedish. He hadn't prepared his lesson for students of other languages.

Rune shouldn't have worried. Before three minutes had passed into the exercise, Anders was already having coffee and cake with the girl with the braided hair. Rune stood at the head of his class, sipping his coffee, watching, wishing he possessed the easiness of Anders.

Anders walked back over to Rune. "Her name is Catarin Guillet. She has a nickname, something that begins with an L. But her name is Catarin."

Rune looked at him. Anders continued, "She lives over in Railroad Island. Quit looking at me like that, Rune. Like you weren't dying to know her name. Go and say hello."

"She isn't Swedish."

"No, French. A friend of hers suggested she come here to practice her English though. Your teaching is getting famous, not only with the Swedes," Anders said, elbowing Rune.

Rune didn't know what to say about the compliment, or about the girl. Anders didn't let up. "Follow your own directions, Rune. It's part of the class, introduce yourself, and practice that easy American tongue of yours. And smile, *röv.* You aren't half bad looking when you smile."

For some reason, maybe it was the sweet jolt of the coffee that pushed him over the edge, or the way Rune felt so stupid and out of place standing at the head of the class, but Rune did it. He walked over to the young girl, all sixteen years of himself, and he introduced himself.

"I am Catarin," the young girl said in difficult, stuttered English. "How many years?"

"I am sixteen years old," Rune said. "And you?"

"Eighteen," she said, after careful consideration. "Your English is easy."

"It comes easy for me. Many other things don't."

"Like?"

"Talking to you," he said, and a blush rose to Rune's cheeks, and he couldn't for the life of himself figure out how his tongue had become so loosened in front of this girl. He wondered for a split-second if Anders could've slipped some of his liquor into his coffee.

"Do not be . . . *nerveux*," Catarin whispered, mixing her English with her native tongue. But Rune liked it. She spoke conspiratorially. "I was . . . *nerveux*, but now I am . . . not." She gave him a quick glance. "Your eye is not . . . *mal*." Rune's expression tightened, and Catarin immediately interjected, "*Excusez moi.*" She averted her eyes and her cheeks bloomed in pink color. Rune knew she felt embarrassed, and he didn't want that.

She had been brave to come here, braver even to talk to him, to try and make him feel better about his eye.

But when Rune tried to think of something to say, to smooth over this bumpy exchange, he was interrupted. The burly man sitting next to Catarin interrupted them politely, and asked in stilted, practiced English. "What is your name?"

Rune smiled encouragingly as they swapped small talk.

And when Rune stood to return to the front of the class, Catarin held up her cup of coffee in some kind of a salute. "Good meeting of you, Rune," she said with her smile back in place, her deep dimples making another appearance, and Rune was transfixed.

Catarin.

Three syllables. Even her name was like music. Everything about her seemed to be beckoning him: her open face, her easy, friendly nature, her ridiculously luminous smile. He returned the smile, and tore himself away, moving onto the next exercise for the class.

The rest of the class went by in a blur for Rune. The vocabulary work. The pronoun game he'd planned so painstakingly.

The back half of his mind wasn't working on teaching English. It was simply reveling in its newest revealed truth.

Rune understood it now.

Why his brothers were never home, why they were moony-eyed and unable to concentrate. He understood what he hadn't so many years ago when he had first learned of the birds and the bees, even when he'd first entered puberty.

Everything prior to this night, prior to this class and his few exchanged sentences with Catarin seemed as though it had occurred in black and white.

But now. Upon seeing Catarin, meeting her, everything was in bold color.

Something in his body had awoken; some latent desire in his body chemistry or blood had become AWARE, and he got it now, all of it.

Why sex was everywhere, why it seemed to drive everything

Because there was nothing, absolutely nothing that could've prepared him for the way that Catarin's dimpled smile would affect him.

The way his knees nearly buckled out from under himself, the way his blood seemed to pump faster, harder through his veins, the way everything in his vision seemed to sharpen and focus when he looked at her.

Her smile. Just that one intimate act, it had snagged something inside his chest, deep under his breastbone and given it life.

He wanted to see her smile again. He needed to see that smile again.

He knew that he might see many other beautiful things in his life, he might hear arias, might listen to recitations of Thoreau or T.S. Eliot, he might hum along to the cicadas with their evening song, and these things would all be beautiful in their own right. But nothing would ever beat the sound of her singsong voice saying his name.

Good meeting of you, Rune, she had said.

And that was all it took.

• • •

"SOMEBODY'S GOTTA TAKE IT up there." The foreman was a gruff man, always irritated, red-faced, and Rune often wondered if he ever bathed, from the smell of him.

"Rune and I will do it," Anders offered. They had just finished their shift, but their foreman had a delivery that needed to go up to the brewery horse barns.

"Fine. Drive the smaller truck and bring it directly back. Be back no later than an hour."

Anders waggled his eyebrows at Rune. Rune knew that Anders had a fix on everything about him. Catarin had come to his class several weeks in a row, and Rune had mooned when he came home, surely.

Anders had found out, after various inquiries, that Catarin's family had a business relationship and friendship with the Minnesota royalty of the Hamm family, Catarin being friends with Gillian Hamm. The Guillets came to America for myriad reasons: business dealings in the railroad, to expand their empire and begin a *parfumerie* here in the states. However, rumor had it that Monsieur Guillet's only child had fought stubbornly, willfully to stay in France, and had only been convinced to make the move if, and only if, her father would guarantee her continued work in the *parfumerie*. And a pony. Rune had laughed out loud when Anders had told him that.

The gall!

Anders had laughed as well.

Anders watched Rune now as they made the trip up to the horse barn. He knew that Rune thought about Catarin constantly, that it was rainy today and no one else would want to make the trip to the barn, that the horses were bound to be inside, along with their owners or trainers or whatever it was you called someone who rode a horse.

The roads were muddy and wet, and Rune had tried to cover the hay with a tarp, but when it flew off halfway there, Rune hopped out and sat in the back holding the tarp down. He would now look like a drowned rat for Catarin, should she be at the barn. But when Anders had slowed down, Rune hadn't even asked Anders to get out and do it. There were limits to Anders' generosity of spirit. There were barely any limits to his vanity.

The barn itself was more than a barn, and Rune often wondered why they didn't refer to it as something grander, with a better name, more majestic. It was an old building, made from quarry stones, tall, rounded, maybe more octagon in shape, with a barnboard roof. The horse stalls sat around the outer edge, with an indoor ring in the center, where they trained and exercised the beautiful Percherons. These select few were kept for show, rather than work. See, the brewery kept these magnificent horses, speckled white and gray, to pull kegs of beer through the streets of St. Paul and Minneapolis; it was a Hamm's Brewery tradition. Until of course, Prohibition.

The horses, apparently, were still trained, groomed, doted on like royalty.

When Rune was younger, he used to come here often, thinking he was unseen, and perch just behind the ring half-wall and watch the beautiful beasts. The old, limp-legged Irishman who used to train the show horses yelled over to Rune one day. "Kid! You feel like helping me out or you just want to stare?"

It had been before Rune talked much, before his acute studying with the ear trumpet, before he'd perfected his speech. He had wanted to answer, to hop the half-wall and answer confidently. In a flash, Rune had seen how it could play out: He would help Mr. Jones, holding the rope or shoveling the shit, and Rune would become his sidekick, and he would learn how to work the horses, become something. But Rune couldn't unstick his tongue from the roof of his mouth.

He stammered on the first syllable. "Sssss . . ."

Then he saw things play out a different way. After he hopped the fence, Rune would get closer, and the old Irishman would lock in on Rune's face, his brow would furrow, and he would say something like. "How'd you come upon that scar?" or "You not one of those kids that are soft in the head, are ya?"

And Rune would answer, with his hollowed-out, imperfect sounding voice. The dead giveaway.

So Rune didn't hop the half-wall at all.

He ran fast out through the back exit, and he didn't visit again.

Rune pushed this memory away as he unloaded the bags of feed and rounds of hay from the rain-soaked, earthworm smelling gravel road up onto the dock. He saw the same Irishman, stooped now and graying. His gaze seemed to linger on Rune for a moment, but Anders elbowed Rune. "Hurry up so we can get in there and say hello."

"Who is it you want to say hello to?" Rune asked, worrying for a moment that maybe Anders might like Catarin, that Rune might have been misreading his intentions.

"No one, you dolt. Don't be thick, Rune. I'm trying to help you out."

They finished the job, and they followed the Irishman into the round barn. And surely, right there in the round barn, Rune caught sight of her. She wore black jodhpurs and a collared, white shirt. Her hair was golden, tied at the nape of her neck. She was a tiny thing.

She leaned into the gray and white speckled Percheron, stroking its mane, and speaking to her under her breath, a quiet conversation. Rune found himself jealous of the horse, of its proximity to her.

Rune turned. He was going to bolt, like all those long days ago. She was his student; he was her tutor, nothing more. How could he read anything into anything? He knew what he looked like.

Anders caught him by the collar, spun him back around. "Catarin!" he called. "Heya!"

She turned, noticing the pair of them for the first time. Anders waved her over. "How are you?" he said to her, smiling warmly as she approached.

"What are you . . . here?" she said, speaking in English, smiling, her eyes not leaving Rune's.

"Dropping off some feed and hay, a favor. Actually," Anders said, looking over his shoulder, "I need to go sneak a smoke. Pardon me." And Anders hightailed it out of there, leaving Rune with Catarin.

Rune swallowed hard, looking for his voice, trying to summon it back to its rightful place in the back of his throat, for it seemed to take permanent residence at the bottoms of his feet when he was around Catarin.

If Catarin thought it was weird or uncomfortable that Anders left them alone, that Rune stood silently, worrying his hat, dripping with rainwater, with his bad eye turned away from her, she gave no indication.

"I have studied much," she said, with a proud tilt of her chin. "Mother says my English better."

Rune nodded in agreement. She had made great strides. He tried once more to force the words from his toes. "You are good with the horses." His voice was a croak.

"*Merci*," she reached out and touched his hand. "You were at library, *oui*?" Rune nodded. "Maybe I see you."

"You read a lot?"

She nodded enthusiastically. "Easy read English. Speak? No."

"I thought that also at first," he said. "It's excellent practice."

"Will you . . . tonight?"

"What?" Rune asked.

"The library."

Did Rune imagine it, or did Catarin blush here?

"Yes, I will be," Rune answered. He could hardly believe what was happening, and the fact that he had told Miss Vendela he would patch a hole in her outhouse roof, well, that wasn't going to keep him from the library. Nothing would. Rune would go to the library every last moment he could now.

The mare whinnied and Catarin tossed her a look over her shoulder. "*Un moment*!" she called. "I go. See you . . . library," she said to Rune, and she did something then that Rune would replay in his mind over and over, that night, and every night after. She reached over to the half wall, where Rune's hands rested, holding onto his hat, and she laid her right hand on top of his, just for an instant. It was light, like a bird, warm from the sun, and she squeezed his hand.

"Goodbye," he called, his voice barely a whisper, again it had dropped to his feet, and it cracked mercilessly on the last syllable.

"No goodbye!" she called over her shoulder. "See you!"

Rune turned and walked slowly toward the exit, and out of nowhere, Anders came and clapped him on the back. "I didn't think you had it in you, brother," he said, beaming.

Rune smiled too. "Me neither."

• • •

HE SCRUBBED AND SCRUBBED AT his hands, his face, and the thick, dirt-stained skin of his neck. He couldn't seem to get clean enough. He couldn't eat his dinner. His stomach rolled and his hands shook as he added sugar to his *kaffe*.

Gunnar watched him from across the table. "Brother, what are you nervous about?"

Rune looked up at him and shook his head, sighed.

Anders came into the room, tying his tie. "He's meeting a girl at the library."

"*Skit*!" Gunnar laughed. "A real live girl!?" He clapped Rune on the shoulder.

Inger clucked her tongue and sat down at the table. "Rune! You secret keeper. You must tell us. Who is she?"

Anders answered, "A girl from his class. Catarin."

Just the sound of her name sent a new shiver of nerves down Rune's spine. He spilled his coffee with his shaking hands. "I can't go. I can't do it. I'm too much a brute."

Inger retrieved Rune a kitchen rag. Rune mopped up the mess and tried to dry what had gotten on his trousers. All of sudden, for the first time since Mama, Rune felt like he might cry. It was hard enough to think about what he was doing, to find that courage, but to think his brothers might be poking fun at him. He couldn't.

Gunnar poured Rune another cup of coffee. "Hey," he said, but Rune wouldn't look at him. He breathed deeply, trying to fight the tears, trying to steady himself. Gunnar put a hand on Rune's shoulder. "Rune, what is it?"

Rune fought against his tears and lost. He felt hot shame at his inability to control his emotions, especially in front of Inger.

"Rune," Anders said, sitting next to him. "What's wrong?"

Rune wanted to answer Gunnar and Anders. But how did you explain to your two perfect brothers, with their beautiful golden hair and their handsome jaws and their devil-may-care smiles that it was dangerous to . . . hope.

When you were Rune, when you were . . . used to how things were, it was dangerous. Scary. Frightening. To hope.

Rune cried into his hands, and Inger handed him her handkerchief, touching his hair gently. "Shh," she said. Rune blew his nose noisily.

Anders grabbed his hand. "Rune, you must talk to us." There was a worried tone to his brother's voice. Rune settled himself down. Embarrassed and feeling childish.

"I can't go."

"You will go," Anders said. "Look at me, Rune."

Rune hesitated, then lifted his gaze.

"I won't let you disappear inside yourself like that. I won't let you . . . hide."

"Anders is right, Rune. What he means is . . ." And Gunnar scratched at his jaw. "It's scary for all of us. We're just a bunch of low-life, poor Swedes, same as you, you know? Nobody expects shit out of us. We're all three of us a bunch of bums, and nobody in Swede Hollow or anywhere else really expects anything of us, except to put our head down and work shit jobs and like it, then drink ourselves into a stupor." Gunnar grabbed Rune's shoulder. "We're all three better than that. We're not Papa."

"We all have things . . . that make us *different*," Anders said, and his faced looked dark then, secret even. And his eyes couldn't quite meet Rune's. Gone was the open face of his most handsome brother. It shocked Rune for a moment.

Suddenly, Rune understood his brothers. For Rune, it was his looks holding him back, the defects he had acquired at birth, his speech, but he realized then that maybe . . . his brothers each had something inside them, some crippling doubt over something that held them back in a way.

And he wondered, was it possible to look like Gunnar or, especially, Anders, and feel even a sliver of the gut-wrenching insecurity that had a hold of Rune right now?

Gunnar wasn't going to let him think about it. He grabbed Rune's shoulders. "Listen, you're gonna go meet this girl, and you're going to take a deep breath, and you are going to talk with her, and you are going to be yourself, and you are going to enjoy it, damn it! And Inger and I will stop by the library later."

"Yes, we will visit and take the edge off," Inger agreed, giving Rune's hand a squeeze.

"Okay," Rune said, gathering himself. He liked the Inger part of the idea. She took the edge off things. Inger was an easy person to be around, chatty and friendly. She was much like her mother in that way. He could imagine Catarin liking Inger very much.

Rune downed his coffee, and he straightened his shoulders. He washed his face once more, and he combed his hair for the tenth time.

Then he walked quickly to the library, giving himself no opportunity to dally, to change his mind, to turn around.

She was already there, sitting at a table in the front, right near the reference desk, her head bent over a volume. Rune stood for a moment, and he watched her. Her lips moved a bit when she read, and she twirled her finger in her hair. The desk lamp angled in such a way that she had a halo of light behind her head. She looked like an angel.

Rune swallowed, and he stopped to say hello to Mrs. Krall at the desk. "Hello, Rune," she said, barely even lifting her eyes from her paperwork.

He cleared his throat when he approached. Catarin looked up with a smile already on her lips. "Hello! I worry you not come!" she whispered. "Please sit!"

And Rune sat down where she motioned, not across from her, although that would've given Rune more room, would've made him more comfortable. But she had motioned for the seat right next to her, and Rune couldn't seem to find it in himself to disobey her.

"What are you reading?" he asked, his low voice more vibration than sound when he tried to keep it quiet.

Catarin closed the book to show him the cover, keeping her finger on her page. Rune smiled when he saw what it was. Hemingway's *The Sun Also*

Rises. She was a serious reader. He had known she would be. "I read first in French. Now I try English. You have read?"

Rune nodded. "Yes."

"You are my . . . English helper. *If* I need the help." She looked at him with such a playful expression that all Rune could do was smile and wonder what he had done right in his life to deserve the sunshine from her gaze.

"Of course," he answered. He pulled his copy of T.S. Eliot from his jacket, and he tried to find his place. He did. He then read the same poem four times without understanding a word, as he sat next to Catarin, aware of every one of her breaths, each movement, a tiny sigh as she worked over some turn of phrase in her mind.

"Why are you smile?" she whispered, elbowing him in the ribs.

"Why are you smiling?" he corrected, and he realized that he *was* smiling. Sitting there smiling like a fool.

"*Alors?*" she asked, and he stole a glance at her face. Her dimples. She was smiling too, and she was teasing him.

"I like being here," he said, following it up cowardly with, "The library is one of my favorite places."

"Why?" She put her elbow on the table and rested her chin in her hand. She leaned toward him then, and her hair fell on her shoulder, and Rune caught a whiff of lavender.

"The stories and poems, they have . . . happiness, heartbreak, trials," Rune said, feeling the blush rise in his cheeks. "It's good to know we're not alone."

"You . . . feel alone?" she asked, her voice so quiet, her accent like music.

"Sometimes," he answered.

"Not now?"

"Not now."

She turned back to her book then, with a nod, and Rune did too, his eyes reading, his mind reeling.

• • •

IT BECAME HABIT. THEY MET at the library the nights that Rune didn't tutor, although some Fridays Catarin and Inger went dancing, with Anders and Maeve. The girls had indeed hit it off, and they became fast friends.

Rune tried to console himself with the thought that she was *his* the other nights. On their third night together at the library, Mrs. Krall even pulled Rune aside and asked him to move to one of the tables in the back near the fireplace, for their whispers and laughing were not as quiet as they assumed. But Rune was too busy being happy about the turn his life had taken, to feel too abashed.

What he found with Catarin, at that back table in the library over the course of the fall and winter of 1932 was not just company, was not just attraction. What he found was a kindred spirit. She read Frost's "A Prayer in Spring" over and over again, and she teared up each time. She underlined one line in pencil, in her library book.

For this is love and nothing else is love

She loved Emily Dickinson, had memorized many of her poems, and she argued with Rune over Eliot, calling him inaccessible. Even *pompeux!* And Rune loved it. Every word from her mouth, every challenge.

He learned of her love for perfuming, how she used chemistry to mix *absolue* in her own private lab at her father's *parfumerie*. She spoke of her home in Grasse, France, with a longing, a wistful tone in her voice that struck a chord in Rune's own heart for the way he felt about Sweden. She'd been to London, to the Vatican, had seen the Mona Lisa in the Louvre.

There was no topic she could speak upon that Rune wasn't interested.

He helped her perfect her English, and Catarin handed him much, much more. Aside from his brothers, she was his first real friend.

She introduced his mind to Carl Sandburg, specifically a poem "A Father to His Son" that damn near put into words every question, every yearning in Rune's young soul. How had he missed this gem? This Swedish immigrant himself, who seemed to speak so specifically to Rune's heart?

But what really got Rune, what he couldn't believe, was when he read aloud Whitman's "O Me! O Life!" to Catarin.

O ME! O *life! . . . of the questions of these recurring.*
Of the endless trains of the faithless–of cities fill'd with the foolish;
Of myself forever reproaching myself, (for who more foolish than I,
and who more faithless?)
Of eyes that vainly crave the light–of the objects mean–of the
struggle ever renew'd;
Of the poor results of all–of the plodding and sordid crowds I see
around me;
Of the empty and useless years of the rest–with the rest me
intertwined;
The question, O *me! so sad, recurring–What good amid these,* O
me, O *life?*
Answer.
That you are here–that life exists, and identity;
That the powerful play goes on, and you will contribute a verse.

When it was finished, Catarin sniffled. She looked at him in the eyes, and she said, "You will contribute a verse, Rune. Of that I am certain."

And Rune's heart skipped a beat because that's exactly what he wanted out of life. To contribute a verse.

Rune had found his other half.

Catarin had pressed herself into a space in his life, and she had molded exactly into it, like it had been waiting there for her, and only her, for a very long time.

And Rune felt the space next to him fill, press against him, warm him. And he was thankful.

Catarin. She became the first thing he thought of when he woke in the morning, the last thing he thought of before his mind wandered off into the oblivion of sleep. And he was aware, back in the recesses of his brain, that there was a part of him that wanted to make plans, to put a name to what they were, to . . . hope.

But the rest of Rune, the practical Rune, the real Rune—not the dreamer—he wouldn't let himself.

This was enough.

To have her near him.

To watch the words come forth from her lips. To hear her French accent roll over the hard Rs of English. To listen to her jingle bell laugh, see the arch of her neck when she threw her head back and really laughed.

She was the one who suggested they meet in the meadow, when the spring finally broke. "We won't need to be so quiet," she said.

She brought the braided Swedish *kaffe* cake that Inger had taught her to make, and she brought a blanket for them to sit on, and books to read—a bottle of a new scent she had mastered in her lab. She had wanted his opinion. Rune had brought nothing. But that romantic Rune, back in the far edges of his brain, wanted to call this a date. He wanted to use this as evidence to the stubborn, practical Rune.

He wanted to call out to the world, "Catarin Guillet is my girl!"

But practical Rune always won out. He made Rune stand in front of the chipped mirror above the washbin in their tin shack, and he made himself stare at his asymmetrical face, the sharp angle of his nose, the forever-shadowed chin, no matter how often he shaved, and the sad, blue eyes that no one usually noticed, because it was the eye, with its forever dilated pupil and its ravaged eyelid that drew people's attention. He knew that.

He was ugly.

Catarin made him feel like he wasn't.

But all Rune had to do was stare in the mirror, and then turn behind him and see the handsome, untouched profile of one of his brothers. He knew.

He couldn't kid himself.

The physical mattered.

He and Catarin, their minds were a match, a glorious match. But she was small and delicate, round and soft, red-lipped and always smelled of freshly cut lavender, with hair the shade of barley at sunset.

Rune was Rune.

And he understood what he was not.

He understood what turned the gears behind things now: the heated, relentless longing that a boy, a man, could have to press his lips and his body to a girl. *The* girl.

The throb that he would wake to in the morning, the want, the sheer force of it, what he wanted to do, it kept him from keeping his thoughts chaste.

He let his mind wander once or twice. Only just. He didn't want to be dishonorable, but it hurt, both inside his ribs, underneath in his heart, and then, of course, in his loins.

He was fixated by the back of her neck. When she wore her hair in a braid, he would get a glimpse of the nape of her neck, the bare stretch of skin there, and that's what he thought of often, drifting off to sleep in his bed. The beautiful, creamy white of her skin, and what her shoulders would look like bared. The curve of her bare back as she would look over her shoulder at him, eyes half lidded in lust.

Because certainly girls had at least a taste of this desire too, didn't they?

They must.

Or babies would never be made.

Marriages never forged.

The world wouldn't go around.

So. Of course, Rune understood that in this way, he could never be what she, Catarin, dreamt about each night. She was, indeed, his mind's other half, his body's dream, but Rune knew that he could never compete against the other boys who must take her dancing on Fridays with Inger—who must look pristine like Anders.

With their unblemished profiles.

Their hand at her waist.

Rune could barely think on the subject. For it incensed him.

So Rune told himself to be thankful for this. For the moments in the library, the way she laid her hand on his cheek when they read in the meadow. The sound of her voice saying his name.

These were more than he had a right to, and these were the things that would sustain him.

Chapter 25

"COME ON, RUNE. THINK ABOUT IT AT LEAST."

"No."

"You keep stashing away all your money, in the lutefisk can under your bed. Yes, we all know it's there. What are you saving for?"

Rune stopped polishing his shoes, stood stock still for a moment, angered, agitated, which was not usually the case in how he felt with Anders. But Anders had become worse lately, out till all hours and living wild. Rune had heard rumors too, from Miss Vendela, from the blind man at the railyard who sold apples. Anders was running with the wrong crowd. And Rune knew he needed to keep the money safe.

Isak had warned him.

Plus, Anders wanted Rune to come work with him, for the Thranes, of all people. Rune sighed. "I'm not sure anymore what I am saving for," Rune finally answered.

"Really? Or do you just not want to tell Gunnar and me?"

Gunnar lifted his head from his washing. "Rune, don't get mixed up with the Thranes."

"I think I was saving it for a trip to Sweden," Rune explained. "Or for a rainy day." But his brothers weren't listening now.

"Gunnar!" Anders said. "Why do you have no problem with your other brother being mixed up with the Thranes?"

"You wouldn't listen to what I say anyway," Gunnar offered. "And anyway, you can handle yourself with those guys. Rune . . ." He let his voice trail off. Anders had quit the railroad a few weeks beforehand, and now he was working for the Thranes. What he did, Rune didn't quite understand.

But much of it seemed to have to do with meetings and gambling in Miss Vendela's front room, being out to all hours, and wearing brand-new expensive suits. Rune didn't know how Anders afforded these suits. He didn't want to ask. He figured it had to do with the Thranes. Everyone else in St. Paul was getting poorer. Not Ian Thrane.

"Well, Sweden or not, Rune, you could get there twice as fast if you threw your hand in with the Thranes."

"I like the railroad."

"No you don't," Gunnar interjected, spreading out his shirt on the ironing board.

"You wouldn't stop working there, Rune," Anders explained. "You'd come out with me and Ian, do a few hours here and there. Be the muscle."

If the money had started to sound good, if he had started to be swayed by the idea of showing Gunnar that he could handle it too, the door definitely closed on it when Anders said that: the muscle.

Rune didn't want to be the muscle. He didn't want to be a coward, true. But he didn't want to be anybody's heavy either. Rune liked to think he had sharper weapons than brute force.

Rune said, "Either I'll go to Sweden or maybe I'll go to university. But I don't need any money from the Thranes."

Neither Anders nor Gunnar had any immediate response to that. After a long moment, Anders clapped him on the back. "You should, Rune. You should go to university. What would you study?"

"Poetry."

"Of course." Anders let out a gruff little laugh and Gunnar shot him a look. "Two hundred and twenty pounds of brawn and the guy wants to *rhyme.*"

Gunnar threw his iron down then and he took a few steps right toward Anders, grabbed him by the collar. "How about shutting your mouth once in a while?" He pushed Anders and let go of his collar.

"Jesus, cool it, Guns. Rune knows I'm only teasing."

Gunnar shook his head. "Get out of here."

"You know I was just giving you a hard time."

Rune went back to his shoes. "Get out of here, Anders."

• • •

IN THAT SUMMER, THE SUMMER of 1932, Catarin mastered English, and Gunnar finally asked Inger to marry him. Uncle Isak sent a short note and fifty dollars to the brothers, with a Canadian return address. Anders went a little wilder, and most importantly, most life-changing, and maybe not unexpectedly, Rune, well, he fell deeply, deeply in love.

If at first, he held back, tried to keep himself from falling too completely for Catarin, now it was a moot point.

She favored the color yellow for her dresses. She was an only child. She was fascinated with the new synthetic fragrances that some perfume houses were using, yet also thought it was a kind of "cheating." Her left dimple was more deep-set than her right one. She loved lemon candies. Her coffee was always just black. And she smelled endlessly of a lavender field, all cool and calm and delicious.

She had six freckles across the pale expanse of her nose, between her wide-set blue eyes, and her hair had a way of fraying into a halo of frizz around her face, no matter the weather. Her cheeks were round apples, her eyes squinting into half-moons when she smiled. She was smart, capable, yet delicate too. Confident, but complicated. She had moments of insecurity with the new language at times, and in keeping up with Rune on their hikes up the bluffs.

She worked afternoons in her perfumery lab, and once in a while at the brewery's stables, taking care of her Percheron, not to be paid, exactly, but because her father thought it was a good use of her skills, and good for her constitution, she said, cryptically. She had also said that the peace of the horses, their *sérénité*, was good for her.

She often met Rune for coffee afterward, smelling of sweet hay, her light sweet sweat, and of course, lavender.

She loved to talk about the West, ideas of travel and seeing the Grand Canyon. She sang Billie Holiday songs off-key and mumbled to herself when she made the old-world braided coffee cake for Rune and his brothers on Sunday morning in their kitchen. Anders always begged her. He said she did it better than Inger.

Catarin got along well with Inger too, baking their Swedish delicacies or little French cookies called *macarons*, filling the Folkeson home with good smells, familiar smells, and new sweet ones as well, giving Rune an ache, so tender, so strong, something felt as if it pressed against his ribs from the inside. His heart swollen with affection.

She laughed hard at Anders' jokes, she admonished him for his crazy hours and wild, pin-striped suits, his slicked-back hair and the way he spent most of his paycheck on cigarettes and that ever-present, ever-illegal moonshine that all the clubs pretended not to have.

She checked out so many books from the library, many Rune had already read, and when she would leave her library book lying around, Rune would take the small blue card out of the front pocket, where it held her signature with that little flourish at the beginning of the C, and Rune would look at the card, running his finger over her signature. Often, her name would be directly below his, and he liked how her name looked so close in proximity to his. Sometimes, they were the only two readers to have checked out a volume, and Rune loved those cards best.

A few times, he checked out books directly after her, just to scrawl his name directly beneath hers.

Catarin Guillet.

Rune Folkeson.

He liked it very much.

Sometimes she signed her library cards with her nickname, *Lolotte Guillet,* but he didn't like that as much. Lolotte meant petite or small, and although she was, she loomed large in Rune's life. She was a powerful person in personality, in intellect, in vitality. Catarin seemed to fit her better.

He liked her so much, it was a punishment and a reward at the same time, to see her, to feel his heart thumping in his temples at her presence, to feel his hands become slick with sweat, his body aware of hers always, his skin taut and alive in her presence.

She awakened him.

He loved her, everything about her. He lived for her, the moments they had together. But, of course, he never told her this.

Everything was strictly above-board and platonic.

She became part of their Swede Hollow world, a friend to all the brothers, close with Inger, part of their social structure, part of their days.

But she became Rune's world.

He was hers, his mind, his heart. Even his dreams were hers—both bright shiny dreams of tomorrow, and dark, unbidden dreams of things unspoken.

• • •

"WHY DON'T YOU ASK HER ON a proper date?" Anders prodded one Saturday evening, as he got ready to go out on the town, his hair slick with pomade, his new trousers held up by jaunty suspenders. He looked like something out of a Sears catalog, so handsome, with his dark blue eyes, and this new swagger.

Rune couldn't exactly put a finger on when Anders had grown into himself, when that small, tearful boy had turned into this man before him, but Rune was glad for him. Even though, sometimes, in an odd moment, a stolen moment, Rune would see his brother, maybe on a Sunday morning, in nothing but his boxers and undershirt, smoking a cigarette and looking out the window, and he would see something cross his face, some kind of private worry in his brow, and Rune would be reminded of that small, sensitive boy he was, underneath all of the bluster.

Rune would know then that his suspicions were right; that some of this new Anders was just an act. One that seemed to be working, but an act just the same.

"She would never go out with me," Rune said, dismissing the idea of asking Catarin out properly, before even giving it any serious thought.

"She goes out with you all the time, Rune. To the coffee shop, to the library. This is nothing to asking her out, but a declaration of intentions."

"If I had intentions, I surely should meet her parents."

"I've heard her ask you to do that, to see the perfumery."

"That's different."

"No, it's not."

"There is something there, with her parents. She is . . ." Rune didn't know quite how to put it into words. He worried that she didn't want Rune to meet them, not really, because, well, Rune was Rune. But in his heart of hearts, he felt there was more to it.

"It is odd that she has so much freedom. Don't you think? Without her parents knowing us, knowing Inger," Anders said.

Gunnar joined the conversation then, pouring himself a cup of coffee. "Inger has met her parents. Doesn't like them."

"Really?" Rune asked. He was glad at this; his intuition had told him so.

Gunnar shook his head. "Inger said they are . . . hoity-toity, that they want Catarin to be a debutante, that her working in the perfumery is a bone of contention."

Rune had gathered as much.

Gunnar went on, "But Catarin gets her freedom bargaining over something with them. Inger said she has to agree to see doctors? She couldn't get the details. I thought you'd know." He looked at Rune.

Rune didn't know.

Doctors?

He shrugged, but now he was worried.

"She might have asthma or any other sort of commonplace ailment. Stop your worry, Rune. I can feel it coming off you in waves already, brother."

Gunnar drained his cup of coffee. "For the record, Anders is right, Rune. You need to ask her out on a proper date. You don't give yourself enough credit. Sometimes you have to take a risk."

"You better do it, Rune. Or someone else is going to come along and snatch her right up." Anders waggled his eyebrows at Rune. And Rune knew what he was supposed to take from it. That Anders himself might just do it, but Rune knew that wasn't true, and it wasn't just the fact that he would never encroach on Rune's declared love. Rune saw Anders with his girls. With Tally Killearn from the Patch, and, of course, the ever-present Maeve from the rich neighborhood on Summit. Rune couldn't exactly put his finger on it, but he knew Anders wasn't falling in love. Not now. Not with any of these girls.

Rune swallowed, looking to his oldest brother. Anders was Rune's biggest supporter, but Gunnar, he spoke the truth. "Gunnar, do you think she will say yes?" Rune asked, his voice sounding stretched thin.

"I think so, Rune."

"But you don't know for sure."

"Of course, who knows a woman's heart for sure? You think I wasn't nervous when I asked Inger to marry me?"

"You were nervous?" Rune asked. Gunnar nodded. "But you were together for years. She was your shadow since we came here and—"

Gunnar put up his hand. "If you're not nervous, you're doing something wrong. When you find the right girl, Rune, you're nervous, because you know she is better, too much for you. You don't deserve her, you know?" He leaned in across the table toward Rune. "But you want to spend your life trying to *earn* her, right?"

Rune nodded. He wanted to earn the affections of Catarin. More than anything, and this little speech from Gunnar put words to Rune's feelings about her.

He didn't deserve her.

Rune sat at the table with his coffee, contemplating this. The minutes ticked away, and Rune knew if he didn't get moving, he would be late for work.

Anders laced up his shoes, put his hat on his head, and then he put a hand on Rune's shoulder. "Don't listen to him, Rune."

"No?"

"No," Anders said. "Gunnar—most guys—me, we don't deserve girls like Catarin. But you, Rune, you do. You're the best of us, brother."

• • •

EVER SINCE HE HAD FALLEN IN love with Catarin, Rune wrote desperately, as if in a fever. At his desk at the library, in his bed at night with only a candle glowing, at the table in the wee hours of the morning, a quilt wrapped around him, the wood in the stove beginning to spark and jump with life.

Before Catarin, he had written. It had been a tool of self-expression, a way to deal with emotions, after Mama, after everything. He wrote poems, short essays, letters to his beloved uncle.

But now, he wrote because he had to. He had so much inside him, so much more than he ever thought possible. He had thought, in many ways, he was a simple man.

He had thought that he was simple, at least, in want, in need.

Now, as he brought pencil to any scrap of paper he could find, he knew he wasn't simple in any way. He was filled to the brim with emotion, with the desire to create and love, and dream and do. All for Catarin.

Words are nil
If not for your eyes upon them

He wrote and he wrote, transcribing some of his favorite bits from famous poets just to feel their words grace his hand, but he wrote his own lines also. Tentatively, at first, but then with a strange, unknown-to-Rune abandon.

He began to write poetry always, in his mind, as he worked on the railway, as he chopped wood for the fire, as he stared into Catarin's thoughtful face, her brows pulled together as she read a particularly difficult passage in English.

A felling of heaven
A promise knocked from the sky

But his poems, he couldn't just keep them in his mind; they demanded to be written. To be brought forth into the world. Otherwise, the emotion of them, the force behind them, became too much for Rune to bear, keeping him up at night, darkening his mood, worrying his conscience.

He *had* to do it. There was no choice involved. He was always jotting them here and there: in the margin of the newspaper, upon the receipt for more coffee beans, inside the cover of the family Bible.

Rune Folkeson was in love. It deepened with each meeting at the library, each tiny new detail he discovered about her past, each new affectation he found in her mannerism, each quiet moment they shared.

Soon, he began to feel too restless with his feelings, even after the writing of the poems. It was enough no longer. He couldn't just leave them lying around the house, on scraps of paper, in margins of books.

These words needed a life somehow. They were the shaky tendrils of connection from his heart to Catarin's. And somehow, unconsciously even, he thought that maybe, maybe, if he kept weaving these threads, with his heartfelt words, they might bolster and thicken, manifest something out of nothing, and maybe Catarin might notice them. Might notice him.

It was a fool's dream, but he couldn't stop. He went on with it. He began to rip the little pieces of paper from the margins of his books, from the newspapers, and he would deposit them places. Not in trash cans or the firepit, but other places, where they could stay alive.

Under a rock in the cave where he and Catarin sometimes would seek shade after they fished.

In the small alcove of the deep tunnel under the brewery, where he had often hidden to stay away from Papa back in those early days.

Inside the bird house on Miss Vendela's back porch.

Rune felt daring.

Anyone could find them.

Catarin might. She very well might.

She could find a shred of his poetry, of his heart, and she could read those words, in her mind, in her heart, and he knew she might not even know they were his. Probably she wouldn't.

But . . . no. She would know. It was his heart on the page, and she would know.

The possibility both frightened and exhilarated him.

Rune wrote in a fever.

Notes of music, chords, and harmonies.

The melody of her walk.

The sharpened note, the point of her chin.

The words helped him live through the fever that had gotten ahold of him. Every thought, every moment, it thrummed through his veins, like a pulse, beating her name. Catarin.

Catarin.

He knew it was a futile love. She could never love him back.

But that notion, of his love being unrequited, all it did was fuel the intensity, the purity of it. It wasn't for himself, really. He had nothing to gain in it.

It was worship, almost.

I slip from my body then, seeing as the gods see
I am above, between, within,
My attention goes only to you
I find you, I find you, I find you.
I perch, I watch and worship.
For only a moment, it is worth it, to see,
To feel the heat of your blaze.

There were so many words.

This one, scribbled on the edge of a newspaper, he ripped and folded neatly, pressing it between the boards of his front stoop, a tiny corner of the paper sticking up, stubborn.

Rune left it.

He began to get reckless about it even, sometimes ripping a line from a page, and standing on his back porch, letting the wind take the paper from his hand. He'd watch it blow, twirl and rise, fall and skitter, across the Hollow.

At night, in his bed, by the light of the candle, they were often scandalous words, but he wrote them, nonetheless.

Petals, plumage, fruit
Lips, hair, tongue
Want, taste, need

That one he burned, with a match in their woodstove, and he promised himself he would get himself to church this Sunday too.

• • •

RUNE COMBED HIS HAIR, adding some of Anders' citrus-smelling pomade and he tried to take his face in. He studied, tried to judge it objectively. Was it a good face? If one could get past the scar? And the droop of his eyelid?

He could recognize his Uncle Isak's jawline, the heavy shadow of stubble that returned as quickly as noon each day even when he shaved in the morning. He had the same deep-set eyes as Gunnar, but nothing so handsome to look as if it were borrowed from Anders. No mischievous twinkle in the eye, no jaunty angle of his hat, no cocksure swagger. That was not Rune.

When he had asked Catarin to the dance at the VFW, his heart had nearly beat out of his chest, and surely she could have seen each pulse of it in both his throat and the blood vessels in his eyes. They sat under the pear tree near the river. She was mending his shirtwaist for him, as she had promised. He'd torn it the previous week at work, and she had seen his fumbled attempt at patching it.

Rune worked quietly carving small pieces of wood. The blind man at the railyard had taught him the mechanism for a puzzle box, and he was determined to make one for Catarin.

As he worked, Rune watched Catarin's petite hands as they made quick work of the patch. She shot him a glance from under her concentrated brow. She looked tired today, pale. "Are you feeling well?" he asked.

"I'm weary is all. This happens to me sometimes," she said, not meeting his eyes. "I just need some fresh air. Why are you so quiet today?"

Rune shrugged, swallowing hard. Rune knew she was suspicious. "I am hoping to finish the puzzle box soon." But this was not what was on his mind.

Anders had given Rune the news only this morning that he had heard from several different sources that Ian Thrane was planning on asking Catarin to the dance. He planned to call on her this very evening.

Ian Thrane lived up on Plank Street, in one of the Victorian houses. His father worked at the bank, had surely dealt with Catarin's own father, with his many investments. Ian Thrane was handsome, not in the Anders way, but in the unpolished, ruddy way of redheads, and he owned an actual automobile, which he drove constantly, even if he was only driving from the bank on Third Street to his home on Plank three blocks away.

Rune tried not to let his blood boil over the idea of Ian Thrane and Catarin, but it was hardly possible.

"It's now or never, brother," Anders had told Rune this morning.

Rune bolstered himself with the memory, his favorite one ever, of how Catarin had kissed him, just a peck, her lips brushed against his wounded eye, of all places, when he'd had his head bent over this puzzle box a few weeks ago.

It had surprised him.

Of course it had.

The kiss.

Her kiss.

He tried not to let himself explain it away, that it was pity, or merely friendship.

When Catarin had finished the mending, Rune set aside his pocketknife and his carving. He reached for the shirtwaist from her hand, and Catarin held onto his fingers for a minute, the pressure and heat of her skin against his made the longing that he carried secretly for her—right there, under his ribs—thump and come to life, beating out of his chest, and Rune thought that he might pass out from it, right there, under the pear tree.

"What is it, Rune?" she asked gently, her dainty little hand holding onto three of his fingers, giving them a squeeze before she let it go. He watched the blush rise in her cheeks for a moment, and then she dropped her eyes from his.

He had touched Catarin Guillet exactly two other times, not counting her kiss, but neither of them had been so purposeful, for such a long moment, and today her touch emboldened him.

He thought of Ian Thrane with Catarin in his automobile, riding to the VFW dance hall. It was too much for Rune to take. He had to act, for he knew that if not, he would regret it always, forever. He wasn't sure of much, but in that moment, with the pressure of her hand on his fingers still fresh in his memory, he was sure of this. And he heard Uncle Isak's words.

You find love like that, you seize it.

He told himself it was too bold to apply that advice to himself and Catarin. It felt presumptuous, but it was Isak's advice that pushed him to the edge.

"Catarin, I was thinking of the dance?" Rune waited then, hoping she would help him out, waiting for her eyes to come back up to his. She only nodded.

"Gunnar and Inger are going of course, and Anders will take Maeve, but I . . ." Jesus, Mary, and Joseph, he couldn't believe the sound of his pulse in his own ears. "Would you go with me? Do me the honor?"

He said it. He could now die a brave man, one who had seized his destiny, and he was so relieved, so fully relieved, that he almost missed the sound of her answer. Almost missed the way her mouth tipped up at the corners, in what? Surprise?

Could she really *not know*? Could she really have no clue as to what she meant to him? After all this time?

Surely she had to know, surely she was aware of his love for her, as it was a fact in this world, like the sun rising, and the seasons changing. It had been steadfast and dependable for so long now, surely she had to know.

But that little tilt of her head, the expression before she said that glorious word. It was even better than her answer itself. Even better than the yes.

Rune thanked her for her answer, and for the first time in his life, he babbled. He actually *babbled*. "I'll probably purchase a new tie for the dance. Maybe from the White Store or possibly Klein's."

"Will you?" Catarin asked, a smile playing at her lips.

"I'll pick you up, not meet you there. Picking you up is appropriate, not that I have an automobile, but we'll walk together." Rune felt his ears heat at that word—*together*. He pushed on. "Would seven o'clock be the best time? I believe the dance begins at 7:30. Maybe 8:00. No, 7:30."

"7:00 would be perfect."

"We will have a fine evening. Inger and Gunnar will walk with us, of course."

Catarin watched him, and Rune watched her watching him as he blathered on, and inside his mind, Rune was replaying the way she had looked up at him, that moment, that gift. It was something he would return to, again and again.

Not only had she said yes, but she also seemed to genuinely want to, had seemed relieved, pleased even. And that, that was more than Rune Folkeson ever had dared himself to dream.

But that was nearly a week ago, and as Rune stared at himself in the mirror above the washbin, he challenged that memory. The tip of Catarin's face. The pleased smile. The slight intake of breath. He twisted it, this way and that. Doubted it.

For he was Rune. The big dumb Swede, wasn't he?

Anders pushed him out of the way with his shoulder and primped himself in the mirror, now adding a little pomade to the pencil-thin mustache that was Anders' new affectation. "Don't be nervous, Rune. We'll all be there. It will be fun."

"Who did Ian Thrane end up asking?"

"Jesus, how should I know?" And then it was like Anders remembered. "Oh," he laughed. "I don't know, brother. I just made that story up that he wanted to take Catarin." Anders waggled his eyebrows in his way, and Rune stood staring at Anders.

"You dolt."

"Really? It got you off your ass, didn't it?"

"Seriously, Rune," Gunnar offered, now splashing his face from the water in the tin, cleaning his neck, his arms. "You should be grateful for Anders. Sometimes we all need a good prod."

"I'll *prod* you," Rune told Anders. But Rune was too excited to be angry. He would dance with Catarin tonight. He would hold her in his arms. He and Anders had spent the last week trying to get Rune to move to the music in some way that could be described other than plodding.

Rune didn't know if he was passable or not, but he would do his best. Jesus, he would do his best for Catarin. He thought of her small waist under the flat of his palm, her breath on his neck, and he pulled at his collar, feeling hot and nearly indecent.

He sat down at the kitchen table, looked up at his brothers. "I don't know if I can do it," he said.

"Rune, you can do it. I'm making you do it," Anders said. "If I have to watch you mooning over her anymore, and not doing a lick about it, I'm gonna drown myself in the Irish end of the crick. Now, get up and handle this like a man. Don't be ridiculous."

Anders seemed truly a little angry, and this surprised Rune. He did as he said, stood up, tied his tie, and he held onto Anders' little smirk of disappointment in him. Rune was a lot of things, but he was not ridiculous. He would have to keep himself together if he wanted any chance with Catarin.

"By the way, "Anders said, offering Rune his flask of homemade whiskey that always seemed to accompany him and Maeve. Rune shook his head, but Gunnar took a swig. "Tonight, if people are asking about me, or you hear anything. You tell them you don't know anything . . . about anything."

"About what?" Gunnar asked, soaping up his chin and dragging the razor across it quickly, evenly.

"Exactly," Anders said, giving Rune a wink.

"You in some kind of trouble?" Gunnar asked, turning from the mirror.

"Not yet, big brother," Anders told him. "Not yet." And with that answer, Anders jumped up, kicking his heels together, and turned toward the door, grabbing his hat. "Catch you guys at the hall. And Rune?"

"What?"

"Tell her she looks pretty. Girls love that."

Rune nodded. "Of course."

"You think we need to give him the talk, big brother?" Anders called to Gunnar, making him nick his chin.

"Anders, jeez. What talk?"

Anders waggled his eyebrows.

Gunnar laughed a throaty laugh. "You thinking of getting lucky tonight, little brother?" He looked at Rune.

"I'm already lucky," Rune answered, but then he understood their insinuation, felt the blush run up his neck, into his cheeks, even his ears. "You guys do that? Catarin isn't that kind . . ."

Gunnar held up his hand. "Calm down. Just listen, if you wind up, or *when* . . . whenever you do, remember this. Pulling out. Or using one of those . . ." he motioned to Anders who was now tossing a sheepskin condom onto the table. "Just be prepared. And know this, anytime you do, it could mean you become a father." Gunnar looked at Rune. "Understand?"

"I understand," Rune said.

He couldn't believe this conversation was happening. The thought of this, let alone the actual words, was enough to burn his cheeks with embarrassment. More than embarrassment, with desire.

It all suddenly seemed too real. Like it was a possibility. Any of it. With Catarin.

"Anders?" Rune called. "Could I have a drink after all?"

Anders tossed him his flask.

It was to be a night of firsts.

Chapter 26

CATARIN AND INGER WERE WAITING AT INGER'S house. Just yesterday, when Rune had asked Catarin if he should arrive a bit earlier than planned to meet her parents, she had gone quiet.

"My mother worries about me too much lately," she said. "I think it would be best if we just meet at Inger's." Rune tried not to read into that too much, but of course he did.

Catarin's hair was freshly washed and fell loose on her shoulders, with the front pinned back in the way that all the movie stars wore it. She had added something else to her face, some kind of makeup, Rune figured. Her eyes were lined with something dark, and her lips a cherry red.

Her dress was a pale yellow and skimmed her waist so perfectly. In his mind, he called Catarin his *skönhet*, his beauty.

When they left Miss Vendela's, Inger and Gunnar walked hurriedly in front of them, and when Inger hooked her arm through Gunnar's, Rune playfully stuck his elbow out as well, offering it to Catarin.

She took it with a giggle, and then she was touching him. He could feel her hand as it curved around his bent elbow. The heat of her traveled through his jacket, through his shirtsleeves. It made him feel heady. "You look beautiful tonight, Catarin," he said, quickly, quietly, as they walked in the moonlight.

"Thank you," she said, and she squeezed his arm, just above the elbow. This emboldened him, and when they got to the stairway that took them up to Plank, he grabbed her hand in a ruse to help her up the rough-hewn stairs in her fancy heeled shoes, but once they climbed it, he didn't let go, and she didn't either. She laced her fingers through his, and he pressed his palm into hers.

It was fifteen minutes into the date and already it had surpassed his expectations. It was all so much more than he could've imagined, and he found that he couldn't look at her face. His bold moves had cost him that luxury.

"You bought a new tie," she said.

"I did," he answered, eyes cast down, watching the shadows of Gunnar and Inger move in front of them.

"Why did you choose red?" she asked.

"Don't you like red?"

"I do," she said. "I like any color on you."

He couldn't find his voice then, and so he squeezed her hand instead. Again, she giggled, and Rune's chest filled with such pure joy that he it took him a few seconds to register what happened next.

Up ahead of him, Ian Thrane and his group of friends pulled up to Gunnar and Inger in their car. Ian leaned out and asked Gunnar something. Rune studied the interaction. They were too far behind to hear the conversation, but Rune saw Gunnar shake his head, then throw his hands up in the air in some kind of I-don't-know gesture.

"What was that about?" Catarin asked, as they caught up with them entering into the Dance Hall.

"Nothing," Gunnar said, giving Rune a look.

"They were asking about Anders," Inger said.

Rune and Catarin surveyed the dance hall, the paper streamers, the five-piece band, the punch bowl. Catarin let go of Rune's hand when she saw some girls from the brewery stables, and she introduced Rune to them. He shook hands with each of them, and he spoke pleasantries. He watched Catarin as she bounced from group to group, saying her hellos, her sing-song voice and light twitter of a laugh rising above the din of everything to his ears. It was her voice that mattered, and he would've been able to pick it out anywhere, bad ear and all.

After several long minutes, Rune began to get anxious. Maybe this was what the dance was supposed to be to her, he thought. Maybe he had imagined the walk here, blown it out of proportion in his mind.

But when Catarin reappeared, her eyes flitted nervously away from his. "Are you going to ask me to dance?"

Just then one of her favorite Billie Holiday songs came on. Rune smiled. "May I please have this dance?" And he held out his hand. He mimicked the fellows in the moving pictures. She took his hand, and he pulled her onto the dance floor, and the noise and the people and the din, all of it fell away, and it was only her hand in his, his hand resting on her small waist, and her upturned nose tipped to his face.

"Hi," she said in a whisper. She blinked at him.

He swallowed hard. "Hi," he answered. They danced like that for a long while. Eyes locked. And when the song changed, the swaying slowed. The beat was different, more melancholy, and Catarin pulled closer to him, curled her hand up around the back of his neck. The press of her fingers there shot a thrill down his spine, and she nuzzled her cheek into that spot between his collar and his shoulder, pressed her cheek there, and Rune figured if he lived another thousand years he would never feel anything better than this, right here, right now.

After so many afternoons by the creek, walks downtown by the library, shared books at the study carrels, after all of his dissections of her body language around him, all of his guesswork, his insecurities, his worries, she was here, in his arms. Could he enjoy it? Let it be them, in this moment, without worrying that it meant nothing to her?

Because it scared him how much it meant to him.

He thought how this was the secret, the thing that grown-ups never told you, that parents never let on. It was all around you: this power that lit things up around you, kept things in motion, motivated people, exacted change, leveled mountains.

It was that attraction between man and woman. Sex.

It made everything go around.

But then, as the dance ended, and Catarin stood up on her toes, and she brought both her hands to Rune's shoulders and kissed his cheek, sweetly, tenderly, just a brush of her lips across his stubbled jaw, he went momentarily weak in the knees.

Lost. Grateful. Strong. Virile. Hopeful. So many things, and suddenly he realized that he was wrong. It wasn't sex or attraction or hormones that were powering anything.

It was deeper than that, and as he looked down into the deep blue of Catarin's eyes, he knew that it was instead *love.*

This was the depth of his feeling for her.

It was most certainly unrequited, foolish even, but it was true. His ribs ached with it.

He loved her.

"Thank you for coming with me tonight, Catarin," he said. He brought her hand to his mouth, and he kissed the soft skin of the back of her hand. And she stared at him, smiling. She took a deep breath, opened her mouth to say something, but then Gunnar was there.

"Come with me," he said, and something in Gunnar's voice made Rune listen.

"I'll just be a minute," he said to Catarin. He held up his finger in a just-wait gesture. And he let Gunnar pull him by the elbow back toward the rear exit of the dance hall.

"It's Anders," Gunnar said, hissing out their brother's name. "He's in a whole shitheap of trouble, and he never told us. We gotta head him off before he comes in here, or he's going to truly get the beating of his life."

"What's going on?" Rune asked bewildered. "By who?"

"Thrane," he said. "Anders has been cheating him." Gunnar lowered his voice, met Rune's eyes. "You know he sells bootleg for Thrane's pop, who happens to be a lackey to Old Man Lassiter? You know that, right? That's big time."

Rune nodded. He had suspected, but he didn't really know that. "Well, he's been skimming the money off the top. Charging more, keeping it for himself. Jesus," Gunnar said, running a hand through his thick blonde hair. "How could he be so stupid?"

Gunnar pushed open the back door, and Rune and Gunnar stepped into the cool night air, and before long, an early model-T crunched over the gravel drive. A tipsy Anders and a red-lipped Maeve got out, and Gunnar wasted no time.

"You can't come in here," Gunnar snapped. "They're waiting, the whole lot of them. They're likely to string you up on the telephone pole. And please tell me this business with Lassiter isn't true."

"Oh, they're full of hot air."

But the rear door opened then, and it was Thrane, and Smith, Cleary and McMillan. They were angry, their shirtsleeves were rolled up, and they smelled like a brewery.

The color drained from Anders' face, and the swagger left his step. "I'll pay back every dime." One of Thrane's gang grabbed Maeve roughly from behind, holding her at her elbows.

Gunnar stepped forward. "Let her go. Let's talk about this. Anders is good for the money."

"Your brother is a pansy and a liar."

Thrane moved quickly, with the off-balance movements of someone who had too much to drink. Anders' attention was on Maeve, his head bent to hers, saying something, and he didn't protect himself at all. The punch to his gut came with a deafening thud. Anders fell to his knees.

Gunnar was on him in a shot, an uppercut to Thrane's chin, and then

Rune saw the guy with the leather jacket kick Anders hard once, twice. Then he reared back for a third time.

Rune didn't make a decision. Rune just moved. First, Rune pulled the kid off Anders, sending him backwards onto his butt with a right hook. Rune turned and it was a combination to the belly of the guy working over Gunnar, and he knew the one holding Maeve was right behind him. He sensed him. He grabbed Rune around the neck, but Rune was too big, too powerful. It was like these other soon-to-be men were nothing compared to Rune. Rune towered over them, outweighed them by at least twenty-five pounds. It was a losing battle, but of course, they came back for more. Between Rune and Gunnar, they kept them at bay, wearing them down.

Maeve hovered over Anders, as he lay unconscious. But Gunnar and Rune kept brawling until they backed off, one by one, all except for Cleary. He came at Rune with a broken bottle, and Rune reacted. He caught him with a sharp fist to his throat. Cleary went to his knees.

From the corner of his eye, Rune saw yellow, just as he finished Cleary off with a punch to his jaw.

He turned then.

On the steps to the rear entrance, he saw Catarin. She stood open-mouthed. She looked—and Rune's entire body went numb with the look of it—she looked *scared.*

Of the fighting. Of the police sirens wailing in the distance.

Of *him.*

Rune shook his head. "I just . . ." He took a few steps toward her, but she put up her hand, just a fraction, a little, tiny gesture.

And Rune stopped. He looked where she was staring, at his own hand, the bloodied knuckles. And he took in a shaky breath. His knees knocked beneath him. "No," he started. He couldn't find the words to explain. This wasn't him. This didn't usually happen.

But as he searched for the words, the magic words that might turn back time and put him back on that dance floor with Catarin, back in her arms, he came up empty.

She looked green now, sickened. Her hand went to her brow. He moved so slowly, like moving in a dream. He couldn't get there, couldn't reach her. And when he was almost there, just another step or two, he watched her eyes roll back, with only the whites visible. And then her body shook. No, it jarred and jerked, spasmed.

And then it crumpled, as if it were made of nothing but cheesecloth, or linen. She crumpled, standing there on the dance hall steps. He caught her just before her head hit the concrete.

He held her to him as she jerked and moved, convulsed and shook, some kind of horrible dance to some kind of silent, torturous music. Gunnar waved over one of the police officers, who in turn grabbed a paramedic.

The rest of the moments were a blur, a frightening, heart-in-his-throat blur, and he didn't realize that he'd been crying, not until the ambulance itself rounded the corner to the hospital. And that was when her body finally settled and stilled, the tiny muscles in her face relaxing, her fists unclenching. It was then that Rune heard himself sob, a small cry, caught in his throat, caught in there with all of the tumultuous emotions of the evening.

The best and worst night of his young life.

Chapter 27

HE HAD NO TRUE CONCEPT OF TIME, EXCEPT that it stopped and stretched out, turning the scene at the gravel lot into an eternity, a purgatory, a burning moment he would have to live in forever. He was trapped there, in his mind, as he sat in the hospital waiting room. The worst image replayed in his mind: Catarin, her eyes rolling back, her body quaking.

He watched what he assumed to be Catarin's parents come in frazzled and grim-faced. They disappeared quickly into Catarin's room. No one called for Rune, gave him any information. Gunnar silently joined him in the waiting room, a hand on Rune's shoulder.

They sat there for what seemed like hours. As the sun came up and the nurses changed into different nurses, Gunnar cleared his throat. "You should go into the washroom. Clean yourself up." He looked purposefully at Rune's knuckles.

And it was then that finally Rune found his voice. "Is Anders okay?"

"He was awake when I left him. Just got clocked is all. His jaw will be sore today. Maeve will take care of him."

Rune nodded and stood, went into the bathroom. He scrubbed hard at his knuckles with the pungent powder soap in the bathroom dispenser. He washed his face as well. He smoothed his angry hair, and he made himself look at his reflection. Really stare.

He needed a shave. He had purple smudges underneath his eyes. It was the same face he had stared at before the dance, the same scar on his eyelid. The same person. But he had been able to trick himself somehow.

To convince himself he was something *other*.

That he was that man that Catarin sat with under the birches, listening to him read poetry. That he was the man who chose a red tie and kissed Catarin's hand. The man worthy of Catarin's smiles, that glint in her eye. The one who got to press his palm to hers.

Rune pressed his face into his hands, and he tried not to replay the image of her body turning on itself, the tight and angry constrictions of her muscles. What had the paramedics called it?

A fit.

Surely he had brought that on. Surely he was responsible. Surely that's what happened to a girl like Catarin when she saw the boy who read her poetry, the boy who had kissed her hand, when she saw him beating someone half to death with his fists, his face surely contorted into some kind of monstrous sneer.

He wasn't anything but a monster. A big dumb Swede. Bigger than everyone else. Uglier. Stronger.

As much as he had tried to deceive himself, he was Papa, wasn't he? The same as Folke Kasparsson. The enemy.

For the first time in his life, he did not feel like Isak's son.

Rune grabbed hold of each side of the sink, gripping it hard. "*Röv!*"

He had to get Catarin to see him, so he could apologize. He had to do that; he hoped she could afford him that courtesy. And then he could let her go. He wouldn't bother her anymore.

He would let her live her life of poetry and flower petals and perfumes, of horses and beauty. The kind of life someone like Rune could only watch from the outside, but not the kind of life he could ever *have*. How could he have kidded himself?

Rune rolled the bloodstained cuffs of his shirt to his elbows. He took off his tie and pocketed it. He undid the first button of his collar, and he gave himself one last glance. He looked as respectable as he could right now.

When he got out to the waiting area, he saw Gunnar standing, speaking with Catarin's parents. Her father held on to Gunnar's hand with both of his, but the mother stood back a bit, wringing her hands. She was a small woman, with a straight back, perfect posture, expensive clothes. Her eyes narrowed into slits when she spotted Rune.

"There he is," Gunnar said as Rune approached.

Rune bent his head forward in deference, trying to make himself smaller, a habit so ingrained in him, he didn't even think about it. "Rune, we've heard so much about you," the father said, and he shook his hand. Next, the mother held out her hand and Rune gripped it lightly. The mother said nothing.

Rune said nothing.

Gunnar cleared his throat. Rune knew he had to speak, knew that this was expected of him, but there was so much inside him, and he didn't know how to apologize for it.

"Is she okay?" he asked, his voice a shaky rasp. And before he knew it, the tears sprang to his eyes, and his one bad eyelid, it couldn't blink them back that well, and one fell. He was so embarrassed. Real men, real Swedes, didn't cry.

He brushed at the tear with the back of his hand, and then he found he couldn't stand. He apologized, but he sat down on the waiting room chair, and before he knew it, Catarin's father was next to him, a hand on his shoulder. "Son, she is fine. I thought she told you. This happens sometimes."

"She has the fits, you know? It is a . . . condition," the mother said, her first words to Rune.

"Epilepsy," the father corrected. "It's merely a misfiring in her brain, not a disability. Her cognitive function is fine. More than fine." He waved his hands in the air, angry at something, someone, as if they had challenged this fact.

Rune thought on this. He had heard of this kind of thing. There had been a child back in Sweden, a neighborhood boy, who had this, though he'd never seen it in effect. Rune had never pictured it as so . . . savage.

And hadn't Catarin told him something, in her own small way. *This happens to me. I get tired.*

Rune sat, considering. "I didn't cause . . . this fit?"

"No," Catarin's father answered. "No, you mustn't think that."

"And she is . . . awake?" Rune asked. He dared not ask if he could see her. It seemed too much.

"She is, and she's asking to see you, Rune," her father said. "Thank goodness you were there. You did everything right. You kept her from hitting her head when she fell, which is the biggest fear. And of course, swallowing her tongue. But that's neither here nor there, because it didn't happen."

She wanted to see him.

He knew that her father had said more, was still talking. But this was all Rune could hold in his mind, in his heart. Catarin *wanted* to see him.

Gunnar cleared his throat again. "Rune, don't you want to go in?" Gunnar gave him a look.

"I do," Rune answered, but he didn't get up.

"I told you he wasn't *all there*," the mother whispered, too loudly. Mr. Guillet shushed her.

Gunnar laughed, a bitter laugh. "Ma'am, no disrespect, but Rune could think circles around every one of us. Don't underestimate him." By now, Rune had gained his bearings, and he stood, ready to see Catarin. He was going to get to see her, and there was a tender spot, right in his ribs that dared to whisper at him, telling him that maybe, just maybe, Catarin didn't want to just say goodbye. Maybe she wanted to see him, because he was still the Rune who had danced with her last night. He was still that man in the mirror *before* the dance, who Rune had dared to hope he might be good enough for a girl like Catarin.

But Rune tamped down that voice, refused to give it space in his mind, because he had seen how Catarin had looked at him, there on the step. How her mouth had fallen open at the sight of his bloodied knuckles, at his fighting stance, at his curled fists.

He knocked on the door with those same bruised knuckles.

"Come in." Her voice was small, and his heart skipped at the sound of it.

He stepped inside, worrying his hat in his hand. She sat up in bed, her hands folded on her lap, a light green hospital gown on, the white blanket pulled up to her chest. Her golden hair fell around her shoulders, and her eyes looked up to him brightly, but then looked away, unsure for a moment.

She smiled, looking back up at him. "Hi."

"Catarin," he began, his voice shaky. "I apologize for what you saw. A gentleman shouldn't . . . I never . . ." But he couldn't find the words, and he couldn't keep her gaze. He fumbled around trying to say what he had to say, but finally he said, "I'm so sorry." And he turned to leave, his head hung, his face contorted in emotion.

"Rune!" she said. He turned. Her face had fallen, with high patches of color on her cheeks, her eyes wet. "Can you bring me my purse?" She pointed to the windowsill, to the beaded yellow bag that she'd brought with her last night.

Rune got it for her and handed her the bag, then he turned to go.

"Who are these about?" Her voice shook. Rune turned then to see what she held in her hands. There were three scraps of paper. All of them were scraps of his poems, of his heart.

A flurry of emotions pushed up against his ribs: love, embarrassment, shame. He saw that one of the scraps was on the yellow paper he'd written on, an old playbill. He remembered that one particularly.

If you could tunnel deep
Within the labyrinth of me
Hidden under the fears, beneath the ugly, behind the scarred,
You would only find
My thoughts of you, unspoiled.

"I found one a while back, deep in the brewery tunnels, in a little alcove near the file cabinets," Catarin said.

Rune nodded, scared.

"And then I saw you place one under a brick near the Hollow ladder, and I realized they were yours. I've found five total. Who are they about?"

Her voice was harder now, demanding.

Rune swallowed. He couldn't lie to her. Surely she thought he was so far from a gentleman. Surely she was angry with him. But, Rune couldn't lie to her. "They are about you, of course." He couldn't meet her eyes. "I apologize."

"Don't apologize!" she said, exasperated. Then her voice got so quiet. "I *want* them to be about me." His head snapped up then. He met her eyes. She was crying now. "Rune, don't you want me now . . . ?" Her face crumpled. Her voice became a whisper. "Is it because of my *fits*?" She spat out that last word like it was poison on her tongue.

Rune took a step toward her. It took a long moment for his mind to catch up to what was going on here. He had been so sure that he was unworthy, scarred and unfit, too imperfect for such a girl.

He watched her dab at her eyes with a tissue, her little face contorted in emotion. Could she possibly, truly, be thinking that he would ever, ever feel too good for her? That *she* might be imperfect?

He saw then that this was exactly what was going on. He cursed himself for not being able to see past his insecurities. And he let his doubts go. He turned them loose. Just like that. A decision.

He would not let his own insecurities keep him from giving her what she needed. Because he could see what she needed. He could see her truth, and he knew if he did anything in this world, it was that he had to make her see, could spend his whole life making her see, that, *no, Catarin, there is no one more perfect than you.* Fits or no fits.

He closed the distance to her bed, and he fell on his knees next to her. He reached for her hand, and she for his. He grabbed it, pressed it between both of his palms, and he looked at her, leaned toward her, their face inches from each other.

"You," Rune said, his voice low, twisted with emotion, "are perfect to me." He wanted to look away from her eyes, to tilt his bad eye away from her. He felt his own imperfections too acutely, but he knew that she needed his steady gaze. She needed to believe him. "I could write a thousand poems about you, and it would never be enough."

He needed her to believe him. More than anything in the world.

She cried then, with a jagged intake of breath, and her little face crumpled. She took her hand from his, and she pressed them to her face, crying. "Rune," she said, through her tears.

Rune knew, then, her heart, seeing her emotion, seeing how much she cared, knowing she wanted this, wanted him. He couldn't believe it, but he saw it now, in the way her shoulders shook, in the relief that flooded her face, how she smiled at him through her tears. Rune understood that she had been trapped in the same insecurity that he had.

He wore his plain as day, on his face, but hers were hidden, waiting to come out, ready to sneak out and ruin her. In her eyes anyway.

Once Rune had this puzzle put together, things became very clear to him. He was emboldened. He could be brave for her.

When she dried her eyes, and she grabbed his hand again, he leaned closer still, and he whispered to Catarin, his sweet Catarin.

"Don't you know I am in love with you, Catarin? Deeply, foolishly, desperately in love with you."

Her breath caught. She fought against the tears again, but then she brought both her hands to Rune's face, and she brought him closer to her. And she gently kissed his good eye. Then his scarred one. She lingered on it, let her lips press against that sensitive scar. It was Rune's turn to shudder with a sob, but he caught it in his throat, and when she pulled back, he pressed his lips to hers, gently, so gently.

"Rune," she said, his name a prayer on her lips, and she kissed him back. "*Mon chou.*"

Part III
Alice

Chapter 28

SERENA AND I SAT ON OPPOSITE ENDS OF MY BED, leafing through magazines. I ripped out each of the perfume samples, then mentally deconstructed each one down to its original components, their respective ratios, even whether or not they used absolutes or synthetics.

I knew that if I checked, I'd be surprisingly close. My previous life had left me with a perfumer's nose, among other things.

"Miss Alice! You have a visitor!" Mrs. Signy called from downstairs.

I looked up at Serena. "Who in the world?"

"Well, you have to go down," Serena said, shrugging. "What am I saying? I gotta go too." She tossed her magazine on the bedside table.

"But who could—"

Serena scoffed. "Please, Miss Molly probably invited over half of St. Paul for tea and erotica, telling them to come meet us, you know?"

"Yeah, I'm sure you're right." But I thought I knew who it could be. Maybe.

I'd run into Eli exactly three times over the last week. Once, I was at the historical society, then at the St. Catherine library, and again at the Starbucks on Summit. (He took his coffee black, only black ever. Of course he did.) I'd chatted with him quickly each time, but I'd abruptly shut down any inquiries into my strange reaction to finding that poem in the tunnels with him. I couldn't get into how I'd clammed up about it, barely holding in my inner freak-out.

I didn't want to talk to Eli about it, at all.

And I found it difficult to lie to Eli. There was something very honest in the way he looked at me, and I had this natural inclination to give it right back to him. So, avoidance was the name of the game.

But St. Paul was a little big town, and I found that when you were studying history in St. Paul, Eli Braithwaite was kind of everywhere inside it. When I was at the St. Catherine Library, I had many sources spread out on a table, notes on the Hollow, hand-drawn maps of the tunnels, and I was deep in thought, making plans for visiting the railroad station.

I recognized his voice. I heard a laugh, and recognition prickled at me. There was something so attractive in its smoky depth.

Then, he appeared as if from another world. Gone were the jeans and t-shirt. No, he wore a three-piece navy suit, his hair slicked back. But the truly appealing part was the engrossed look he had on his face as he stared down into the face of a little girl, a tiny elf of a child, all owl eyes, dark hair, and ears that tipped out at the top.

He walked right by my table with his daughter, her hand in his. His body leaned over toward her a bit, and he bent his head as he spoke to her. And I watched, so transfixed.

"Hey," I said before I could stop myself. It was like I couldn't help but get up from my table and insert myself into what they had going on between them, this sunny moment between father and daughter. I felt . . . compelled.

He saw me, and his reaction was a good one. He looked surprised, stopped in his tracks, and nodded his head, like, *Of course*. I didn't know if that meant, like, *Of course you're in the library*. Or, *Of course, you're going to meet my daughter*. I couldn't tell.

"How are you, Alice?" he asked.

"Good. Fine." I gave the little girl a smile. "Hello."

He spoke to her. "Persi, this is Alice, a friend of mine."

"Hi," she said, staring at the floor, and she held her hand that wasn't in her father's clasp, right in front of her mouth when she spoke. I could tell right then, right there, that she was desperately shy. I understood. I had been that child once.

"Very nice to meet you, Persi," I said. She nodded, still no eye contact.

"We're here to stock up on books," Eli offered. "Persi is going on a weekend trip with her mom, so she needs a lot to keep her busy."

I guessed her to be about eight. "Have you read *Matilda?*"

She shook her head.

"Maybe we'll try it," Eli said. "Good to see you," he said, and with that, he led her toward the children's department. I watched them leave, Eli's big frame, stooping over toward Persi's little body, deep in conversation. And I felt strangely left out, strangely upset with myself that I had avoided him all week. And, I guess, I was upset that he didn't try harder to engage me. When I'd run into him the other times, he was all about asking me questions, bringing up the poem, even asking if I'd been down in the tunnels since.

But today, well. It was like he'd given up. And to be honest, it didn't sit right.

I hadn't been able to stop thinking about Eli since.

So, I was hoping it was him who was interrupting my pajama party with Serena.

We were in our pjs already. It wasn't late, probably 9 PM, but Serena and I had been busy with our individual projects the past week, and we hadn't had much time to catch up. So, Serena had suggested a magazine, wine, and chocolate slumber party. And I was all in, but really, I spent 90% of the time with Serena feeling terribly guilty for not telling her about my discoveries.

My past life.

I felt dishonest. Disloyal.

I had the ivory pocketknife, the scrap of Rune's poetry, and even the puzzle box shoved in my suitcase. I was a terrible, terrible liar.

A worse friend.

But . . ..

Anyway, we turned the corner in the hallway to the top of the staircase, and the thing is, I knew it was going to be him.

No, I didn't know it. I *hoped.*

He stood at the foot of the stairs talking with Mrs. Signy, as if they were old friends. They probably were, weren't they? He tilted his head back and laughed at something she said, and my heart did this little lift.

Oh, to be so comfortable in my own skin.

And the sight of his bearded chin and neck thrown back like that, it did something to me.

"Who is that?" Serena asked, with no small amount of lust in her voice.

And at the sound of her voice, he looked up, his eyes barely catching on my gorgeous head-turner of a friend. "Hi," he said. He didn't smile, but his face, the gruff exterior, it softened a bit. He'd let his beard grow fully in.

"Hi," I said, but I didn't make a move to walk down the stairs until Serena gave me a little push.

Mrs. Signy's voice called up to us. "Serena, there was a . . . something in the kitchen that I just imagined that you . . . um . . . Just come on."

"Ha!" Serena said, and as she walked past Eli, she stuck out her hand. "I'm *the friend*. Serena."

"Very nice to meet you," he said, shaking her hand. But after just a beat or two, his eyes were back to me.

And then we were left alone in the foyer. I leaned onto the carved-acorn newel post. And I tried not to stare at how handsome he was. I knew he wasn't actually perfection. I told myself to tally his imperfections: his nose had a bump at the ridge, and his brow was heavy. His hair was cut short but not styled. His jeans were raggedy, and his eyes . . . Jesus they were beyond beautiful. The eyes of a thinker.

To be honest, there was something between us, and it was kind of electric. I wanted to be above that, felt myself too much of an intellectual to admit it fully, but it was there. That something.

But now he was looking at me, brow furrowed, practically scowling. Now that it was just us, he was back to his grumpy façade. And I didn't know what to make it of it exactly. My back went up, and I was ready to snark at him, but then I realized something.

Maybe he wasn't grumpy at all. He was something else.

His eyes skittered past mine. "So," he said.

Was I making him nervous? Was he shy? Like his daughter?

Could that be it? Was Eli's grumpy façade simply nothing more than his time-worn attempts at disguising his shyness?

"I um . . ." He cleared his throat then, pressed his hand to the back of his neck—a nervous gesture?—and I further thought that maybe I was on to something here. Was that it? Was Eli Braithwaite simply . . . *shy*? "Alice, I didn't want you to spelunk on your own. Seemed like a dangerous idea. I came over to make sure you weren't . . . doing that."

I looked down at my jammies then. "I'm in my pajamas," I said by way of answer. "I won't be going anywhere, not tonight at least. I haven't . . . since . . . with you."

"Well, I suppose you still won't tell me what spooked you so badly about the poem we found the other night."

"No, I won't."

"Okay, well, maybe it scared you enough to keep you out of the tunnels by yourself."

"Maybe," was all I offered.

"So, this was a wasted trip."

"At least you got to see Molly," I teased. "You keep popping over here and she might think you have a thing for her."

"Hmm. Maybe I do."

He looked at me then, up from under his furrowed brow, and suddenly, I didn't know if we were talking about Molly anymore.

He'd walked up the first few steps toward me, during our conversation, and I suddenly couldn't meet his eyes. It was then I spied a backpack sitting on the foyer floor, near the umbrella stand. A blue backpack.

His?

"Oh!" I said. "You came here to spelunk with me *now*?"

He nodded. "Well, yeah . . ."

"I thought you were stopping here to tattle on me, warn me off, because you didn't need your research project getting shut down because of another stupid tourist getting stuck in there or—"

"I'm not worried about my project, Alice. And," he said, clearing his throat quickly, "to be honest, I'm not that worried about you either. You're smart, capable. You'd be safe. I just thought . . . I kind of wanted to . . ." He ran his knuckles over his beard then, and it took me a moment to realize that this supremely confident-seeming man, was . . . uncertain . . . nervous?

He spoke, his eyes not leaving mine. "I wanted to go back to the tunnels with you. If you wanted to." He cleared his throat. "Do you want to?"

Just then Serena appeared in the foyer again, under some pretense of putting an umbrella back into the umbrella stand. Jesus, she was creative. She spoke to Eli, "You could take her swing dancing, I mean, if she's turning you down. She loves to swing dance."

"Serena!"

"Just an idea!" Serena disappeared toward the kitchen again, and I shook my head at Eli.

"I'm sorry."

Eli didn't say anything. He looked up at me with those intense eyes. He was waiting for my answer.

I didn't answer right away, because I found that I couldn't really put together what I was feeling. I'd had plenty of . . . boyfriends, here in this life. Romances. But they were all very . . . easy.

Safe somehow. Because I knew they weren't going anywhere.

I knew love. I knew that spark that people dreamed about. That simple yet complicated click, that instant compatibility with someone that you knew was the basis for . . . possibility. I knew that from my previous life.

And it was scary, looking down at Eli, standing there on the steps, waiting for my answer, because I knew that he was different than the other guys I'd dated. I felt a snippet of fear, because I could have something with Eli. It wouldn't be *easy*.

There was a spark.

A possibility. An intensity.

And I felt like Eli would demand honesty from me, not just small talk, not just anything on the surface. If I was to fall into anything with him, it would be serious, real. He would demand honesty, and there would be so much I couldn't tell him. And he wouldn't . . . he wouldn't let me get away with . . . what?

Anything.

Anything at all.

Suddenly, I surprised myself by answering, "I'll go change." He tipped his chin in a nod, the corner of his mouth curling up just a bit. If I would've blinked, I would've missed it.

I told myself it was because I'd finally recovered enough after holding Rune's poem in my hand, that I was ready to go back down in the tunnels, find more information, find the spot.

And that was part of it.

But was it all?

Did I maybe just want to spend more time with Eli, talking about history, listening to the rumble of his laugh? Yes, I could admit that. But I could also admit that it was an uphill climb for any guy—if Eli was truly interested.

For this is love and nothing else is love

"Porcupines?" Eli asked when I reached the second-floor landing.

I looked down at the print on my flannel jammies. "Yeah. Porcupines in love," I corrected. "Even prickly things need love too." And then suddenly, I didn't know why I added that part. I hurried toward my bedroom, but when I turned the corner, I chanced a look down at Eli. And he was shaking his head, a grin on his face.

And he was watching me.

And my heart thudded against my rib cage at the sight of his smile. Jesus.

I'd never . . ..

He was . . ..

This was dangerous.

• • •

IT WAS A HUMID NIGHT, the air close, the fireflies flitting close to the ground, blinking on, off, on, off—a telltale rhythm.

"So you've read about Swede Hollow?" Eli asked. We were walking down Summit Street, toward the Phalen river, heading into the gulley near the river, the actual site of the old Swedish neighborhood. The Hollow. Eli said he wanted to take a roundabout way into the tunnels, that he wanted me to see the memorial park, and the only structure that still stood from that time, a covered, arched bridge near the Irish end of the Hollow. Connemara Bridge.

"I've read a lot," I told him. *And I was there eighty years ago*. "It's intriguing, the story itself. The whole way of life wiped away by a fire, on purpose, no less. I'm going to include it in my research. I've even found some first-hand accounts of the decision for the controlled burn at the historical society."

"You said something the other day that made me sit up and take notice. About intertwining the history of these structures with actual human stories of loss and triumph, something about growth and death, the buildings and structures mirroring the circle of life."

I made a face at Eli. "I'm surprisingly eloquent."

"Hmm. You are."

"You liked that, Professor?"

"Well, you get into teaching for the love of your subject, you know?" I nodded, hoping he'd continue. "Then, you do this as long as I've been doing it, you get jaded by all the kids—you know the ones—who need to fulfill a requirement. Check a box." He shrugged his shoulders. "You start to appreciate anyone who looks at history as more than a bunch of dates to memorize."

"You sound a bit cynical," I teased.

"Hmm."

He swung his flashlight down and around, and he shined it in front of us, onto the grassy area that sloped downward toward the river. The light shone on an old, grown-over man-made staircase of sorts that had been built into the earth itself. Railroad ties, bricks, things I couldn't identify, they were buried within the slope of the earth, to give people traction to step on when climbing this tough incline.

"The Hollow ladder," Eli explained. "We'll have to come back here when you can photograph it in the daylight. The steps were put in by some of the earliest immigrants."

I was about to walk down into the actual Hollow.

I shivered, even though the night wasn't cool. Eli noticed, but I didn't give him a chance to ask about it.

"How long exactly have you been doing this history professor thing?" I asked him as I took the first step down the "ladder." He followed on my heels.

"Well, I got my doctorate in '94 from U of Minnesota."

I waited.

He sighed. "I'm thirty-four. Is that what you really want to know?"

I nodded. "I'm twenty-five."

"I know."

"You know I'm twenty-five?" I stumbled a little, and he grabbed onto my hand, and caught up to me, tucked my arm into his elbow.

"Molly Signy isn't stingy with the details."

I laughed then, and the corner of his mouth turned up. He led us the rest of the way down the ladder.

"I'm sorry to hear that your mother passed recently."

"Thank you."

"Your father still around?"

"No, it was only ever my mom and me."

"Even harder," he said. "I only ever had a father, and it was . . . difficult when I lost him."

I nodded, embarrassed by the tears that threatened. "My mother was . . . singular."

Eli asked, "What does that mean?"

I shrugged. I started to answer, but then said, "Actually, I don't want to talk about her."

I watched as Eli bristled, and then suddenly I wanted to take it back. But he spoke, smoothing over the moment, "My father could be a mean bastard, but I still miss him."

I nodded, and I could tell Eli was waiting for more information, for me to volunteer details about my mother.

I didn't.

"You have brothers and sisters?" I asked.

"An older brother. You?"

I shook my head.

He continued, "I have an uncle too. He's getting up there, but he's still around. Lives in Eden Prairie."

I was having trouble focusing on what Eli was saying though, as we were down the steep slope now, and on level ground. I swung my flashlight around, and I took my first real look at the Hollow. It was a great green expanse. A community park now, with a kids' playground off toward the east, where I assumed the river curved, a swath of cattails and prairie grass growing near the edge. A shadow of something hung over the water, further south down the river's edge. I wondered if that was the covered bridge.

A cobblestone walkway meandered around the area. Old-fashioned streetlights modeled to look like gaslights lighting it up, with cozy wrought-iron benches dotting the path. A handful of picnic tables sat under a small pavilion. Up ahead of us, an older couple walked the dimly lit path, hand-in-hand.

I tried to imagine Rune here. Anders. Gunnar. Inger. I tried to wipe away everything that was here now and picture the Hollow back in the day.

Where had Rune's tin-roofed house been situated? I spun around, looking. But I couldn't get my bearings. North toward the bluffs? Or was it further down the river?

I couldn't see the layout in my mind's eye. With so many things, my mind had details trapped and cemented on constant replay, but with other things, my mind was stingy. This frustrated me.

Just like I'd always known I'd come to America, from France, but not exactly where.

I mean, shouldn't I know this place like the back of my hand? I wanted to be able to stand right in the spot of Rune's porch, where I'd watched him carve the puzzle box.

I wanted to see and touch that earth, feel it under my palm.

You could hear the river in the distance, a hush of white noise. I closed my eyes, let the sound of it soothe over my exposed nerves. I pushed my mind to remember, but there was no forcing it. An owl hooted in the distance, and I opened my eyes, spying a structure off to the far end of the park.

"What's that?" I asked, thinking of how I'd seen this structure before, when I'd been looking out from the tunnel opening above, up in the bluff.

Eli turned and in the soft light of the streetlight, he cocked an eyebrow at me, and I liked the way it made me feel. Like I was in his confidence, like he was the master of a lot of the history here, and he would let me partake.

"That is Swedehenge."

The wind was soft, breezy, the air humid, sticking to my skin like a memory.

Eli continued, "The rocks, it's kind of a memento to all the immigrants who lived here, struggled here." He led me closer.

There were a dozen large rocks set in a rough circle around the center monument. Each rock probably weighed a couple hundred pounds each. How had the people gotten them here? By machine? Surely, they couldn't have been carried. Some of the rocks were gray, boring. But a few of them were striated with silver, maroon, black sparkling deposits of some gem-like mineral.

What was it that the maker of this monument was trying to convey? Remembrance?

Was the artist marking that, yes, people had lived here, died here, suffered here. It was worthy of remembrance. Of respect. Of mourning?

My hand went to my throat. Something was sneaking up on me, a memory, a thought, an idea. Something. The hairs on my neck prickled. The wind teased at them. And I realized that right here, right now, that Rune had helped build this memorial.

I just knew.

His roughened woodworker's hands, his drooped eyelid, his loping walk.

Rune as a middle-aged man.

He existed here, in this gully, and this took my breath away.

This. This is what I wanted.

To feel that I was here with Rune. To *know*.

Rune's feet walked this earth. Here.

He helped to move these rocks. To honor the life he had here.

I looked up at Eli, saw the softness in his eyes. He thought I was emotional over the monument. I was.

And I wasn't.

"Come on," he said, reaching out his hand for me to take. "Let's get into the tunnels. I know that's where you really want to go."

I nodded.

I did. I really did.

"If you don't mind climbing a little bit, we can go in over here, by my old fishing hole."

Chapter 29

America, 1933

MY DRESS WAS COMFORTABLE. I THANKED THE *fashion gods in Paris and New York City for their invention of the drop-waist shift. I breathed in and out, easily, with no corsets or under garments made for discreet torture.*

The piano player in the grand ballroom played a festive Christmas tune, and I walked easily among the guests, nodding here and there, clasping hands with the older women, giving air kisses on both cheeks. "And how is Florencia?" I said, hating how my voice sounded so much like my mother's, but I knew this was something I could never miss. The Guillet Christmas Party was a must, especially as we were new to America, and this was a social entrée.

I spotted Gillian in the corner and I waved her over. She wore gold dress on, in the same general style as I did, with a fancy, feathered headband on her newly bobbed white-blonde hair. And so many rhinestones. Everything about her sparkled. "You look happening," I said.

"So do you," she said, "but when do we get to cut your hair?"

"Soon." As a slender boy, whose very rich father had business dealings with mine, came up to both of us, I said, "Good evening, Pascal."

Mother appeared as if from nowhere, her lipstick perfectly red on her perfectly pouted lips, her face freshly powdered and rouged. "Well, Catarin," she cooed, "do you know Pascal?"

"I do."

"The band has just finished setting up," Mother said. "Do dance with us," she intoned, laying a hand quickly on Pascal's arm before she disappeared into the crowd. And sure enough, as if on cue, the bass player pulled his bow across the strings of his instrument, tuning a note to his ear.

The main singer counted, "a un, a deux, a trois–" *The band joined in with a flourish. The crowd came alive on the dance floor. I was trying to come up with some kind of excuse. Could I excuse myself to use the bathroom? Could I–*

Then Pascal reached his hand out, but not for me. "Gillian," he said, "would you like to dance?"

Gillian lit up like a Christmas candle. "Of course, as long as Catarin doesn't mind."

"No. Of course not," I said, and although I was relieved. I was also . . . annoyed that my mother wasn't there to see this. She needed to know that even Pascal Monparte didn't uphold the line between the classes anymore. Especially in America. Even he was free to dance with his own choice. True, Gillian was only a notch below us, if you prescribed to all that silliness. She had no lineage though, so this was scandalous. Pascal might as well have asked one of the aproned waitresses to dance.

Oh, how I'd wanted to invite Rune.

Since the hospital, since the introductions, life had become . . . more difficult. Maman wasn't pleased with my choices, but I had my bargaining chips.

I would only see the doctor, do his fancy brain-reading tests, partake in his tonics, if and only if I kept my freedoms. I was eighteen years old. I was in love.

I watched as Gillian and Pascal took to the dance floor.

I took a flute of champagne from one of the tuxedoed waiters, drinking it down in one gulp, the crisp surprise of the bubbles always making me want to inexplicably giggle. I stood there, tapping my patent-leathered foot, thinking of how I would write Martine-Marie about this night, how I would detail the entire evening for her, from the gold and silver crepe streamers and mistletoe decorating the doorways, to the light dusting of snow on our beloved fields, to the funny flapper dances that even the mothers were trying out.

I knew I would also tell her of the dance, not just the Charleston or the waltz, but the other kind, the one of society, of rules, of liberties limited by the pull of corset strings. The give and take, ebb and flow of the classes, the sexes, the keeping of the ancient rhythm and rhyme of upper-crust patriarchal society intact.

Martine-Marie had a baby boy now.

I didn't have to dance with Pascal Monparte if I didn't want to.

I stole another flute of champagne from a silver filigreed tray and fled the ballroom. I grabbed my boots and cloak, and I rushed out the servants' entrance.

On my way to Rune.

Chapter 30

THE TUNNELS SEEMED DISQUIETED TONIGHT, like something was coming, the feeling akin to an incoming thunderstorm. I didn't like it. Didn't like the pressure I felt on my eardrums, the hum of some kind of energy just out of my perception's reach, the twitching feeling of déjà vu that threatened with each step further underground.

"The poem," Eli said, as we hiked deeper, "from the other night. You knew who wrote it?"

For a second, a moment, before I answered, I thought he was asking me the real question. Did I know *whose hand* had written the poem? And my stomach had dropped at the thought, the idea, that Eli knew my secret somehow. But then I understood.

"Of course. It was Emily Dickinson," I answered.

"You like poetry?"

"No," I said.

"No?"

"I love it, Eli."

He stopped then, opened his backpack and took out a bottle of water, handed it to me. I drank greedily, handed it to him and he did the same.

He wiped his mouth with the back of his hand. "I like it too. I like things that get right to the point."

"Most people wouldn't say poetry gets right to the point." I laughed.

"Maybe I misspoke. I don't mean that it gets right to the point." He tilted his head and thought for a moment. "I like things that get right to the important things, to the heart of what's at stake. No bullshit."

I nodded. I liked this theory. "What are the important things?" I asked before I could censor myself. I moved my flashlight then, away from his face, and I surveyed the tunnel around me, suddenly feeling too brash.

I didn't miss his shrug though. He moved his broad shoulders up and down, a coward's answer, but maybe, then again maybe, it was an unfair question. Especially when I was holding so much close to the vest.

He threw his backpack back on, started to move forward again, but then, surprising me, he answered my question. "I'll tell you what's important: good coffee. Wisdom. Courage. Moderation. Justice."

"Ah, of course. The Greek virtues. Plus coffee."

"I have trouble with moderation," he said. "In terms of coffee."

I laughed, following him through the tunnel.

"And cheese. I really like my cheese." But then he added, "The Greeks though. They . . . forgot one. Love. Yeah, love, most of all, which is really only shown in selflessness."

I followed him in silence for a while, turning his answer over in my mind.

Love, most of all.

Selflessness.

Who was this man? And how did he cut through it all? So easily, and why did I feel that sting of emotion behind my eyes?

I asked, "Wasn't it Plato who said that love was the cure for our wound? The wound of human nature?"

"Ah," Eli said, "a student of the Greek. So close, but it wasn't Plato. Aristophanes wrote that."

Suddenly, the tunnel curved hard to the right. He slowed then, and he motioned for me to stop. "We have to jump down here."

"Again? Didn't we do this last time?"

"Last time it was just a shimmy or a hop. This . . . ah, it's a jump. See, that's the thing about deep underground caves, sometimes you have to move downward to get into them."

He shone his flashlight in front of us, to show the abyss below. This drop was bigger than the one the other day, twenty or twenty-five feet.

"I'll jump down first, and then I'll catch you. Make sure you don't land badly."

I nodded. I would need help with this jump.

Eli did just as he said, making a smooth landing, but when it was my turn, after I'd passed him my backpack, tossed down my flashlight, and I was standing on the precipice, I balked.

"I won't let you get hurt."

I laughed this scoffing laugh that reminded me instantly of Isabel. She laughed at me like that when I didn't want to speak to her newest boyfriend that she brought home. When I'd stare at the ground, hand in front of my mouth, a lot like Eli's little daughter.

Isabel's laugh echoed in my ears then, and revulsion coiled in my stomach. I never wanted to treat anyone like that, with that laughing scoff.

And Eli had been nothing but wonderful to me. Ugh, I wanted to take it back, that awful sounding laugh, just swallow it down the second I heard it in my ears.

"Really," Eli said. "I won't let you get hurt."

"Okay," I said.

"Okay then."

"I'm going to jump."

"Whenever you're ready. You can trust me." He moved closer, motioned with his arms.

"I do trust you." But God, did it take all my will power to let go, to jump. I leaped then, flailing as I went down, panicking a bit, but true to his word, Eli caught me, let my body fall into his. He stumbled, but grabbed me to him, and we didn't fall to the ground.

His arms had locked around me and he steadied us. He released me when he knew I was steady on my feet. "Not so bad, yeah?"

I nodded. But I was shaking. I didn't know why I was so freaked out. I had too much adrenaline going or something. Or maybe . . . maybe it was just that with Eli it felt impossible to live like I usually did, just gliding over the surface of things, never delving in deep.

"Hey, you okay?" he asked. He gently let go of me after he'd steadied us, but I hadn't let go of him. I realized I was still holding on to his shoulders. I took a deep, shuddering breath.

"You okay?"

"I sounded like my mom," I said. "When I . . . forget it. I . . . just . . ." I finally let go of him, took a step away, leaned down to grab my flashlight.

"You could tell me about her," Eli said, as he picked up his own flashlight, began to look around the cave.

"My mother was kind of awful," I said, grabbing my backpack. "I was being evasive earlier when you brought her up. I don't know. It's a sore spot. She had a new man around every other week, a new get-rich-quick scheme right along with it, and she just . . . One time left me home alone for an entire weekend so she could jet to Vegas with her then-boyfriend, using my little nest-egg of money I'd squirreled away."

"How old were you?"

"Eleven."

"I'm sorry, Alice."

"I loved her. God, I loved her, though. And she was a liar. A terrible, vicious liar. She took me to all the museums, snuck us in the back door if it wasn't the free day. She dreamed about big things and never had a dime for anything I might need. She made me shop at Salvation Army when her dresses were new. She used to paint my nails, and she would read me T.S.

Eliot and make me watch all these old French movies. And . . . and she'd pluck my eyebrows into neat little arches, and tell me that if Rembrandt were alive, he would have me in a tutu, painting the look on my face, the curve of my shoulder. She said I had that look, of his ballerinas. That I was aching for something just out of reach." I laughed because I didn't want to cry. What was wrong with me tonight?

Why did I want to bare so much of my soul to Eli?

He didn't fill the silence between us, just reached out and touched my hand, a laying of his fingers on mine, for a moment, then two.

"If you would've told me a year ago that I'd be this sad over her passing, that I'd feel so goddamn anchorless, I don't know. I wouldn't have believed you."

"She was your mother. I get it."

I nodded. I looked around the cavern. It was huge, absolutely enormous. "What do we have here? What is this place?"

"Well, it's the dance hall."

I chuckled. "Why is it called that?"

"Because it really was a dance hall. Legend has it they'd set up a little three-piece band over there. Acoustics were great." Eli pointed toward the far wall.

"And it would be invite-only," I said, walking deeper into the dance hall, looking around. It was surprisingly empty, no junk stored here, no obvious folded-up poetry for a lovelorn historian to find. "There would be a super-secret code word to get into the door, or a secret knock! One with several steps, maybe a bird-call in there."

"You're close," Eli said. "You had to get a map. Hand-drawn on the back of a church bulletin. Only seven or eight were made, so people rounded up their friends."

"Are you making this up?"

"Nope. Well, it's legend. Urban myth. Word-of-mouth stories. So I'm sure it's embellished."

"But why would this be the dance hall when you could go to Wabasha upstairs?"

"Liquor."

"Ah ha!"

"And skin color didn't matter here. Race. Sexual preference. It was . . . progressive."

"I like progressive," I said, and as I heard the flirty note in my voice, I remembered those exact words coming from my mouth as Lolotte.

And suddenly, Eli was right next to me. "Dance with me?" he asked, offering his hand.

"But . . . there's no music."

He shrugged. "Please? Serena said you liked to."

He blinked once, twice, those gorgeous eyelashes, and I saw in those eyes that it cost him something to ask me, to be light like this, to be silly. But he did it anyway, shy or not, he pressed onward, and I appreciated it.

I set my flashlight down next to his, and they both pointed toward the ceiling, giving off just enough light. Eli put a hand at my waist, took my right hand in his, and brought it to his chest, covered my hand there, and this move. Gah!

He was a romantic. My suspicions were correct.

Love, most of all.

I had this sensation inside my chest then, like something had cracked open, a gush of something warm. Honestly, right then, swaying to no music, in this dark, hallowed space with Eli, I realized I hadn't thought of Rune for minutes.

I felt suddenly . . . disloyal.

But . . . what was I supposed to do with that information, that feeling?

Eli broke me from my thoughts, pulling back a little, so I could see the lightest flicker of light reflecting off his eyes. "My daughter loved the book, you know. *Matilda*."

"Oh," I said. "I'm so glad."

"Persi is short for Persephone."

"What a pretty name. But of course, the Greek." I smiled, then asked,

"What other kinds of books does she like?" I wondered more about the little girl. Was she a Barbie kind of girl, or a dinosaur lover? Both?

Eli chuckled. "Most people, when I bring up Persi, the first thing they ask is, why did you divorce? Or how often do you see her?"

"Oh, sorry, I didn't . . ."

He pulled back then, looked me in the eye. "No, I like it. Your question is . . . better. And to answer it. She just started the first Harry Potter."

"Ah, score."

"And to answer the other questions, her mother and I met in undergrad, nearly married at first, but it was pretty apparent that was going to be a mistake. So."

"You don't have to tell me."

He *hmmed* an assent then, and he pulled me closer. "And I don't get to see Persi enough. That's the other answer."

"I'm sorry."

"Don't be. Persi is . . . a gem."

"She seems like it."

"Any other recommendations?"

"Yeah. *A Wrinkle in Time*. She'll love that one pretty soon."

"Okay." He squeezed my hand. Then, he pushed me out, spun me away in a little swing move, and I was surprised. But I admonished myself. Why should I be?

Eli Braithwaite was full of surprises.

I sighed then, curled back into him, turned my cheek, and let my head rest against Eli's chest. I wasn't sure why or how I was so comfortable with him, but I was.

He pulled back then, spun me away from him, and brought me back into a dramatic dip. I smiled up at him, and he returned it.

But then something changed; my vision went hazy. Eli's face blurred. He wasn't Eli anymore but he was Rune.

My body was mine, but not. I wasn't really here.

I was suspended, as if I sat on my own shoulder, watching. A bird, tiny and unassuming, perched above, looking down.

I was dancing with Rune. His dark hair, his blue eyes, his face uncertain. He wore a dark suit, a red tie. And I was Catarin, with my fringed, blue dress, the one I'd found in the shop in Paris with Martine-Marie.

This memory was new to me. I didn't know it.

Rune pulled me up and swung me out, brought me in for a pretzel twist. I twirled under his arms, and suddenly, it was Eli again, his mouth turned down into a frown, watching me too closely.

I watched, as a bird, as we danced, lazily, side-to-side, then, he spun me out again, a tuck-turn, and the cavern sandstone walls turned into the tulle-draped arches of a nondescript ballroom, the tuxedoed waiters standing at the ready, other couples sashaying around us.

The bird-version of me blinked my eyes, trying to unsee what was going on.

I couldn't do it.

Then, I was back in my body.

I stumbled on the next dance step, tripping over something or nothing on the sandstone floor. I let go of Eli. "I'm sorry, I—"

His face was his own—dark eyes, knuckles worrying his beard—but then it morphed into Rune's face for a flash, a blink.

I closed my eyes, steadied myself.

My old life was there, always, just barely under the surface, waiting. I was too scared to open my eyes. Would it be Rune?

Who did I want it to be?

"Alice, are you okay?"

It was Eli's voice.

I opened my eyes. I shook my head. "I just . . . got dizzy," I lied. "I haven't eaten much today. I think I'm lightheaded."

My God, things were getting worse.

Eli looked me up and down, settling on my face, staring at me like he didn't quite believe me, but he let it go. "Let's get out of here then."

Chapter 31

LIKE ANY CHIVALROUS KNIGHT-IN-SHINING-ARMOR, he took me to his house to feed me. And I let him. I was too zapped of energy to argue. Something had happened back there, this crossing over of the present and the past, this superimposing of one life onto the other, it scared me.

In a very serious way.

I started to question my big things, huge things, like the quantum mechanics of all of this. Could my past life just reach out its claws, grab me and throw me back into it? Or could the line between the now and then, blur and smear repeatedly until I lost my bearings completely?

These were the kinds of questions that circled my mind while I sat in Eli's little craftsman house, on his worn leather couch, a Chinese food container in my lap, eating orange chicken and eggrolls, but not tasting much. I looked around Eli's family room. It was warm and cozy, all leather upholstery and natural wood, with bookshelves lining two of the family room walls. I spotted some of the classics—*Catcher in the Rye*, *Gatsby*, James Joyce even.

One corner of the family room had a toy box, but what spilled out of there too was a pile of books. I recognized the covers of the Baby-Sitters Club mysteries, Percy Jackson, a stack of graphic novels. Persi was my kind of girl.

I finished eating, and I topped it off with a sugary soda-pop, and I started to feel at least a little better, the jolt of sugar bringing me around a bit. Eli had been watching me closely, too closely, since we'd gotten here. So, when he said that there was something he wanted to show me in his basement, I agreed, quickly, hoping to avoid any of his questions.

But as soon as we started down the stairs, as soon as I could smell the sawdust, I tensed. I knew I had made a mistake.

Once we got to the bottom, I saw that the basement, which was only partially finished, held some exercise equipment and an old TV with an ancient Atari attached to it, and most importantly, one wall held a homemade workbench built into it. On it sat wood scraps, carving tools, a sander and electric saw.

"You work with wood? You're a carpenter?" It was an accusation. I couldn't help the tone of my voice. It was like I had walked into some kind of second dimension, some kind of fun house where Isabel had come back from the grave to tease me, to make me feel like I was going crazy.

Here, Alice. Here's your past life, showing up inside your real one. Have fun!

"I'm not a carpenter," Eli said.

"Then what's this?" I walked over to the workbench and I held up one of the planes.

"It's a wood plane," he said, shrugging and shaking his head.

"It certainly looks like you work with wood." I was sweating. And a zing of adrenaline had me heading for the stairs.

"Where are you going?" he asked.

"I remembered . . . I have something."

"No you don't."

"I really—"

"I goof around with wood. I'm terrible at it. But Persi likes it. I carved her a flock of birds when she was little, and . . . Why are you freaking out?"

I crossed my arms over my chest, standing at the bottom of the stairs.

"So you do carve wood. So you technically are some kind of carpenter."

"Yes, I suppose so, if you're putting me on the spot."

"Then why'd you say no?"

"I'm not, like, professional or anything. And Jesus, I guess just because of the way you asked me, like it was a cardinal sin." He had come closer now, and his hand was on my elbow. "Can you not leave?" He gave me a look then, his eyes flashing.

"I should–" He let go of my arm then, turned around.

"Fine." He sat down on the stool in front of the Atari, and he shrugged to himself. He reached over and turned the TV on. He said something under his breath.

"What did you say?"

He looked up then, and I saw a look of hurt in his eyes before he shuttered it away. It surprised me. "You're making me work awful hard, Alice. I don't want you to go, but it's clear you want to. I had some rare maps of the area, from just before 1900, and I thought we could look at them. I thought we could talk shop, you know? You could bounce your thesis ideas off me. But . . . I don't know why I'm scaring you. Or whatever. So let me walk you out." He got up then, his jaw tight, and he moved in front of me, headed for the stairs.

"No, wait," I said. "I don't really want to go. I'm just . . ."

He turned back around then, came back down. He was very close to me. I backed up so that he could come all the way down the stairs, but he still advanced. "No, finish your sentence. You're just . . . what? What's going on?"

I shrugged, tried to play it off. "Can we just skip past all this and have the impromptu date we were going to have, maybe watch a movie, maybe you kiss me, and we swap stories about our childhoods, and I kiss you back?" I tapped him on his chest with two fingers and gave him my flirtiest smile. "I thought you promised wine after the Chinese food."

But Eli wasn't smiling. No, back was the serious Eli. The near-grouch. He just shook his head. "I want you to finish your sentence. You're just *what*?"

"You're not going to let me get away with this are you?"

"No, I'm not."

He motioned for me to take a seat on the battered sofa in front of the TV. I did, and he followed, taking the stool from near the TV, sitting across from me, with a stern look on his face.

He didn't say anything, just gave me a look, like, *I'm waiting.*

"I guess I'm scared," I answered.

He nodded like this actually meant something. "What are you scared of, Alice?"

"You. This." He raised his eyebrows for me to continue. "You and me together."

"Listen, I like you, Alice. It troubles me that you're feeling . . . afraid."

I shook my head. "I'm not afraid of you." I cringed a little. If I was going to tell the truth, I was going to tell the whole truth. "That's not true," I admitted. But I didn't meet his eyes. "I'm a little bit scared of you, but I'm more scared that you make me . . . You make me . . ."

He got up then and sat next to me on the couch. He took one of my hands from my lap and held it in between his. "Look at me." He waited until I did. "What do I make you do?"

"Admit things."

He nodded, and the look he gave me, the genuine concern, everything, I could barely handle it. And his touch, the callused pads of his fingers dragging across the tops of my knuckles, it was like a balm somehow, that friction. This man.

I didn't know what it was about him.

It was like he looked at me, and he saw through the years and years of a veneer that I'd worked so hard to establish, to keep myself in working order. *He saw me.*

Not Lolotte, or Catarin.

Not Isabel's daughter.

Not the mess of constructed walls and booby-traps that I'd set up for most everyone else.

No, he saw *me.*

"You make me want to tell you my secrets," I whispered.

He let out a deep, slow breath, his shoulders relaxing. "I want your secrets, Alice. I'm not going to lie. I want them so badly."

If I turned to look at him now, my face would be right near his. I knew it wasn't the right choice. The temptation was too much.

But there was a part of me, in the back of mind, telling me not to. That I should be thinking of Rune.

I always would've been, if I was with a different guy, if I was *anywhere* else with *anyone* else, I would see these woodworking tools and I would smell this cut lumber and sawdust, and my heart and head would be back in my *parfumerie*, and nothing would ever compare to the way that Rune and his one good eye looked at Catarin, as she bent her head over her test tubes and her *clinking-clanking* pipettes.

But sitting here with Eli, with his thumb rubbing across my knuckles, his breath on my neck, his quiet sage and almond scent. And his easy, steady stillness, I . . . felt. I . . . wanted . . ..

I was Alice.

I was me, and I was no one else.

Because when Eli looked at me, it was like he saw me down to my roots, my essence, my heart note. And more than that, it was like he could never get enough, he was mesmerized, all in, and all I had to do was surrender.

I turned my head an inch, a fraction.

His brow was furrowed, his eyes soft. "Alice," he murmured, and it was permission, his gaze dipping to my mouth.

"Eli," I answered, and our lips met. Soft, so soft. A tryout, a question. Was this okay? He hummed then, a sound of pleasure, and I smiled behind the kiss. He smiled too, and our teeth clacked gently. Then he opened his lips over mine, and the kiss became new, his tongue tasting mine, his hands on the sides of my face, bracing me like I was precious. Suddenly it was a different kiss, it was him asking me if I knew.

Did I know? Could I tell? That this was rare, this sparking electric thing between us. My fingertips went to his jawline and curled into his beard.

I know, I know. I know now, they said.

When he pulled away, he pressed his forehead to mine. I heard myself give a shaky exhale. "Alice," he said. And we stayed that way for a long time, his forehead on mine, my fingertips tracing the muscles on his shoulders, the column of his neck, the jut of his Adam's apple.

He hummed deep in his throat again when I stroked his beard, and I knew that his silence, his arms around me, they were asking a question now. They were saying, *So now where are your secrets, Alice? Let me have them in my greedy, greedy paws, and I swear that I'll carry them around, treat them as million-dollar Faberge eggs, protect them like the crown jewels. Just let me have them, Alice.*

I was thinking of how to start. Somehow the decision had been made. I was going to tell someone.

I was going to tell Eli.

But just when I thought he'd wait me out, he spoke, "From the beginning, I knew you had a secret, that you held something tight that scared you."

Before I even realized I was going to say it, I did. "I think I learned from my mom and from this secret that the things I want the most . . . they're not for me."

"What could possibly not be for you?" he asked, his voice low, a grumble, disbelieving.

I shook my head and pulled back. "You know when I found the poem?" My voice cracked then.

"Yes?"

I sat up straight, and I took a deep breath. "Please let me tell you the whole story before you say anything. Okay?"

He nodded. I spread my hands out on my knees, then pressed my thumb into my birth-marked palm, a nervous gesture. I exhaled slowly.

Eli took my hand. "You know that . . . I'm *here*, whatever you're about to tell me. You know that?"

I nodded. And then I told him my story. The story of Catarin. Of Rune. Of how I had already lived and loved, how I'd already died, how I was a different person now, but not completely. I told him all the big parts, the main ideas, and I even highlighted some of the missing information, the conundrums, the questions.

I told him how Mom had sold it to me as a ruse; I told him everything.

All of it wrapped up into a succinct twenty-minute story, it wasn't much. But it was. It was too much. It was an entire life, in all its glory, just like it was only a blip on the radar. It all sounded inconsequential, yet preposterous, ridiculous, mundane, made-up, like some fairy-tale. Or a nightmare.

He listened to me the whole time, his jaw grinding in places, his chin tipping into a nod in others.

"So, now is the time for you to tell me that this can't possibly be true, that there's got to be a different explanation."

He shook his head, sighed. "Jesus."

And in that moment, I saw myself through his eyes. He knew.

Eli *knew.*

The heart of me, the mystery, the . . . story behind the regular, closed-off girl.

He stood up slowly, and he turned away from me. He stretched his arms up above his head. He leaned back and cracked his back.

Was he putting space between us on purpose? I swallowed hard and gave him a few moments to digest all this.

But I was in a near-panic.

He *knew.*

He turned back around, squinted at me. "And this happened here. In Swede Hollow."

"Yeah."

"You believe it all?"

I nodded.

"But your mother told you it was a fraud, a set-up? That doesn't sit right."

"Yep. I know. I mean why would she do that? I have no idea."

He rubbed at his beard. "That's . . . beyond anything I could . . . But I guess it makes some kind of sense." He turned and looked at me. "I'm sorry, Alice."

"Makes sense?" I scoffed.

He nodded. "Yeah. You were little, and you had all this love for a life before your mother. You . . . longed for it. Maybe she was just tired of . . . coming in second, watching you hurt for something she couldn't give you. Like by denying it, maybe she thought she was protecting you from the heartbreak of it somehow."

This startled me. I hadn't considered this. I'd only seen any of this from my own selfish viewpoint. Could Eli be right? Could Isabel truly have thought she was doing me a favor?

And also, could she ever have felt second-rate in my life? I considered this. Isabel with the red lipstick, with the beautiful flame-red hair, with all of my adoration. No, she couldn't have. Could she?

Eli sat back down next to me. "So you're telling me you're a history scholar who's had an actual previous life nearly a hundred years ago." He stopped then, looked like he was considering. "It's kind of amazing. Tough to believe."

I nodded. "I know."

"And in this past life, you loved someone."

"More than that, I think."

"More than love?" he scoffed, leveled me with a look.

How could I explain it? That I belonged to Rune? Or at least I thought I had for so long, that I wasn't a separate person from Catarin, that, at times, I was more her than Alice Grier even.

My voice was a whisper, "I'm scared I'm kinda ruined."

"Yeah? Explain that." He turned toward me, angled his body just so.

"Because I saw what true love was, the tenderness, the complete selflessness, the magic . . . the heartbreak."

He nodded then, and I saw anger flash in his eyes. He ran his hands through his hair. "I don't like to hear you say that."

"With my mother, all I ever saw was how awful men and women could be to each other, manipulative. It all seemed so unnecessary and dramatic. And not something I'd ever want." It was my turn to stand up then. I didn't even really know what I was saying, just confessing everything, or trying to scare him away? I didn't know exactly. I walked over to the workbench, with Eli's eyes on me, and studied his woodworking tools. I gave him a moment, because I thought he might be trying to make up his mind if I was just a nut.

But all of a sudden, he was right behind me. "Just one question."

I turned around. "Sure." He was so very close.

He swallowed hard, and he looked at me for a long moment. He reached out and held my cheek in his hand. He stepped closer even, then pulled me to him. He dipped his face toward mine. "Do you want to kiss me?"

I nodded. "Very much."

"Okay then," he said, and then he kissed me. His lips were soft, just brushing mine at first. But then, he was kissing me deeply, hungrily, and I was kissing him back in the same way. He lifted me then, and he set me on the workbench, so he could stand between my legs, kiss me more thoroughly.

I was proving something to myself. I wasn't exactly sure what.

And I sighed into his kiss, into the strength that was his body, the weight of my secret of my past life of my fears, all of it, for that moment, in Eli's arms, it disappeared. And I was just Alice.

Kissing this man who carved wood, who held me like I was precious, who made me see, made me feel the difference between then . . . and now.

And there was a rhythm to our kisses. A beat.

And the beat was poetry.

Chapter 32

America, 1934

THE EARLY MORNING MINNESOTA SUN HUNG IN THE sky, like an unblemished egg-yolk, full and orange, as we bent over the lavender blooms, sickles in hand. You had to get the buds only an hour or so after dawn, otherwise they were too hot, they didn't hold the fragrance. Our field was small, so small compared to that in Grasse, but it had thrived surprisingly well this first season.

"Catarin!" I heard and turned.

I turned and there he was, in his work clothes, his smile wide, those two front, overlapping teeth. My Rune. I ran to him, and I threw my arms around his neck. I kissed his cheek in greeting.

"This is a first, a hug with a sickle in hand," he joked.

I dropped the sickle on the ground, and we walked hand in hand, over toward the roundabout, where our gravel road ended and our fields began. I pulled the paper from my apron pocket.

"What do you think?" I asked proudly, opening the brochure for the lavender harvester. Here it was. The first heavy piece of industrial equipment, a complicated machine that I'd begged Father to invest in. Mr. Abraham had been on my side. He of the synthetic absolutes, knew what progress could mean for a place like this new American Guillet Parfumerie.

Rune pressed a finger to his lower lip as he did when he was thinking. He looked at the harvester. "It must weigh a ton. And does anyone know how to work the thing?"

"Not yet," I said, "but the man from the company should be here soon."

Father came barreling over the hill, from the main house, wearing his white linen suit, looking both in charge and out of place. "How are you, Rune, son?" he asked, reaching his hand out for a shake.

"Catarin here has lots of ideas," Rune said, motioning to the brochure.

"Some of them fairly good," Father joked.

I smiled at them both. "This should save us a lot of money," I said.

"Yes," Father agreed. "It should give us an edge to hire someone who can get us up to speed here. A real chemist, from New York, who can teach about synthetics, who can keep Abraham and Catarin here from damn-near blowing the place up." Father chuckled then added seriously, "She knows more than Abraham now. She needs a proper teacher." I loved how proud he seemed of me.

A horn honked in the distance, and we turned to see a large panel truck, pulling something on a flatbed trailer. The truck had green lettering on its side, Bournival Manufacturing. It rambled down the lane. Papa waved him over. "That's Anton now."

"Would you like me to go get Mr. Abraham?" I asked. "I believe he's in the distillery."

"No, no, I will go," Rune said, donning his hat. "You stay with your father." He took off in his long-legged, loping gait, and I shaded my eyes from the sun, watching.

"He is besotted," Father said, and he said it so softly, it was almost like he didn't even expect a response.

I just looked at him. My father, his eyes crinkled at the corners, his hair blond like mine, now graying at the temples. My confidante. My silent supporter. How he knew my heart without any words. Suddenly I needed him to know. "I love him, Father."

"Thank God. Because . . . the way he looks at you. He might not make it otherwise."

"We'll have to work on Maman, you know. I mean to marry him."

Father's face fell a bit, but he disguised it well, recovering.

Anton pulled up then, and he and his assistant hopped out. "Monsieur," Anton said, shaking hands with Father. He tipped his hat to me. "This is Francois, my son. He is going to help us demonstrate the usefulness here." Francois also tipped his hat in an exaggerated fashion. He was all of maybe twelve years old, and I didn't like the way he looked at me, giving me a cheeky wink, no less.

"Francois," Anton said, oblivious to his son's dramatics, "can you unhitch the machine for Catarin here?" He turned to Father. "Would you like it here? Or should we drop it somewhere else?"

"Here seems fine. Catarin?"

"Yes, we will try it tomorrow morning, after I figure out how to drive the thing."

"You?" Anton said.

"She may be small in size, but not in power. She is in charge," Father said, and I gave him a nod.

"I've driven the tractor, and I know how to drive a motorcar. Will I have much trouble?"

Anton moved to unhitch the trailer from the panel truck, and I followed, excited to have this equipment. It signaled such change for us, the beginning of something great. Something new.

My tenure at the Guillet Parfumerie.

"You will have no problem, Mademoiselle. You seem to know your way around." He struggled with the hook of the hitch, and he stood up, sweating with his pot belly sticking out in front of him.

"Yes, I do. Let me," I said. I moved between the trailer and the panel truck, and I bent over to unhook the trailer.

That moment–before the accident–played out slowly for me. I saw the lacy pattern of rust on the latch to the flat-bed trailer. I watched a drop of sweat drip from my forehead onto the dusty gray ground, as I reached for the hitch. The crunch of the gravel underfoot reverberated in my ears, and I smelled the lavender, ready to be harvested, the calm, sweet, soothing scent of our land's purpose.

It happened quickly, a terrible mistake. That's all it was. The consensus afterward was that Anton signaled Francois to move forward and he accidentally went in reverse, but how doesn't really matter. Why doesn't matter either.

At the moment I unhooked the trailer, with my left hand still placed on the ball of the trailer hitch, the panel truck reared back, with angry force, smashing my hand between the hitch and bumper.

The pain was instant, fiery hot and blinding. I heard yelling. I felt the gravel underneath me, then someone lifting me, and the grass was cool on the back of my neck. My grass. The calming scent of lavender nearby, along with the iron scent of blood.

And someone was crying, screaming, terrible sounds of agony. Before I lost consciousness, I realized it was me.

Chapter 33

"SHE'S COMING FOR BRUNCH, DEAR," Mrs. Signy explained. I was helping her set out several settings of fancy crystal and china, and I hadn't been tracking on exactly who was coming over, as I thought Mrs. Signy understood that I had an appointment at the railyard.

"Oh today? Mary Nearhouse is coming today?"

"Yes, did I forget to mention it to you? Serena said you'd be overjoyed. I invited Eli as well. I have to remember the cheeseboard. Eli loves cheese."

"Oh." I wrung my hands. Suddenly, this was a conundrum. I wanted to talk to Mary Nearhouse. Dear God, I wanted to see the love letter. But Eli too?

I wasn't yet sure what to do with this information. I didn't want to see Eli again so quickly, and definitely not in the context of the Lovers' Legend. The intimacy I'd felt with him the other night was . . . overwhelming.

"Well . . . goodness," I said looking down at my scrubby workout clothes, coming to grips with how I wasn't going to get any railway photographs taken today. I was instead about to have a very Swedish brunch with the woman who had the actual love letter found in the caves, one that could very well have been written between Rune and Catarin. I felt a bit lightheaded, as I filled up a coffee cup.

Serena flounced into the room wearing a gorgeous wrap dress, her hair piled high on her head. "Did you thank Molly for getting this altogether? Smells delightful, Molly. What can I help with?"

"Yes, thank you, Mrs. Signy." I eyed Serena, feeling a little queasy.

"Alice was just saying last night how much she wanted to hear about the letter, how she could enter that into her research. History needs some spice too! Right, Molly? Not just dilapidated old caves and whatnot." Serena sidled up to me. "What is wrong? You look like you've seen a ghost."

I swallowed hard. I'd told Eli everything.

I'd never told Serena even an inkling. But here she was, checking on me, knowing me. She could obviously tell I was not . . . *normal* right now.

How much did she wonder about? Did she have any clue? Why hadn't I ever told her anything?

I knew why.

I loved, absolutely adored that Serena loved me enough to leave me alone, to respect my boundaries.

But after last night with Eli, I wondered. I wondered if that could possibly be true. If that put the onus on the right party.

"I need to go upstairs and change," I told Serena.

The doorbell rang. "Hurry!" Mrs. Signy said, wiping her hands on her apron. "That'll be Mary. Never a second late."

I ran up the stairs and slipped into a cotton sundress and my Docs. It was a wrinkled mess, so I took it off and spent a good few minutes ironing it to perfect. Then, I smoothed out my ponytail and I looked into the mirror.

Nerves were getting to me.

Was I going to be able to keep it together when Mary Nearhouse showed me the letter?

Would I recognize it? Sob?

Would I somehow understand how the end had come for Rune and Catarin?

And just as importantly, how was I supposed to keep up this façade that this was all just a research project? Especially now that Eli knew.

He *knew.*

And he was still coming today?

And Serena didn't know a thing.

I could barely process the delicate layers of lying and omission that I would have to navigate.

And Jesus, Mary, and Joseph, now that I understood what it was like to tell someone, to feel that intimacy, this connection I had with Eli, how was I supposed to settle for anything less ever again?

How was I supposed to look Serena in the eye and think that I was anything more than a terrible best friend, keeping the dirtiest details, the most complicated connections to myself, letting our friendship only skim over the surface, never diving in, never disturbing the calm tension of the water.

I swiped on some lip gloss and slipped on my favorite sandals.

I had a feeling this whole brunch was going to be a very Swedish disaster.

• • •

MARY NEARHOUSE WAS A TINY THING, aged and wizened, especially next to Mrs. Signy's size and vitality. Mary used a walker, complete with the tennis-balls fastened on the ends. She held an enormous yellow vinyl purse that she patted when she was introduced. "I'm the town romantic. Have all my priceless preciouses in here."

I could barely contain myself.

The letter.

We sat in the parlor, and I helped Mrs. Signy pour the tea. I insisted on her letting me set the brunch items out on her sideboard, slicing the coffeecake, the fruit tart, so that Mrs. Signy could chat. She'd done so much cooking and preparation: her *vertebrod*, of course, a fragrant fruit soup, and some kind of homemade spicy sausages.

I listened as Mrs. Signy and Mary swapped pleasantries about the neighborhood, shared acquaintances, with Serena interjecting here and there. Didn't Howard Newell know his dog pooped only in Mary's parkway? Of course he knew, that was the problem.

When the doorbell rang, I stopped fiddling around with my food, and I answered it.

When I swung the door open, I wasn't prepared for the sight of Eli Braithwaite in a shirt and tie. Jesus, Mary, and Joseph. He'd slicked his hair back and he smelled like literal almonds and heaven. And I realized then, *almonds.*

Was there a deep, primitive part of me that recognized this similarity to Rune? Did it draw me to Eli?

I realized I was staring, and I opened my mouth to say hello, but all I said was "Um." Like some kind of moron.

But even though we'd left things strange and unfinished last night, even though I'd told him such deep, twisted, unbelievable secret, he stepped into Mrs. Signy's foyer with confidence, closing the door behind him, and he said my name, low. "Alice." A greeting that the other ladies couldn't hear from their perch in the parlor, although their eyes were glued.

He stepped toward me, closing the distance between us, pressing a kiss near my ear, his hand coming up around me, and resting between my shoulders blades. He held us there, the rough scratch of his beard on my cheek for a beat. Two. Three. Surely longer than was innocent.

He must've felt my smile curve into his cheek.

"Every time I'm away from you, I convince myself it isn't . . ." He didn't finish his sentence.

"What *isn't?*" I asked.

"This thing between us." His voice was right in my ear now. "I convince myself it isn't. But . . . it . . . *is*. It definitely is."

I swallowed hard, unsure how to answer. Because I did know what he was talking about. And I did agree. "They're watching."

"I know." He said. And he pulled back again, pressing the lightest of kisses to my lips.

I might have sighed loudly, and he chuckled.

"Molly," he said, turning toward the parlor. "Thank you for inviting me here. Mrs. Nearhouse, Serena, good afternoon." He tipped his chin in greeting. I followed after him, trying to compose myself. What was this Mary lady here for again?

We ate our brunch. Molly asked after Eli's uncle who lived in Eden Prairie, whom she knew from many years back. Mrs. Nearhouse asked Eli about Persi. We ate our fill of spicy sausage and Swedish pastry.

At one point, Eli explained that he had heard the best Swedish joke the other day.

"Are you Swedish?" I asked.

He nodded. "Yes, half. My father was Italian, but my mother's side is all Swedish."

"What's the joke?" Molly asked.

"The other day, I met a Swede, and he loved his wife so much, guess what he did?"

"What's that?" Mrs. Nearhouse asked, scooting toward Eli.

"Well, he loved her so much, he almost told her." Molly erupted in laughter, and Mrs. Nearhouse chuckled too. But Serena just looked at me. "I don't get it."

I shook my head. "It's a thing. Swedes are . . . stoic."

The small talk went on. And we sipped our coffee.

But I only wanted to watch Eli.

The way his eyelashes grazed his cheek when he blinked. The easiness he had with the older women, even with Serena and her DILF jokes once she learned about little Persi. I watched him maneuver through each minefield with ease, and I noticed that although he wasn't the grumpy version of himself that I'd first met at the caverns, he only had smiles for me.

He was pleasant, he was polite, but his smiles, that little fishhook of a turn that the corner of his mouth would make when he looked at me. It was almost too much to bear.

Even here, now, when I was supposed to be thinking only of the love letter, of Rune, Of Catarin. Of our star-crossed paths, I really only wanted to trace the planes of Eli's face with my eyes.

The pads of my fingers, my lips.

After coffee, Mary Nearhouse began the business portion of our brunch, which I was grateful for and dreading in equal measure.

"So Molly told me you've heard our ghost," Mary said.

"I have," I nodded. "Although we may not be able to call it a ghost much longer."

"Why's that?" Serena asked.

"Eli has a team of experts digging into that."

Eli shrugged, giving me a tiny shake of his head. I wasn't sure why he didn't want to talk about it. But I moved on.

"So, Molly tells me you brought the letter?" I asked Mrs. Nearhouse.

"Yes, darling, let me show you our Lovers' Legend's most prized possession." She rummaged through that bag of hers, and she pulled out a blue three-ring binder that had seen better days.

"When did you find it exactly?"

"1952 or 53."

My hands were itching to take the binder from her, especially as she flipped through it, and instead of handing me anything, she began to read, in her warbling old-lady voice:

My love,

Without you, I wither.

The words you spoke to me on the bridge, under the flower moon, they sustain me.

My heart constricts with what could happen to you, to us, and all because I could not be more careful about us.

You were right about it all, my love.

I will meet you in the cavern, the one above the Hollow. You know the one of which I speak. At midnight on the third Sunday of this month. We will go away.

If you, for whatever reason, are not there, my love, I will not hold it against your memory. I bid you courage, I bid you strength. I hope you know the depth of my love for you.

Stay safe.

Yours

I felt Serena's eyes on me, smiling, interested, entertained. I felt Eli's on me too, but hot and full of questions, testing my reaction. Molly sat, dotting her eyes with a scrunched-up tissue.

I understood her reaction. Especially coupled with the romantic, desperateness of the poems that were also found. This letter left me breathless.

The absolute seriousness of it. The stakes. The feeling.

But it didn't spark anything in me. I searched my memories, forced myself to block out Eli and the way my mind wanted to run with details of him instead of what was at hand.

I forced my attention on the letter.

I wasn't getting anything. Not the way I wanted. No memories came flooding back. No explanations.

Of Rune, of our split. Of our end.

"May I see it?" I asked Mrs. Nearhouse.

Mary handed over the binder. I swallowed hard and gazed at the letter. The hand was written in ink, dark from a tight grip that pressed hard, scratched deeply into the paper. The script was looping and leaned to the left. A southpaw maybe?

It didn't look familiar.

I was at a loss.

I knew Rune's handwriting, the hurried printing of the Dickinson poem. I could press my eyes closed and see his hand curled around the pencil, just in a similar way that he gripped his ivory pocketknife. I knew Rune.

This cursive penmanship was not his.

And although I couldn't quite bring up a picture of Catarin's handwriting, I didn't feel like it was hers either.

I lifted my eyes up and immediately met Eli's eyes. Whatever he saw there, it comforted him as he gave me a little nod. His shoulders relaxed a tad.

Mrs. Nearhouse spoke, "There are St. Paulites who believe the letter was a ploy, a red herring maybe, just to trap someone, to get them into the tunnels, a grudge gone wrong. You know, during Prohibition, so much criminal activity going on. Others believe it's a true love story, with hopes that they met, lived happily ever after."

"Hmm," I answered.

I flipped the page then. "Do you mind if I look through your scrapbook or is this—"

"Of course, my dear," Mary said, patting my knee. "I would be honored."

Next, Mary had a detailed map of the Swede Hollow in its prime. Then, handwritten testaments from relatives of immigrant family members.

"This is a gold mine of information." I said. "The description of the covered bridge alone is like poetry. Could I quote this in my research?"

"Oh!" Mrs. Nearhouse twittered, bringing her hand to her throat. "My goodness."

"I would give you credit in the article, certainly. And if it ever published for money, I would certainly pay."

"Well, my dear, I would be absolutely honored."

She had several black-and-white photos of children standing knee-deep in the shallows of the river, their clothes period specific, the two girls in flapper dresses, their hair cut at their chin, the small boy dressed in shortpants.

Then I turned to the last page of the binder.

I gasped.

Mary Nearhouse had one more black-and-white photo.

Sitting within the plastic sleeve of this hobbled-together scrapbook sat a photo of a young man, one who's just lost all the softness of youth.

Tall and broad, wide in the chest, with a thick strap of curly dark hair. He wasn't smiling into the photo, but looks straight at the camera, his chin tipped in a challenge.

He had his arm hanging around a slightly shorter young man who had been cut out of the frame, although you can see a glimpse of his blonde hair.

Rune's eye drooped, worse than I remembered, the scar more prominent in the photo than I recalled.

The suspender over his right shoulder had slipped some. I could remember the feel of that suspender under my index finger when I slipped it back into place, moved it back on his shoulder for him.

I became aware that I'd been quiet for a long time, that Mrs. Signy, Eli, everyone in the parlor was waiting for me to say something. A question had been asked.

I wasn't able to though.

I couldn't . . ..

It was Rune.

"What is it?" And it was Eli, kneeling next to me, looking at the photo with me.

"It's him," I whispered.

Eli looked up at me, his eyes confused. "No."

"It's Rune."

"You never told me his name, Alice."

"His brother saved me from drowning once, many years ago," Mrs.

Signy was saying, but I couldn't follow the conversation, could only marvel at the photo.

Rune.

"You never said his name," Eli said again.

"Who is this? What's going on?" Serena was asking.

I didn't know how to answer. I looked at Eli. I didn't like the tightness around his eyes, the stress around his mouth. What was it that bothered him about Rune?

"Let me show you this," Mrs. Nearhouse was saying, and she reached over then, flipping the page. "It's got writing on the back."

It was Rune's writing again.

And dear God, I remembered his love of this poem. It was Frost again.

A voice said, Look me in the stars
And tell me, truly, men of earth
If all the soul-and-body scars
Were not too much to pay for birth.

"It's his handwriting."

"Jesus Christ," Eli said, and he stood, running his hands through his hair, and he loosened the knot on his tie. I watched him, a little afraid of his reaction.

"What is it? What in the world is wrong?" Serena asked.

I flipped back to Rune's face in that photo, and I couldn't quite catch my breath. He was older here, a bit thinner. This was after I'd known him.

Eli was pacing, rubbing at his beard.

I handed the binder back to Mrs. Nearhouse, and I stood on shaky legs. "Eli?" I said, going toward him. "What is it? Why are you upset with me? I don't want–"

He turned toward me, his face ashen.

"Rune . . . that's . . ."

"What is it?" I asked.

"Rune is my uncle."

"Your uncle?"

"Great uncle. He lives in Eden Prairie. He's alive."

I tried to reach for Eli, I did. But I saw stars, bright sparks in front of my eyes, and my knees knocked.

Then next thing I knew, my vision faded from the edges, and it all went black.

Chapter 34

America, 1934

THE LAVENDER ROWS MOVED IN THE BREEZE, *all timed together like a well-choreographed ballet. They bent and swirled, giving and swaying to the silent music of the wind coming off the faraway lake.*

Catarin stooped her head, walked more quickly through the rows of lavender, toward the small orchard on the hill. She could hide there, slip away, and sit in the cool shade of a pear tree and read her book, and she could avoid her father, her mother, Gillian, the lot of them.

Mrs. Abraham waved at her from over near the small enfleurage, *where she was handing out red-and-white striped paper bags of fresh popcorn. They were celebrating the American Independence Day here at the new Guillet Parfumerie, with a fried-chicken picnic at noon, complete with a band and hayrack rides, and fireworks to come after dark.*

Catarin hurried toward the edge of the orchard, whispering under her breath, "Please, please, please." She hoped Mrs. Abraham wouldn't call out her name. She needed privacy, solitude, to nurse her sadness.

Catarin scurried farther into the small orchard, near the climbing tree that she and Rune had found earlier in the summer, the weeping willow, with its skinny hanging leaves that hung like a privacy curtain.

Catarin adjusted the leather cord of her sunhat below her chin, listening to the chatter of the field workers, of the chemists, all of them, as they assembled outside, under the tent eating their celebratory lunch. All of it made her stomach ache. She knew it had been Father's idea, the whole picnic. All of it was a ruse. A thinly veiled attempt at cheering her up, as if a picnic was all it should take.

Catarin settled herself at the foot of her tree, and she stretched her legs out in front of her. Two good legs.

She pulled her book from her apron pocket, a volume of poetry from the library. Another idea for cheering her up. From Rune. She opened the book to the stalk of lavender that served as her bookmark, but even this, this mundane everyday task, was difficult. It would get easier once her wound healed, the doctors told her. She still had her thumb.

This apparently was a blessing beyond all blessings.

She supposed they were right. She knew this in a logical way, but why did it make her want to laugh, just cackle in their pinched, doctorly faces.

Lucky? Ha!

Merde.

All of it. Gone to shit. She couldn't even open the lid on a jam jar or twist the top off of iris absolue. *How was she supposed to mix* parfum, *that delicate work, with pipettes and measurements that forced you to have such tiny, delicate motor control?*

Merde.

She was wallowing in her own self-pity. She knew it.

And she'd had so many staring spells while recovering. A dozen. More.

And they were vicious, savage, not the still-as-stone episodes of before.

There was one upside, however. She'd been disfigured for two weeks now and Mother hadn't mentioned any suitors, any teas, any dinner parties. "Maybe I should've mangled myself earlier," she had grumbled bitterly to her father.

But he had only given her a hard look, a tired look.

Catarin stared at the words on the page of her book, orderly and in line, patterned and predictable, with punctuation and capitalization. She flipped through the pages haphazardly and found a new poem, one that didn't make as much sense. Just words in different typefaces, placed oddly about the pages, no phrases, no lines, no order. Free form.

Catarin liked this; it mirrored her feelings now. But she heard the band start up, out there, under the white canvas tent. She listened as the wind brought her the tail end of laughing voices, of twanging banjo music, and the scent of the buttered popcorn in greasy paper bags.

Catarin froze as she registered a shadow, a snapping twig, movement at the edge of the orchard, just beyond the shady canopy of the apple trees.

"Catarin?" he called out. And she knew then that it was Rune. Of course it was Rune.

He stepped into view, and she hoped that she would stay invisible, hidden in the shade of the tree. She sat stock-still and watched, her breath still in her throat, her ravaged hand throbbing, a dull pain with every pulse of her heartbeat.

He stepped into her sight then, and the sun hit him just right, put him in shadow, with only his outline in view. For a sliver of a moment, she wondered if it was really him. Could she have been wrong? This man, this silhouette, was too movie-star-esque, his shoulders too broad, and his profile strong against the setting sun.

Catarin recognized his gait as he took two, three steps into the shade of the orchard, and she knew it was him. Catarin felt the rhythm of her body hitch and respond to the familiarity in his walk.

And Catarin felt the familiar connection toward Rune, the pull toward him. But also . . . an unsettling feeling. She knew that something had shifted and changed. Not in Rune himself. Not in his gait or his silhouette.

Catarin had changed. And not just her hand. But inside, the value she placed on herself. That feeling that she was worth someone as good as Rune. That had plummeted.

"Catarin?" he called once more.

She didn't answer, and in that moment, she realized something in her heart, something she had never quite admitted to herself. It was this: Before the accident, she was going to marry him. When it suited her. Marry him because he understood.

She would still run the parfumerie, *and she would still flourish. She would live a life of freedom with Rune.*

But now.

Now, she would never . . . She would be nothing now. Unable to work as a perfumer. She would be nothing.

Her self was lost, her most precious inner self, and she couldn't, wouldn't settle for an empty life, a domestic one that trapped her somehow. With coffee spoons and menu planning and trips to the modiste. She would have to find another way. Or she wouldn't . . ..

Then she would be bitter and worthy of nothing from Rune.

She watched Rune worry his hat in his hands for a long moment. But then he turned, his large form moving out into the sun, toward the lavender fields, back to the crowd and the picnic.

Catarin breathed a sigh of relief. She was not ready to see him yet, to brave his pity.

But she knew. She knew she had just seen the man, the only man, she would ever love.

Chapter 35

SERENA AND I SAT IN MRS. SIGNY'S PARLOR, in our pajamas, the guests now gone, including a thoroughly freaked-out Eli. Even Mrs. Signy had gone to bed. She let Serena and I have some privacy.

After everyone's worrying and tongue-clucking, I had finally convinced them all I was indeed fine and didn't need to go to the hospital. I just needed some time to . . . absorb. To think.

I hadn't offered up any explanations to Mrs. Signy or to Mrs. Nearhouse, but after they left, I explained it all to Serena.

It was only early evening. It felt much later. Too much had happened.

I lay on the sofa, with my feet on top of Serena's lap, who sat at the opposite end.

"I'm supposed to be a therapist," Serena said, scooping ice cream out of the container and leaning over to feed me a spoonful. Chocolate chip. "I'm supposed to be a really good one, for Christ sake. I mean, in a matter of months, I'll be licensed, and I didn't know this was going on. I mean, I knew there was something. I knew you kept some things close, but I just thought it was the depths of Isabel's neglect, you know?" She ate a spoonful of ice cream.

"I'm sorry."

She hit me with the spoon, a light tap on the leg. "You shouldn't be sorry!"

"Well, I can tell you're mad at me. I don't want you to be upset with me. I need you too much. I need you. I wish that—"

"It's just that I tell you everything. We've been friends for a decade, Alice. And you told *him*."

"I know." I let this sink in. Of course she would think of this as a betrayal. If I were on the other side, if I was her, I'd think so too. "I'm sorry."

Serena waved this away. "My grandmother, when her blood pressure would get real high, she would see this little repeating image of a chimney sweep—old fashioned top hat and tails—and the chimney sweep would dance this little jig. She'd see it just superimposed over her field of vision, down in the right-hand corner."

"Really?" I asked. I didn't know what this had to do with anything.

"At first, it freaked her out, of course. She thought it was really there. But of course, she couldn't ever touch it. It was just an image. It would disappear out of reach, fade away or dissolve, when she reached for it. But then, she started to realize it was only happening when, well, she wasn't feeling well. She went to the doctor, told them a little bit about it, reluctantly, for fear she would be put into an asylum. I mean, this was years ago. But, it turns out, she saw the right doctor—progressive enough to understand. To know. It's a thing, a diagnosis. Visual projection, a type of pareidolia. She'd seen the image sometime, in a movie, on TV, something. It was pressed into her memory, and then, somehow, some way, when her blood pressure increased to a certain point—actually, dangerously high, when she got it checked—her brain would fire up this image."

"That's supremely weird."

Serena shook her head. "It is. But that's the thing, Alice. The human mind is supremely weird, with many tricks up its sleeve. It's a machine, you know? All electrical impulses and imperfect electrical connections, synapses and neurons firing. Things mess up. There are glitches. I would know. I deal with them in their many forms day in and day out."

"So, you think that my thing, my glitch is something else. Not a previous life?"

"No," Serena answered. "I'm not saying that at all. I'm just saying that . . . I *believe* you, that something is going on. The human brain can produce some weird shit. I just had to read this case about two identical twins, how one burned her right hand, like seriously bad, talking second-degree burns, and the other twin lives like three states away, she goes to the hospital with pain in the exact area, howling so much she had to be sedated."

"Okay, but what's that got to do with me?"

"I don't know. But we don't understand *everything*, you know? Not anywhere near everything. Doesn't make it less true."

I liked that. Just because we didn't understand something didn't make it less true.

"I've read some about previous lives," she explained. "Spent a few hours watching someone participate in regression therapy in order to remember theirs. It's not that *out there*, Alice."

"I know that. But that's only when you read about it in some textbook. Like the six-year-old kid who told his mother exactly how to operate a World War II drop tank?"

Serena nodded. "Exactly. He was a Navy fighter pilot. We had to read that case. It was really thorough. Totally believable. The details that kid knew, it was uncanny." She gave me a look. "Usually, the death in the previous life is violent or unexpected. What's your death memory? How did you . . ."

I shook my head. "I don't know. I hurt my hand in *the before*, like I told you, exactly where I have this birthmark. I know that. I remember . . . the pain of that. Then that's about it. It all falls away. I remember a moment in the tunnels a bit later, a meeting with Rune. It's hazy. It was a goodbye of sorts, there was blood, and the scent of gunpowder, but I don't know. Did I maybe . . . did I die there? Or did I wallow in sorrow because of my hand, and push away Rune after I mangled my hand in the harvester accident? I don't know. I have no real death memory."

"Hmm."

I had given Serena a lot of the details, the same kind of overview I'd given Eli, and I felt exhausted. Utterly wrung out.

Rune was alive? And 89 years old?

What was I supposed to do with that information?

"You know you don't fit the profile exactly though. Most past-life memories, or what are perceived as past-life memories, fade by the time the kid is school age. That's well documented." Serena ate another spoonful of ice cream. "But you still have yours."

"I know. " I said, taking the ice cream from her and finishing off the carton. "Do you think my mother could've been trying to protect me? Did she know it was all real? She must've, right? She had the puzzle box."

"How did she get it, though?"

"I don't know. I can't seem to . . ."

"Your French back in high school. I mean, Jesus, Alice! You lucky dog. No wonder your grades always blew me out of the water. I should've suspected."

I laughed. "I know. I barely studied."

"No one understood the irregular verbs. You got 'em every time!"

"That's me. I'm a cheater."

Serena looked at me, suddenly serious. "You going to go meet Rune? Really?"

"I think I have to." God, the thought twisted my insides. Serena looked deep in thought. "So, you believe this whole thing?"

Serena tilted her head. "I'm not sure."

"Do you think it hurt Isabel? Did she feel second best? Jealous of it all? That's Eli's theory. Is that why she did what she did? So she could be the boss of me, all of me?"

"Well," Serena said, "as a therapist, I think it's safe to say that we can explain away a previous life a whole lot easier than we can explain Isabel Grier's behavior."

This earned Serena a chuckle.

"I'm sorry this happened. I'm sorry I didn't know," she said.

"I'm sorry I wasn't brave enough to tell you before. You know, you've often been the only thing that has kept me . . . sane these past years."

She nodded. "A good thing to say to an aspiring therapist." She gave me a look. "Have you investigated Catarin at all?"

"Yes. The *parfumerie* existed. I inter-library-loaned every book in the world about French perfumeries. I don't know anything about her specifically though. Or their trial *parfumerie* in America. I think that mustn't have lasted. I don't know the details, the demise of the thing with Rune. I hate it. I hate that I don't have closure. And I hate that my research has been spotty. I mean . . . I want answers."

"Well, it was a long time ago." Serena stopped, considered. "I wonder if your mother ever talked to any professionals. Maybe I could search some of our psychology databases, with some of your specific details, see if I can come up with any hits. Maybe you were written about, you know, anonymously or something. That might be possible."

I nodded. I didn't have a lot of faith in that idea. But I could see that Serena was interested.

"When I first started to get more memories, they were coming at me so fast and hard, right around fifteen, and I almost told you when—"

"Wait. You discovered more memories as you aged, like, as you grew up?"

I nodded.

"That is . . . not how these cases usually work."

"No?"

"No. Nobody gets more memories as they age. That's, like, completely counter intuitive. I wonder . . . why yours is different."

"I can't even get my previous life right."

"Hey," she said, shaking my foot a little. "Can I ask you one more thing?"

"What?"

"Does it make you hate your mother?"

I shook my head. But then I answered, "Yes. A little."

"Did you really love him? Rune?"

I waited. Then I answered, "Yes."

Chapter 36

America, 1934

HE SAT DANGEROUSLY CLOSE TO HER, HIS TROUSERS brushing the loose fabric of her dirty dungarees. They sat in the tiny round enfleurage*, recently repurposed from its days as an old grain silo. The scents of tuberose, of jasmine, of rose, edged out the stale wheat fragrance.*

It was a reunion, but not a wholly happy one. Catarin had begrudgingly agreed to see Rune. It had been nearly three weeks.

"Do you want to see it?" she asked.

"Catarin, of course I do."

"It's healing well, they say. But I keep it covered so people don't have to look at it. It's a mess. An unholy mess."

Rune gave her a hard look then, and he nodded once. "It is my fault. I took off to get Abraham. I should've hitched the harvester for you." She wanted to argue with him on this point, she did. But he took her arm from her lap and began to slowly unravel the cloth around her damaged hand. Catarin couldn't find her voice. It fled, along with all of her bluster and bravery. She struggled not to cry. She pressed her lips together hard in a line, and she let him look.

But when her ravaged hand was bare, Rune took it in both of his hands gently.

He brought it to his lips, and he kissed the fresh healing scar. He stood up carefully, still holding her wounded hand, and then he knelt on the ground.

"No," Catarin said.

"Marry me, Catarin. Please."

"No."

"I knew you would say no."

"There is no other answer I can give." Something changed in Catarin then, hardened and solidified. She wiped her tears, and she jerked her hand away from him and turned her back.

Rune sighed heavily, his breath shuddering. "You didn't return the letters I wrote when you wouldn't see me."

"I was very busy."

"With what? Ignoring me?"

"Learning to be one-handed."

"I wrote you often."

"Letters are paper only."

"I think they are more." He touched her shoulder, turned her toward him, gently, patiently.

Catarin turned to Rune and studied his face, the pity there, the horrible, endless pity. She looked away from his eyes, the pools of emotion there, and she studied his scar. What he hated about himself.

Just another thing about him she loved. Mon chou.

She wanted to explain it all to him, how he deserved better. A whole woman, a beautiful woman, one without fits, one with both hands, someone who knew to how to give, how to say yes, how to be happy. But she understood the double standard, the way that she only wanted to press her lips to his scar. To his eye. To the pink skin in the part of his hair, from the hot summer days of working the rails. "You should wear a hat," she said. "You're sunburnt."

"You will . . . adjust, and the parfumerie *will flourish with you here, and my tutoring is growing. You have to know this has been my plan, my hope. Your father has given his consent."*

"I haven't given mine."

Rune balled his fists then, brought them to his eyes, rubbed hard. "Catarin," he said, his voice thick with emotion, "is this going to be the end of us? Are these your real feelings? After all these weeks of refusing to see me, I'm inclined to think maybe you . . . blame me. Or you really don't want me."

Catarin took a step closer to Rune. She pointed her finger right in his face. "That is exactly what I am saying." But her voice broke, and Rune grabbed her pointed fingers, brought them to his lips, kissed each of her good fingers. Then, his mouth was on hers, and she kissed him back, putting her arms around his neck. He pulled her to him, one hand in her hair, another at the small of her back.

Catarin closed her eyes then, and she smelled the enfleurage, *the power of all the scents given over in that room. The tuberose, the lavender, the jasmine. And also the smell of cedar coming off of Rune. The smell of his skin, as he kissed her neck, her collarbone. She tried to unbutton his shirt, but before she could get frustrated, Rune grabbed both of her hands, and he kissed them slowly. The good one, and the bad.*

He placed both of his hands on either side of her face, and he kissed her purposefully, properly. And then he laid her down on the soft dirt floor of the enfleurage. *Catarin wouldn't agree to marry him, and she couldn't say the words he wanted to hear. Catarin wouldn't profess her love for Rune. Not now, not when she felt so . . . broken. Even when he whispered his most private nickname for her,* "Skönhet." *But Catarin's actions spoke for her heart. Her lips and her body played out the words, there on the dirt floor of the* enfleurage. *Surrounded by her most favorite scents in the world.*

Chapter 37

SERENA BARGED INTO MY BEDROOM AT MRS. SIGNY'S. I sat on my bed, staring down at the puzzle box. I had made it to Move 11. I was one away from opening it, and I was contemplating setting it on the ground and using the heel of my Doc Marten to end the suspense. "Jesus, Alice, you're not going to believe what I found."

"What is it?"

"Sit down. I had it couriered from Chicago today. Paid a mint, but Jesus, you gotta sit down." She pulled a video tape from her bag.

She pushed it into the tiny television on the boardinghouse bedroom bookshelf.

I moved closer.

Serena and I sat on the floor together in front of the TV, cross-legged. The videotape was grainy and poor quality, the sound was tinny and the production value low, but I quickly understood that none of that mattered.

A toddler, a strawberry-blonde girl bounced on a rocking horse at a playground. a serious-sounding voiceover giving a quick introduction to previous-life experience, or PLE as it was known in scholarly circles. It was some kind of documentary.

And after a few shots, especially a close-up of the girl eating an ice-cream cone, I realized the tiny girl, it was me.

Alice Grier at age three or four.

Tiny Me.

"Fucking hell," I said.

"I know. Watch. This was never aired, but . . . it almost did."

The show was certainly edited to make the audience fall in love with Tiny Me from the get-go, with shots of Tiny Me laughing, Tiny Me running and stumbling at a playground. Tiny Me was adorable and sympathetic, real and believable, and whoever was behind this knew what they were doing.

The tape then focused onto Tiny Me sitting in an office chair.

I smiled into the camera.

"I can play *le piano*!" Tiny Me said.

I heard the plucky melody of *Frére Jacques*, and then the fancy piece, the one that had made them all go silent, the one that had freaked out Mom. I suddenly remembered this.

I forced myself to look at the television, even though I knew what was coming. A sharp pain hit me in the breadbasket.

There she was.

My mother in the frame. Isabel Grier.

So young and beautiful, her red hair tied at the nape of her neck. The dress, made of silky purple material, cinched at the waist with a black leather belt. It was her only good dress.

I had buried her in that dress.

Something deep underneath my ribs throbbed.

The sound of Mom's voice saying my name. "Alice," she said, running her hand over Tiny Me's curls as I played the keyboard. *Alice,* it echoed in my head. I wanted to keep that sound in my head. Mom's voice. I didn't want to forget it again. It was like a pocket of home, found unexpectedly in the strangest of places.

Tiny Me finished the difficult piece of music effortlessly. I recognized it now as "Für Elise." In the before, I had had to endure tutors of all kinds, to civilize me.

Tiny Me hit a wrong note.

"Oh, the cow!" Tiny Me squawked.

"I think you mean, Holy Cow, Alice," Mom said. "She always gets that saying wrong."

I watched as the blonde woman came into the frame, correcting Mom, explaining the origin of that saying. "*Ah la vaca*," she explained. I remembered that. How it had freaked Mom out.

"*Oui. Ah, la vaca*," Tiny Me said.

Mom shook her head. "I need a break. Turn it off. Please," she said, and then, the camera went black.

I wrestled with myself inside. Wrestled with the ghost of my mother. Of how she had . . . what? Backed out of this documentary?

Why? How?

The tape skipped then, blurred, and came back on. Focused.

My body tensed, and Tiny Me appeared again. I sat on the blue couch, back in our old apartment on Delaney Square. I sucked on my lower lip, and I brushed a stuffed giraffe's mane across my lips, my eyes watery and wide. I had been crying.

"I miss him."

"Alice?" It was a man's voice. Off-camera. "Who is it that you miss?"

"Rune."

I stared hard at the Tiny Me, my stomach plummeting, bottoming out. Even then I had missed Rune.

"He ran for the doctor. Gillian told me."

"Show Dr. Lewellyn your hand, honey," Mom said. And Tiny Me shook her head. Mom sat on the couch with Tiny Me, whispered something, and then Tiny Me held up her left hand, palm up for the camera. The camera zoomed, and there was my tiny, chubby left-hand, a smaller version of my very own palm. The red-wine stain, jagged and zig-zagging, going from the fleshy spot between my forefinger and thumb, diagonal across the palm and up onto my fingers.

"She used to hold her hand still, in a fist, close to her chest, when she was a baby. I thought she might have some kind of cerebral palsy, a birth defect," Mom explained. "Although, in the end, they told me it was only a birthmark. She did some physical therapy, and her hand was fine."

"But this is what caused you to seek help for your daughter. Her hand, the way it looked, how she favored it," the doctor said.

Mom sucked in a deep breath and nodded. "Yes. That and the drawings. She drew the scene of when her hand was ravaged. A bloody mess on a field of green."

"And you don't know a Rune?"

"No, Sir."

"And she has mentioned him before?"

Mom sighed deeply. "If I'm being honest here . . . it was her first word."

On the television screen, Mom said something in my ear. Tiny Me scratched at the inside of her elbow, pressed her thumb into her opposite palm, my nervous gesture. Mom motioned off camera, and someone came into the frame, handing Mom her old patchwork hobo bag. She dug around inside and handed me two knitting needles, with a small ball of yellow yarn, dangling in Tiny Me's lap.

Tiny Me did it. She picked up the needles and began to knit. I mimed the motion, with my own hands, right then, there in my boardinghouse room. I did it on instinct, watching her. I didn't think. I just let my hands move. It was a reflexive memory, ingrained, something I didn't have to think about—like tying shoes, or speaking French. That's how I knew how to knit, one-handed.

I used my left hand only minimally, like a dead weight, a malformed claw. It held the needle, but my right hand did all the work.

There I was on screen. Tiny Me. Doing it as well. In the same stilted, one-handed fashion: knit one, purl two.

Like Catarin, surely.

"Why are you doing it one-handed?" Serena asked.

"It's how I learned," I explained, without really explaining. "After my accident."

On the screen, Mom watched Tiny Me. "How do you know how to do that?"

"My tutor taught me. In the before," Tiny Me said.

I was suddenly awash in memories, snippets of this and that.

Martine-Marie and I wading knee-deep in the *Riviere d'Argent*. Rune laughing as we tried to catch a tiny gray mouse in the back of the gardening shed. My piano tutor, the one with the eyepatch, and how she'd rapped my knuckles with a candy cane when I hit a wrong note.

A flashcard adorned with a blue umbrella with white polka dots. *Parapluie.*

Mom smoking a cigarette at the kitchen counter in our old apartment, a stack of those flashcards on the counter. She was just trying to keep up with me, keep up with my French. That's all.

There was no sinister ruse.

My heart had known it for so long.

It was all true. Mom had taken me to be interviewed by these specialists, to star in this documentary, but when it was all confirmed for her, why did Mom back out? Why did she pull the plug?

The tape went to static again, and I stood, pushed the OFF button.

"I think . . ." Serena said, "maybe it just scared your mom. Maybe we're being too harsh toward Isabel."

I flopped on the bed then, and I laid my arm over my eyes, and I cried. Because I thought maybe Serena was right.

"Have you heard from Eli? Has he set the meeting up with Rune yet?"

I didn't take my arm away from my face, I just shook my head. "I'm scared, Serena. I'm not even sure I want to anymore."

Serena plopped on the bed then, curled up next to me. "I know. I know."

"I don't know what to do with any of this."

"I know." Then she chuckled. "We could always go on Jerry Springer."

I sat up and hit her with a pillow.

Chapter 38

"HE PUTS THE RADIO UP HIGH LIKE THAT when he's crabby and doesn't want to talk," Persi said.

"Does he now?" I asked.

I was happy to be sitting in the back seat with Eli's daughter. When they'd shown up at Mrs. Signy's, I was glad. I needed to end this torturous waiting, this in-between. I'd been here for years, really. A lifetime of the purgatory.

I knew I had to meet Rune Folkeson.

I was both ready and not. How could I ever really be prepared for such a task?

Cosmically, I knew it was fated, destined, and I was thrilled. But also, dreading it. What in the world was I supposed to say to him? I mean, he was alive. Flesh and blood.

Rune.

Eli's own uncle.

When I had answered the door, Eli had seemed polite, all business, his eyes skittering from mine. I was so relieved to see he had brought Persi with him, I nearly hugged her. She turned this entire dramatic event into something bearable somehow, especially since her shyness seemed tempered. Apparently, my reading recommendations had done much in the way of endearing me to her.

She sat next to me in the back seat, her dark hair braided into two French braids that fell over her shoulders. They were immaculate, and I kept wondering if Eli had done this for her this morning.

But he was . . . quiet. Looking exactly like he was fighting a surliness about this whole matter.

Eli.

I wanted to reassure him. But what was I supposed to say?

Who was I to him anyway?

But God, he was so unbelievably wonderful with his daughter.

When we were getting into the car, I had made a move to sit into the front seat. Persi had made a little noise, like a startled squeak, and Eli froze in the movement of getting into the front seat.

He sighed. "Would you mind sitting in the back?" he asked me, his eyes not meeting mine, his mouth setting in a hard line. "It's important to Persi." He lowered his voice then. "She . . . *worries*."

Persi had heard him though. But she didn't seem to mind. She leaned her face between the front car seats and spoke up, "The passenger seat is also known as the death seat. I saw it on 20/20."

Eli scowled. "I don't know why your mother lets you—"

"I don't mind at all," I told Persi. "I prefer it actually." So I got out and I resituated myself into the back seat, and I didn't miss the look that Persi gave her dad, something akin to I-told-you-so.

Anyway, that was how Eli ended up turning the radio up too loud. But Persi and I talked about books, anyway, just pitching our voices a tad louder.

"But my favorite one so far has been *The Girl with the Silver Eyes*, because I like magic. I might even like it more than Harry Potter. But I don't know. I'm like that. I like too many books. Have too many favorites. Mom says I'm fickle. But I don't think so. Do you ever have trouble deciding because you like two things so much, and it's hard to pick your favorite?"

I looked up then and I saw Eli's eyes meet mine in the rearview mirror.

I wanted to look away. I did.

But I couldn't. It's like he caught me there, held my eyes against my will. But eventually, I broke away with a blink. "I know exactly what you mean, Persi."

"Dad bought this car because I worry," she offered. "It's the safest one on the market, according to Kelley Blue Book and Better Business Bureau."

"You know what I do when I worry a lot?" I offered.

"What?"

"I write my worries down, the worst things I can think of, and then I fold them up real tight into the tiniest little scraps of paper. Then I make myself stare at them, those tiny scraps, and I tell my worries with a real mean face. I mean, I squint my eyes and scowl real hard and I tell them, *I'm bigger than you*."

Persi nodded at me, and she tried out her mean face, pinching it all tight. "It's like a metaphor."

"Ha!" I said. "Yeah, something like that."

This time, when I caught Eli's eyes in the rearview mirror, I saw that he still had his clenched jaw, his somber expression, but something in his eyes smiled, just a tiny bit.

I grinned at him.

• • •

WHEN WE PULLED UP TO THE condo complex, I tried not to freak out. I really did.

But Rune was here.

In this world.

In this time.

Not some parallel universe that only existed in my memory.

He was living his life here just a few hours from Chicago, growing old. All these years. Still remembering Catarin?

Thinking daily of her?

Hating how it all ended?

How had it ended? And why? I still didn't know. I was so very nervous, thrilled to meet him, this man who had loomed so large in my life. This perfect, idealistic version of love that I had upheld in my mind for so long. Frozen in time and memory, unable to be blemished by real life.

I mean, I wasn't silly enough to think that I would meet him and I would feel . . . that same . . . feeling. He was sixty years older than me. And I was literally a different person now.

But at one time, a time so close to my heart, we weren't different people at all. We had been in love. And Rune, he epitomized what a man could be. Especially when I only had Isabel's oft drunk and ridiculous suitors to compare him to.

That wasn't true though, was it?

My eyes shot to Eli as he helped Persi out of the car, carrying her little pink sequin backpack. He was silent as we walked up the sidewalk of the complex. It wasn't a depressing place, even though it was specifically made for senior living. There was a golf course attached, a swimming pool, all kinds of amenities. There were ramps, not steps, but there were also cheery window boxes of red geraniums, perfect manicured lawns.

But Jesus, Rune lived here.

My Rune.

And he had lived his entire life alone, had never married. I'd asked Eli.

What had his years consisted of? His days? His hours?

He was facing the end of his life by himself. And . . . suddenly, I panicked. I stopped short on the sidewalk, and I pressed my thumb into my left palm, and I made a little noise of hysterical anxiety.

I wanted to forget the conversations Rune and Catarin had discussed about life, about its meaning. I wanted to forget the way he looked at her, like she hung the moon.

And why had I ever let Eli bring me here?

My hands shook as I clenched my fists, my breath felt tight in my chest, and I kind of wanted to run away, but I didn't. I forced myself to stand still and reconfigure.

Everything had been leading to this. All my sorrows and trials, all the heartache, my mother's gift of the puzzle box, which, of course, I'd brought with me.

I was supposed to come here and meet Rune.

Eli had told me when he called and said he'd be picking me up that Rune knew what I claimed, to know of Catarin's past life.

Rune wanted to meet me, was a willing participant for this meeting.

He wasn't being blindsided.

But Eli warned me that he was in poor health. He had emphysema, and well, he was nearing ninety, so I should keep my expectations in check. And this meeting, this first meeting, as Eli put it, would have to be brief.

Other meetings would be up to Rune.

He'd raised horses as a second career, Eli had told me. Never married. Taught English in his younger years, of course.

Eli held the building door open for me, up ahead twenty or so feet, but when Persi saw that I had stopped in the sidewalk, that I was balking, she ran back to me, offered me her hand.

"Uncle Rune has a dog," Persi said. "And Uncle Rune is very nice, not at all like the crabby old man at the post office who sells the candy." Eli smiled.

I took Persi's hand and I let her lead me in. I could be brave. I could do that for Persi, for Eli.

For Catarin.

I walked in, and as I brushed by Eli, I caught a whiff of his almond sent. My memories went to Rune.

Rune.

Eli.

Cut from the same cloth.

Stoic and Swedish and tenderhearted.

It felt incestuous almost, the feelings I had toward them both. But I supposed there were no rules when it came to being reincarnated, when it came to remembering your soul's first time around.

I steeled myself while Eli knocked on Rune's door.

I was shaking so hard my teeth chattered. I couldn't seem to calm myself down. But as we waited for Rune to answer, sweet little Persi grabbed my hand in hers again, just as Eli took pity on me and placed a hand lightly on my shoulder.

"I'm here," he said, and when I looked up at Eli in that second, my stomach bottomed out.

Eli. Even when he was upset with me, part of this complicated unforgiving situation that he'd never asked to be in, he was . . . *kind* to me.

God, I wanted to kiss those worry lines away from the corners of his mouth.

I wanted to fling my arms around his neck and beg him to get me out of this place. In that second, that moment, he could've carried me out of that hallway, and I would've never looked back.

I could've forgotten about Rune Folkeson forever, if Eli would've asked me to.

Instead, he gave my shoulder a little squeeze and went to knock on the door again, just as it swung open.

My body went numb from the shock of him.

I expected him to be smaller in stature now that he was eighty-nine years old.

He wasn't. He had the same presence.

His shoulders a bit stooped, only a tad, but he was broader, thicker around the middle, and his face had aged with thick, deep wrinkles near his mouth, at his neck. His wounded eye drooped so much now that it was nearly closed.

He was clean-shaven and his hair was a dirty pewter color now, thick as ever, curled a bit over the ears.

His eyes. His good one.

Jesus, looking into that blue eye, the color of a spring Swede Hollow morning, I couldn't tell you if it was 1998 or 1933. They were ageless and all-knowing; they were calm and surreal.

They were sad. So sad.

Phalen Creek skipping rocks, Miss Vendela's homemade toffee, the freshly cut green grass of upper Plank homes, Rune's hand in mine on the way to the VFW.

It was too much, all of it.

"Morning, Rune," Eli said, shaking his hand, breaking me from my reverie.

"Well, you might as well come in."

His accent. The singular sharp Swedish consonants, his nasal vowels, just shy of perfect.

"It's you," I said.

He turned back around then, and he took a step closer to me, looked my face over. "You can come in and you can ask me questions, but don't try to tell me you're Catarin."

I swallowed.

My eyes shot to Eli who gave me a soft look.

"How's my Persephone Juniper?" Rune asked, as the little girl grabbed his hand.

"Is Sötnos here? I don't hear his barking. And I like his barking, not like Daddy."

"He's on the porch. Didn't want him to slobber too much on our guest."

Persi ran over to me, just as Eli and I settled onto the couch. "I will be right back," she said in a very serious voice, and I could tell that she knew I was nervous. She was looking out for me.

"Don't let him lick you all over your face," Eli said.

"Yes, Daddy," she said, and she was out the sliding glass doors in a flash, where we could see her enthusiastically greeted by a shaggy and geriatric sheep dog. She scratched his neck, and he licked her face.

Eli watched and sighed.

"You've brought the puzzle box?" Rune asked.

I nodded, somehow unable to find my voice. I slipped the box from my bag, and I handed it over to him.

"Ah, this was my first one." He sat down across from us in a recliner, and now he put on a pair of reading glasses as he examined the workmanship and details of his creation. "Not bad," he mumbled. I noticed there were oxygen canisters next to his chair, a length of clear tubing resting on the side table.

"He's made many other boxes since," Eli offered. Eli gave me a soft smile.

"So you are Gunnar's great grandson?" I asked Eli, finding it easier to ask him a question than to truly face Rune.

Eli nodded. "Gunnar's daughter Kirsten was my mother." Eli gestured for me to talk to Rune. "Rune here, he's skeptical, Alice. You'll have to tell him some of the details you know. Convince him you're not some kind of phony." Eli gave me a look of apology, and he surprised me then by reaching out and grabbing my hand, giving it a quick squeeze. I was so very thankful for that anchor in that moment.

I racked my brain with what to start with. How Rune and Catarin met? A description of Catarin's family? That first tutoring session when Anders had teased Rune into speaking with Catarin?

I stopped short then, realizing something very specific. In the past weeks, I'd started to think of Catarin in the third person.

Not the first anymore.

More and more, it was Rune and Catarin. Not Rune and me.

I wondered at what this meant, but I pushed the thought away, and rather than start with any of the stories that I'd tried out in my head over and over, when contemplating this meeting, I did something else.

I pushed up the sleeve of my cardigan, and I showed him my birthmark. Rune eyed it from afar at first. Then I moved closer, sitting on the edge of his coffee table, so he could see the birthmark.

Then he scooted forward, sat on the edge of his recliner. And he reached out, "May I?"

I nodded.

He touched my fingers, grabbed two of them to study the mottled strawberry mark.

If I was waiting for some kind of electric sparks, a confirmation of knowing, anything, when he touched me, I got nothing.

He let my hand go, and he nodded. I'd seen his first reaction, just a brief, momentary startle. If I would've blinked, I'd have missed it.

But I'd seen it. It was there.

The birthmark meant something to him too.

"I don't know *everything*," I offered.

"No, you don't," he said, his voice gruff, unfriendly, but underneath there was an uneven emotion. I knew this was hard for him. He had loved Catarin.

He had, no matter why he had chosen to leave her that day in the tunnels. No matter what transpired between them that I didn't quite know about, he had loved her.

I knew it. I believed it.

"I can remember to Move 11," I explained.

He handed the puzzle box back to me, with a "show me" gesture, so I proceeded to move the slats and pieces this way and that, getting so near the ending move, so close to actually opening it, but, yet, nothing.

"You had a kitten. Aprikos."

"A veritable sphinx that one."

"You loved Whitman and Frost. You used to read poems, when you were underneath the willow behind the perfumery."

So many things flashed over his face then, and I was sorry for what I was doing to Rune.

"I have this too," I said, and I passed him the pocketknife from my backpack. "I found it in the tunnels."

His brow furrowed, and I watched something dark flash over his face. Regret? Then, another emotion, and another. His face told a story, one so private, I had to look away for a moment. He reached and took the knife from me. "Ah," he said. "This was useful. I think I left it there, that last night . . ." His voice caught in his throat, but then he continued, "Miss Vendela . . . she kept me from the law. All of her connections. I . . ." Rune stopped then, with a shake of his head.

What did he mean? The law?

What had happened? I wanted to ask; I wanted all the answers.

But I couldn't bring myself to push. Instead, I filled the silence, moved the topic slightly. "You wore a red tie to the dance at the VFW. You bought it new for that dance."

He blinked several times.

"She tripped on the Hollow ladder, and you grabbed her hand, and you didn't let go."

He took a shuddering breath.

And here I was again, back at the question: *What happened that night?* "You made promises to Catarin, maybe not in words, but in other ways. And then . . . in the tunnels . . ."

We sat there staring at each other, Rune and I, for what seemed like a long moment, my eyes caught in his. Eli, at this exchange, stood abruptly, leaving us alone.

And I wanted to call him back. I did.

But this was Rune. Here we were, and maybe I could finally know?

I had to know.

But I did want to call Eli back and explain something about Rune and me.

This was otherworldly and hard to believe. This was all so strangely predestined, our fates so intertwined, but . . ..

But it was not romantic.

I understood something meeting Rune, saying the things I'd said to him. I was a passenger, an extra, a third wheel privy to the gorgeous, star-crossed romance of Catarin and Rune.

I was close to it, buried in its details, drowning in its drama at times.

But I was not part of it.

I was extra.

This was at once a shift in my thinking, and a sudden realization, and it was a relief. A disappointment too. Both at once, and really neither. A complicated epiphany.

I was not Catarin, although I knew her thoughts, her desires, felt myself in her skin.

"I remember your face in the tunnel. The way you wanted her to leave. I still wake up gasping for breath."

His eyes left mine. "It was the worst day of my life, those moments in the tunnel."

"Then why did you leave me . . . her?"

Rune took in a deep, shaking breath. He started to say something, but then reconsidered.

He grasped the clear tubing on the side table and adjusted it to his nose. He turned a valve on one of the oxygen canisters and took a deep inhale. He got up then and moved toward the kitchen, dragging the wheeled tank behind him. But then he abruptly turned. "Do you remember what Catarin said was wrong about the new synthetic fragrances when she first got here to America? Can you tell me that?"

I knew this was some kind of test. The synthetics? The chemical versions of the essences of the flowers, the plants. Did I know how she felt about these? She loved them, how they were progress itself, but she could spot their shortfalls. Sniff them out certainly, for she loved the *enfleurage*, the distillery, the natural processes for taking the scent from the bloom.

But in the moment, under the pressure, with Rune staring down at me, testing me, I couldn't quite put these intricacies into words. So instead, I shook my head, and I let him speak.

"You were right, what you said when you first got here. When you said you don't know everything. You can know some of Catarin's life, you can know her story, and I don't know *how* you know. I don't claim to be able to understand the birthmark, or your uncanny details, but I am humble enough to admit there are mysteries yet to be explained, in this fractured human experience." He rubbed a fist into one eye then, in a gesture so familiar, I felt my breath catch. He continued, "I am also smart enough, certain enough about the important things, to know some truths. So you listen to me, young lady, there was only one Catarin Guillet. You are *not* her."

He turned, his face red with emotion, and he went into the kitchen, his gait heavy, loping, the oxygen tank dragged behind him.

I sat on the edge of the coffee table, blinking back tears, feeling what I had to feel, a myriad of emotions. I let the complexities, the surreal quality of my conversation with Rune wash over me, and I just felt. I let myself feel. The honesty of it.

The depth. The reality.

Rune was right.

I was not Catarin.

I had been.

I was *in some way*, but not in maybe the most important ways. I was . . . other. I was of a different essence, a different heart note.

Eli came out from the kitchen, after a moment. "I don't know what happened. But he said that's all for today." He gave me a tender look then.

Persi and Sötnos entered through the sliding glass door then, muddy from wrestling in the yard. I smiled at their haphazard appearance, one of Persis's braids had come out almost completely. I wanted to chuckle at her, the abandon at which she was pleading with her father about the unruly dog, who now left muddy pawprints on the tile and shook his coat, spraying little muddy droplets everywhere. *Could Sötnos come for a visit?* Persi was asking.

But then before I understood what was happening, the smile I had for Persi, the tenderness with which Eli spoke with her, it all became too much. I had upset Rune. I'd come here and I'd discovered I was not Catarin *exactly*.

Things had shifted for me, my identity, my past.

I became overcome with emotion, and before I had consciously made any decision to move, I stood up and moved toward Eli. Somehow I was crying, and then Eli noticed me, startled, and was pulling me to him.

"Shh," he said, and he tugged me closer, slid his hand up and down my back in a soothing gesture.

The dog barked once and pushed his friendly nose into my knees, and Persi nudged her little head in between Eli and I, her arms around us both. "It's okay, Alice," she said to me. "Daddy will let Sötnos come over another time."

I cried more.

I didn't know what else to do.

Jesus, I was so exhausted. I was.

Because it was difficult to let go of the idea that I had lived as Catarin. I had understood the importance of life and love through her, and I had thought that I'd done it all before, known the limits of the human heart, life's one great love.

But now I understood, I knew nothing.

I was only me.

With someone else's knowledge, third-hand.

It was, at once, invigorating and terrifying.

Chapter 39

SERENA FOUND ME IN MY BOARDINGHOUSE bedroom with all the lights off, the curtains drawn, curled up on my side on the bed.

I had met Rune.

In the flesh.

And I angered him with my overconfidence, my oversimplification of our situation. How arrogant to think that I understood any of it. I upset him, and I hadn't gotten anywhere near any of the conversations I wanted to have with him.

And I didn't love him.

Not the way that I thought I did.

Because I wasn't Catarin.

And now I still had a puzzle box that I couldn't open. And I had a wide, open expanse of self-discovery to delve into, because when you didn't feel like you were living a rerun, if you didn't feel cheated from what *should've been*, didn't feel prisoner to the what-ifs, you could start to look out in front of you at the great big swathe of possibility that surrounded you.

It was a brand-new thought for me.

Is this what Isabel thought she was giving me? By trying to tell me so long ago that it was all a ruse?

Jesus, could Isabel have been right to do so?

But that was my mother, a woman caught smack in the middle of an ethical dilemma, finding the grayest, most difficult parts of a problem to nestle into, the corner in which nothing seemed clean-cut, easy-to-solve, or blank. That's where she lived.

Serena didn't let me wallow. I knew she wouldn't. She flipped on the lights. "Alice. You gotta get up."

"It's been a shit day, Serena. I can't—"

"Nope. Not gonna listen to you. This is too important. The human mind is a labyrinthine maze with many twists and turns, hiding places, operating on both flesh and blood levels with a component of an actual electric current. It isn't immune from interference from outside sources, okay? It makes sense that sometimes our wires get crossed, you know?"

I sat up. "What are you even talking about?"

Serena sat on the bed too, began unpacking stacks of papers from her bag, placing them around me on the bed, shoving some into my hands. "There are a few really convincing cases. Sometimes they're related, other times they've been through some kind of intense trauma together, and then some people don't even know each other. It's rare, of course. But cases are known, studied, proven, insomuch as science will consent to it."

"Cases of what?"

"Can I write a paper about you? A case study? Would you let me? I think you could—"

"Serena!"

"Here, just read it."

"Psychic connection," I said out loud.

Psychic Connection. I focused on the article.

I skimmed the first couple of paragraphs. My heart sped faster. I could barely focus on the words on the page, the ideas presented there.

Whoa. I slowed down, read it again.

Then I slowed down even more, read it more thoroughly, absorbing the details, how it worked, the way this could possibly explain me. Explain Catarin.

It worked like a direct line into someone's brain, so that you see right into his or her mind and memories.

There weren't any logical explanations or theories as to how or why this occurs, but there were several well-documented case studies. These were strangely comforting to me. The more I read, the more I realized that this could possibly be *the* explanation.

An out-there, flimsy explanation, but of course, wasn't a past life just as flimsy? Just as unbelievable?

How could I believe one, so gung-ho, and yet discount the other?

A case from Pepperdine University dated from 1974. A man in Utah thought quite sanely that he was having a break with reality—some kind of schizophrenic episode. He was in his mid-thirties when he started having these visions or memories of traveling with what he thought was a carnival, maintaining the animals. He had specific memories of trying to medicate a chimpanzee while it pulled on his hair. Only after he had gone through many different medications trying to stop the visions did he find it was *a psychic connection*. He stumbled upon the fact that he had a twin brother, whom he had been separated from at birth, and this led to the discovery that the man worked for Barnum and Bailey's.

Another case cited a woman in Korea who had a story a lot like mine, except that her connections spanned a few different people, all in a specific rural region of South Korea, over several different decades.

I tried this theory out.

So, I wasn't Catarin exactly. Had never been.

I was just tied into her psyche, her memories, in this otherworldly, inexplicable way.

I pictured some kind of twine or cord, a cable of neurons, sparking and alive, stretching across continents, through oceans, from Catarin to me. It was impossible and ridiculous, and seemed very much like it could be true.

I was not Catarin, even though it felt like I was.

And wasn't that exactly what I had discovered when meeting Rune? That it was one thing to know all these things, be a witness to so much, a little bird on Catarin's shoulder through thick and thin, years of life and love and loss. It was another thing completely to *be* her.

"But . . . wait," I said, "Wait. But why me and Catarin?"

"Why anyone? Why anything?"

"But why do I only know some of the memories?"

"There are certain memories that people revisit often, the most traumatic sometimes, or when they were the happiest." Serena shrugged.

I read some more. A case of two young girls, studied thoroughly at the University of Virginia, were raised in foster care together, then separated for a decade. They weren't blood related. One began to have visions—hallucinations, she thought—of falling from the sky, repeatedly. Eventually, she reconnected with her fellow foster-sister and found she was a sky-diving instructor. The details, emotions, and vivid experience of jumping from a plane were just some of the many "memories" these girls shared over the course of their lifetimes.

"Serena, how did you stumble across this? I mean, I've never heard of it, not even—"

Serena gave me a look. "No one wants to believe things like this, because it's a little discomfiting, isn't it? Our minds are our own or are supposed to be. Plus, we can't quite explain it scientifically. It's all part of parapsychology, which people want to dub garbage. But there's a little too much to a lot of these things for us to just dismiss it all. There are serious college departments who study this stuff, University of Virginia being the most respectable." Serena gave me a look. "The human mind, the human experience, there are a lot of dark corners within it, lots of misunderstood possibilities. I believe that wholeheartedly."

I sat there, having another realization.

One I could barely wrap my head around.

But Serena kept talking. "You are paired with Catarin, dialed into her for some reason. It says in one paper I read that you might have similar genetic markers, and that's why you're connected. Or epigenetic anomalies, types of—"

"Serena."

"What?"

"For me to be psychically connected to Catarin, doesn't that mean that she has to be still alive? Like Rune?"

"I think that's exactly what it means. In fact, I *know* it."

"What do you mean?"

Serena rifled through her bag, and she handed me a few Xeroxed pages. "The university has a great connection to the internet, with a few international databases, and it's amazing how much data is available. Seriously, I was able to do some searching. There wasn't much, but there was something."

I took the paper.

She was old. Of course, she was old. She wore a sunhat, a red kerchief tied at her neck, as she squinted into the sun. It was Catarin. The ski-slope nose, the point of her chin. The freckles.

There was no doubting it.

My God.

She was alive.

"It says here that she took over the family *parfumerie*, rehabbed, reinvented—even renamed—the whole business in 1941. Alice, really, she's like a serious entrepreneur in the field of synthetic perfumes. She's given money to studies that link olfactory sensation with memory recollection, trying to explain scent-connection to the mind's ability for recall. She's lived in France her whole life with a brief respite in the United States during the 30s. And she breeds Percheron ponies."

I grabbed the paper again from Serena, greedy for the details, reading about her charity work, her expansion into several chemist labs in the 1950s, at the height of her career where she had conceived her most famous scent, a man's cologne. *Willow.*

It sold for many years, in department stores such as Marshall Field's and Barney's, being produced even into the early 1980s.

I felt like I'd had the wind knocked out of me. I could barely take this all in.

Catarin.

I stared at her photo.

She had overcome her injury. Of course she had. And her dreams, they were realized, fulfilled, surpassed in so many ways.

But . . ..

No Rune?

Had she ever married?

Had children?

I wanted more, every single detail of her life. Did she ever travel? Did she reconnect with Martine-Marie when she went back?

Did she miss Rune?

Did she still have her staring spells?

"Serena, I can't believe this."

"Yes, you can. You don't get to be a skeptic, not after what you've . . . lived. You can believe it."

I considered this, nodded. "Yes, I can. It's just so much to . . . digest. And I still don't know what happened with Rune and—" I sat up then with a sharp realization. "Maybe it's not my business though. My God, she's alive. Maybe that's what I'm supposed to realize, that it's not really my heartache to recall or investigate or thoroughly understand."

"Or, maybe it's shared with you for a reason. I don't know, Alice."

"I'm haunted by the scene in the tunnel that night."

Serena gave me a soft smile. "I know you are. And you know what I think?"

I looked up at her. "What?"

"I think you and I, *we* should go to France—and soon, like now—and we should ask Catarin all about it."

Part IV
Rune

Chapter 40

RUNE KNEW THAT CATARIN NEEDED TIME and space to heal, her wounds, her heart, her perception of herself.

But Rune had a hard time giving it to her. To know that Catarin was near, and that she was hurting, and for him to not go to her, it was a Herculean task beyond him. He visited the *parfumerie* every day he could, after his shift at the railyard. Most days he was turned away by one of her parents or by one of the white-uniformed staff, and even sometimes by Catarin herself.

But once in a while, usually when he was nearing his wit's end, Catarin would greet him at the door of the main house, and maybe she would smile, a shadow of her old exuberance, but his heart would leap and recover, filling again with that most dangerous fickle friend: hope.

He and Catarin would then walk into the small orchard, and there beneath her favorite willow tree, he would read to her. She would listen mostly, her words few. She held her shoulders tightly, as if bracing for something, and her eyes would have smudges of lavender-gray beneath them, evidence of her worry, her wrestling with this new version of herself and her limited capabilities.

Rune's heart broke anew each time he watched her attempt some trivial task, something that required two hands, such as tying her boot, or extracting a paper from an envelope.

Her father had told Rune that Catarin was working with a fellow from the nearby hospital, a studying physician. She was retraining the motion in her hand, her wounded one, to build up her muscles, exercise her fine motor skills. And because she still had her thumb, she would be able to do most everything again. The fine work of perfuming, the chemist's small motor motions. It was only time and training that was needed.

Rune didn't ask Catarin about it though.

Catarin did not speak of it.

Rune figured he was doing exactly the right thing, waiting for Catarin in this way. Not forcing anything.

Or, he was stupid.

So very stupid, allowing this cleaving, this months-long goodbye to stretch between them, Catarin giving him up one inch at a time. One moment of silence blending into the next.

Oh, how Rune wished and hoped for Catarin's spirit to return, the way she had poked him in his chest in the refurbished silo of the *enfleurage*. The way she had said that she didn't want him anymore. At the time, he'd been so very sure she didn't mean it.

And now, he replayed that moment in his mind often.

He just wanted her fiery spirit back, even if it meant . . . No, he couldn't make himself wish that.

He wanted her.

Only her. Always.

Catarin was his. They had lain together, there on the *enfleurage* floor, and Rune would never, ever be the same.

If there had been anything left of himself that didn't belong to Catarin before that act, well, now, it was all surely hers: his soul, his dreams, his most secret self, the deep inside secret parts of his heart. They were all Catarin's, and he gave it all gladly.

For his daily visits, he chose his poems carefully, always trying to reinvigorate her spirit, to remind her of her feelings for him, her lust for life, but he had promised himself he would be patient, he would be what she needed. And that he would not bring up marriage again, not until he felt she was ready.

This was Catarin.

He could be patient.

He chose Byron, because of course he had to.

She walks in beauty, like the night
Of cloudless climes and starry skies;
And all that's best of dark and bright
Meet in her aspect and her eyes;
Thus mellowed to that tender light
Which heaven to gaudy day denies.

And he chose Eliot, because he wanted her to argue with him again. Lord, if she would only argue.

Let us go then, you and I,
When the evening is spread out against the sky

And when she didn't argue, didn't complain that Eliot was difficult, obtuse on purpose, a sham of an academic, he chose Eliot again.

April is the cruelest month, breeding
Lilacs out of the dead land, mixing
Memory and desire, stirring
Dull roots with spring rain.

He thought he saw something twitch across her face when he read the word *desire*, but maybe Rune had only imagined it. For Catarin was not herself, and Rune had an itch, a nervousness that he couldn't seem to quell.

He couldn't lose Catarin inside herself. Not because of a scar.

No.

The irony would be too much for even him to bear.

But when he finished this particular Eliot poem, for it was a long one, he turned to see that she had fallen asleep with her head on his shoulder, her breath turning into the lightest whistle of a snore, and Rune thought he had never seen anything so beautiful in his life than her profile in the orange glow of the sunset. He wrapped his arm around her shoulders, and he held her to him, relishing her every breath.

Those afternoons that Catarin would see Rune, they would pass quickly, a moment, a blink, and soon, they would be walking back to the main house, in time for dinner, sometimes hand in hand, most times not, and Catarin would leave Rune with a sweet peck on the cheek, if he was lucky. Oftentimes, he only received a smile, a polite thank-you, and Rune would leave the Guillet Parfumerie, his hat in his hands, his heart in his throat.

And he would worry. And he would worry.

Until the next afternoon, when he would knock on her door again. Surely, this would be the time that his sweet, energetic Catarin would return. She'd call him *mon chou*.

Surely. This day. She'd come back to him fully.

And on went the summer, until it nearly turned to fall.

Chapter 41

ANDERS' GIRLFRIEND MAEVE HAD TWO BROTHERS. Rune would hear them talking about both of the brothers often. One was running for mayor of a Minnesota city up north, and the other was some kind of doctor, working at Our Lady Hospital in downtown St. Paul.

This brother of Maeve's in particular also seemed to know everyone of any importance in the twin cities. His name was Declan, and he could get Maeve and her friends into any of the speakeasies they wanted. Age wasn't a problem. Money either. Or the fact that booze was still illegal. Declan Mills was high society. He took care of Maeve and all of her decadent habits, but he also took care of Anders' problem with the Thranes.

Somehow, Anders was untouchable. He went right back to work for the Thranes, right back to his same wild ways. Everything was forgotten by Ian, by his bootlegging father, and when Gunnar asked Anders how this could be, how they could just pick up and move forward, Anders leveled Gunnar with a look. "I've made the right friends."

One night, not long after the debacle with Anders, Rune woke from his dream of Catarin to hear a racket outside their house in the lane. He knew it was Anders, could hear his throaty laugh. He was trying hard to be quiet, but Rune heard another voice, a man's voice, so he got up and looked out the front window. He saw a wobbly-legged Anders standing in the middle of the lane, his hat in hand. He was making some kind of sweeping gestures, blowing kisses this way and that.

Anders. It made Rune smile in spite of himself.

Maeve's Citroën sat idling, and Maeve grabbed Anders, moving him toward the steps. She didn't look her normal good-time self, instead she looked tired, weary of this behavior.

The other fellow had a medium build with dark hair. He was handsome in a broad-shouldered way, not the movie-star looks of Anders. He stood leaning on the car.

Rune knew at once this must be the brother, Declan, so much of him resembled Maeve. Rune could see the same line to their noses, the hard curve of their chin. Maeve said something to Anders then, pulled herself out from under his arm. Anders was obviously drunk.

Rune was just about to reach for the front door, to say hello to Maeve and help Anders in, when something happened.

Anders kissed Maeve goodbye, the standard chaste on-the-lips kiss that Rune had seen many times before, but then he turned to Declan, for he had climbed the stoop as well, and Declan leaned down to be eye-level with Anders.

Declan reached out gently, tenderly, and with his thumb and forefinger on Anders' chin. He brought Anders' eyes to his own. "Good night, you." Rune read his lips through the front window.

Then Declan shot a glance up and down the Hollow, and seemingly satisfied, he turned back to Anders. He kissed Anders, full, on the mouth, and there was none of the chaste, platonic sense of Maeve's kiss. This one lasted much longer, with Anders bringing his hands to Declan's face, holding him tenderly.

After a long moment, Anders pulled from the kiss, breathless. "Get in the house, you," Declan said, planting another quick kiss to Anders' lips.

Rune turned from the window and froze.

Was he surprised? Should he be surprised?

Anders rattled the knob of the front door, and Rune grabbed it, and swung it open.

"Heya, Rune," Anders mumbled, and he stumbled to their room, humming a tune Rune couldn't place. Anders fell face-first onto his bed.

Rune shut the front door and watched as Maeve's *Citroën* took off. Rune looked up and down the Hollow. *No one had seen*, he thought, anyway.

He stood for a moment in the kitchen, and his breath was heavy, hard in his chest.

Anders.

So many things fell into place then. So many times Rune had wondered at Anders' secret center, at what forced him to become all bluster-and-brash, at what had happened to the tender, sensitive heart of his youth.

It was still there. Hidden, along with the true yearnings of his heart.

Rune waded through his feelings for his brother. And once he got over the semi-shock of it, what he really felt was fear.

Not *of* his brother. No. Rune fancied he was above anything as trifling and small-minded as that. But fear *for* his brother.

It was difficult to be different in Swede Hollow.

Rune knew. He was kind of an expert on the subject.

Chapter 42

TODAY, RUNE BROUGHT HER FLOWERS, picked from their field of wildflowers up above the Hollow, Queen Anne's lace and chicory, lilacs and crane's bills. Inger and Gunnar's wedding was fast approaching, and he wanted to talk to Catarin about it today. Surely, he wouldn't be able to convince her to attend. But he had to try.

But today, Catarin swung her front door open with vigor, and Rune saw something in her, a spark, a light, an energy that had been missing. A knot, deep inside of him, loosened, even before she pulled him close.

"Rune," she said, standing on her tiptoes, fisting the labels of his jacket in her hands. She pressed her lips to his.

Rune smiled like a fool and returned the kiss, at first tentatively. Then, it turned deeper, and in mere moments, Rune had forgotten himself, pressed her body against the doorjamb.

Catarin kissed him hungrily, until Rune realized he had crushed the flowers between them. He pulled back reluctantly. So reluctantly, but Catarin! Her eyes danced as she watched him attempt to freshen the now-crushed bouquet. She reached out and took them from him, burying her nose in the soft petals, her cheeks a high pink color. And Rune very nearly wanted to drop to his knee, throw his arms around her waist and sing hallelujah.

A sharp clearing of a throat made Rune jump away from Catarin, and he turned to see Mrs. Guillet in the doorway, her face pinched and irritated, its most common state.

Mr. Guillet appeared then from the parlor, a newspaper in hand. "Clemence," Mr. Guillet chastised his wife. "Have a heart."

"We are going for a walk!" Catarin announced, and Rune could see the disapproval in her mother's eyes, the tilt of her chin, in every angle of her posture. "Mother, could you put these in some water?" She handed her mother the flowers.

"You feel it is best to exert yourself?" her mother asked. "We do not want another *incident*."

"I am feeling perfectly fine, and I must get out of this house! Rune will have me back by dinner."

"Should you like to stay for dinner, Rune?" Mr. Guillet asked.

"I would love to. Thank you."

Rune stuck his elbow out for Catarin to grab, and he once again felt the heat of her touch through his shirtsleeves and jacket. Rune averted his eyes from Mrs. Guillet, and instead focused on Catarin's father.

"There is a chill," her mother said. "Please take your sweater."

Catarin grabbed her light green sweater from the coat tree near the door, and then, in a matter of moments, Rune and Catarin were out on the sidewalk, with Catarin turning them toward Swede Hollow, toward the meadow, at a brisk pace.

Although they were certainly on a public street, in a public city, and there were others even as close as across the street, Rune thought, *I have her back and I am alone with her. For the first time in so many weeks, she has returned. To herself. To me.*

Rune felt brave as they walked past the hardware store, where Mr. Watkins nodded a greeting in hello. He brought his other hand up across his body, and he placed it on top of Catarin's own hand at his elbow. He felt the heat of her skin, against his own palm, and he nearly forgot to keep his feet moving. She let go of his arm then, and she dragged her hand down his arm until she reached his hand, clasping it in his own.

"I like this better," she said, squeezing his hand. Rune dared to glance down at her, at his Catarin.

"I do too," he whispered, not trusting his voice.

Part of him had accepted that she was drifting away from him, little by little, piece by piece. Dear Lord, it felt good to be wrong.

When they reached Hollow's Ladder, they walked down. Catarin was not chatty, but she smiled, she leaned into him. They traded looks.

Rune understood somehow. Rune knew that Catarin didn't want to speak, and he knew instinctively that she was leading him somewhere.

She walked them past Rune's tin house, their hands swinging between them. She walked them by Inger's house, waving hello to Miss Vendela on the porch. Soon, they were at the creek, the lower end, the arched Connemara bridge marking the end of Swede's Hollow and the beginning of the Irish Patch.

She walked them up to the bridge, and she looked around this way and that, surreptitiously, and there were no kids loitering at this moment—no teens with their hidden cigarettes. Catarin pulled Rune by the hand behind the archway of the bridge, behind the multi-colored assortment of limestone, and she pulled him to her, with her back leaning against the stones themselves.

Here, they were hidden from view. Here, they were alone, in their own little world, their own little moment.

This.

This was sweeter than their time in the *enfleurage*, for if that was frenzied emotion, this was Rune taking care of her, being gentle with her, showing her what he could be.

And all Rune could see was her eyes. "*Mon chou*," she said, breathless. He lost his footing as she pulled him closer still, her hands on the collar of his jacket. He fell into her, catching himself on the stone behind her, and he straightened up, his arms on either side of her.

He looked down into her eyes, and Catarin bit her lip. "*Mon chou* means 'my cabbage.' I looked it up at the library. Why am I your cabbage?" he teased.

Catarin smiled, a real one, her dimples deep and her eyes crinkling with mirth. "It is a term of endearment. It doesn't exactly translate."

"So I am your green, leafy vegetable?"

"It means . . . It's more like . . . *my one, my only*." Her eyes slipped from his.

Was she . . . embarrassed?

A swell of emotion welled in Rune's chest. "Catarin."

"Will you kiss me again, Rune?" she asked, and her eyes stayed lowered. She was indeed shy on him, and Rune could not answer her question, for the emotion in his throat, for the want in his body.

Part of him had resigned himself to living the rest of his days with only the memory of her body against his, rather than the real thing.

But now, here she was. Back in his arms. Rune took a shaky breath, and he dipped his head lower, and he caught her eyes with his. One last question of permission, and when she leaned in, he caught her lips in his. It was nothing, just a brush of lips against one another.

It was everything, soft and tentative, but then he leaned in again, parting his lips, truly kissing her, and she brought her arms up around his neck, pushed her warm body up against his. "Rune," she whispered behind the kiss.

He shivered as their kiss deepened, only wondering for a moment if he should be embarrassed at his arousal, so blatant, as she pressed her body against his. But then Catarin pressed her tongue in his mouth, and Rune forgot about being self-conscious. He pressed her gently up against the stone wall, and he kissed her, his hands on her cheek, her neck, her collarbone, in reverence.

Everything about her was soft, the creamy white of her skin, so pure.

He pulled from the kiss only when he was scared he would embarrass himself. "I'm sorry," he said. "It's too much. We cannot again without . . ."

"Rune," she said, pulling him into an embrace, her hands underneath his jacket, her fingertips tracing the knobs of his spine. She pressed her cheek to his chest. Her voice was fevered, full of something Rune understood. "Rune, I love you."

As she held him, he heard the sound of his own breathing, rapid, shallow. Had he truly heard what she said? He inhaled a shaky breath. "Say it again," he whispered into her hair. "Please."

"I love you, Rune." He heard the smile in her voice.

He let out a deep sigh. He thought of Wordsworth:

How great delight from those sweet lips I taste
Whether I hear them speak or feel them kiss!

He hadn't even known he was going to say it, but then he did. "Catarin, when will you marry me?"

Chapter 43

THE FOLLOWING FRIDAY AFTERNOON, Rune sat across from Mrs. Guillet in an office at the Downtown Bank of St. Paul. A young man had come to the railyard to fetch Rune, during his shift, and he had little information for Rune, saying it was an emergency, that Mrs. Guillet must see him right now, that it was of the utmost importance.

Rune's mind and emotions had gone into a frenzy. It was Catarin, of that he was certain. Had she had another episode? Was she okay? He had run the entire way, hadn't bothered to change from his work clothes, his dirty boots, his hands still stained from the grease and filth of the track.

When he'd been shown into the back room of the bank, just a small conference room with a table and chairs, Mrs. Guillet had been waiting for him, sitting there, with her legs crossed, smoking a cigarette. She didn't look frantic.

"Please tell me she is okay."

Mrs. Guillet waved her hand in a motion of dismissal. "Catarin is fine. For now. Please, I only wanted to talk to you."

"She has not suffered another episode?"

Mrs. Guillet pursed her mouth. She shook her head in response. "She is actually in the chemist lab for the first time since her injury. She has been able to handle the glassware, the pipettes. She is encouraged by her progress with the physician from the hospital." Mrs. Guillet stubbed out her cigarette.

So, Rune's shoulders released some tension, for what could possibly be truly wrong if Catarin was okay?

"Please sit, Rune."

Rune did so, beginning to perceive the tension in the room with them.

"But to answer your question, Rune, actually Catarin has actually had several episodes. Fourteen since her accident."

And Rune's stomach dropped, because this was his Catarin. "She hadn't told me."

"Someday you will have a daughter, Rune. And you will understand me." Mrs. Guillet's eyes squinted at Rune as she said this. And Rune broke out in a sweat then.

"What will I understand?"

"She needs to go back to France with us. We are leaving soon. In London, there is a doctor there who specializes in *épilépsié*. He treats it with a series of bromides, and he has had much success, especially in his younger patients. We have to do this for Catarin. Do you understand?"

"I want what is best for Catarin, of course I do." But for Catarin to leave? This was something he didn't know if he could survive. Could he leave and go with her? Would she ever just agree, and marry him first?

But he didn't have time to think through all of this information, for Mrs. Guillet was still speaking. Rune had to focus his mind.

"So, Rune, you have a brother."

This seemed neither here nor there, and really, all Rune could think of now was getting to Catarin, speaking with her, making plans. He wiped his hands on his handkerchief, and he answered Mrs. Guillet.

"Actually two of them. I have two brothers. Both older than me. Gunnar and Anders."

"One of them is getting married soon, yes?"

"Yes, Ma'am. Gunnar."

"Miss Vendela has invited us."

Rune nodded, and he watched Mrs. Guillet. He didn't like the way that she watched him back, looking down her nose at him.

"Your brother is marrying Miss Vendela's girl, yes? Miss Vendela, who runs the Hollow illegal alcohol trade."

Rune sat silently, beginning to understand now. He was slow on the uptake. Very slow obviously, as he didn't think, hadn't suspected that Mrs. Guillet had this in her. The color slowly drained from Rune's face.

"So it is the other brother, he is the homosexual, is he not?"

She held Rune's gaze then, and Rune felt his rage ignite, fast and fiery inside his belly. How did she know?

"He is also wrapped up with the lowlife gangsters in the area, yes?"

What on earth could she do?

He had drastically underestimated her. He knew she was a domineering mother with ideas for Catarin that dealt in taffeta dresses and society ballrooms, but he had no idea that she was capable of . . . this.

He had not expected this woman to be a wolf in sheep's clothing. He had thought the enemy was Catarin's healing, the threat of her disappearing inside herself.

But now, Rune was beginning to understand.

His pulse thudded in his skull, pounded at his temples. He had been outwitted. He asked, "What do you want from me?"

But he thought he already knew.

Chapter 44

IT WAS LATE, AND RUNE WAS A PACING, jangly-nerved mess. Rune heard his front door open. He hoped it was Gunnar. God, he needed to talk to Gunnar. He had to formulate some kind of plan, something to put into immediate action, and he needed his oldest brother—his practical advice—desperately.

But, no, it was Anders. He smelled of tobacco and of liquor. He came noisily into the bedroom that they shared, and he stood in silhouette next to his bed, not moving, for a long moment. Then, Anders began to pull of his clothes, replacing them with his pajamas.

Anders' motions were heavy, thick. There was a sadness there, a weight to his movements, a contemplative line to his brow. Rune could see it even in the dark, in the way that Anders heaved himself into bed, sighed deeply.

Part of Rune wanted to chastise Anders, bark at him for ever working with such lowlifes as Ian Thrane or Old Man Lassiter. He wanted to get up and shake him by the shoulders, but something inside himself stopped him.

He would be gentler with his brother.

Take care of Anders. He is special. His mother had implored, on her deathbed.

And Rune also thought of Uncle Isak then, in that moment, how just today he'd received a letter from him, the first in many months. Isak was home in Sweden, this they knew from Aunt Malin. But Uncle Isak himself now wrote that he had a new bride, Dahlia, and a baby on the way. He had written, "Proof that life can manage to surprise you even upon a late hour. I never found your father, you know, in my travels north to Canada. I am glad, for violence is only ever triumphed over through selflessness, through love."

The letter had been ripped, taped together, ripped again, delivered to the wrong address, stamped, and sent again. It had been postmarked ten months ago. Rune understood it must've been lost in the mail.

He'd only gotten this letter today.

So Rune wondered at the timing of this letter. What he was meant to glean?

Was it a sign?

He knew his Uncle Isak. He would tell him to be brave, to talk to Anders. For there was a time for action, and there was a time for forbearance. And Rune understood that he must decipher the thin line between them, in order to truly be a man.

Rune chose action.

"I know, Anders," Rune said into the dark.

Anders sat up in bed, fluffed his pillow behind him.

"Rune. What do you know, brother?"

"All of it."

"You know I'm different, yes?" And his voice was not thick with drink, but some kind of emotion. Rune couldn't tell at first what it was. Worry? Guilt? Had Anders been crying?

"I know," Rune answered quietly, into the darkness between their two beds.

"I'm different in a way that makes people scared."

"Talk to me, Anders." Rune sat up then, swung his legs over the side of his bed, the same bed he had slept in since he was a child.

Anders sniffled, brought his fists to his eyes, a gesture so much like the small-child version of Anders that Rune could barely bear it. Rune got up and sat next to him, on his bed, their knees touching.

"People love you, Anders. You're everyone's favorite. You are handsome and likeable, too charming for your own good." But even as Rune said the words, it was like he knew, somehow, somewhere deep inside himself, he knew that these things, these qualities that made Anders so wonderful, they would mean nothing to many people, cruel people, small-minded people, when they found out about Anders, about Declan.

"I don't want to be different, but I am."

Rune placed his arm around Anders shoulders, and Anders let himself relax into Rune, and Rune heard Anders sob, felt his shoulders shaking. Rune's heart broke for the secret his brother had carried for so long. How it must've weighed on him for so many endless times. Rune had not known. He let Anders cry.

And suddenly, Rune felt so scared, absolutely terrified for his brother. He knew that this thing with Thrane, his involvement with these characters, it was only the start of it for Anders. If they could solve that problem, it would only be on to another one. The world wasn't going to take kindly to Anders and his difference.

"It isn't going to be easy for you," Rune said.

"No, it's not," Anders said, pulling away, wiping at his eyes. "I know that. I don't need it to be easy. I just need to know that you don't think I'm an aberration. Something unholy, a monster or—"

Rune cut him off. "I have spent a lot of time knowing people have thought those things of me, Anders. You know this. And I tell you, I am somewhat of an expert on aberrations." Anders smiled a little then, in the moonlight. "You are no monster," Rune repeated. "I love you no more, no less, because of this secret. Come now, Anders, did you really even need to hear me say those words? Do you not know?"

Anders threw his arms around Rune then, and Rune tried to find something else to soothe his brother's heart.

Rune had thought a lot about what he'd seen that night with Maeve's brother and Anders on the porch, and he had been uncomfortable at first, of course. Scared for his brother.

But he had come to this: if Rune's want, his passion for Catarin, was seen as wrong or taboo, would he be able to stop it? Change it? Reverse the course of it for society's sake? For the church's sake?

He knew he couldn't.

He knew that Anders couldn't change what was inside him either.

"We are one in the same, Anders," Rune told him. "I think of you as my other half, brother. Growing up, you taught me to be a man as much as Isak or Gunnar. You were my guide in this life. You still are, in many ways. I love you. And I know this life, it won't be easy, but what is?"

"That's true," Anders said. "You sound like Mama."

Rune needed Anders to hear truly him. "You are pure, brother. Don't let anyone tell you different. But I still think working as you do, with Thrane and those lummoxes, it isn't a good mix."

"I am . . . working on fixing that."

"How bad is it, Anders?"

"Bad."

"I have the lutefisk can. I have some money."

Anders swallowed hard, cleared his throat. "I fear it is so very much worse than that."

Chapter 45

THE WEDDING WAS A BIG AFFAIR FOR EVERYONE in the Hollow. Miss Vendela knew how to throw a party.

Catarin looked healthy and glowing on his arm, wearing a pink bridesmaid dress, with short white fashionable gloves, a way for her to hide her injury, as this was her first appearance in public since the harvester accident. She had a healthy pink glow in her cheeks, and a secret smile for Rune, teasing him in his ear, "Maybe you should ask me again tonight," she said.

He knew she meant proposing marriage. It had become a game between them. "One of these times, I will say yes," she teased.

Rune smiled at her, his chest twisting with emotion. Didn't she know about her mother's plans? Her threats? He'd hadn't had the heart to discuss any of it with her. Not yet.

Rune sighed. He'd put off any action, thinking he would solve this easily by going to Catarin's father, which he had done just this morning.

Many years from now, Rune would look back on this night, Gunnar and Inger's wedding, and he would realize that the heartbreak of his life, all of his aching sorrow could be brought back to this night, when he had failed to act first, act bravely, act at all. When he had relied on his intelligence, on his ability to mold a situation into something new, rather than act.

But the thing is, he had thought he had time.

He had underestimated Clemence Guillet.

He had gone to Mr. Guillet, of course, in order to keep Mrs. Guillet from interfering in their life, and he had assumed Catarin's father would be on his side, would align with Rune. Would carry out Catarin's wishes. Would be Rune's champion in keeping her here.

But Rune had found that there were several very glowing success stories in treating the *épilepsie* with this London doctor, and as such, Mr. Guillet didn't want to hear much about any other plans for his daughter right now. He waved away his wife's threats as well, giving them no credence.

He only said over and over, that he wanted to take Catarin back to France, to visit London frequently. Maybe only for a year. Two. For her health.

And didn't Rune want Catarin to be well?

Of course he did.

Of course.

Give her time, her father had said. *Give us time, as a family to get her well.*

• • •

GUNNAR AND INGER MARRIED IN A simple ceremony at the St. Paul Lutheran Church, and the reception afterward was at the adjoining park. Miss Vendela called in every favor she had, and the park had been transformed. A large, white canvas tent stood over a freshly laid dining and dance floor, and it was lit with hundreds of twinkling jam-jar lanterns, hanging from twine that stretched across the struts of the tent. Guests were served Swedish delicacies from potato sausage to pig's feet, rice pudding to fruit soup, and the cake was a thing of Scandinavian beauty. It stood three tiers tall, decorated with tiny rosette pastries.

On each table, Miss Vendela placed a bud vase holding Hollow lilac blooms, plus a special, personal touch. She explained this special centerpiece during her pre-dinner toast, in which she spoke words of love and admiration for both her daughter and her new son-in-law. What Vendela had done was she borrowed photos from many of the Hollow residents, wedding photos, engagement photos, family shots, so that on each table, the guests, and the bride and groom, could see who it was that they had in their heritage, who was rooting for them, supporting them, and who had gone before them down this matrimonial road.

"I want you to look at these photos, Gunnar and Inger, and I want you to remember that we, in the Hollow, stick together. So look at these photographs, and know you are loved." Miss Vendela kissed her daughter on the cheek, leaving not a dry eye in the house.

Rune felt a special pride for his brother this day. Gunnar and Inger had a new apartment up on Walters Lane, and they were beginning their life. It gave Rune a feeling of closure, but also a feeling of anticipation, for the new, grown-up lives in front of them. Gunnar had told them, so many years ago, that the Hollow would turn out to be a blessing, that they would flourish. And Rune told this story during his toast to the couple. "We are here today, all of us Folkesons, because of you, Gunnar. You have led us here, turned us into grown men. And you, Inger, are our sister, through and through, and have been for so long. So, From the Folkeson family, we give you a belated, *Valkommen!*"

Rune watched Anders a lot during the wedding and the reception, and although he was still suave, still everyone's favorite guest, he saw that Anders was . . . sad. He didn't have his usual spark.

He also seemed to be looking for someone, checking over his shoulder often. Was Maeve supposed to meet him, maybe? Or even Declan?

Rune watched as Anders sneaked a drink from his flask at the dinner table, and he vowed to ask Anders about Declan specifically, about what was truly going on in his heart, because looking at Anders, sitting there in his fancy wedding suit, he looked heartsick. That's all there was to it.

Uncle Isak would know the words to help Anders, to soothe his heart, but Isak was not here. Rune would have to try. Anders always did for him. It was the three brothers in this together.

Rune knew that.

He would never, ever forget that.

Miss Vendela asked Anders to dance as soon as the band began to play, and Rune watched as Anders nodded, his mouth turned up at the corners. He was acting the part, but Rune knew. Anders' heart was not in the festivities.

"Shall we say hello to your parents?" Rune asked Catarin.

Catarin had a lilac pinned in her hair, giving her an exotic look. She gave Rune a nod, squeezing his arm in response. Rune could hardly believe that he got to have her on his arm.

"Good evening," Rune said to Catarin's parents, as she kissed her hellos.

"Good to see you," Mr. Guillet told Rune. "Could I speak with you a moment, Catarin? I wanted to introduce you to a man from the bluff who works with the Percherons." Catarin excused them, and it left Rune face-to-face with her mother.

"I see we are at an impasse," Mrs. Guillet said, her eyes boring into Rune's.

He didn't want to have to argue with Catarin's mother here of all places, but he wouldn't be bullied. "Ma'am, I wanted—"

"You will find on Monday morning that you are no longer employed by the railway, Rune," she said.

Rune took an actual step back, feeling as if he had been punched in the gut. "But . . . that's not . . ."

"Pick your jaw up off the floor, boy. Did you really not think I was playing a game? That I would just roll over? My daughter will not marry an immigrant gutter rat. You break it off tonight with my daughter. Or you will find all of your family in the deepest of trouble. We have the resources. Don't think we are not able."

Rune looked at Mrs. Guillet, and he was incensed, truly. But more than that, he didn't understand it. "Is it really so important to you that she not marry for love? Can't you see that I make her happy? That we will live a life of poetry and fragrance, of love and laughter, one that would be worthy of the romantic poets? I will go back to France with her, for her treatments. I would do . . . anything."

Mrs. Guillet narrowed her eyes at Rune. She spit her next words. "Grow up, Son. You think that you're good for her? You are blind. She is too thin, a nervous skeleton of her past self, she has lost a limb, she has had sixteen epileptic episodes in the past two weeks, certainly from the stress of your constant marriage proposals. Yes, she has told me of this."

Rune took a step back. This couldn't be true. "You're lying."

"Am I? Look at her arm, see the needle marks, Rune. The inside of her elbow. Tonight just to be well enough for the wedding, she spent the afternoon in the hospital with an intravenous drip in order to feel healthy enough to be with you."

Rune couldn't believe this. Had she looked ill?

Mrs. Guillet continued, "This trip to America has been nothing but a disaster for her. She lost her hand, for God's sake, her fits are exacerbated by the climate, by the stress of your *intentions*. We will travel back to France in a month. She will go unencumbered by the likes of you."

"This isn't true. You–"

"I knew you'd be too selfish to see reason. You break it off tonight. Or Anders' secret is public tomorrow morning. Your job is gone and you will be unemployable."

"I don't believe you–"

"You will *not* marry her."

The celebratory scene around Rune seemed to slow and blur around him. Rune steeled himself, clenching his jaw, realizing he had terribly, terribly underestimated Clemence Guillet once again. "No, this cannot be. Mrs. Guillet, there has got to be a way for us to come to an agreement. Catarin–"

"This is our agreement. I've already stated it," Mrs. Guillet said, taking a step closer to Rune, putting her hand on his shoulder momentarily. "I will not negotiate."

Mrs. Guillet walked away, and Rune stood still, his pulse pounding in his ears, his throat constricting.

How could he fix this? He had to steady himself on the back of a chair. He saw Catarin and her father returning to him, and Catarin's brow furrowed when she saw him. She picked up her pace to get to him.

He had thought earlier she looked healthy?

Did she really?

Was he . . . hurting her with his intentions, his pressure? That was all it took, one doubt, one sliver of an opening, and so many of Rune's old insecurities found their way back in. Circling, like birds of prey, finding their old stoop. Nesting.

Of course, he wasn't good for Catarin. He was just himself, a smudge of nothingness, a dumb Swede, and Catarin was a summer garden, the vibrancy of every color in bloom.

But then, Anders was at his elbow. "Rune." He pulled at his arm. "Rune," Anders said again. And the seriousness in his voice stopped Rune from taking the few steps to meet Catarin. "Rune, I need to speak with you." Rune held his hand up to Catarin, motioning he would be with her in a moment. He let his brother pull him away, outside the tent, under the purple-grey evening sky.

"I have to leave. See those men over there?" Anders jerked his thumb toward a black car parked in front of the church.

Rune tried to clear his mind for a moment. He was still shaken from his encounter with Mrs. Guillet. "Wait, wait, are you telling me you're in trouble again?"

Rune hadn't meant to sound angry. But he did.

"I am. It's not good, brother. I just wanted to say goodbye . . . in case." Anders swallowed visibly then, and Rune took in Anders' face. He had dark patches beneath his eyes, and there was a stillness about Anders that wasn't usual.

What was it that he was accepting?

Oh God, things were happening too fast. Rune had thought he had time.

"Are you skimming money from them still?" Rune asked.

Anders scratched at his jaw, and Rune saw his eyes tear up. "Worse than that. I kind of made it look like it was one of Lassiter's guys."

Rune gasped. "Anders, my God." Did Anders hate himself, the truth of himself, so much that he would set himself up for such disaster?

"I know. I know. It's not going to go well tonight." Anders withdrew his matchbook from his pocket, and his hands shook so much, he couldn't light the match. Rune took it from him, struck the match and lit Anders' cigarette, all the while trying to figure out how things had gotten here, how they had gone from Gunnar's wedding celebration to absolute, utter shit.

"They're gonna hurt you again," Rune stated.

Anders took a long pull on the cigarette, then exhaled slowly. "Yeah."

"Worse this time, you know that?"

Rune heard a car door open, and he saw a man, large and dressed in a black leather jacket, appear from the inside.

"I have to go."

"Anders, there's got to be something we can do."

"There isn't."

"Could Declan help? Pay them off again?"

Anders shook his head. "I haven't seen Declan. I'm trying to lie low, keep him from trouble, and . . . this has gone too far."

"Maybe I could talk to Thrane, get him to intervene or . . ." Rune ran a hand through his hair. He couldn't just let his brother walk away. He couldn't just say goodbye to Anders and watch him get into that car.

Rune began to panic. "Anders, tell me, what can I do? There's got to be something."

"I tried to talk to Thrane, to appeal to his Hollow loyalty. I saved his cousin Mary or Molly in the lake that one summer, you remember that?" Rune nodded. "Anyway, we can't count on Thrane."

"I'll try again. Let me talk to him. Who else? Anyone else have any weight with Lassiter?"

"Do you remember the red barns, back home?"

Rune was caught off guard for a moment. "In Sweden?"

"Yeah."

"Anders, you've got to tell me how I can help you. This—"

"Rune, stop. Please." Anders held up his finger to the man at the car, to signal he was coming. He stubbed out his cigarette. "I miss the way the sun used to hit the roof of the barn in the morning, making the whole thing look like it was catching fire. Do you remember that, Rune?"

"I do."

Anders clapped Rune on the shoulder then. "Goodbye, brother." Rune pulled him into an embrace then. When Anders tried to pull away, Rune held on. Dear God, this was Anders. And he couldn't let him go.

"Anders, they could kill you. Is that what you're telling me?" Rune's voice sounded unhinged.

Anders didn't look at him, just pulled away slowly. Then he walked toward the car, without looking back. Rune stood, unable to do anything. Anders had gotten mixed up with Old Man Lassiter. He watched Anders get into the back of the car, and then the car pulled away.

Rune had to think.

He had to do something.

He hurried into the tent and he found Catarin. "I can't explain it right now, but I need to go."

"What is it, Rune?" She searched his face. "It's Anders?"

Rune gave her a grave nod, and he turned and he ran for the Hollow, in the direction of the black car. If any of the gangster stories he heard were true, then Rune knew that Lassiter would take Anders into the caves.

Rune's stomach clenched at the thought of what he might do to Anders there, but that was not at the forefront of Rune's mind. He just had to get there. He had to talk to Lassiter, he had to do something.

Action.

Not forbearance.

This couldn't be the end. This wasn't how Anders' story would come to a close. But just as Rune was slipping into the dark of the Hollow, off the path of the streetlights, toward the sandstone cliffs, the caves, and all the menace that they held for him, a man appeared in his path.

"Rune."

Rune stopped short, not recognizing him at first.

"It's me, Declan."

"I need to go. Anders is in trouble."

Declan nodded, he handed Rune a piece of paper. "Please give him this. I haven't been able to speak with him, Rune. He hasn't let me near him, and it's. . . He's mule-headed, as you know. I've left notes like this in all our spots, tried to get word to him. It's like he thinks he's . . . deserving of this. Like he's saving me . . . by cutting me out." Declan's voice cracked here and shuddered with emotion. "Please don't let him get hurt."

Rune took the paper from Declan, shoving it in his pocket, knowing he had no time to think, to comfort Declan. He clasped him on the shoulder, giving him a nod. "I will do my best." And Rune left, running toward the tunnels.

He had to get to his brother.

"I owe you," Declan called.

"Between brothers there are no debts."

My love,

Without you, I wither.

The words you spoke to me on the bridge, under the flower moon, they sustain me.

My heart constricts with what could happen to you, to us, and all because I could not be more careful about us.

You were right about it all, my love.

I will meet you in the cavern, the one above the Hollow. You know the one of which I speak. At midnight on the third Sunday of this month. We will go away.

If you, for whatever reason, are not there, my love, I will not hold it against your memory. I bid you courage, I bid you strength. I hope you know the depth of my love for you.

Stay safe.

Yours

Chapter 46

RUNE RAN THROUGH THE NEARLY DESERTED Hollow. He splashed through the creek.

Rune knew he had to move quickly. He had to intervene. He had only this one chance to step in for his brother.

If he could only get him away somehow, he could send him off. Send him back to Sweden with the money from the lutefisk can under his bed. There was nothing more important that this money could do for him.

His dearest brother. The other half of his Folkeson soul.

God, how had he wasted away the past few days trying for a solution that would keep everyone happy and safe, when he just needed action? He hadn't understood the seriousness of Anders's situation, hadn't wanted to. And he'd ignored how horrible the Catarin situation was too.

Wanted to believe Mr. Guillet would iron it all out.

Foolish. He'd been so foolish to not see how desperate things had become.

Anders.

Dear God.

They were going to hurt him.

No.

Worse.

Anders had sought him out, said goodbye, for Christ's sake. Rune had to face reality. The world of his brother had been crashing down around him while he spent his days pining over Catarin.

His dear Anders.

The brother who had stuck up for him in their new American classroom, the brother who had held him during his nightmares of the bear, the brother who had helped free him from his mother's womb, with only seconds to spare.

Sweat dripped in his eyes, and his lungs burned but Rune ran on. He tried to stay quiet, listening only to the thud of his heartbeat in his ears. He sucked in a quiet breath, and he scanned the dim outline of the brush field, the silhouette of the sandstone wall, the mouth of the nearest caves.

He saw the momentary flash of a lantern, up in the highest of the caves. Once. Twice. He decided it had to be them.

He flattened his body against the bluff and he listened. He couldn't be spotted.

In a split-second, Rune made a decision, for better or worse. He couldn't scale the front of the bluff. They would see him coming.

He would run through the tunnels, squeezing through the small opening in the lip of the limestone at the base of the nearest bluff, and he would make his way past the big Arch, and up into that top cave. Coming in the back way.

It was his only chance to save his brother.

He moved quickly, as quietly as possible, his large body hunched, his shoulders scraping the sides of the tunnels as he moved. He knew these tunnels from his days of exploring as a boy. He would get there quickly, coming up behind them. Surprising them.

When he was ascending quickly, in the tightest section of tunnel, flat on his belly, pushing forward, it was black, inky and dark, and it was then that he thought of his mother's vision. He pushed it away, but it was there, unbidden, in the front of his brain.

Death was chasing him in these tunnels, Mama had told him that. Mama had seen it the day he was born and many times after.

Rune pressed forward. He knew Mama had it wrong.

Because death wasn't behind him in these tunnels, but it very well might be waiting for him at the end of it. His or Anders.

Maybe both.

Chapter 47

HE CAME UPON THEM QUIETLY, JUST AS HE had planned. He peered around the last turn of the tunnel into the cave. Old Man Lassiter was white-haired and pot-bellied, and he sat on a boulder, with his back up against the wall of the cave. His man, the man from the car in the black leather jacket, held a small pistol.

This pistol was pointed at Anders.

Anders was on his knees, in the middle of the cave, his head hanging low, his chin on his chest. Rune could see even from here that his eye was a bloody, raw mess, swollen shut.

Rune pulled back around the corner into the tunnel to keep from being seen. It took all his will power not to sob.

His brother. *My God.*

Rune listened as Lassiter spoke.

"This is about honor, now," he said, in an accent Rune couldn't quite place. "You have pissed on my honor, and that is not allowed. A bullet? Or do you want to be bricked into the tunnel, lad? Your choice."

Rune knew it was now or never. He summoned all of his courage. He understood that his size, his bearing, his strength, these were things he had left at the wayside for so long. But they were strengths that Anders needed now.

Violence.

Rune would not let Anders be killed.

He was Folke Kasparsson's son, even as much as he didn't want to be. He had violence in him.

He barreled through the entry into the cave, startling the man in black with the gun.

The man froze for an instant.

But Rune charged on.

The gun went off, just as Rune tackled him to the ground. Rune barely registered a piercing pain in his leg, as he wrestled the pistol from the man. Rune was aware of Anders and Lassiter scuffling behind him, but Rune could not give his attention to them. Finally, Rune centered his weight on the man beneath him, pinning his arms to the ground under the weight of his own knees. He wrestled the gun from the man's grip. He reached back and brought the butt of the gun down onto the man's head, knocking him unconscious.

This happened at the same time that something hit Rune from behind, grazing his skull and landing its full weight on his shoulders. Rune toppled backward. Lassiter stood in front of him, a wooden baseball bat in his hands, cocked and ready to be brought down on him again. Rune spied Anders sprawled on the ground out of the corner of his eye.

Rune pointed and pulled the trigger of the handgun in his grip, and nothing happened.

A small clicking sound. Nothing else.

Old Man Lassiter lunged for him then, with a wild sneer and chortle of a laugh, and the baseball bat came down on Rune's arm, popping the gun from his grip.

Rune reacted as a true violent Folkeson would.

He maneuvered his hand low, toward his boot, and he grabbed his carving pocketknife from his boot. He flicked it open one-handed as he had done a hundred times before, and when Lassiter came back at him with the bat, Rune reached up for him, grabbing his shirt, bringing him down on top of him, the knife plunging deep, deep into Lassiter's rib cage.

Rune wrestled with him, until the man's body went limp. Rune threw Lassiter's still body from him, and he scuffled backward. He caught his breath. Dear God.

He had . . ..

He shuffled forward on his knees and checked the pulse of both of the men. The one in black was only unconscious, Lassiter's pulse was barely there, nearly expired.

Taking life. The worst of sin.

Rune stood up, on shaking legs, but once he bore all of his weight, he felt the gunshot, a hot pain in the meaty spot of his leg just above his knee. Like his entire leg had been hollowed out and replaced with an ache, white-hot and piercing. He leaned onto the cavern wall and he surveyed the horrible mess in front of him. He limped over to his brother. He bent onto his knees, letting out a wail with the pain in his leg. He leaned over and shook Anders' shoulder.

Please be okay. Please be fine.

Blood stained his swollen eye, dripping down his neck.

When he didn't move, Run pressed his forehead to his brother's chest. His heartbeat was a steady drum. "Anders!"

He came to with a start, and Rune sobbed. Grabbing his brother to him, holding his head to his chest.

"You have to go. You have to run. Here," and he shoved the paper to him, the one from Declan he'd put in his pocket. "Take this, so you don't doubt his love for you. Find him right now. No waiting. You go to Chicago tonight. Ride the rails. Take the money left in my lutefisk can. Hide out. Lie low. And then as soon as you can, board a ship. Get back to Sweden. Help Isak with his soon-to-be-born child. Isak can keep you two safe."

"You are talking nonsense. I will bear the responsibility for this."

A noise in the tunnel turned their heads. Was Anders not to get away? Were the Thranes coming so soon?

Ah, Rune had to get Anders to leave!

But when Rune got up on his shaking legs, he turned, and it wasn't Ian Thrane who appeared through the tunnel.

No, she was there, her beautiful pink bridesmaid dress and her pristine white gloves scuffed, her face flushed, her eyes wide with worry.

Catarin.

It was the same terrible memory of the night of the VFW dance all over again. Here he was, a bloodied violent mess.

He knew in that moment, that Mrs. Guillet was at least partially correct. Rune was no good for Catarin, not all of him.

Not the part of him that could do this.

The violent part, the Folkeson part.

Seize that love. Protect it, Isak had told him.

He would protect Catarin. From this part of him.

She would go to London. She would get free from her epilepsy.

He would protect his dear, dear Anders too.

It all made so much sense when he just gave in. When his own wants, his own needs, his own heart were of no consequence. The plan, the world, fell into place.

He couldn't keep Catarin here. He loved her too much. In that moment, that blink of an eye, when Catarin looked at him, and he looked at Catarin, Rune felt it last forever, a lifetime. All the love he had for her, all of his hopes, his plans, they played out over his heart, like a sad song, an epic poem, of love and loss.

He knew endings. This one was upon them.

And Rune understood two important things in that moment, that flash of time that would be forever branded on him, this moment, here in the Swede Hollow tunnel.

First, he would change his name. He wasn't Folke's son. He would never be.

And second, no one would ever love Catarin as he did, no one would ever love anyone as much as he did her. Not in the history of all the loves in the world.

The depth of the feeling he had for her.

It was love.

For this is love and nothing else is love.

It was selflessness, and it was sacrifice, and it was love in action.

It was all solved so simply now, but she just had to go. Leave him. She had to. He had to make her. He schooled his features, steeled his voice, "Catarin, you must go. Now. Hurry. With Anders."

True love. Selfless love.

Good God, he could barely make himself do it. He almost tried to reconsider, testing the weight on his leg, if he could run. He tried to think of some way, any way, he could get to be with her. But then he shook his head.

The look on Catarin's face—shock and fear, how she abhorred the scene in front of her, the violence, the blood, the dark, violent part of him—told him that she must know, she understood. That he was not worthy of her.

That he had to do this.

That she would be better off.

"I'm sorry," he said. "You must go."

But then the VFW dance scene replayed in another way. Another detail.

Catarin went rigid, her eyes rolling back. *No,* he thought. *Not again.*

And he went to her, he rescued her, holding her in his arms, her body convulsing, the jerky stiff contractions, this ugly dance. God, how he hated it for her.

He turned to Anders. "You must leave. There is no time!"

Rune kept Catarin in his arms, held her convulsing body close to his, wishing he could absorb this pain, this aberration.

He ordered Anders, "Send the police. Send back the paramedics for Catarin. I will take care of this. All of this."

"What are you going to do, Rune? Take the blame? No, this can't be done this way. I have to stay, and—"

"I will take responsibility. I will explain I used you as a scapegoat. You must go. Now, Anders!"

"You cannot do that, Rune. I won't let you."

"It's already done. Now please go, before it's too late for Catarin. You must leave for her as much as for yourself. Run as fast as you can. I cannot go, with my leg like this. You have to do this to save her. This is how you repay me. You save her life, Anders. Now go!"

Anders brought his fists to his eyes, then rubbed. He keened a loud, animal sound, of pain, or terrible choices. "Rune! You are not supposed to pay for my crimes."

Rune leveled him with his eyes. "Don't make me pay with Catarin's life. Now go."

"Her seizure is finished. You are trying—"

"My leg is bleeding. I cannot leave. Either you get the police and the paramedics or we wait for Lassiter's cronies to come here and kill us all. Now go!"

"Brother," Anders said, and he knelt down next to Rune. He pressed his face into Rune's neck, and he breathed in. His shoulders racked with a silent sob. "Brother."

"Go!" Rune barked.

And Anders left. He ran.

Rune held Catarin in his arms. He rocked her gently. He pressed his lips to hers. He checked the tender skin of the inside of her elbow. There were indeed marks, bruises. She was a bird in his arms, feather-light, and she wanted to go home.

She would go home.

He would stay and face the consequences of this night.

He would go to prison, if need be.

He would live knowing she would be well.

Without jarring her, he reached into his jacket pocket, he found the velvet box. The money from the lutefisk can was not all spent. He had hoped to have enough for a honeymoon too.

It wasn't anything fancy, just one small pearl set in a white gold band. But he knew that baubles were not what Catarin cared about.

Catarin would have her home, her *parfumerie*, her health. And she would always have his love.

He took her right hand, and he slipped the ring onto her fourth finger.

When she awoke in the hospital, she would know it was from him. She would never see him again.

As he waited for the police, he memorized her face, the thin, nearly translucent skin of her eyelids, the six small freckles across the bridge of her nose.

He thought of Anders too, prayed he'd gotten away.

He couldn't help but think of all those first nights in *Svenska Dalen*, of the scary times when Papa would be violent and a monster—a bear in his imagination—and Anders would climb into his bed with him, hold him tightly, be the other half of his Folkeson soul.

Rune made his decision. He would never regret it.

For this is love, and nothing else is love.

Part V
Alice and Lolotte

Chapter 48

SERENA AND I FLEW INTO *NICE CÔTE D'AZUR*.

We phoned the *parfumerie* beforehand, of course, speaking to an assistant, Pauline. We had an appointment with Catarin later today. We were expected at the main house at 4:00.

As the morning brightened into day, the views from the train leading from the airport into Grasse became familiar, and my nerves jangled an unsettling rhythm.

Each view was prettier than the last. The countryside was singular, beautiful, with the train stopping at a few small French provincial towns along the way, with head-scarfed women bent in fields of jasmine, pulling weeds, and young children running barefoot around in the dirt, playing jacks, like something out of the last century.

I began to recognize things. The old mill against the rising sun. The sway of the wheat field in the wind. The stone-arch bridge over the Pommier Lake. The way the tracks wound toward the east near a small patch of scrubby overgrown lavender hills.

Things clashed in my head, memories and viewpoints, and my breathing became erratic. "Slow down. Put your head between knees," Serena said.

And I did. I breathed long pulls of air. Serena went and bought us ham and cheese melts from the dining car. We ate, and I felt a little better.

"I lived here," I said, resting my forehead on the window of the train, pointing to the perfumery. There it was, a speck in the distance, but it loomed so large in my life. Serena threw her arm around me, squeezing my shoulder. "It's hard to realize that I didn't live here, that it wasn't happening to me. I mean, I was happy here." I took a deep breath. "And sad. Both."

"We can turn around. Just say the word."

"No." I shook my head. We had to do this. I knew that. It was just that I'd spent years thinking I was Catarin Guillet reincarnated. I'd only had days to absorb that this wasn't true, that my connection to Catarin was something else, something more, something alive.

Not something long dead.

The future, the past, one long ribbon turning in on itself. Life. Mine and Catarin's intertwined.

One in the same, but separate, singular.

It was a half-mile walk from the train station and every step we took, I felt like I slipped back into Catarin's skin again, into her mind, her memories. I was retracing a path, footsteps I had taken many times, and it was a coming home of sorts.

The rich, balmy scent of the late-summer air came off the nearby fields. The click-clack of our heels on the flagstone pathway echoed near the chapel, where I had scraped my knees as a child. The *patisserie* where they sold the blueberry muffins I loved so much still sat on the corner, with cakes in the window. A white kitten lay sprawled out on the stoop, looking at us with expectant blue eyes, the pinkest of noses.

• • •

A MIDDLE-AGED WOMAN IN A LINEN suit met us in front of the main house, at precisely 4:00, a sprig of lavender tucked in her braided hair. "Good afternoon," she spoke in English, with a heavy French accent. If she was curious or surprised to see two Americans, she gave no indication. "My name is Pauline, and I am Ms. Monparte's assistant."

"It's nice to meet you," Serena said, offering her hand.

She shook both of our hands in a business-like manner. "Catarin will be ready to see you shortly. However, she suggested a tour for you, of the grounds?" I looked at Serena, who lifted her eyebrows. Pauline continued, "I would offer to take you later, after your appointment, but they are calling for rain in a bit."

"Yes, I think we would love to have a tour," I said.

We followed Pauline down the cobblestone path toward the *enfleurage*, one I had traveled many times before, with the swirling, curling rows of lavender extending up and away in the fields past the *parfumerie* outbuildings, their precision and grandeur giving the whole backdrop a surreal look.

I could hardly take it all in. I was here. The landscape, its shape and scent just as I remembered, but weathered from time and use, softer at the edges. The cobblestone faded by the sun; the equipment sheds faded to a lighter gray.

My *parfumerie*.

The grand oak near the eastern outbuildings had grown so large, shading the walkway, its limbs gnarled and turning in on themselves, its bark thick and healthy. The old gravel turnaround had now been paved, gone were the tiny pea-gravel stones, on which my knees and elbows had been scraped so many countless times.

Past the distillery, the rest of the ground came into view. "The lab is gone," I said, shocked, as we rounded the path.

"This new building was erected in the eighties." Pauline stopped then, turned toward Serena and me. The new structure was sleek and modern, all steel and windows; it didn't fit. A sharp pang of loss erupted in my chest for the old ramshackle stone building, where I had mixed my recipes. It was gone.

Pauline touched my wrist lightly, "Miss Grier, may I say something?"

"Yes, of course," I said, snapping back into the here and now.

"I have worked for the Guillet family for many years. I just want you to know that Catarin has been waiting for you for such a long, long time. Let me say on her behalf, Welcome."

I froze, not trusting my voice. *Waiting for me?* My heart hammered in my ears, and I held onto Serena's hand in a death grip. *What is going on?*

Serena and I exchanged a look. "She's been waiting for you," Serena repeated. "Could your mother have written to her?"

I shrugged, absolutely overwhelmed, as Pauline turned and led us up the steps of the revered *enfleurage*.

The *enfleurage* itself, the outside of it, looked mostly the same, small and unassuming, with whitewashed barnboards and the tin-slatted roof. Pauline unlocked the newly painted peach door, with its tarnished brass knocker. She pushed it open, gesturing for us to go inside. "It's been remodeled into guest accommodations."

I gasped. The scents still lingered. The walls were freshly painted, with waist-high wainscoting. It was all completely renovated, but the sweetness of the rose, the floral fullness of the gardenia, the fleeting freshness of the tulip, it was all still there. Caught in the building itself or . . . caught in my memories of it.

"There's an adjoining kitchen down the hall to the right, as well as a bath, two small bedrooms." Pauline continued.

We stood inside a cozy sitting room, with two high-backed upholstered chairs and a cushioned window seat. The room held all the charm and history of the perfumery itself. Upon every surface sat an old glass bottle, which in turn held some kind of bloom native to the Grasse countryside—the probable cause for the head-rush of scents.

Or was it? This place was so full of memories.

"Do you smell it?" I whispered to Serena.

She nodded, closed her eyes, and breathed in through her nose. "Of course."

I moved toward the far wall; it pulled me like a magnet. It was covered by dozens of the *enfleurage* frames: thick pine frames, small mahogany frames. Frames of many woods, in different sizes, all of them vintage, all with the original yellowed linen stretched within them. But in place of the flower petals giving over their scents, there were beautiful watercolor renderings of the blooms painted by hand on the linen itself. Gorgeous little white star-shaped jasmine, big blooming pink gardenia, fuzzy gray-purple buds of lavender. It was a beautiful repurposing of these historical objects.

Something chirped and Pauline took a walkie-talkie from her pocket. She spoke in French for a moment, and then she turned to us. "She is ready for you."

I gave the *enfleurage* one last look.

"Are you ready?" Serena asked, grabbing my hand.

I nodded. "Ready as I'll ever be."

• • •

WE CLIMBED THE STAIRS OF THE grand porch. I was going to meet Catarin. It seemed both impossible and inevitable. Cosmically fated, yet all a dream.

Pauline led us quickly into the hall. "She will meet you in the study."

The study. It would have ivy-wallpapered walls, heavy mahogany furniture and drapes the color of Queen Anne's lace. I took a deep breath and squeezed Serena's hand.

My knees knocked together as we walked down the main entrance hall, with its pillared entryway, and its Italian tilework. Then we turned left, opening heavy wood-paneled doors. It was all as I remembered it. The room, the furnishings, the smell of furniture polish with an undercurrent of firewood.

She sat in the red floral-upholstered chair near the window.

She stood slowly in greeting. She was small and hunched, with the wizened look of the very old, but her eyes were bright and full of questions before she spoke a word.

I knew this place, the grounds, the buildings, yes, but mostly I knew this tiny woman. Those eyes, her mind. My second home.

"Dear," she said, and it was in English, and I watched her from across the room.

"Do you know me?" I asked, but I knew she did, and I was walking toward her. She met me in the middle of the study, in an embrace, pulled me close, with her one good hand, and her disfigured one, the hand with only a thumb. She gave me two kisses, one on each cheek.

"Catarin," I said, and it was a statement, a question, a greeting. Everything in between.

"Alice," she said, pulling me out at arm's length, taking a good look at me. "You've made it. Welcome to Grasse." Her voice was high, heavily accented, the sound of so many of my memories.

And in that moment, I was in my mind and hers, and I saw myself through her eyes, standing there in my purple dress. I saw her as well, sensed her absolute contentment at having us here, and we were one for a moment, and then I began to get a headache, a sharp swelling ache in between my eyes. "I'm sorry," I said. "I just . . ."

Serena was at my elbow, and she led me to the red settee. I sat down, and a piercing pressure built slowly in my skull, and then it dissolved, several times, like a volcano erupting repeatedly behind my eyes. I would try to speak, to apologize for my behavior, but then it was there again, building.

I sat with my head in my hands, pressing my palms against the growing surge of pressure in my forehead. Serena and Catarin spoke a worried exchanged, but then, the pain exploded in a bright flash behind my eyes. The force disintegrated and burned away like fireworks, and in a moment, my mind was unclouded, silent, solitary, with my viewpoint only.

I looked up. Serena sat down next to me. "You okay?" she asked.

I nodded. Catarin eyed me carefully, as if she was going to say something. But then Pauline appeared with a rolling tray, topped with a teapot, small finger-sandwiches, and cheese, lots of cheese.

Catarin settled on the red toile chair again, and she spoke. "I was confused. I thought before that maybe Eli was coming as well—back when I had Pauline do some shopping."

The cheese. Many kinds, gorgeous choices of French handmade cheese.

Eli loved cheese.

She knew me. She knew us.

My vision blurred for a moment, with a sharp pain in my temple, and then, it was gone again.

Catarin cleared her throat. "I've studied birds in my later years." Her accent rolled over the r's.

I nodded, still reeling, not knowing what this had to do with anything.

"The grey-blue heron is often on its own, and it is a regal bird. I like to think of myself as a heron, but the hummingbird may be a better choice. Its ability to hover in place. The way it doesn't draw attention to itself."

"I'm sorry, I don't—"

"When I am seeing your world, your life, your memories, I feel like a bird, perched high on a fencepost, watching, involved but not involved, part of you but not." She took a sip of tea. "I'm a bird in America," she said, with a chuckle.

I wanted to say something. But I was shocked. I had not expected . . . to be so completely expected.

So what we had . . . this was . . . *reciprocal.* Of course it was.

It made a strange kind of sense, within such a nonsensical story.

Catarin knew me, as I knew her.

I had come here with trepidation, not knowing how I would ever introduce myself. But here I was, with Catarin, my other self, and she knew me. Really knew me. All the questions I had, they flew away for now, like a bird surprised from its nest. I marveled at Catarin, this situation, where we were.

What we were, two halves of some kind of whole.

Catarin leaned toward me, reaching her hands out to me. "Can you show me your birthmark?" she asked, pointing to my left hand, which I had curled into my chest, in that weird way. I opened it, displaying my birthmarked fingers and palm. "*Ah la vaca*!" she exclaimed. Then she stood slowly and sat down now on the settee, next to me.

She smelled of . . . oh, the scent was glorious: tuberose and jasmine, lavender and a touch of coffee. It was Catarin, and it was my past, and it was . . . home.

We sat there, knee to knee for a long moment, looking into each other's eyes. "It seems unbelievable to me that you have this physical manifestation of our connection, this birthmark. I have read of no other cases with such physical symptoms."

"So you know?"

"I cried when your mother died," she said. "It was too soon."

I nodded, touched, overwhelmed. "I thought for so long you were my past life . . . memories of myself. How did you know?"

Catarin waved this question away with her hand.

"It's been a treat for an old woman like me to live a few moments of youth, through your eyes. I have enjoyed knowing you, Alice. But it was confusing to me for a long while as well. I thought I had some sort of mental illness. What began as a series of snapshots in my mind, well, it turned into a wonderful mystery for an old woman to solve."

I thought of all that was in my mind, in my heart, all that Catarin had access to, the old arguments I'd have with Mom over stupid things, my obsessive preoccupation with my father a few years back, the way I replayed my most recent kisses, the ones I planted on Eli's Adam's apple.

The color rushed to my cheeks.

"There is no need for embarrassment here," Catarin said. "We are better than that. We are more than family."

I calmed myself. I wasn't connected with Catarin right now; it was like it had turned off or blown a fuse a few moments ago, with the headache. I continued, giddy with the idea that I could ask my questions. "I know a lot of your childhood, of your days with Rune, then not much more. After the tunnel, the day of Gunnar's wedding . . . nothing."

"Oh!" she said, her face flushing, and then I was apologizing.

"I'm sorry. I shouldn't pry and I just didn't know—"

"Your knowledge has been incomplete. It's a mystery. It's just . . . I think maybe you know the best things . . . the strongest memories. The moments that have lasted me a lifetime."

These questions I had, what happened between her and Rune. The answers were hers. I wouldn't force them.

I looked around her library. There were silver-framed photos of a young girl as she grew up. Had Catarin had a daughter? I wanted to ask so much.

But it was all hers.

Her life.

Her decisions. Her heartache.

Not mine.

I was free from it. I was. And it was so weird, because I kind of didn't want to be.

"You should stay on here, for the summer, Alice. You can work the lavender fields, learn to truly mix a *parfum*."

I considered this. "It's almost like coming home."

"Eli decided not to come?" she asked. "His beard is so handsome. I've always wanted to touch it."

Catarin and I had switched to French, and I hadn't even noticed. Serena sat listening, but she looked like she didn't have any idea what we were talking about. She gave me a slight smile.

"Could I please see the puzzle box?" Catarin asked, in English now.

"Oh, I . . . I never got it open. Do you think you could show me?"

"Of course!"

I produced it from my backpack. I began to work on the moves I knew. Then I asked Catarin. "Do you maybe know how my mother ever got it in the first place?"

She tilted her head, gave me a look. "I sent it to her, of course."

"You sent it to her? Huh." I rolled this around in my brain, considered it. Of course she had. I handed her the puzzle box.

"When was that?" I asked.

"Hmmm. Not long after the Christmas holiday, if I recall correctly. I waited until I had it mostly figured out—who you were, our strange connection. For years it gave me something to ponder, a puzzle of my own, perhaps—after I convinced myself I wasn't hallucinating it. When I saw that your mother wasn't going to make it, I hurried." Catarin reached for the puzzle box. "You haven't seen what I put inside for you?"

She opened it with the last move. She had to move the entire base, screw it around 180 degrees on its axis, while holding the lid still. Huh. I'd forgotten.

"Please, look," Catarin said. "There was an airline ticket inside for you. I wrote you a letter, explaining." I lifted up the papers.

"Did my mother write you back?" Every last thing was sliding into place for me now.

"Why, yes, she did." Catarin gave me a soft look. "She wrote saying that you would probably be coming, that I should wait until the end of the summer if you did not, then contact you myself."

My mother had known she was sending me on this journey. And she had set up a back-up plan, in case I hadn't acted on the mystery.

"She didn't tell me, you know. Just left me the box," I explained. Catarin nodded, as if she knew. "I think maybe . . . she just ran out of time."

"Maybe so."

"Or maybe she just didn't want her last months . . ." I let my voice trail off.

Maybe Mom had done the best she could with an impossible situation.

Catarin spoke quietly as she pressed her fingertips to her bottom lip. "I watched Rune carving that box in the summer of '32."

"I remember."

"When I sent you the airline ticket, I almost also put in the *étoile de mer*.

It was blown from blue glass, from when Rune and I went shopping in the open market of Linden Hills? The day his shoe fell in the lake?"

"I don't remember that."

"It's always been a favorite memory of mine. We stuck our bare feet in the lake and—"

"Rune was yours," I said. "I understand that now . . . well . . . You are allowed to keep those memories just for yourself, you know. I don't—"

"Having lived so long, Alice," Catarin said, "I think I have had an advantage. From the beginning of this strange connection, I knew what was real versus what was yours. I could tell the difference between my own self, and the specific, strange vicarious feeling of being you."

"I couldn't tell the difference for a long while."

"It is a lot like the synthetic scents," Catarin explained. And I scooted forward on my chair, understanding that this was going to be an important explanation. "The synthetics are so very close to the natural essence. Most noses cannot tell them apart, but you and I, we know the difference. We sense when it is not the *exactement* absolute. We know the synthetic by its façade. We see it for what it is: not quite the real thing. There is nothing as exquisite as the real, actual absolute. You know this." She looked to me, and she smiled. She reached over and squeezed my hand, intertwined her fingers in mine.

"I completely agree, Lolotte."

"Lolotte. This is a funny name for an old woman," she said. "I was called Lolotte in my youth—it means little, petite, and—"

"I apologize," I said. "I will call you—"

"No, no. It is good to hear. I just . . . I gave that nickname up when I came to America. I was trying to punctuate the event, become a grown-up. Sometimes, I think we need to mark the big changes in life, like you did when you cut your hair after your mother passed."

"Yes." I nodded.

I had a flash in my mind then, just an image: a middle-aged Catarin standing on the bow of a large ship in a rainstorm, staring stoically toward the shore.

Catarin looked at me carefully, and it was like I could *feel* what was going on behind her eyes. There was some kind of invisible tether between us. She knew what I'd just seen, and she'd seen something in me as well, dipped into my memory. We'd had some kind of *exchange*.

It left a slight buzz at the base of my skull, an aftershock.

"I went to Japan to see the cherry blossoms," Catarin said. "It's how I said goodbye to Rune, before I married Pascal. It was a business venture, a settlement." She pressed her eyes shut. "I had no idea how hard this whole adventure has been for you. How much pain it has brought you, when you've already had so much at such a young age. Alice, I am sorry that you had to question your mother, her motives."

"I wouldn't trade this, what we have," I whispered. "Ever."

"I have something else for you." She reached into the side-table drawer. Catarin cleared her throat, pulled something from her side table. "Your mother sent something for you, when she wrote to me."

She handed me a folded-up piece of stationary paper. "She gave me instructions to keep this for you, until you came here to meet me."

I opened it, and sure enough, there was Isabel's handwriting. My mother. Mom. A new piece of her.

I only half-registered Catarin turning her attention to Serena then, giving me privacy. A moment to myself.

To read this note from my mother.

I scanned the paper. It was a numbered list, not a letter. There were only ten points. I let out a little chuckle.

My mother. No lengthy goodbye, no maudlin apology.

I hadn't even read it yet, and I was already wishing there were more words on the page. More of my mother here.

I sat back on the settee, and I fought against that sting of tears in my throat. "Mom," I whispered. And then I read my mother's list to me.

"Things You Can Do For Me *by Isabel Rosemarie Grier.*"

1. *Try caviar.*
2. *Scuba dive.*
3. *Travel.*
4. *Forgive me for trying to spare you any of life's losses.*
5. *Don't be afraid.*
6. *Fall in love. Over and over.*
7. *Remember.*
8. *Forget.*
9. *Love even when it's scary.*
10. *Live. Right now. Live.*

Chapter 49

I REREAD ISABEL'S LIST TWICE. A THIRD TIME. I laughed at her absurdity. At how much I loved her, despite everything.

Then, I registered Serena's voice. "Alice? You okay?"

"Yes," I said, pocketing the precious letter, rejoining their conversation.

"Alice, why don't you and Serena stay a few days. I think you could learn to love the *parfumerie* here. You may take it over for me, this old woman, *oui*? You could learn to run the *parfumerie*, own it for me, take over my duties? For when I pass on." Catarin waited here for an answer, and I stumbled, still in shock from my mother's words, still coming to terms with Isabel's confession.

Was Catarin even serious?

The *parfumerie*?

Serena caught my eye, and I know I looked bewildered.

Catarin continued, "My own daughter has her own life, is uninterested in scents. And I see by your face I have scandalized you. Think about it, *ma chere*. I am an old woman, with ailing health, and I will not live forever, contrary to the belief of the workers of my *parfumerie*." She laughed then, like the trill of a songbird. "Alice, you are the closest thing to my own flesh and blood besides my dear daughter."

"Catarin, I could never . . . This place is . . ." My throat felt clogged with emotion.

"Think about it. I am serious," she said. "If you stay a bit this summer, and fall in love with the land, with the work, it is yours if you want it. Maybe in a few years? I do not say that lightly. My life's work resides in the buildings on this land and in the reputation the scents from this land have produced. Nothing would give me greater pleasure than to know that you, in particular, would be looking after it when I am gone."

"Okay, I'll consider it," I said, surprising even myself, thinking of my mother's list, of the endless possibilities in front of me now.

Serena asked then, "Do you ever wonder why it's you two? Not someone else? Why the two of you were chosen for this?"

Catarin considered this, and she shook her head. "Why does the bitter orange tree bear fruit only in winter? Why do we love whom we love? These are strange questions, I think, questions that cannot be answered head on. But rather through the twists and turns of time and life. Only then, later, will we extract some hint of an answer, some whisper of a reason."

I nodded, stricken with Catarin's words, with her wisdom, with this whole situation. "I will make it matter," I told her, and I meant it, like a promise. I would learn from her life, from her memories.

"I think you already have," Catarin said, holding my gaze. She meant this whole adventure that my mother had started by leaving me that puzzle box. I was grasping life and living. Is that what all of this was for? To appreciate the *now* in our lives?

Each day.

Each *moment?*

Each person?

My mind flitted to Eli—his handsome profile, the tenderness he had for his daughter, the thrilling beginning that seemed to stretch out in front of us.

I had told Eli of my plans for this trip. I'd even hinted that Rune might like to come, but Eli hadn't agreed. He said Rune was . . . adamant, that this story had ended long ago for him.

"I am feeling fatigued," Catarin offered, standing from her chair. "If you'll excuse me. But please let's have breakfast together tomorrow, *oui*?"

Serena and I exchanged a look. I knew she was wondering how I could leave this room without telling her Rune was alive, but I . . . I was feeling as if I was overwhelming her.

And I was feeling chicken.

I didn't know how to form the words. Would she be amazed? Upset? Angry? Or did she maybe know?

I was through assuming I knew the depth of her emotions simply because I was linked to her memories. *Some* of her memories.

So I just thanked Catarin. I let her walk out of the library.

I would tell her tomorrow.

And I would ask about the tunnels, that fateful day, tomorrow. And I would ask her of Pascal, of her daughter.

I had waited this long.

Chapter 50

I WOKE EARLIER IN THE MORNING AND MADE coffee in the tiny kitchenette inside the guesthouse *enfleurage.* Serena still slept in her little bedroom. So I dressed and walked out to the lavender fields, lightly dragging my hands over the fuzzy gray buds on their stalks. I looked out onto the rows and rows of lavender, curling up onto the plateaus in the distance. I shielded my eyes from the bright light, and I watched the sun rise, pink and swollen, emerging from the horizon like a victory torch.

I took a leisurely walk through the lavender aisles, and I paid little attention when a car horn sounded in the direction of the main house. But then I heard my name being called.

"Alice!"

I turned abruptly.

It was a man's voice.

Not just any man's.

Disbelieving, I watched as Eli jogged across the gravel lot of the *parfumerie,* his limbs lithe and graceful. He looked like something out of a dream. And soon, I was moving toward him, meeting him at the edges of the lavender field. Eli, with his beard fully grown in now, and his tousled hair, as if he'd come straight from the airport. He shoved his hands nervously in his pockets. "Hi."

"You're here?" My heart fluttered in my chest. He'd really come.

"*We're* here."

This took me a moment to figure out. "Rune is here?"

Eli nodded.

"But when I told you that she was alive, you told me to mind my own business, not in so many words. You said that—"

"I was wrong. I talked it over with Rune, and after the initial shock. Well, he wanted to come."

"He's in there now. Right now, with Catarin?"

He nodded.

We had met each other, walked toward each other down a lavender row. The sun was just peeking up over the horizon. All pinks and oranges, yellow and gold, casting an eerie light over the fields, over the planes of Eli's handsome face.

"You want to go in there, hear what they have to say to each other? See their reunion?"

I shook my head. "I'm good."

"Really?" He made a face.

"I'm where I want to be." I stepped closer to him. God, almonds and sage. Eli was here. "You *flew* here? But you don't like planes. You *really* don't like planes."

He nodded, his fishhook smile turning up at the corner. "Barely made it. Uncle Rune poured me a scotch from his flask after the first five minutes."

I laughed.

He reached out, tucked a curl of my hair behind my ear.

"I've learned so much," I told him.

"About the tunnels, about what happened with—"

I shook my head. "I mean, I've learned so much . . . about life. In the past few weeks."

"Yeah?"

"I thought I understood what it was like to care for someone, to feel that electric spark, that thing that's in the movies, in books, that people write poems about. You know, finding your other half, all that stuff. The Greeks, they said we're born with two heads, four arms, all that. And Zeus split us, right in half, right? Out of jealousy and fear."

Eli nodded, a smirk on his face. He liked that I was relating this to the Greeks.

I continued, talking fast. I had to get this out, had to explain. "That's supposed to be true love, finding your destined other half. And I thought I understood that. I thought I had that." I stepped closer to Eli, and I grabbed the lapels of his jacket, pulled myself up to him, pressed my lips to his. "I thought I'd experienced it all in the before, you know? I was jaded."

"Go on."

"And I figured that I'd never have anything close to it again, that nothing would ever compare." I lifted my arms around his neck. One of his hands rested on the small of his back, the other came up to cup my face, his thumb rubbing across my cheekbone. His eyes were so dark and full of emotion. I thought of Catarin's explanation, that slight difference between absolutes and their synthetics. Between real and *not quite*. "Eli, I thought I knew everything, had experienced it all. I didn't. I was wrong. What I remember from Catarin's life ~ Rune, the *parfumerie* ~ it all pales, it all falls away, seems unreal and fake, merely a set on a stage, when I'm next to you."

He leaned down then, kissed my lips, just a brush and then a peck. Then he smiled behind it, sighing deeply. "Thank God."

"Why's that?"

He pulled me closer to him, our bodies flush, and he pressed his face into my neck. "Thank God," he repeated, pressing kisses on my throat, underneath my ear. "I can't explain it, Alice. Not really. But when I'm away from you, I try to convince myself that this . . . us . . . it *isn't* . . ."

I pulled back and met his eyes, finished the thought for him, "But it *is*."

Chapter 51

SHE SAT IN THE STUDY, A CUP OF HOT CHOCOLATE in front of her, the morning paper folded on the side table. This was her morning ritual. Pauline had it set up for her each day. She was a woman over ninety years old. She had her health. She had her mind, but she wasn't stupid. She knew what was around the bend.

And she appreciated the little moments. She worked at the crossword, her glasses at the end of her nose. A bowl of granola sat to her right, on the settee cushion, where she picked out the cranberries and almonds, ate only her favorite parts. Life was indeed too short.

A knock on the doorjamb startled her. "Pauline?" she said. "What do you need?" She looked up, and she startled. It wasn't Pauline.

He stepped into the doorframe, overtaking it, overtaking the whole of her view. Of her mind.

Her heart.

But in truth, he'd always been there, and always, always first and foremost in her heart.

She took off her glasses, placed them on the table, rubbed at her eyes with her good hand and her bad.

He was still there. Not a figment of her imagination. They stared at each other for a long while, each taking in the details of the other, cataloging not the evidence of age, but instead the perpetuity of beauty, of the heart's reaction to what it loves so very deeply.

"Rune?"

Two syllables. A question.

Her whole life.

He nodded and moved into the room. She'd forgotten exactly how large he was. For everyone was bigger than she was, but Rune was a force.

Rune looked as if he were choosing his words.

He knew there were many choices, had indeed imagined this moment so many times, played it out so many different ways, in his mind's eye. Today, here, in the real reunion, this blessed event, he decided to forego conversation completely. There were other ways to communicate. Rune chose first Ezra Pound. But then he found his throat had clogged with emotion. He stood only feet from her, from Catarin, and he attempted to compose himself. He cleared his throat and spoke:

"I looked and saw a sea
roofed over with rainbows–"

Catarin interrupted him and finished the verse:

"In the midst of each,
two lovers met and departed."

He moved closer to her, a step. But Catarin didn't trust herself to stand and greet him. *Was this a dream?*

But then Rune chose Frost, and she knew it was real.

"A voice said, Look me in the stars
And tell me, truly, men of earth

If all the soul-and-body scars

Were not too much to pay for birth."

Catarin swallowed, unglued her tongue from the roof of her mouth. "Was it too much to pay?" Catarin asked, her voice thin, stilted with emotion.

But the music of her accent, the same as it always was, it nestled into the farthest corners of Rune's heart. It was a coming home. It transported him in a way that nothing else could.

Her voice filled the room, his ear, his heart.

"It was all worth it, everything, to know you, my Catarin, to love you, even if it was . . . from afar."

He pulled the armchair closer to her settee. He sat down, their eyes never leaving each other's. So many years, so much time, so much life lived, all of it pushed aside, left by the wayside because it didn't matter.

Rune was here.

Catarin sat across from him. The tender slope of her nose, the bright searching of her eyes. The freckles on the bridge of her nose. They made Rune feel as if he were a young man again, capable of anything. Rune also felt he might weep.

He was home in her presence, under her searching gaze.

How had he ever left her?

He tried to remember the why, made his heart and his memory think of Anders, broken, beaten, on his knees in that cave inside the tunnel.

Catarin fought a sob, her small shoulders heaving. He reached across to her and he grabbed her hand. Her tiny, wrinkled hand settled into Rune's knobbed arthritic fingers. She squeezed them.

Over the years, she had tried to piece it together. She had figured it mostly came down to his brother in trouble. Rune's loyalty. His selflessness. Her own mother's threats surely giving weight and credence to Rune's deep-seated insecurities. But the whys were not important anymore. Were they?

"You are here," she said.

She reached for his other hand. He held both of hers in both of his. "I came for you once before," he confessed.

"When?"

"1946. The spring. I came to the *parfumerie*, here. I saw you in the field, your hair tied back with a red scarf. You turned, and your profile, I saw—"

Catarin gasped. "I was with child. I had been married two years already."

The moment passed into silence. Catarin blinked back tears.

She and Martine-Marie had lived only blocks from each other, raising their children to tend to the lavender, to play in the orchard, to be children as they had once been.

"You must have been angry with me, to have found me married."

Rune shook his head. "Your husband treated you well? And you continued your work?"

"*Oui.*"

"And you have been healthy."

"*Oui.*"

Rune's thumb rubbed across Catarin's knuckles, stopping over the pearl ring she still wore. Rune stilled at the sight of it.

"Of course I still wear it."

Rune swallowed around the emotion in his throat, then spoke. "I wanted your happiness more than anything, Catarin. Please know that."

Catarin nodded, unable to speak. She squeezed his hands in hers, a soft sob escaped her.

Rune produced a handkerchief then and blotted her tears. "What is your daughter's name?" He motioned to the photos on the bookshelf.

"Oh, Rune." She exhaled a shaky breath. "I named her Birgit . . . for you."

He tried to remain stoic, but he didn't succeed. He had to let go of her hands and bring his own to his face. This surprise. He couldn't mask how deeply it affected him.

What Catarin had been to him—what she still was—he knew it was . . . singular.

But for her to have done this, it cemented to him, that after all these years, he, too, had been this to her. It was reciprocal in all ways. She had named her only daughter after his mother.

Rune pressed his fists to his eyes, like a child, fighting back the tears, but the years had sneaked up on him, the emotions right with them. Catarin reached out, and she pressed her good hand to his cheek. She pulled him closer to her. And he moved off the chair, kneeling in front of her. They were now face to face.

She asked, "What kept you from speaking with me that day you came?"

"Pride."

She shook her head. "Selflessness." She clucked her tongue. "My Rune, I too looked for you," she said. "I hired an investigator before I married Pascal. I tried to find you. Rune Folkeson was not to be found."

He nodded. "Ah. I changed my name. Isakson. Son of Isak."

"Rune," she said, understanding. For Catarin was the only other person he had ever told, besides his brothers. Catarin knew all of his secrets.

"My Rune," she said. "I should have known." And she leaned toward him, staring into his eyes, blue as a Swede Hollow spring sky, and she pressed a kiss to the scar on his eye.

Then she kissed his other eye, his good eye.

"I write you a poem, every year, on your birthday," he explained. "This was this year's."

He cleared the emotion from his throat and recited from memory:

All I ever wanted was to contribute a verse

A simple couplet

With you, dear Catarin, I write a ballad across the skies,

Sonnets dance on my tongue

Every blink of your eyes is an ode to beauty,

Every curve of your smile, a hymn of thanks to the gods,

For you, dear Catarin, I live

I contribute a verse

Its rhythm is, Catarin, Catarin, Catarin . . ..

She was crying then, wiping the tears as they fell to her cheeks.

He hated that he upset her, but she had to know. They were nearing the end, both of them, and he had this chance. He had to make it known.

"I don't kid myself," Rune said, looking at Catarin. "I've had the best of lives, because I held you in my heart. Anything I've done here on earth, I did with your name beating its rhythm against my heart."

Catarin sobbed then, and Rune handed her his handkerchief. Her tiny shoulders shook, and Rune understood. It was too much. It was, but it was nothing but truth.

He pulled her into an embrace then, held her to him, and it was his greatest joy to have her in his arms, a torture too, for all the years lost.

Finally, when she could, she pulled away and asked, "And what did you do, all the years. Did you take no wife, have no children?" she asked, her face crumpling into tears again.

She pressed the handkerchief to her eyes, and he answered her. "I never married. Gunnar lost Inger early on from polio. I helped raise his children. Two girls and three boys."

"Of course you did. And Anders? What of him?"

"He is still alive, living with Declan near Goteborg. They run the farm that Isak left them."

"You gave them that gift, somehow, I know this much, Rune, although I only can imagine the details. And what else has filled your days and hours for all of these many years?"

"I raised Percherons. I began a ranch for youngsters without . . . good parents. And I made a summer camp for children who struggle with epilepsy, who need the peace of those animals. Like you did."

"Rune."

"The horses do not care if the old man has a scary looking face or needs his spirit tended to also."

"Rune, you humble me. I cannot believe you are here. Oh, how I have missed you. Not a day has gone by that I haven't thought of you. You have always, always been *mon chou,* Rune."

And he had one more verse to recite to her, one he had held in his heart, knowing that when this day came, if it ever did, decades and decades in the making, he would say it to her. It was an apology, a declaration, a homecoming, his only real truth:

For this is love, and nothing else is love.

Acknowledgments

Special thanks to the editors at TouchPoint Press for taking a chance on this novel, especially Sheri Williams and Jennifer Haskin. I also want to thank ColbieMyles.com for the beautiful cover art.

Of course, I owe a debt of gratitude to Rune's favorite poets—those who strip life down to its barest essentials and whisper its truths in your ear:

Byron, George Gordon Byron, Baron, *1788-1824. Hebrew Melodies.* London: printed for John Murray, 1815. Print.

Dickinson, Emily, and Thomas H. Johnson. *The Complete Poems of Emily Dickinson*, 1960. Print.

Eliot, T S, and Frank Kermode. *The Waste Land and Other Poems*. New York, N.Y., U.S.A: Penguin Books, 1998. Print.

Frost, Robert, Edward Connery Lathem, and Edward Connery Lathem. *The Poetry of Robert Frost: The Collected Poems, Complete and Unabridged.* 1st Owl Book ed. New York: H. Holt, 1979. Print.

Hughes, Langston, Arnold Rampersad, and David E. Roessel. *The Collected Poems of Langston Hughes.* New York: Knopf, 1994. Print.

Pound, Ezra, 1885-1972. *Make It New.* London: Faber and Faber, 1934. Print.

Sandburg, Carl. *Chicago Poems.* New York: Henry Holt and Company, 1916. Print.

Whitman, Walt. *Walt Whitman's Leaves of Grass: The First (1855) Edition.* New York: Penguin Books, 2005.

Wordsworth, William. *Lyrical Ballads.* London: Oxford UP, 1967. Print.

The title of this book comes from Frost's famous poem, "A Prayer in Spring."

Oh, give us pleasure in the flowers to-day;
And give us not to think so far away

I wish for you flowers, dear readers, and the beauty of now.

About the Author

GINA LINKO is the granddaughter of Swedish immigrants. She has a master's degree from DePaul University in creative writing, as well as several published novels for kids. She lives in a south suburb of Chicago with her husband and three children. *Nothing Else Is Love* is a love letter to her Swedish ancestors, and it is her first novel written for adults.

Visit her at ginalinko.com

Made in the USA
Monee, IL
07 November 2021